A FLUTTER IN THE COLONY

Praise for *A Flutter in the Colony*

'Ray weaves an expansive tale, at the heart of which lies a cavernous longing for the homes and histories we leave behind. *A Flutter in the Colony* is an evocative and sonorous debut.'

– Aanchal Malhotra, author

'Sandeep Ray crosses geographies, from what used to be Malaya during that complex, tragic and instructive time called the Emergency, to Bengal in the final years of the Raj. A story of this magnitude needs a dexterity and felicity in writing that goes beyond the mere demands of rigour in understanding history. Ray combines this rigour, and an informed, reflective mastery over the nuances of historical processes, with a keen insight into the human condition, and sets his characters within a multi-layered canvas. And yet, there is more. Ray has a visual aesthetic that creates memorable, detailed images. As an introduction to the lives of Indians in Southeast Asia and to the recent history of Malaya, this novel is to be cherished.'

– Siddhartha Sarma, author, historian

A FLUTTER IN THE COLONY

SANDEEP RAY

HarperCollins *Publishers* India

First published in India by
HarperCollins *Publishers* in 2019
A-75, Sector 57, Noida, Uttar Pradesh 201301, India
www.harpercollins.co.in

2 4 6 8 10 9 7 5 3 1

Copyright © Sandeep Ray 2019

Cover image: *A Bumbung Belanda House at the Lake Front* (2009)
by John Wong

P-ISBN: 978-93-5357-101-6
E-ISBN: 978-93-5357-102-3

Typeset in 11/14.8 Warnock Pro at
Manipal Digital Systems, Manipal

Printed and bound at
Thomson Press (India) Ltd

To my parents who took ships

CONTENTS

THE ROAD INLAND

Maloti saw it in the distance. A giant, dense, lush, green hill that dropped several thousand feet, right down to the shoreline. Penang was a sight to behold. She could soon make out the small fishing villages on stilts as they moved past them, speeding up time. On the last dawn of a week-long voyage that had taken them through the Bay of Bengal and past the Andaman Sea, she had remained on deck, jostled around and drenched, as they passed through a storm. When the splendent sun finally bobbed over the Strait of Malacca, she looked at the choppy, shimmering waters and felt her heart lift. They were close. Wet and shivering, she ran back to their cabin, where her husband and son still lay asleep. Ducking behind a makeshift curtain – a sari hung from a taut rope – she changed quietly.

Maloti knew the river, but not the ocean. At thirteen, she had left her village, swum across the Ichamoti – a fissure off the Ganges – and walked westward towards Calcutta. She had escaped the famine barefoot. Now, a decade later, she was on an eastward course on an enormous ship, travelling farther than she had ever imagined possible. After clearing the crumbs off the makeshift table from their hurried morning meal, Maloti accompanied her son, Jonaki, around the large ship. They skirted around a clumsy promenade of Europeans sprawled along the deck, making the best use of the last hours of sunbathing on the ocean liner. Maloti's husband spent most of his time reading in bed. He took frequent cigarette breaks, strolling along the deck. The young man had been on a ship once before. But that journey had passed by in a drunken stupor.

'Are those clock towers?' he said squinting, as Georgetown appeared within sight. The liner berthed within startling proximity of the main street, almost as though it had entered the island. Maloti hesitated as they stepped off the gangplank, staring at the hundreds of men milling on the dock. 'What if they aren't nice to us?' she mouthed silently, clutching Jonaki. A thin, bent, bare-bodied elderly Indian coolie in a short, fading lyongi trailed them, carrying their luggage. The contents of two dented trunks and a large cloth holdall was all they had brought to start anew. Jonaki recognized his father's plump friend Palash in the crowd, waving dramatically.

The people would be nice. For the most part.

The drive went on, across the bridge, past the limestone crests and inland into the peninsula for several hours. Large, loud timber trucks passed within inches of the car. Buxom women in colourful clothes sat by the roadside, swatting flies off fruits. The road eventually became narrower, frequently winding around small, serrated hills flanked by tall trees. Jonaki felt carsick and laid his head on Maloti's lap. She spoke softly, caressing him, describing the passing landscape as Palash chattered on.

'Monkey!' she screamed. A troop, ambling along slowly, appeared as the car took a sharp bend. The sudden, loud honk sent them scampering. 'Did any of them get hit?' asked Maloti as they sped on.

'No. But I think there's one riding on the roof now,' said Palash, laughing. Jonaki sat up, his nausea gone.

Hours later, as the sun cast longer shadows, they took a turn off the main road and went down a dusty red lane before stopping in front of an old, corroding metal gate, adorned with fresh, bright pink and white bougainvillea. A short distance in was a wooden bungalow, raised on concrete pillars. Maloti stared in silence – her family's own home. It was large and had a hollow but sturdy appearance.

A pimpled youth of about eighteen appeared out of nowhere and introduced himself, 'I am Mamat, this one my property to jagah. I take care of all, eh?' He seemed anxious. Mamat offered to be guard, gardener and shopper for a small salary and the shed to live in. His legs buckled as he hoisted one of the trunks out of the car.

'Let him do it,' said Palash, as Mamat made his way to the house, grunting. Maloti took Jonaki's hand and followed him inside.

'Palash, will they be safe in there? Are there any lights?' asked the young man.

'Just wait here a minute. That wife of yours would be safe anywhere. Now if it were you, I'd be worried,' said Palash laughing, as he reached into his trouser pocket. He handed the young man a wad of folded bills secured with a rubber band. 'Pay me back only when you can. No rush.' The young man nodded.

'I don't know how to thank you for arranging all this,' he said softly.

'Shut up and have a cigarette with me. Let them take a look around.'

The young man took the cigarette.

'How do you like it here?' he asked, sounding tired.

'I like it here. It's peaceful.'

'Do you really? Aren't you and Reba lonely?'

Palash sighed. 'Listen to me. There is this saying in many cultures, well at least in some of them – if you aren't a rebel in your twenties, you have no heart; but if you don't seek lucre in your thirties, you have no brain. I believe this to be true. And if you don't follow this rule of the world, things fall apart very quickly. Especially for dreamy aristocrats like you.'

'But I wasn't much of a rebel. And I'm not an aristocrat.'

'None of us were. But the world changed faster than we could have ever imagined while you were cooped up in your old house in Calcutta, didn't it? Things are better now. In fact, things are good.'

'Are they? And what if I let us all down again?'

'Look, stop pondering over these pointless matters. Just do your work and make peace with yourself. This is a decent country with decent accommodation for riff-raff like us. Reba is quite happy here. I'm sure Maloti will be too.'

'You're not riff-raff, Palash. You're a dentist.'

'We're all riff-raff here. No one knows who we are. Back home, your father could have gotten us out of jail with a snap of his fingers.'

Maloti stepped out, perspiring. 'It is musty inside.'

'But did you like your new house, madam?'

'Bhaloi,' she smiled, politely tipping her head to one side.

'And would you like a cigarette now, madam?'

'Dhath!' she slapped Palash on his arm playfully. 'How is it that you have lost weight? And when is Reba-di coming?'

'I think I will gain it all back now that you are here. I would have brought her today, but we weren't sure if there would be enough room in my chariot.'

'Bring her here as soon as you can,' said Maloti. 'I got to meet her so few times after your wedding. And I'd never even seen her before that.'

'Neither had I!' said Palash, laughing. 'We're just simple people. When my parents chose her, she mumbled, "I have no objections." Done. No objections! Not everyone gets married in mysterious ways like the two of you.' He winked.

Mamat peeked from inside a shed at the edge of the unkempt garden. 'Don't pay him more than thirty dollars,' said Palash.

'How much is that in our money?' asked Maloti.

'It's about one-and-a-half times more here.'

'So forty-five taka?' asked Maloti immediately.

'Ah-ha, you're still the financial mind of the family,' Palash laughed. 'Good. Some things shouldn't change.'

'Where's Jonaki?' asked the young man.

'I think he went out back to investigate the neighbour's quarters.' His mother called for him, raising her voice for the first time in their new home. Jonaki was in the overgrown area behind the house, treading carefully through the unkempt grass, surveying his new environs.

'By the way,' said Palash, lowering his voice, 'I was wondering on the drive over ... does Jonaki know? Did you ever tell him? He's so much older now.'

Maloti looked up at the young man.

'No. He doesn't know,' he said softly. Maloti felt a pang of sadness as Palash got into his car. He was a familiar, comforting face; someone who had seen them through strange, difficult days.

'Can we come visit soon?' he asked, popping his head out the window. 'No objections!' yelled Maloti.

Mamat gave Palash a one-time-only salute and closed the rusty gate.

The Senguptas were now truly on their own.

Later that afternoon, the young man followed the narrow red path that curved away from their new home. As it approached the main street, he spied a few Indian men squatting on the pavement, smoking. A board hung above them, displaying large, squiggly Tamil letters முத்துசாமி மற்றும் மகன்கள். The English lettering below read, 'MUTTUSWAMY & BOYS. SPICE & CARRY'. Piled by the entrance were several large, open sacks containing dry red chilli, onions, garlic, curry leaves and spices labelled in English – kura, sambar, charu, pacchadi, pulusu. He realized that dishes broken down to their basic unit was something he knew little about.

Sensing his confusion, the shop owner, dressed in a bright white shirt and blue lyongi, said, 'I pack you ready food, sir. Ready to eat. Maybe for one, two days ... not go busuk. Then when house is ready, you come carry the meats and very fresh vegetables.'

'Do you have any soap?'

'Yes, got the soap. How many soaps?'

'Three soaps.'

The shopkeeper leaned over and opened a carton of Girl of the Moon soap. The food came to one dollar and eighty cents. The soap was another seventy-five cents. This didn't worry the young man. He had brought some money with him and Palash had lent him a thousand. If food was about three dollars a day, then he could feed his family for less than a 100 a month.

'You need any joss sticks, mister?'

'Joss stick?'

The shopkeeper plucked a lit incense stick from a wedge in the wall. 'For the holy fragrance. You want tea?' The young man did want tea, but was unsure as to how he would take some home for Maloti. But before he could say anything, the shopkeeper handed him an empty milk bottle, filled halfway with steaming tea. 'Return bottle and glass tomorrow only. Hold from the top.'

It grew dark sooner than he expected. When he reached home, he could barely see inside the house. 'Lampu, lampu,' muttered Mamat and ran to his shed. The young man put the packets of food down on the table in the dining room and called for Maloti. 'Where is Jonaki? I have some Coca-Cola for him.'

'He has fallen asleep,' said Maloti, appearing out of the darkness, sounding hoarse. He noticed that her eyes were moist. They walked out to the veranda. The young man poured some of the tea from the milk bottle into the small glass and handed it to Maloti.

'Imagine,' he said gently, 'back home we'd have a servant bring out our tea on a tray.'

'But it is quiet here,' said Maloti, taking a sip. 'And you've never served me anything before.'

'Do you like it?'

'Too sweet.'

She went inside and lit the holy fragrance.

The next morning, the young man woke up to find Maloti arranging the kitchen.

'I've bathed outside. The taps in the bathroom don't work,' she said.

'No water in the bathroom?' exclaimed the young man.

While it was easy for Maloti to bathe in a makeshift arrangement, the young man knew he would face challenges – they had grown up in different worlds. He walked outdoors to where the drum of water was. He stuck his right hand in and shuddered. It would be inappropriate to be fully naked. Yet, soaking his pyjama seemed unnecessary. Maloti appeared with a large towel and one of his loose underpants. 'You can change into this and bathe. I'll dry it afterwards. There is a bar of soap on the ledge.'

He began timidly. Small splashes.

At about nine, a jeep pulled up to the house. A thin, balding, sunburnt, middle-aged Indian man wearing frayed rubber slippers hopped out, nearly twisting his ankle. Walking carefully down the cobbled entryway, he took in the young man.

'Ah ... a handsome fellow. Still so young. On the better side of thirty if I would have to guess. Just wait till you see what this tropical sun does to you. It will shrink you into an old prune like me.'

'Nomoshkaar,' greeted the young man.

'My name is Utpal. Utpal Nag. Wife?'

'Yes, I have a wife.'

'Arré baba, I know. But where is she?'

'She is inside,' he said.

'So, you brought her with you ... very good, very good. Otherwise you would have been bored out of your mind. And worse.'

'Worse?'

'Your character would deteriorate,' Nag whispered.

'Oh.'

'The fellow before you – a Bengali party like us – went almost mad after his wife returned home. She said she couldn't stand it here any more. Claimed she saw ghosts. So, he became lonely and his character deteriorated.' He kept looking into the house, hoping to catch a glimpse of Maloti.

'He took to drink?'

'No. The other character.'

'Oh. I see. A mistress ...' mumbled the young man uncomfortably.

'Worse.'

'Worse?'

'Servant boy,' Nag whispered. 'They called him the Bengali Buggerer.' Nag looked at the young man's feet. 'Arré, why shoes? You are overdressed. We are clerks after all, sir.'

'But I don't have anything else to wear,' said the young man, embarrassed.

'No problem, my dear man. Anyway, let's go now. Not good to keep the sahib waiting. He has a habit of returning home for a morning toilet break and gets into a foul mood if he is delayed. Those estate buggers need to be out in the fields very early, so there isn't time for all the business before leaving the house.'

Nag kept chuntering on as the jeep made its way through the small town. The young man felt comforted by the volley of Bengali that had ambushed him early in the day.

'Have you been here for a long time?' he asked.

'Oh yes ... about twenty years.'

'Twenty years, sir ... You must know everything about this place.'

'Oh yes, I've seen them all – rascals, saints, English, Irish, Scottish, Tamil, Bengali, Malays, Japanese, Chinese, baniyas, communists ... they all love the rubber here.'

'Communists?'

'Surprised, mister? Wherever there are Chinese, there are communists, my friend. But now you can't tell any more. Just the other day they caught an Indian tapper with four guns. He had a job, a wife, and a brood of twelve children, but in the middle of the night, he would go out ...' Nag widened his eyes for dramatic effect and didn't finish the sentence.

They were soon driving on even, asphalted roads. 'These are the estates. Look to your left, look to your right. Look behind and look ahead. Rubber, rubber everywhere, but not a ...' Nag didn't finish his sentence again.

The young man was taken by the symmetry of the plantations. The trees were arranged, diagonally, in impeccable rows. The area was completely deserted, except for the odd cyclist.

'The smaller estates are a couple of thousand acres and the largest maybe fifteen. Ours is about six. And the labour – mostly from our southern brothers. This is slavery of the new kind. But then most of these poor chaps are better off here than their families back home. You'll see where they live soon.'

The car turned off the main road onto a dirt lane. They stopped in front of a wooden building with three jeeps parked out front.

'Estate!' shouted the driver, startling Nag and the young man.

'There is your fellow,' said Nag, pointing at a slender, rakish man in his early thirties.

Milne wore light khaki-cotton clothes, mud boots, and kept his sunglasses on. 'Mr Sengupta,' he said loudly, extending his arm to the young man. 'You've made a long journey from a big city to come to the boonies. I hope Naag here hasn't had you packing your bags already.'

'For the hundredth time, sir, it is "Nag", not "Naag".'

Milne laughed. 'Apologies. I will not deny that I have a terrible drawl.' Nag shook his head in playful disapproval, and then got up to leave the room. He said to the young man in English, 'Ask them to locate me after you're done here, and I'll walk you around. Now you talk with your manager. "Naag" will take your leave, sir.' With that, he sauntered off, slippers flapping.

Milne got to the point immediately. 'Sengupta, why do you feel you are here?'

'To work hard and use my acumen to improve the plantation, sir.'

Milne smiled and embarked on a managerial speech peppered with personal anecdotes. 'Sengupta, the first thing I will tell you is that we need you here not so much for your knowledge or expert skills, but for your integrity. The work here is not complicated; you'll get the hang of it quickly and, frankly, you're rather overqualified for this sort of stuff.'

The young man nodded earnestly; he liked Milne already. He accepted the Pall Mall he was offered.

'I was terrified about coming here, you know. I have an older brother who served in Burma and he used to write home sometimes ... My old man would read his letters out to us. God, the horrors that went on there ... But it's nothing like that here now. There are a few pesky chaps out there and technically we're still in the middle of an "Emergency", but it's nothing really – just a bunch of ragtags taking potshots once in a while.'

'Who are shooting, sir?'

'Oh well, there are some insurgents. We call them CTs, or communist terrorists. The Japs finally surrendered and left in '45 and it was good and peaceful again. But a leftover group of local bandits couldn't make up their minds as to who the enemy was.

They fought the Japs alongside us and then they turned on us. Imagine that if you can. Forest dwellers making mischief is all it is. You'll notice some small roadblocks when you leave or enter the town in the evenings, but they don't bother plantation vehicles any more.'

Milne spent about half an hour explaining to the young man his basic responsibilities. He was to keep an eye on the short-term contractors hired for building fences, constructing houses for workers, digging, removing trees, and supplying water drums.

'You'll pick up the language quickly ... You know they say that Malay is the easiest language to speak badly,' said Milne, laughing. 'Seriously, you'll be speaking it in a couple of months, but it'll never improve beyond a certain point. You Indians have a way with numbers, though.'

The pay was 375 dollars a month and the contract was temporary for the first six months. The house was provided for. Milne assured him that someone would be sent immediately to look into the matter of the electricity and running water.

'One last thing,' he said getting up. 'Naag will show you the job, but you report to me. Any problems, you come here. I keep every conversation in this office confidential, even personal ones. I once had someone who got a young tapper pregnant ...' Milne stopped himself.

He leaned in a little closer and said, 'You know, you have a gentleman's face. The sort that could be ... persuaded. Some of these chaps are pretty damn shrewd and they can sniff out a nice guy quickly. So, be a little careful, will ya? And like I said, just come to me if anything worries you.'

The young man left the office feeling lighter.

Nag was waiting for him at the canteen.

'What did he say?'

'He said I could be persuaded.'

'Persuaded to do what?'

The young man shrugged. 'He said something about the "Emergency" also.'

'Rubbish talk. All fighting finished now. "Emergency" my foot.' The young man looked at him.

'The English are clever. They call it "Emergency" because if it was called "war", then they couldn't claim the insurance for the estates and other businesses. Also, no one could accuse them of torture. Sly foxes underneath all that big-big talk. Did he offer you a cigarette?'

The young man nodded.

'Sala never offers me one. What's the pay?' asked Nag. 'Don't look at me like that. I am a direct-speaking fellow.' The young man lifted four fingers and then bent the last one. 'That's not bad, but you could have asked for a full 400. Anyway, you'll be able to save a lot here. Let me know when you're ready to send money home; I'll help you with that. Now let's eat lunch and then we'll find you a lift back.'

Nag produced his own tiffin box. 'Unfortunately, I don't have lunch for the both of us. You have some ringgits with you? Have you ever eaten sambal?'

They walked over to a counter where a cracked piece of hard plastic shielded four large bowls. A boy was waving away flies. 'Open, open, lah,' said Nag. 'Okay, give this one, and this one over there, and extra nasi.'

They returned to the table. Nag said, 'Try it.' The young man tried the red paste along with some chicken with some glutinous curry sticking to it.

'Aah, good, na? The food here is a bastard of Indian, Chinese, and Malay. But it has produced good bastards.'

A teenaged boy entered the room and ran over to their table. 'They looking for you, Nag sir! Asking what to do with extra fence wire? Sell it?'

'Go away, we are eating,' said Nag with a curtness that surprised the young man. Nag dropped his voice and said, 'I will talk to you about some other things later. You get started first.'

After lunch, Nag left the young man in the canteen with the promise of a pickup jeep. No jeep appeared. An hour later, a dark, sweaty, hefty man walked in and said 'so hot' to no one in particular. He noticed the young man and smiled, 'Hello, mister. Working with Nag?'

The young man nodded.

'Just coming from the India?'

The young man nodded again.

'I am Ganesh,' the perspiring man said, picking up a bottle of Coca-Cola. 'My father has worked here for very long time. This is good place.'

The young man nodded politely.

Ganesh immediately walked over to his table and looked right into his eyes, soliciting conversation. 'Just tell me how I can help.'

Realizing he had been cornered into making small talk, the young man considered what Milne had said about learning Malay. 'Mr Ganesh, can you teach me to count from one to ten?'

'Indeed! Hokay, you repeat after me:

Satu,

Du-ah,

Tee-gah,

Empat,

Lee-mah,

Enam,

Tuu-juh,

Laa-pan,

Sem-bee-lan,

Se-pu-luh!'

The young man repeated the numbers. The canteen boy recited along like a child in kindergarten. Ganesh asked a barrage of questions as he sipped his Coca-Cola. Half an hour later, the driver from the morning jeep ride stopped in front of the canteen and waved at the young man.

'I come one day to see you,' informed Ganesh, lifting up his half-empty bottle.

'Yes, do come by,' said the young man and left the canteen, anxious to get home.

'Encik,' Ganesh called out, as the young man got into the jeep, 'how you say 1956?'

The young man mumbled to himself and then said, 'Satu-sembilan-lima-enam...'

'You Bengalian chaps very clever fellas.'

'Thank you, Mr Ganesh,' said the young man and hopped onto the jeep.

It was still dark when Maloti shook him gently. 'Five more minutes,' he begged and rolled over. Maloti returned with a cup of tea. He sipped the tea and heard the chatter of birds.

'There is a bucket of warm water ready for you. Hurry up or it will get cold.'

This brought a smile to his face; it was that cold morning bath that he was dreading. Soon, he was splashing himself, singing and quivering despite the lukewarm water.

He emerged dripping in a towel and opened the door to the veranda. There was enough light for him to comb his hair, but a crack across the top of the mirror got in the way. He managed by crouching. 'A bold, confident hair parting is the mark of a gentleman,' his decrepit, debonair Uncle Potol had once remarked. He sat on a chair in the veranda and tied his shoelaces while Maloti swept the bedroom floor. He looked at his watch: 5.30. He walked down the narrow stairs to the unkempt garden and stretched. He walked over to Mamat's shed and peered in. There seemed to be a lump on the floor, under a blanket. He noticed a basket in the corner, full of a fruit that resembled mangoes. The jeep honked. There were four people seated inside, all asleep. The young man waved to Maloti as they drove away.

The jeep took the same route, passing quickly through the town, a main road and narrow side streets that felt disproportionately small compared to the large plantation lands surrounding it. They crossed the rail tracks and got onto the wider, smooth asphalt leading to the estates. The tall rubber trees emerged on both sides again – thousands of them, leaves swaying gently in the quiet breeze of dawn. The night lingered in patches under the gigantic canopy. The young man could see the tappers with lamps on their heads walking in file. They were mostly men, bare bodied, holding short blades, chattering amongst themselves. The other passengers were still dozing when the vehicle came to an abrupt stop.

'Estate!' shouted the driver. Milne was already pacing.

While the young man was out at the estate, Mamat engaged Maloti in conversation. He tried to convince her that they needed to make arrangements immediately to rid the house of ghosts.

'Ghosts?'

'Eh. Hantu. I see the one sometime. Before you people come. Eh, it come at night and looking, looking. That one Hantu Pontianak.' He put his arms out in front of him and swayed, making a whooshing sound.

'You see ghost?'

'Eh, I see sometimes. Very scary one. Is looking, looking, looking...'

'Looking for?'

'Eh, that one cannot tell. Blood.'

'Then what?'

'Must call a bomoh.'

'Bomoh?'

'Yes. He come and see house and do the white magic. Then no more hantu. All gone already, eh.'

'Okay. I ask mister.'

When she broached the subject with him, the young man teased Maloti for being a superstitious village girl. Then he said that he had seen a hantu himself the previous evening. But on closer inspection, it had turned out to be Maloti sweeping the veranda. Eventually, when she argued that they had not had the traditional ceremony to bless the new house, especially done with the local customs, he relented.

On Sunday morning, the young man saw an unknown person squatting outside the house, urinating. Realizing that he had been seen, the man shook himself and stood up, smoothening his flowing garb. Then he stood by the front gate and started smoking.

'Mamat!' The young man called out. The stranger did not turn. Mamat came out running. He noticed the man at the gate.

'Oi, Tok Modin!' Mamat clasped the man with both hands, dragging him towards the house. 'Eh, this one the bomoh.'

In his peci and flowing one-piece black garb, the man did resemble someone who could have connections to the occult. He spent some time trying to relight his cheroot. Then he whirled it like an incense stick and mumbled something. Maloti and Jonaki appeared on the front stoop. The bomoh pointed to Jonaki and whispered to Mamat, shaking his head.

'He telling the boy cannot play outside in the evening.'

'Why?' asked Maloti, alarmed. The bomoh whispered again, this time for about a minute.

'Eh, because of Hantu Tetek. She steal the childrens. Hide you underneath her very big tetek and run away fast,' said Mamat, confidently taking on the role of interpreter.

'What is tetek?' asked the young man. Mamat looked embarrassed and turned to the bomoh. The bomoh laughed and cupped his hands in front of his chest.

'Okay, what does he need to do now?' asked the young man impatiently. The bomoh understood this. He pulled out a kris from somewhere inside his robe. He fastened it to a rope and dangled it.

'This one got magic power,' said Mamat, pointing to the rusted, jagged, silver blade with Arabic inscriptions. The kris swayed as the bomoh watched it sternly. He walked over to the side of the house and began some sort of incantation.

'Can I follow?' asked Jonaki.

'No!' said Maloti immediately. The young man laughed. After about five minutes, the bomoh and Mamat reappeared. He pointed to Maloti and whispered something. Mamat looked puzzled.

'What is he saying?' asked Maloti

'Eh, he say ... where is your small girl?'

'No small girl in our house.' The bomoh checked his pendulum-cum-weapon again and whispered to Mamat.

'He say all okay now. The old people make the spirit angry.'

'What happened?' asked the young man.

'Some people put spell on them. They use egg and dirt from the kubor. So that's why the Hantu Pontianak comes here,' said Mamat, without consulting the bomoh this time.

'Okay, okay. How much money, Mamat?' asked the young man sharply, eager to end the mystical circus that had taken over his first proper holiday morning.

'Only ten ringgit. Next time, five,' said Mamat.

'Next time? What next time?'

The bomoh spoke up, 'Must come back, tuan. Hantu Pontianak can come back. Because cari-cari always.'

Mamat walked the bomoh to the street, chattering away. 'What do you think, Jonaki?' asked the young man.

Jonaki shrugged. 'I don't know. He has a strange smell.'

The young man lay awake in bed later that night as Maloti drifted off to sleep. Matters at home were settling down, but it had been a long first week at the estate. He had got acquainted with the plantation business. Milne had sent him to supervise a fencing job and he saw that the quarters where the tappers lived, while lacking in comforts, were better than he had expected. A couple of Chinese contractors had expected him to bend the rules, as they did with Nag. They had wanted to sell the unused supplies. The young man had refused, causing problems. But he had kept the matter to himself, not discussing it with Nag or Milne.

He pondered over how he ought to have been a doctor in Calcutta. How he should have been living in his large ancestral house in one of the oldest enclaves of the city. And while he wasn't really to blame for this turn in his life, he was, undeniably, a wavering sort. Perhaps the only thing he had ever been sure of pursuing was his marriage. Fourteen years ago, on a rainy day in mid-1942, he had walked next to a schoolteacher in a torrential downpour, determined to wed his daughter, the girl he had set his heart on. He had seen her during a function at the village school. Dark, sinewy and sonorous, she had taken his breath away as she had sung. But she wasn't the slender young woman lying next to him now.

THE HEADMASTER'S DAUGHTERS

Calcutta in early 1942 was a metropolis on tenterhooks. Malaya, not so far away, had just succumbed to a rapacious Japanese advance, its white officers bolting like jackrabbits, undermining the public's confidence in the ability of the British to protect them. Colonial troops were performing miserably all over Southeast Asia. News of the Japanese encroaching into Burma spread fast. Would India, especially its eastern front, be the next to fall? For the first time in its history, there was an acute threat of Calcutta being bombed, just like Singapore, Kuala Lumpur, Penang, Rangoon and Mandalay had all been in recent weeks. The government instructed people to switch off their lights at night so the Japanese planes wouldn't be able to gauge the contours of the city. The Victoria Memorial, a huge, lavish, white marble palace, constructed in homage to Queen Victoria in the heart of the city, was coated in tar in order to camouflage it.

For a while, it seemed that the situation would not escalate. And then, one afternoon, a deafening siren went off all over the city. 'Get under the stairs,' people yelled everywhere. Bomber planes circled overhead at a menacingly low altitude. After a while, they flew away. People crawled out and ran to their radio sets. Nirmal Sengupta decided it was not safe to be in the city any longer. People of some means, those who had a second home away from the city, began packing up and leaving. The entire city was caught up in the evacuation fever.

The Sengupta family shifted residence temporarily from Calcutta to their ancestral village in the east. They packed up their belongings, and their servants, and travelled the short distance to the town of Taki, where they crossed the river. Their rural home was a little further inland.

It proved to be a slow interregnum for the young man who had just started college in Calcutta. He made friends with some of the local boys, who, like him, seemed to have absolutely nothing to do. They would walk around, dropping in on random homes. They would have a drink of water while being plied with local gossip: a snake spotted slithering, a husband caught cheating, coconuts stolen in the dead of night. The young man forsook his books and embraced this new desultory life. The one thing that focused him somewhat was a girl in the village whom he had seen roaming in the fields and at the market with her mother. On occasion, she would walk around with her friends, but on seeing the tribe of boys, they would abruptly turn so as not to cross paths. He watched her for weeks from afar, not daring to make further inquiries or speak to her. But he tried his best to run into her as frequently as possible, charting her routine and plotting her exact movements. He was worried about the social implications of such an indiscretion; he was the son of the village landlord, she a village girl. But luck was on his side.

Charity, one constructive by-product of boredom, led to this fortunate set of events when Nirmal Sengupta decided one fine day that he would start a school in the village.

'A school, sir? An *entire* school?' his local manager, or nayib, responded, caught off guard.

'Yes, a school. A school with ... a school bell!'

You didn't question Nirmal Sengupta. His stentorian voice, shock of white hair, ramrod posture and cane with silver cap, all formed his formidable presence. But if you gazed into his eyes, you would find a tender man trapped in there somewhere.

A school had already existed there, but it had been closed for a while. The war had caused hardship in the village, turning much of it into a desolate wasteland. Educating children, even to minimal literacy levels, was not a priority. Inquiries revealed that there were teachers in the village, without employment, whiling away their time. They were grateful to find scope for some income. Nirmal Sengupta galvanized the village, including his own family members, to resurrect a decrepit one-storey structure on his land.

The only person who lost out in this scheme was the nayib who lived in the village. He received a monthly salary from Nirmal Sengupta to look after his rural estate. But he had been supplementing this income by skimming off the land for years, forcing the villagers to hand over most of their produce, only for him to brazenly sell them in the open market. On occasion, he would send a basket of mangoes and lychees to Nirmal Sengupta in Calcutta, falsely claiming that vandals, pests and inclement weather had robbed the family of yet another season's prodigious harvest. He was horrified with this new direction of matters and tried to dissuade the landlord. He insisted that good deeds, such as opening a school, served no purpose; in the end, the people would rob him blind, murder his family and take over his property. He was not wholly unprophetic.

But Nirmal Sengupta remained undeterred. With the little money he fronted, the classrooms were cleaned and the walls whitewashed. Cracks in the building were cemented over and the exterior was painted a dull, patchy pink. The villagers were startled to see members of the landlord's family working alongside them;

they washed the floors, applied coats of paint and went looking for people to assist them.

'The goddess of learning knows no class, tolerates no prejudice,' Nirmal Sengupta would opine softly to those near him – labourers unloading bricks from carts drawn by emaciated bullocks, children helping their mothers prepare the frugal midday meal of a bit of rice and some vegetables, self-made carpenters crafting simple, wobbly benches. When he went on his evening perambulations through the dusty roads, men and women greeted him with a half bow and a full smile. He would respond with a slight lift of his cane.

Once, he accepted a glass of water from an old lady. Several people gathered as she tipped her urn. They asked Nirmal Sengupta about the state of the war and his thoughts on the talks of an independent country. He answered their questions for an hour. Three generations of his family had owned land here, but none before him had ever sat and had a glass of water with its residents. He declined the offer of a meal.

When he arrived home, his wife took his cane.

'I'll serve you dinner soon,' she said, folding his shawl.

'May I have half a cup of tea first?' asked Nirmal Sengupta. 'My throat feels parched. But just half a cup, no more.'

On inauguration day, Nirmal Sengupta waved his stick amidst the clapping and cheering. He broke into an uncharacteristic broad smile and said, 'What are you looking at? School is open.' He ceremoniously handed each of the six teachers a stick of chalk while the children rushed in, elbowing and tripping over each other.

Unbeknownst to the Sengupta family, the villagers had organized a cultural event for the evening. It was a simple affair. A stage-area was created in front of the school, with swathes of old cloth and some benches. The patron family was asked to sit on a raised dais adorned with wilting flowers. There was the customary tea with fried snacks – onions, some mealy muri, and fritters – and then rambling speeches made by the village elders and the headmaster. A show followed.

And it was then that the young man, who had almost fallen asleep, first saw, up close, the girl he was so fascinated by. She sat in the front row, huddled together with the other women in the choir – a dark, gangly adolescent with bright darting eyes. It soon became apparent that she would lead the group.

'My daughter, sir ...' stammered the headmaster by way of introducing the singer. She began in a low tone and the chorus joined in.

The lad stared at her. The girl held several hundred people transfixed with her rich, perfectly modulated voice. When it was over, the elders nodded in appreciation. Nirmal Sengupta beckoned. 'Go on and touch his feet,' her father urged. She leaned over and, in one graceful motion, swiped his feet and planted her hand on her forehead.

'What is your name?'

'Nirupoma,' she replied in a silky voice.

'It is always better to give beauty to the world than to merely inherit it from god. Bless you, child,' said Nirmal Sengupta.

Over the next few days, the young man went to visit the headmaster under any pretext he could come up with – to deliver a note, prepare an inventory of books, create a sign for the school, pick up the unused paint, check on slate supplies. The list went on. His sole purpose was to catch a glimpse of Nirupoma. But what could he do even if he were to come face-to-face with her? He had no inkling. Still, it was thrilling just to see her for a fleeting moment here and there; when she opened the door or chased after her little sister. He lay in his bed in the long, unending evenings, wondering whether she had any idea as to how much she had bedevilled him. He just needed time, he reckoned, to find a way to approach her appropriately.

But one day, Nirmal Sengupta announced abruptly that they were leaving. It had been a couple of months now and he was bored with the rural life. He missed the city and his friends. He decided that Calcutta was safe to return to. The entire village gathered around when everything was finally in place and the short journey of just a few hours was about to commence. The headmaster walked over to the landlord and touched his feet right before he got into the bullock cart that would carry them to the ferry, which would then take them across the narrow river to the small train station.

'I will look after everything, sir. I will send you regular postcards about the school. I will do anything you ask of me ...' his voice faltered. 'And thank you for letting us stay in your home. We will take good care of it in your absence.'

'He'll ask for your son's hand in marriage next,' the nayib smirked.

The young man tried unsuccessfully to catch Nirupoma's eye.

Months away from Calcutta had turned the young man languid. It took him weeks to adjust to city life again. He had fallen behind academically. It was now close to the midway mark of the 1942 school year. Friends who had stayed on had been promoted to the next class. He missed his days in the village and fleeting memories of Nirupoma made him pine for her. He was embarrassed by his listless condition. He turned dull.

He could not speak to a family member for fear they might laugh at him, or worse, berate him for distracting himself from his studies, daydreaming about a girl. He knew how pernicious gossip was, even amongst the people who cared for him deeply; an admission during a moment of weakness could scar him. Schoolboys of his own age could offer little insight into such matters and he did not know a single girl who was not a relative. He clung miserably to his thoughts. He would imagine Nirupoma in his old house, in his room, his bathroom, in his bed – sleeping peacefully, arms around *his* pillow. Sometimes, at dawn, he would slip out the front door and walk through the fresh mist that enveloped the city – to hear the tuning of radio sets, the gurgling of throats, see the sensual washing of shivering bodies, the ironing of creases, smell the smoke from the coal stoves before the whiff of a first meal. He procrastinated, trying to delay the day arriving with unstoppable certainty, as he wondered what his place in it was. He had no job, no school and certainly no sweetheart.

He would wait for news from the village. Every new postcard that carried some information about the school – attendance, accounts, vandalism and illness – meant that he had not imagined those days, that the people from his dreamy rural hiatus were real. As long as there was a school, Nirupoma would have to be playing some role in it. But one day a most disturbing postcard with a streak of sandalwood arrived. As soon as he saw the headmaster's handwriting, he picked it up from the floor under the mail slit.

Dear respected sir,

It is with deep pleasure and unreserved gratitude that I wish to share this good news with you. With the blessings of the Lord above and benevolent souls such as yourselves on this earth, I have been able to secure a groom for my older daughter, Nirupoma. The wedding will take place on a date determined by our priest. I will send you exact details in the following weeks. Of course, I could not even imagine such a joyous day in our lives without the dust of your feet gracing it. Please do keep a request from a younger brother.

May the good Lord bless you and all your family.

He ran to his room, feeling like a fool for not having foreseen this most predictable of events. She was of age. Of course she would be getting married off. And what could he do? What good was his secret, his one-sided obsession? That night, he dreamt of Nirupoma, resplendent on her wedding night, in a bright red sari, facing an older man with a moustache and an intimate smile. His own father seated across them, a guest of honour, nodding gently in approval.

When he woke up, he had a plan. He walked to his parents' bedroom and knocked on the door.

'There was a letter from the headmaster, Father.'

'Oh? Where is it?'

'I actually left it on the bus, I had picked it up on my way out,' he stammered.

'Well, did you get to read it?'

'Yes, sir. Well, he said that they need a framed photograph of you because the one they have hanging at the entrance of the school hallway fell off the nail and is damaged. No one was hurt.'

'Oh, that's good. I hated that photograph. Made me look too regal. We're modern ... We don't sit in velvet chairs any more.'

'Well, since exams are over, I was thinking that I could make the journey and take a new photograph with me. We should visit occasionally, Father. You know, it is ... our school.'

'Ah ... you wish to feel special again ... be an important person ... Calcutta is just too big, isn't it? And you're a nobody here?'

'No, Father,' he stammered, 'I just want to be of use.'

'I'm teasing you, Son! It's a good plan. You deserve a little trip. You've been looking sick lately. Go on, go to the countryside and get some air. We'll go to the studio this afternoon and get a portrait taken.'

The young man was off the next afternoon with a large framed photograph tucked under his arm, a small bag with a change of clothes, and a tiffin container – the contents of which he gave to the first beggar he saw. He savoured train food: greasy luchis, potato, green peas and especially the sweet, frothy tea. The seven cups kept him up and he rehearsed, over and over in his mind, the conversation he was going to have with the headmaster. He would be matter-of-fact, yet resolute.

He was asleep when the train arrived at the station. The man sitting next to him – with whom he had shared a cigarette – woke him up. He jumped up, clutching his bag and ran out of the compartment.

The man shouted from the window. 'The photograph of your father!'

As the whistle blew, the man slid the framed photograph, wrapped in paper, through the window.

'Brother,' he said, 'who knows what lies ahead, but I wish you luck. Four years of luck. I don't have a thumb, you see.' He gave him a sweet smile and held up the four fingers of his right hand as the train pulled away.

But four years of luck it wouldn't be.

When he reached the old house, he put down his bag and ambled around. A lantern, barely illuminating his tentative steps, cast weak, long shadows. There was no one at home. He had prepared himself to meet the headmaster to discuss important life-altering matters. Now he was not sure. He found himself at the back of the house, near the small stable of goats; he smelt them before he could hear them. One of them bleated shrilly, piercing the quiet of the late evening. He found himself making a strange soothing sound. The goat responded.

The absurdity of the situation struck him – he was walking around in his own home, communicating with a stinking, nervous goat while waiting for his imaginary inamorata. He decided to enter the house through a hidden sideway that he had used many times. It led into the kitchen and then to a corridor. He stood there, holding up the lantern, peering at the familiar surroundings. There was new furniture and an enormous calendar with a sketch of Ramkrishna on the wall. He felt exhausted.

'Who's there?' a shrill voice called out. And then something heavy hit him on the torso. His lantern smashed on the floor. Before he could respond, something hit him again, this time on the face. He heard the crunch of glass under his feet as he stumbled. Yet another object landed on the wall next to him. By the thuds, it seemed that large books were being hurled at him.

'Please, stop attacking me!' he yelled. 'I am not a thief ... This is MY HOUSE!'

'What do you mean, this is your house?' The voice in the dark seemed unsure now. But he felt another book fly past him. This time, he slipped and fell on the floor. He slid over to the wall and rested his back against it, feeling a sharp stinging sensation on his palm. He sat wincing and breathing heavily.

Deciding that he had ceased to be a threat, the attacker stopped hurling books at him.

Moments later, he saw a dim light move through the house. He made out the figure of a girl holding a candle.

'I am Nirmal Sengupta's son. I came to meet the headmaster and the house was locked and so I came in through the back ...' he said wearily. 'I think I have cut my hand.'

The girl fled the room so swiftly that the candle she was carrying extinguished. He waited for a moment and then called out, 'Can you bring a light here, please? There's glass everywhere, I think I may have cut myself.'

He heard nothing.

She then walked towards him slowly, holding the candle. He forgot all about the cut in his palm. He could see her face now and was reminded of her beauty. Perhaps it was the anticipation or the dramatic setting of it all, but for the rest of his life, he would never remember her looking lovelier than she did at that instant. She crouched near him, sweating profusely, staring into his face.

'Show me your hand ...' she said gently. He unclenched his palm, opening it for her to inspect. She asked him to follow her to the sink, where she poured water on it to wash away the fresh blood. The faint metallic smell hung in the air.

'What would be dangerous,' she said gravely, 'is if there is a piece of glass lodged inside.'

'Oh, would it?'

She ran the tip of her index finger softly over his palm. When he winced, she said, 'We need to take it out. Wait here.'

She left him in the dark again, and he was now aware of the odour from his body and felt embarrassed. When she returned a few moments later, she saw him smelling his armpits. She asked him to open his palm again. Under the light of the candle, she pricked the area where the speckle of glass had entered.

'Gently,' he said.

'It might hurt a bit, but we need to cut the skin near it, so it comes out.'

He felt a little annoyed that she could touch him so easily. 'There!' she said triumphantly as she dislodged a small piece of glass.

'Look, a diamond,' he said, holding it up.

'Now wash your hand with the Dettol on the sink. Your family had left it behind.'

He walked over to the basin and she walked beside him, holding the candle. He did as he had been told and winced as the raw antiseptic entered the small wound. He noticed that she too winced a little.

He looked at the floor and saw the book that had hit him, *The Wise Words of Swami Vivekananda*. 'I wonder if the great man ever knew the violent use his books would be put to one day.'

'What are they about?' she asked.

He touched a bump on his head and said, 'I'm not sure. But he wrote too many pages.' Nirupoma didn't find the joke funny. Her polite laugh echoed feebly through the large house. And then, as if purposefully ending their odd encounter, she said somewhat formally, 'Please seat yourself in the front room. My parents will return soon.'

He followed her to the large room at the front of the house. It had four hard wooden chairs placed around a large table and an old calendar hanging on the wall. He sat down on one of the chairs and closed his eyes.

The opening of the door and the chatter of the headmaster's younger daughter did not wake him up. The headmaster let out a long, satisfied groan and started to take off his shoes.

He then noticed the young man sleeping. The girl screamed. The shrill sound awoke him.

'Hello,' he said standing up, wiping saliva from his face, 'I am ...' But before he finished, the headmaster's wife exclaimed, 'Oh my god! It is Nirmal-babu's son, isn't it? He must have died!'

'Shut up!' barked the headmaster.

'Or was it your mother?'

'No, no, everyone is alive. I just came to see all of you ... Father wanted me to inquire about the school and about the conditions here and so ...' he was facing three pairs of bewildered eyes.

'What is that?' asked the girl, pointing to the framed photograph – the lone prop in the empty room. He unwrapped the paper explaining that his father had wished to send a new portrait of himself. Everyone peered at the large photograph in the dim light.

'The face of a saint. You will stay with us tonight, won't you?' asked the headmaster's wife.

'I hadn't thought that far ahead ...' the young man mumbled.

'Of course he will. What an odd thing to ask. Where will he go at this hour? He will rest and eat, and return whenever he wishes to,' said the headmaster warmly. He would make a nice father-in-law, thought the young man. Nirupoma's younger sister badgered him with questions. How long did it take to come here? How many storeys high was their house in Calcutta? Did they eat goat meat every day in Calcutta?

Her mother called out from somewhere inside, 'Maloti, stop disturbing him. He is very tired. Come to bed right away.' He heard her speaking softly to Nirupoma, giving her instructions on how to make his bed and how to fasten the mosquito net.

A makeshift dining table had been set up right in the middle of the main hallway, the area where he had been attacked a little while ago. Uneven candles adorned its sides and dishes of food were arranged in an arc in front of a shining silver plate.

'Please sit down and eat. You must be hungry. This is just our everyday food. Sorry that we don't have anything special ...' said the headmaster's wife.

Father, mother and younger daughter sat across from him as he proceeded to eat. The young man was famished. They watched intently as he sampled the dishes – vegetables in season and two types of lentils.

'Vegetables don't taste as good in Calcutta.'

'These are from your own garden! This is what the villagers are planting and selling these days. I shall send your father a couple

of baskets with you, if you don't mind carrying them,' offered the
headmaster.

'Of course not ... He has been pestering mother for some
bitter gourd lately, he brings it up at every meal. But the cooking
is divine too...'

The headmaster's wife lit up. 'Nirupoma ... did you hear that?
He said that your cooking is divine. Why don't you come and sit
with us?'

There was no response from Nirupoma. 'She's shy, except when
she sings, of course. And yes, she can cook really well too. We just
met with her future in-laws. You did receive our letter, didn't you?'

The young man nodded.

A moment later, Nirupoma appeared at the door and stood
there silently. Maloti, the younger one, burst out giggling and said,
'When Didi gets married, she will cook all day for her fat husband.
And he'll eat and eat, and will blow up like a pumpkin. And then
one day he'll just burst!' She ran to her sister and wrapped her thin
arms around her legs. The young man caught Nirupoma's eye and
held her gaze – he strained to find any signs of anxiety or sorrow.
There was none.

The school looked shabby. The exterior had lost its cheerful
pink, and wild shrubbery now covered the walls. The large bell
at the gate was coated with rust. But when he saw the rows of
boys and girls seated at their wooden desks reading aloud, he
felt less discouraged; he was glad that his family had intervened.
The headmaster walked him into classrooms and interrupted
the teachers. They welcomed him warmly, if a little anxiously.
He overheard whispering: 'His father has sent him to assess the
conditions here.'

He was expected to test the students. The headmaster thrust
a textbook into his hands as he entered a bright room with about

twenty children inside. 'Go on,' he urged. 'Ask them something.' He looked at the book for a moment and then put it down.

'Which class are you in?' he asked.

'Class five, sir!' the children yelled.

'Who was the founder of the Indian National Congress?' Three hands shot up. He pointed to the boy nearest to him.

'Gandhiji, sir!'

Another girl shouted out, 'No, sir, it was Octagon.'

'Octagon?'

'Yes, sir. Octagon Whom!'

'Octavium Hume.'

With that, he concluded his tour of the school. He was beginning to feel like an imposter, especially when a lean old man asked him nervously, 'Will I be able to keep my job, young master?'

'Of course, sir,' said the young man. 'I am here merely to say hello.'

'You should come here and be a teacher for some time. And then you will go on to more important things in life. But you will learn all about your country right here. How will we ever win our freedom if young men like you do not serve their own country?'

The headmaster walked up to them and said, 'This young man has to go on with his morning. Why don't you go to the staff room and have a cup of tea, Bikash-babu?'

The old teacher nodded slowly and shuffled away.

'He's getting old ...' the headmaster offered by way of explanation. 'I just don't have the heart to let him go.' They looked at each other for a moment. The young man wasn't sure of what to say. The headmaster spoke softly, 'There is a train later this afternoon. Are you planning to go back today? Should we walk back towards the house?'

A torrential rain had started. It was so loud that the young man couldn't hear the school bell. He was startled to see the boys and girls suddenly get up and run to the door. He stared at the menacing downpour, and at the children being ferried away, huddled under clothes and the rare umbrella.

The headmaster saw him standing at the edge of the corridor and walked up to him, 'We can go home together. Yet another thing your father left behind is this enormous, sturdy umbrella. An entire family can fit under it!'

So, he ducked under his father's gigantic umbrella and together, they made their way through the slushy roads. A dog joined their group and tottered along beside them. The young man reckoned that this was an opportune moment to discuss his prospects as groom.

'Umm, I was thinking … I was wondering about the future, sir. Our families are hardly strangers and you see …' he started stammering.

The headmaster couldn't hear him. 'Strangers? Oh no, we don't encourage strangers at the school.'

The young man decided to raise his voice and took a deep breath. Just as he was about to shout out his fantastic intentions, under a moving umbrella circumscribed by pouring rain, a short, half-naked man ran in from the street and joined their group.

'Oh, what a stroke of luck! I need to open my shop soon. What an enormous umbrella this is! And this … filthy dog!' He gave the dog a sharp kick, but it continued walking with them. The young man trudged on quietly.

It stopped raining just as they arrived at the house. They were greeted with large towels, and were served warm tea and a bowl of vegetable fritters with wedges of raw onion. The headmaster ate noisily, blowing on the steaming hot snack.

Turning to the young man, he asked in a jovial tone, 'So … what will you tell your father when you return home? That everything has fallen to pieces here?' He laughed. 'Things are not so bad here, you know, not too bad. We've had some issues with a few teachers at the school, but nothing that I can't manage.'

'Are you feeling hot?' asked the headmaster's wife. 'You know, people think that it cools down when it rains, but is that really true? I, for one, sweat a lot. Nirupoma! Bring the hand fan and help them cool down a little bit.'

Nirupoma appeared a few moments later out of the dank interior of the house with a small palm frond attached to a thin wooden handle.

'Now sit here and fan them,' instructed the headmaster's wife. Nirupoma sat next to her father and moved her thin arms back and forth, in a swift, effortless arc.

The family and their nervous guest moved into the dining area a little later. This time, the young man ate with the headmaster, as his wife and Nirupoma scurried around. Once again, the young man approved of everything on his plate. Finally, when it was time for him to leave, he crouched down and touched the headmaster's wife's feet. She was embarrassed by the gesture. Nirupoma started giggling and covered her mouth. The younger sister stood by the door, staring at him, sad that their guest was leaving. The young man would remember that moment for many years. As they left for the train station, the downpour began again. Time was of the essence. The young man was determined to have his way. He cleared his throat and clenched his sphincter.

UNIVERSE LOST AND FOUND

Unfortunately, the distance to the station was short. It did not give the young man enough time to attempt the proposal. The platform was deserted when they arrived. As they stood waiting for the train, the headmaster repeated his good wishes for the family back in Calcutta.

'Do you have all your things?' he asked for a third time, glancing at the small bag and the satchel of vegetables.

They heard the train approach.

'Sir, I'd like to marry your daughter,' the young man said.

'What?'

'SIR, I'D LIKE TO MARRY YOUR DAUGHTER.'

'*Which* daughter ...?' the headmaster asked cautiously, after staring at the young man as though he had lost his mind.

'Nirupoma.'

'But you do know that we've arranged for ...' He did not complete his sentence as the young man nodded instantly.

'Does your father know about this?'

'No.'

The train arrived trailing a cloud of smoke. People scurried around them. The headmaster picked up the bag and got into the train. He sat down by a window and motioned to the young man to sit across from him. The young man kept looking at him, waiting for his thoughts on the epic matter he had just broached. The guard blew his whistle. The headmaster remained in his seat. He did not get up even when the train started moving. Finally, when the young man gave him a confused, alarmed look, he said, 'I need to go to Calcutta with you. We cannot waste time. We must talk to your father immediately.'

The young man stared back in disbelief. His plan was working. A few moments later, he looked out the window and saw a thousand fireflies in the dark fields beyond.

An hour later, the headmaster began shivering. The young man heard a soft moan. He leaned over and found his huddled body hot to the touch. 'You're burning up, headmaster-babu ...' he said.

'I don't know where this sudden fever has come from.' He spoke with difficulty.

When the train arrived at Calcutta four hours later, the headmaster was unable to get up on his own. The young man helped him off the train and escorted him to a taxi. He laid him down in the back seat and himself sat next to the driver.

'We'll be home soon, headmaster-babu. We'll get you some medicine when we get there.' He tried to say all this matter-of-factly, but he was nervous.

When they arrived at his house, the young man asked the servant boy sitting on the front stoop to help carry the headmaster in. They managed the short distance to the living room. Nirmal Sengupta had just returned from his post-dinner perambulations and was in the next room, massaging his calves, when he heard the scuffling.

'What's the matter? Who is this man?'

'Father, this is headmaster-babu. He was coming to Calcutta with me and has collapsed with a high fever.'

'Our headmaster ... all the way from our village? But why was he coming here?'

Nirmal Sengupta's wife appeared moments later. She supervised a soft mopping of his forehead while speaking to the old man softly, 'Master-moshai, can you hear me ... Try drinking some water.' The headmaster grunted and lay limp.

The family doctor arrived. Observing the headmaster, he made no attempt to wake him up.

'I'm quite certain he has malaria.'

'Serious case?'

'Maybe. Let's move him to a bed in an airy room and I'll give him an injection. He might have to lie there for a while. I'll call in the morning.'

The lights in the large house dimmed. The whirring of fans ceased and conversations attenuated. Only the occasional sound of a door closing or a tap running was heard. The young man ate a quick meal and returned to the living room. The day had left him exhausted, yet restless. He opened his notebook to write, but stared at the blank pages. He fell asleep.

He woke up in the middle of the night to find a tall, thin figure crouched beside him. When he saw the headmaster's face up close, he drew a sharp breath. The old man was soaking in his sweat, and his eyes were sunken and vacant.

'Sir, you're standing up again!' He tried to sound cheerful.

The headmaster asked in a quivering voice, 'Where am I?'

'You are in our home, sir, in Calcutta.'

The headmaster spoke with some awareness. 'I was completely lost, you know, I was stumbling around ... and then I saw you.'

The young man took the headmaster's hand and slowly walked him back to bed.

'Headmaster, do you remember why you came to Calcutta with me?'

The headmaster peered at him. 'Why don't you sit here with me,' he said unexpectedly.

The young man nodded, but when he returned with a chair, he found that the old man had fallen asleep. He set down the chair next to the bed and curled up in it.

In the morning, his mother gently awakened him. 'Ei ...' she whispered, 'try sleeping in your bed now.'

He stood up groggily. The headmaster was still asleep. As he walked back to his room, his mother said, 'It looks like he woke up in the middle of the night. He changed his clothes and ate an orange in the living room.'

'Orange in the living room?'

'Yes, we found peels this morning. And his water glass. Your father said that he had also written a letter. Thank god the doctor gave him that injection last night. I think he's getting better.'

Her observation was premature. When she went to check in on him later in the morning, she found him wracked with fever. The doctor was sent for again. This time he was grave. 'Sadly, this seems to be a case of malaria *falciparum*. It is a rather aggressive and fatal strain that affects the brain. We've been having quite a few of these of late.'

He administered another injection and said, 'This will reduce the fever, but it won't cure him. I will send his blood out for a test, but my diagnosis is, unfortunately, probably correct.'

'What can we do, doctor?' asked Nirmal Sengupta.

'Send for his family.'

The headmaster's high fever did not abate. He lay in a feverish haze – thin and crumpled on the large bed. The young man came to the room frequently. An odour of rotting breath now lingered in the air. At about seven in the evening, the headmaster's wife arrived at the house. She saw her husband taking shallow breaths. Crying softly, she wiped her tears with the folds of her sari.

'Come with me, Didi, come and eat some food with us,' said the young man's mother gently. But she just sat at the large dining table, unable to eat.

'I don't understand,' she whispered. 'I don't understand at all why he came to Calcutta without telling me.'

The headmaster died that night. His wife had felt his hot body cool too rapidly. She had held him tightly, feeling the heat leave him. Rather than wake the rest of the household up, she lay beside him quietly, cradling his head.

When Nirmal Sengupta's wife entered the room in the morning, she found her sitting on the edge of the bed. 'He is no more,' she said simply. By the time the young man had woken up, arrangements were already under way for their journey back to the village.

The widow was given one of Nirmal Sengupta's mother's white saris. A servant rushed to the market to buy a bier. Another was sent to the Ganges to bring an urn of water. Yet another was dispatched to purchase several train tickets. Finally, the family priest was summoned.

The young man sat around helplessly. His plan was now foiled. He peeked into the room where the headmaster lay, but couldn't bring himself to talk to his wife. When it was time, he carried one of the posts of the bier. The body that he had almost single-handedly brought all the way home just two nights ago, was now much heavier. Between them, they managed to get him onto the train and lay him down across the wooden seats. It was when the conductor walked into their compartment and started counting the number of passengers in the group that the widow burst into tears. A few hours later, the young man saw Nirupoma and her younger sister on the platform as the train pulled in.

Nirupoma got into the compartment before the train came to a complete halt. She had thought for a moment that her father was unconscious. But when she saw her mother in a white sari, she threw her arms around her in confusion. They made their way towards the headmaster's house. The villagers watched silently. Some folded their hands in deference when they realized that Nirmal Sengupta was leading the group.

A small ceremony followed, officiated by the priest who had travelled with them from Calcutta. The body was hoisted up again. This time for its final journey to the cremation ground. With loud, solemn chants of 'bolo-Hari, Hari-bol', the men left the house and turned towards the river. The priest sprinkled a few flowers. They decided to take a detour by the school. 'Headmaster! Look at your beloved school one last time!' someone called out.

On the slow walk back in the falling light, Nirmal Sengupta touched his son's shoulder and said, 'There is something that I've been debating about whether or not to tell you.'

'Why would you not tell me?' the young man asked politely.

'The matter is ... I found a letter in the headmaster's pocket this morning. It was addressed to me. I first thought that they were the words of a dying man – probably irrational and sentimental. Yet, as I read it, I realized that the letter had been written with great clarity. Every sentence was simple and certain ... It was as though he had known precisely what he was about to write.'

The young man stumbled.

'Watch your step.'

'Yes.'

'He said that he would like you to look after the school for a while along with his assistant. He said that he had seen in you a genuine quality to care ... that he trusted you. And then ... this is the strange part: he wishes for *you* to marry his older daughter. You know the dark one ... I forget the name. The singer.'

'He asked me to marry her?'

'Yes! Imagine that...'

'Should I?'

Nirmal Sengupta stopped in the middle of the road. 'Now, I know you are a sensitive boy. And I worry about that sometimes. Listen to me, you don't have to feel any obligation at all towards anything written in that letter. But I thought it was only fair that I tell you about this. And not a word of this to your mother ... she might be superstitious about this sort of thing. Is that clear?'

'But I want to.'

'You want to work in that school?'

'Yes...'

'Well, why not. I suppose you're not doing anything right now ... I didn't realize you cared so much about our village.'

'And the other part too.'

'What are you talking about?'

'Nirupoma ... the girl,' said the young man.

'What?'

His father grasped him by his shoulders. 'Don't be silly. You are not a schoolboy now. Don't get carried away by this.'

'But I want to.'

'Why on earth? She isn't very beautiful, is she?'

'I think I should. I am the right age and she doesn't have a father to take care of her. You should be a father to her now.'

Nirmal Sengupta let go of his son. He walked on quietly towards the house. The young man stood where he was, his heart pounding.

He called out to his father, 'Baba, should I?'

'God help you now,' Nirmal Sengupta hollered back.

It was hard to gauge how Nirupoma felt about her imminent wedding. Her mother had somehow managed to reconcile that the two events – her husband's death and her daughter's fortunate engagement to Nirmal Sengupta's son – were an astral balancing act. 'The lord who gives us sorrow also gives us joy,' she repeated like a mantra.

Nirupoma, however, was guided purely by a sense of duty. Her father's wishes, made clear in a letter composed during his final hours, became a sacred charter for her, much more important than anything a priest could say. So, she was calm at her wedding with a pre-ordained sense of purpose. This was unlike the young man who was overwhelmed with anxiety. In fact, he seemed rather miserable as he sat across from her, looking effete in a plain white singlet and an oversized white cone balanced at an angle on his head.

His mother whispered to him, above the dull thrum of the Sanskrit chants that no one understood but quietly endured: 'Look a little pleasant, or our guests will think that we forced you to marry her.'

The irony of his mother's words made the corners of his mouth twitch. His father had relied on the headmaster's letter to explain the abruptness of the situation to their closest relatives: 'Ordinarily, of course, such a marriage would not occur; however, we felt that we ought to honour the headmaster's wishes. My son did the honourable thing. It can be no other way.' And there he was, sitting honourably at his wedding.

But their priest had raised the issue that it was inauspicious to have a wedding within a year of a death in a family. 'Unless the dying man himself decreed otherwise,' explained Nirmal Sengupta authoritatively. 'It says so in the Vedas,' he added.

The priest quickly agreed, 'Yes, the Vedas do say so. Indeed.' Everyone in the room grunted.

'But Nirmal-babu ... Which shloka? I'm not a learned man, so I don't know about such things,' asked the nayib. He was not afraid to go on record. There were matters at stake. The nayib was worried by this sudden nuptial. He had observed the young man staring foolishly at Nirupoma long before anyone else had, and had anticipated the worst. This new alliance threatened his position.

His troubles had begun when Nirmal Sengupta had decided to rehabilitate the crumbling school, despite his objections. He had been forced to vacate a portion of the house he was living in, free of rent, to accommodate a new family and an administrative office. And now there was this wedding joining the two families. His role – for three decades – as village leader during Nirmal Sengupta's long absences was eroding at an alarming rate.

The landlord shot him a stern look but said nothing. The matter was decided.

It was a modest event, at least by Nirmal Sengupta's standards. Typically, a wedding would of course take place at the bride's home, followed by another ceremony soon after at the groom's residence. But since Nirmal Sengupta owned the house that the headmaster's family lived in, it was a protracted three-day affair, all in one location. Nirmal Sengupta did not spare any expense. It was the last great meal before the wrenching famine that would follow in the coming months, resulting in the deaths of half the village.

On their wedding night, exhausted from the long ritual fast and the heat, the couple fell asleep as soon as they lay down. The young man awoke in the middle of the night to find Nirupoma missing. He found her on the floor. She was clutching a small spindle-shaped container full of the red vermillion she had just been entrusted with.

'Why aren't you in bed?' he whispered.

She stirred sleepily and said, 'It is cooler on the floor.'

The young man crept back in.

After the wedding, they stayed on in the village so the young man could help at the school till a new headmaster was hired. Nirupoma continued to sleep on the floor.

One night, out of sheer exasperation, he asked her, 'Are you going to sleep on the floor all your life?'

'No,' she replied.

The young man stopped dreaming about the universe's elusive secret. He had seen evidence of it in the eyes of every married man and woman he knew. He knew that his real life was on a hiatus. His father had said that he was in the process of collecting enough funds for him to study medicine in Scotland. Nirmal Sengupta distrusted the medical colleges in the city with their rampant diversions to the freedom struggle. 'We will have a generation of revolutionaries with no skills,' he said.

It was not a good time to sell property, but Nirmal Sengupta went about liquidating parts of his estate whenever he was offered a decent price. The young man knew that he would eventually have to part with his wife and leave for several years. After what seemed like an eternity, the seasons changed and a cool breeze began blowing in the mornings and in the late afternoons. Kites appeared in the afternoon sky.

One night, Nirupoma slipped into the bed. The young man was unable to sleep. Her bracelets tinkled and her hair seemed to be everywhere. He also detected a faint snore, which annoyed him. But after a couple of nights he became used to her warm body next to his. When he finally reached for her, she did not resist him. By the time he left for Scotland, she was showing.

Nirupoma moved to the large house in Calcutta at the end of 1942. She soon found herself at the helm of domestic duties. She learnt about the lives of the numerous servants who worked there – the villages they came from, how many children they had and how much their debts were. They found it easy to talk to her because she understood the rural life with its intricate social systems, the constant shadow of penury, and the unrealistic expectations from family members who waited at home.

More significantly, she shared with them a sense of humour. While she was reserved and demure with members of the family, the landlord's wife would often find Nirupoma on her haunches, surrounded by a group of servants laughing at her stories. This made her uncomfortable.

'She needs to understand that she is one of us now,' she complained to her husband.

'Why don't you get me some tea?' asked Nirmal Sengupta, not wholly attentive to his wife's concern. 'Just half a cup, please. It cools too quickly otherwise.'

With his son absent, he was glad to have someone young to talk with, or mostly to just listen to him. He would sit with Nirupoma for hours in the large, wide balcony. She continued with her habit of singing in the evenings, sitting sideways on the floor to safely position her growing belly. Nirmal Sengupta would often invite his friends to the house and they would gather around her, holding onto their canes, eyes closed, swaying their heads gently as she sang.

One evening, the electricity went out, as was often the case due to wartime austerity measures, and the servants were asked to light lamps next to Nirupoma. It was a luminous sight – a group of elderly men in white, sitting in an arc around her. Her silky voice reverberated through the walls of the large house. The women sat on the floor of the balcony. It was Shivratri and Nirupoma sang devotional songs.

When she was done, one of the servants who had been listening from the stairway crawled up to her and wept. 'Forgive me for speaking in front of the elders. Ma, you have brought the lord to our house today.'

Nirupoma knew him well. Entertained by his theatrics, she stifled a giggle.

One of Nirmal Sengupta's friends said, 'You have spoken well, lad. What is your name?'

'I am Budhon,' the servant replied meekly.

One of the elders asked Nirupoma, 'What nonsense has your husband gone to study? If I had a wife like you, I'd have stayed right here in my own home. Write to him and ask him to return.'

Nirmal Sengupta turned to the guest and said, 'Yes, she does write. Every month, I give her an aerogramme and she gives it back to me, sealed. She must be complaining about her old father-in-law: why else seal it with good glue?'

Nirupoma bit the tip of her tongue. 'Please don't say that, Father. I merely do it so there is one less thing for you to do.'

'Aha! They must be love letters then!' exclaimed one of the guests. Nirupoma blushed hotly and left the room.

The truth was that while she did give Nirmal Sengupta sealed aerogrammes, she never wrote anything on them. She was embarrassed about her squiggly handwriting. But when her husband kept replying, bewildered at all the blank letters, begging her to write at least two sentences, she felt terribly guilty. One day, she saw Budhon jotting down the daily shopping list for the bazaar. She noticed that he had a fairly legible script. She called him to her room.

'Can you keep a secret?'

'Yes, Didi.'

'I need you to write something for me.'

She handed him the aerogramme and began pacing around.

'Write this ... I am well. Father is well. Mother is well. Everyone else is well. How are you?'

Budhon scribbled the words.

Nirupoma inspected the letter closely. 'Can't you write in a straight line?'

'Sorry, Didi ... Should I cross it out and try again?'

'No. Now write my name at the bottom.'

'Would you not want to write anything else, Didi?' he asked with a smile. 'When will you return? Or maybe ... the baby is kicking?'

Nirupoma spoke sharply under her breath, 'Did I ask you for your stupid opinion?'

Budhon made a sad face and left the room.

A moment later, Nirupoma called him again from the balcony. 'Budhon! I think there might be a cockroach under my bed, come here right away!'

Budhon came back and stood at the door.

'Alright' she said, gentler this time. 'Go on ... add another line before my name. "The baby is due before Durga Pujo." She took the envelope from him and licked it across the flap. 'One word of this to anyone and I'll make sure you never get a mango to eat.' Budhon grinned.

Nirupoma was confined to her room for the last two months of her pregnancy. She lay in bed all day, often staring at the ceiling. Her mother-in-law supervised her meals and made her finish every morsel of the food on her heaped plate.

'Impossible to fatten you,' she grumbled.

By the time she was due, she had put on a few kilos and looked radiant. The doctor who had attended her father's death, delivered the child. Nirmal Sengupta paced around the balcony while the whole house listened silently as she screamed her lungs out. He rushed up the stairs when he heard the first wail and gasped, 'Boy or girl?' The news of a grandson pleased the ageing man immensely. He grabbed his wife and attempted to hug her in a rare, public display of affection. She shrieked and ran away.

A few days later, Nirupoma's mother and her sister Maloti, now thirteen, arrived at the house. They peered into her bedroom. The windows were shuttered so the baby could sleep through the bright afternoon. 'He's not dark like you,' said her mother softly. 'But he has your lovely eyes.' Nirupoma hugged her family, squeezing her own flesh after months of waiting. Tears fell.

She spent deliriously happy days. A bed was moved into her room. Mother, two daughters and baby all slept close to each other. She awoke one morning and saw her sister softly cradling the little baby, whispering a lullaby, *'Firefly, firefly ... where do you fly? Firefly, firefly ... so bright in the dusky sky.'*

'That's it,' said Nirupoma. 'I will name him Jonaki.'

'But that's a girl's name.'

'Aren't there male fireflies? And it will be my own name for him. They can call him by some important landlord's name.'

They laughed and the baby stirred. Maloti calmed him down instantly.

'You will make a lovely mother someday,' said Nirupoma, observing them.

They left about two weeks later. Her mother buried her head in the baby's belly and said, 'I will miss this sweet smell of my tiny grandson. Come visit us when he is a little older. He is so small now ... A sudden jerk of the train and he might fly out the window.' Nirupoma laughed through her tears. She stood at the balcony with her baby and watched for as long as she could make out the tiny receding figures of her mother and sister, escorted by Budhon carrying their belongings. For the first time since she had arrived in Calcutta, she longed for her village.

She walked away from the balcony and whispered, 'Jonaki, Jonaki ... where will you fly to?'

The baby stared at his mother and sputtered.

RICE

By the early months of 1943, it became evident that a catastrophic shortage of food was looming. Bengal, it seemed, had fallen under the curse of a dual-headed beast loyal to both ill fate and human tyranny. A pernicious crop fungus, followed by massive cyclones, had destroyed the winter harvest the previous year. The Japanese invasion of Burma, just months later, blocked the rice imports urgently needed to cover the shortfall. These reductions, compounded by refugees fleeing from Rangoon, caused a harrowing shortage of essential grains. Yet, the British War Cabinet sequestered food for its own war efforts, building manpower and army garrisons in and around Calcutta while implementing a pre-emptive scorched earth policy to deny the resources to the Japanese, in the event that they were successful in entering India. Tens of thousands of fishing boats were systematically destroyed with no alternative in place, effectively eliminating the local water-transport system. Starvation loomed, especially in rural areas. Usury was rife.

Budhon, Nirupoma's favourite servant and ally, returned from the market one morning and reported that the sellers were speculating that the cost of rice was to rise significantly. This was brought to Nirmal Sengupta's attention over lunch. He too had been discussing the matter with his friends. 'Yes, yes, but we don't need to panic,' he responded calmly. A couple of days later, before Budhon went the market, he gave him enough money to buy an entire month's supply. 'Be very careful that we don't waste a single grain,' he announced as four servants hauled the sacks in. The following week the price doubled, a few days later it trebled, and by the end of a month it had reached five times the usual price.

Budhon was barely awake one morning, lying in his small corner behind the kitchen, when he thought he heard someone call his name. He listened carefully. He sprang up; it was his master's voice. Nirmal Sengupta had never visited the servant's quarters before.

'Sir ... what is it, sir? What may I do for you?' he said, clearing his throat.

'At what time does the first train leave for our village?'

'At eight, sir. A train leaves from Howrah; it is sometimes on time.'

Nirmal Sengupta peered at the clock in the dining room. 'That gives you enough time to get ready. Now, go into the storage room and pick up one sack of rice. You will take that to our daughter-in-law's house. Return immediately.'

He walked back up the stairs and settled in his large armchair on the balcony. Nirupoma was surprised to see her father-in-law up at the early hour.

'Did you sleep well, Father?' she asked.

Nirmal Sengupta asked her to sit next to him. As she crouched on the floor, he explained to her that he had just sent Budhon to her mother with enough grain to last a few days.

Nirupoma ran to the balcony and saw Budhon walking away briskly with a sack of rice balanced on his head. She called out as loudly as she could.

'Please bring back a letter from my sister.'

Budhon nodded, the sack bobbing on his head.

As dusk fell, Nirupoma cradled her baby and waited on the balcony. She stared at the street, anxious to catch Budhon's white singlet in the twilight.

Eventually, it was time for her to serve dinner. She was distracted. She mistakenly served her mother-in-law a piece of fish, a food item she did not consume on Thursday evenings on account of Lokkhi prayers in the house. Moments later, she switched the serving ladles, creating a small pool of green in the vivid yellow dish of lentils. She sat staring at the wall, impervious to her baby's cries.

Nirmal Sengupta leaned over, 'What is it? What is wrong with you today, Ma?'

She started sniffling.

'What is it?' asked the landlord's wife.

'Budhon has not returned yet.'

As she uttered those words, the creaky sound of the large metal gate from the ground floor was heard.

It was Budhon. He looked exhausted.

'Did you see them? Did you deliver the grain? Did you see my mother?'

Budhon nodded. He had also brought back a letter. Nirupoma snatched it from his hand.

'What does it say, Ma ... Read it out. Don't be shy,' said the landlord's wife.

Nirupoma wasn't feeling shy. She read aloud:

Nirupoma of our affections,
    This is a gift from heaven and we are grateful. We shall never forget this generosity in this time of great need – not in

this lifetime. May you and your small son be well and may he never know hunger.

Ma

Nirupoma sank to the floor, clutching the letter. Her mother-in-law put her hands around her and said softly, 'They are well, Ma, don't worry.'

Budhon spoke from his spot a few feet away, 'I saw them. Yes, they are well.'

Nirupoma looked up at Budhon and asked, 'How is everyone else in the village?'

He looked away.

In the following months, the cost of rice kept compounding. People sat on stoops, tired and listless. The loud, animated discussions of war and freedom, of self-rule and foreign expulsion, had attenuated to whispers of worry. The radio looped the same recordings for hours. The sacks of rice were moved from the storage room near the kitchen to a den, with a secure lock, next to Nirmal Sengupta's bedroom. Only Nirupoma had a key to it. She doled out as little as possible every morning. She prayed every night that Nirmal Sengupta would arrange to send more rice to her mother, but she could not bring herself to ask this of him.

Three weeks later, he summoned Budhon again. He asked Nirupoma to unlock the den. She fell at his feet in gratitude. Nirmal Sengupta remained silent. He shuffled away awkwardly and asked Budhon to take it to the village and return immediately. Before Budhon left, Nirupoma brought a crumpled handkerchief from her room. It contained her gold earrings which she placed inside the sack of rice. In the following weeks, it was Budhon who would subtly remind Nirmal Sengupta about Nirupoma's family.

That beastly summer, little effort was made to ease the starvation and rampant deaths of people – mostly those in the countryside.

In August, the *Statesman* carried horrific photographs. 'Look at this, just look at this,' Nirmal Sengupta exclaimed, pointing at the image of an emaciated woman in rags staring blankly at her two dead, skeletal children. 'And that overfed swine of a prime minister and his War Cabinet will do nothing!' Nirmal Sengupta threw the paper down angrily. Indeed, ships laden with wheat had sailed right past Calcutta, on occasion even docking briefly, before being diverted to be stockpiled in Britain.

Soft wails from the streets were heard during the long days. Defeated and starved, people stood in front of large houses asking just for the water that the rice had been boiled in. 'Ma ektu phaen dao, O Ma, ektu phen dao na.' Villagers began arriving in the city, often walking for several days for the empty promise of food. Yet another small sack of rice was sent through Budhon a few days later. Nirupoma slipped off one of her thin gold bracelets and put it in with the coarse, cheap rice. A gaunt Budhon left the house for the train station. This time, she heard her mother-in-law express dissatisfaction.

That night, as Budhon returned, Nirupoma ran to meet him at the top of the stairs. She stared at his face with intensity. Budhon broke into a weak but reassuring smile. It was always the same smile – a confirmation of life, a hint of hope.

Nirupoma couldn't sleep most nights. She would cradle Jonaki and stare out at the street, watching people moving around slowly or lying under the shelter of a tree or building. At times, someone on the street would catch her eye and feebly call out, imploring her for food. Nirupoma would turn her gaze away. Late at night, she would see shadowy creatures move around and hear the blood-curdling squeals of cats and dogs.

One monsoon afternoon, during a torrential downpour, so loud that it assaulted the senses and devoured conversation, there was an insistent clamouring at the front gate that wouldn't stop. A girl was trying to enter the house, and when the servants blocked her from entering, she began to howl. Nirupoma heard her harrowing yells from the second floor where they were having lunch.

'Don't go to check, Ma,' said the landlord's wife. 'These things will only break your heart.'

Nirupoma sat in her chair and stared at the shallow plate of lentils as the hollering continued. She turned her head with a sudden jerk. Her eyes widened; her name was being called out.

'Who is it, Ma?' asked Nirmal Sengupta.

Nirupoma left the room shrieking. She ran into a servant on her way down the stairs. 'Don't worry, we won't let her enter, Didi. This beggar is mad. And she keeps shouting your name.'

When Nirupoma saw the ragged, rail-thin girl, hobbling and croaking on the stoop outside the front door, she ran to her and fell on her frail body. They collapsed in a soaking heap. Everyone in the house gathered around the two sisters, reunited in agony.

Nirmal Sengupta crouched down. Lifting her stick-like arms, he whispered, 'How did this happen?' and then added nervously, 'Where is your mother?'

'Where is Ma?' asked Nirupoma, breathless.

The girl shivered and put her arms around Nirupoma. 'I tried my best, Didi. I really did try.'

'Is she alive, Maloti?'

'Yes.'

'But ... what about the rice?' asked the landlord's wife. 'What about the sacks we sent you?'

The girl lifted her head and looked puzzled. 'Rice? There wasn't ever any rice...'

She started coughing.

'Eat and drink slowly,' someone suggested, but she couldn't eat any of the food Nirupoma had brought in a small bowl. Maloti covered her mouth and made a tight fist after she spat into it. But she was unable to conceal the mixture of saliva and blood that trickled out. Budhon was nowhere to be found. Someone said that he had fled as soon as the emaciated girl had appeared.

Nirupoma laid her dazed sister down on her bed. She looked around the room. 'Where am I, Didi?'

'Try to rest now. I will be by your side.'

The girl nodded obediently and closed her eyes. Soon, she drifted into a haunting sleep that would not lift for days. When she heard her sister's faint, familiar snore, Nirupoma went out into the hallway and walked up the two flights of stairs. At the end of the large terrace was the marble-tiled room where the family held pujas. She tucked her sari in and lowered her body. Sitting on the cool, white floor, Nirupoma stared at the row of gods and goddesses lined up on the shelf. Small figurines, some with chipped edges and faded paint, faced her in trapped, catatonic stares. She took several deep breaths before letting out a scream of vengeance, shattering the sombre afternoon.

GOSSIP

1956. Even in the leanest of times, Malaya had not seen poverty like Bengal. Now, a decade after the war and the Japanese occupation, few were impoverished. Maloti marvelled at the affordability of basic staples – rice, fish and meat. She saw the most menial of men eating a boiled egg with their glutinous rice, a piece of fish with their midday curry or sambal. The children running around in the streets were generally healthy; few exhibited rickety limbs or the distended bellies she had often seen growing up.

The house smelt of smouldering spices when the young man returned from the estate one afternoon. Maloti did not hear him over the crackle of the fish frying. He stood at the top of the stairs that led to the kitchen. She shrieked upon noticing him. 'How did you manage all this?' he asked, looking around the kitchen in amazement. The small wooden table overflowed with packets, each secured with a thin rubber band. Maloti was cooking on two burners at once, deftly alternating pinches of spice while stirring ladles. She had finally been able to force Mamat to take her to the part of town where sellers set up stalls in the mornings.

'The market is really good,' she said excitedly. 'And clean. Just a bit of looking around carefully and I kept finding what I needed.

They have everything here – even our fish! They call our rui "tong sang", but it is the same, really. You know, the Malay girls have such sweet faces and they smile at you for no reason...'

Jonaki walked in and shouted, 'You talk about fish all the time. No more fish! Chicken! Chicken! Chicken!'

'Well, let's catch you and fry you, then,' said the young man and chased the squealing boy through the spartan house.

Later that evening, after eating the tong sang, the young man sat on the veranda jutting out from the bedroom and lit a cigarette with some difficulty because of the wind. He could make out the gentle swaying of the trees. There was a wide, tall one, right in front of the house, that produced a fragrant, mango-like fruit called 'kuini'. He had seen a few of them in Mamat's shed and had plucked a low-hanging one right off the tree once, only to discover that it had not yet ripened. It occurred to him that he would be spending many evenings with little to do. He looked at his raised wooden bungalow with its dark windows and the empty rooms behind them. He wondered how long it would take for the house to feel lived in. He had only known one residence in his life – the huge house in Calcutta, save for his time as a student in Glasgow, and the brief interludes in the village. In a way, the tappers with their simple establishments had a livelier existence despite the sparse furnishing – a few posters and wall calendars, shelves for deities and incense sticks, pots and pans in the open – they had querulous people everywhere, creating a reassuring ruckus. He wished that the local Indian community lived closer to his house. He could have watched the families to entertain himself. Jonaki and Maloti could have had a few friends. While there was an Indian family in the house across the street, the only signs of life emitting from it so far were intermittent high-pitched mechanical noises at odd hours of the day.

He heard a sound resembling the flutter of a small bird's wings. And then he heard another and then yet another, timed slightly apart. The soft whut-whut-whut noises seemed to be settling on the floor of the veranda. He felt a soft, furry touch on his foot and jerked his leg instantly. Something flew away. But moments later, it returned and settled on the floor. As his eyes adjusted to the dark, he noticed that a dozen dark, flat creatures had surrounded him. He watched the veranda gradually fill up, the small pink tiles getting covered over. They were moths of a size he had never imagined possible. He got out of the chair and tiptoed back inside. Maloti was attaching the mosquito net. The young man noticed Jonaki asleep on the wooden floor. 'Get him up and put him on the bed,' he said. 'There might be insects and creatures running around.'

'I don't think he'd wake up if a tiger carried him away,' said Maloti.

'Are you going to the market again tomorrow?' asked the young man.

'Perhaps. Why? Are you worried I'm spending too much money?'

'No. I need something. Can you buy me a pair of rubber slippers?'

'To wear around the house? Yes, I should get pairs for all of us.'

'I need a pair for the estate. My leather shoes don't fit in.'

'You wish to go to work in rubber slippers?'

'Perfect for the warm, tropical weather. Nag wears them.'

Maloti managed to hoist an unresponsive Jonaki onto the bed. 'Nothing will bite us tonight,' she said, encasing her family inside the taut mosquito net.

If Maloti felt lonely in the isolated bungalow, she didn't show it. She maintained an impeccable routine. Up before dawn, she slid quietly out of the net, swept the house, took her bath, said a set of short prayers and then started the three-step process of waking up the others. She would start by cajoling, then threatening, and finally resorting to limb pulling and short slaps on the bum. The young man would be the first to leave the house and a few minutes later, Mamat would appear at the porch, dazed and half-asleep. Jonaki would climb onto Mamat's bicycle, clutching his school bag. They would wobble for a few yards until Mamat picked up speed. As they exited the compound, Maloti would pray again for ten minutes – the time it Jonaki took to reach school.

She would take a short nap after breakfast, but the whirring, mechanical noises from across the street would soon wake her up. Their neighbours operated a machine that crushed spices at all hours of the day. People would come with raw condiments to have them powdered. In time, Maloti too started buying uncrushed spices from the market and making the short trip across the garden, crossing the street, often barefoot. The business was owned by a Mr Kottiyan. He had a friendly, cloying nature. The term 'god-fearing' came to mind. But Kottiyan did have one earthly excess – a second wife. The three of them took turns at the spice grinding machine while their litter of children ran around – the smallest ones naked. The two wives, though of different builds and a few years apart in age, were surprisingly similar looking. Maloti soon realized the reason behind their domestic harmony – they were sisters. Both ladies were extremely nice to Maloti. A game would be played out every time she walked over to avail their service. After the grinding was done, Maloti would pull out a few coins, but they would wave her payment away. Maloti would come home and peer through the kitchen window till she saw one of the children. She would call out to them and when they ran over, she would hand them the money and tell them to pass it on to their mother. A few minutes later, a voice would call out, 'Madam ... madam! Very bad! Very bad!' Sometimes, on Sunday mornings, she would hear a shout from the fence. One of the wives would be standing there with a steel plate heaped with paper-thin dosas or soft pancake-like uttapams. Maloti would accept these graciously while saying, 'Very bad! Very bad!'

Every other day, Maloti would go to the market and Mamat would trudge along about twenty paces behind. He pretended that he was not with her. Unlike the markets she was used to at home, which started brisk business early in the morning, the market here started selling fish only after nine. Despite her reputation as a skilled bargainer, sellers looked forward to her visits. She would instruct them on exactly how she wanted the fish portioned. They marvelled at her knowledge of how to gut, clean, scale and slice any kind of fish. 'You sell fish in India, is it?' asked an old Chinese woman, smiling through her golden crowns. Then they would beckon Mamat to carry the packets, but he would saunter over only after Maloti had left.

'I think people are more honest here,' observed Maloti one day when a boy brought to the house a packet of brinjals that she had paid for and forgotten at the market.

'No,' corrected the young man. 'People who have enough to eat will steal less.' He did not tell her about his experiences in the estates. And the minor issue of Mamat filching fruit.

Jonaki was now moving in a trilingual world – Bengali at home, English and Malay at school. One afternoon, Maloti heard him humming something in Chinese.

'What are you saying?'

'I don't know. My friend Boon Siew sings it when we play marbles.'

'You're speaking *Chinese* now?' asked Maloti. This triggered a sense of alarm in her.

So, every Sunday after lunch, Maloti would open her large, dented green trunk and pull out a thin, crumbling book called

Borno Porichoy (An Introduction to the Alphabet) – a staple for Bengali children. 'If you speak English all the time, how will you talk to your mother?' she would harangue him.

Ganesh, whom the young man had befriended on his first day at work, would usually stop by on Sunday mornings to help Jonaki with his Malay homework. It was unclear whether he had completed any formal education himself. 'School and I were not good friends,' he had once vaguely remarked, but he clearly knew enough to teach the boy simple sentence construction.

'What is your job, Ganesh Uncle?' Jonaki asked while memorizing Malay verbs.

'I don't do the work any more,' Ganesh replied.

'Oh, are you retired?'

'*Re*-tired? No. I am just tired.'

'Ganesh, what is Hantu Pontianak?' asked Maloti when the study session was over.

'Oh, you been talking to local people, na? That one very scary hantu.'

'Mamat mentioned it. Tell, tell.'

'Hokay. That hantu was human before. But she die when giving birth to the little baby. So, in her sadness and anger, she became a hantu and flies to look for the victim. And when she attack, she make a sound like, "hnhnhnhn ..." and then she scratch the person to drink the blood.'

'So we can see her?' asked Jonaki.

'Oh yes, she has long white dress and nails for the scratching. Like vampire. Her face is the ugliest one. One look and you will run, boy! But sometimes this mischievous hantu can go inside people. Become a very beautiful woman. Then marry a man and become wife, mother ... all. No one can know she is a hantu.'

'Then how to catch her?'

'Sometimes can never catch her. She just lives all life with the family. And takes the blood.'

'So the children never found out they had a false mother?'

'Ah. Yes, they have been caught. There is only one way. Sometimes, small children, when they are brushing their mother's hair, they will see a small nail in the back of the neck. That means she is actually the Pontianak. Must take out of her neck quickly. Then she will become Pontianak hantu again.'

Jonaki shuddered.

'Okay. Enough stories. Now go take your mandi. You stink like a hantu,' said Maloti. She asked Ganesh if he would like to stay for lunch. Ganesh appeared touched, but declined the invitation. He did mention, however, that he had heard of her bargaining at the market.

'Nag's wife,' he said, 'never goes to market. Maybe she thinks she is high class. Always send the servant boy. And then complains that he steal from her.'

The young man, now listening in, asked if he had ever met her.

'Oh yes, plenty of times. Nag went to India and brought back his high-class wife when I was in school. It was the talk of the town. There were some rumours about him and one of the tapper girls. So he left for India suddenly and returned three weeks later with the fair and lovely wife. When he married, he already got grey hair. That fellah dark bugger like me, but the wife is so fair. Must have paid her father lot of money.'

'Nag is rich?' asked the young man.

Ganesh nodded. 'But he keeps it secret.'

'How did he become rich?' asked the young man. 'Isn't he a clerk?'

'Okay, I will tell more about the life of Nag.' Ganesh looked at the boy and paused.

'Jonaki, I said go and take your bath right now,' said Maloti sternly.

Ganesh let out a fiendish laugh. 'Never met an Indian – woman and also man – who can say no to the gossip.'

The young man sat down on the steps. Ganesh began.

'Nag came here long time ago, in the 1930s or something. They say that he got into some trouble in India – maybe something criminal or politics, and so he ran away before he was caught. Someone found him a low-paying job as an assistant or something to a clerk here. In the beginning, he used to do everything – lift sacks, drive people, cook, clean – anything to earn the extra money. But he was very good as a clerk's assistant and when the estate expanded, they made him a full clerk. He worked very, very, very hard. My father remembers how the managers used to come to him if they wanted to guarantee that something must get done. Nag got wise and started to make money. Every contractor went through Nag and he took his share. The work was done, the reports were good and the White people were happy.

'Nag got a bigger house and he bought a few nice things – bicycle, radio and all that, you know. Then the rumour started about Nag and the estate girl. The girl's father, a poor tapper, came to the office one day looking for Nag with a sharp parang in hand. I think Nag paid him something and then he took leave from his job. He came back with the fair wife and the people stopped gossiping.

'Everything was going well for him, and then suddenly the Japanese came here; I was still in school then. Those were wretched times, I tell you. Simply miserable days for all of us. The Europeans ran away or were sent to camps and to sweep the streets, and the Japanese took over the estates here.

'Nag soon became very, very important to them – after all, they needed people who knew the operations, na? They could not trust the Malays and certainly not the Chinese, but Nag was a small Indian fellow. And so they kept him on the chain and he ran the show from behind the curtain. He saluted them and spoke to them in Japanese, and we even saw him driving around in the Jeep with some of them. If they wanted any information, Nag could get it for them. The worst was when he supplied the Japanese with the workers to build the railway line in Thailand, Burma and those far places. Hundred and hundred of young men, many with wife and children here, were taken away. Nag said they will be back in few months. They said Nag was given lot of money for supplying the men. They also say that Nag ... supplied women. Most never came back. And then the big bombs were dropped and the great World War was finished everywhere.'

'What happened to Nag?'

'Ah. So, when the Whites came back my father said it was surely the end of Nag. But that fellah is a genius. He told the manager that his loyalty was to the trees, not their owners. Somehow this answer satisfied them. And besides, same problem again – they needed Nag's know-how. So, he was back at his old job and even *more* powerful now. I even think they offered him a job as assistant manager, but Nag, being the genius, knew that he could make more money as a clerk.'

'Does he have any children?' asked Maloti.

'Yes, one son who studies in a boarding school in Singapore. We hear he will go to England soon. Imagine that, son of an estate clerk going to England. So that is the story of Nag.'

'Incredible guts and cunning, I must say,' remarked the young man.

Ganesh nodded and then added, 'Only one problem – he made serious enemies with some of the locals. They did not forgive him for collaborating with the Japanese. That's why Nag never alone, never go out at night. And that's why he sent the boy away.'

'Nag is afraid?'

'Nag is very, very afraid.'

As Ganesh left the kitchen and turned to the front of the house, he noticed a tall ladder leaning against the large kuini tree. He walked up to the tree and saw Mamat high up in it, among clusters of fruit. Debating whether he was just plucking, or worse, stealing the fruit, he went back to the house and asked the young man to come out and investigate the matter.

'Mamat, what are you doing up there?' asked the young man, a bit rudely.

'I am putting number on the buah-buah,' answered Mamat calmly.

'Number?'

'Yes, see this one is 61, then got 62, then 63. Now this big one ... 70.'

'I think he is acting-acting,' whispered Ganesh. 'Doing all this on Sunday for show, so you can see.'

'Why are you numbering the fruit?' asked the young man, confused. The afternoon sun had turned the ground very hot. Barefoot, he was now uncomfortable.

'Because, encik, the people in the other house steal it when the nice smell come. If got number, they cannot dare.' Mamat was leaning into the tree, gently inscribing on the fruits with a pen.

'So how many do we have, Mamat?' asked the young man, squinting, trying to read the numerals.

'120, maybe 125,' said Mamat, concentrating on his task. 'Later, I bring you all the good ones. You count number every time, 1, 2, 3, 4 ... 50, 60, 70 ... like this.'

'Good. I want to try this fruit soon.'

Ganesh waved at the young man and left the house on his cycle, a sceptical look clinging to his face.

Palash called the young man at work one afternoon and asked if he could visit the following Sunday. He had not visited the Senguptas since their first day in Malaya, when he had met them at the dock in Penang and had driven them all the way to their new home.

'Does he want his money back?' said Maloti.

'Mind your own business!' snapped the young man. 'How many years have we known Palash? Why does your mind work like this?' This sort of exchange between them was uncharacteristic and Maloti stayed silent. She had been looking forward to Palash and his wife Reba's visit, feeling hurt that they hadn't come sooner. But her plans for a cosy day with them were shattered when the young man said that he would invite Nag and his wife as well. 'He is my superior at the estate,' he reasoned.

Maloti went on a cooking spree on a Saturday and everyone experienced a rare side of her, one where she was capable of being short. 'I thought you were going to bring fresh sekap for me today,' she yelled at the fish seller. 'Do you expect me to catch a bus to Seremban now?'

She managed to shout enough Malay to galvanize Mamat. 'Air habis! Saya masak! (Water finish! I was cooking!).' She glowered as Mamat ran across the yard to the water tank, holding up his sarong. By Sunday morning, the small, blue refrigerator was packed with dishes. Maloti had a second bath and pulled out a new sari from her trunk. It had a light white print, with a sprinkle of small yellow flowers. She peered at her reflection as she adjusted the throw of the cloth.

'How do I look?' she asked the young man.

'You look like a nervous village girl about to meet her future in-laws,' said the young man chuckling. 'But you look pretty.'

'I wasn't afraid of my in-laws. Not in the least. But I'm afraid of meeting Nag and his wife.'

'Don't worry, we've got Palash to manage him. I hope you've made enough food; sometimes I wonder if Nag gets any at home.'

Maloti heard a car pull into the driveway. As the doors clicked open, a sing-songy voice chanted, 'Haven't eaten in three days, haven't eaten in three days ...' Maloti ran to the porch.

'That's all right, I serve more than tea and fritters nowadays,' she said smiling.

'Yes! That sweet tea of 1946! Hot and steaming, fanned only by the promising breeze of freedom,' said Palash, clutching his chest dramatically. He was dressed in loose, comfortable pyjamas and appeared as though he had just woken up. Maloti had served Palash tea many, many times in her life. She stood at the steps and reminisced for a fleeting moment about the earnest conversations that used to ensue during those long, humid Calcutta evenings when she had taken over the house after her sister had died. She had played her part in the struggle, alongside the charming, excitable, worldly men she had met. But all that had eventually destroyed her husband. And killed a friend.

Reba got out of the car and walked to the front of the house, holding a small Pyrex container. 'For afterwards,' she said, handing it to Maloti. 'And some local fruit,' she added, handing her a bunch.

'What fruit is that?' asked Jonaki.

'They are called rambutan. They taste a bit like litchis. Here, try one,' said Reba, tearing one off.

'A strange furry thing ...' remarked Jonaki, running his fingers over it.

'Reba-di,' exclaimed Maloti. 'You look so lovely, but what's wrong with Palash-da? He looks like he has just woken up. Does he think we're still back home in Bhowanipur?'

'That, my dear, is exactly the point! For the next few hours, I will forget that I am stuck on this narrow peninsula and will transport myself back to good old Calcutta,' said Palash cheerfully.

'Stop being the joker and come on inside, Palash,' said the young man.

Palash commented on the house. 'What a complete transformation! Look at that, Reba. She has wasted no time in arranging a home good enough for our decadent aristocrat.'

'Why, does Reba-di make you sleep in the garage?' asked Maloti.

'Indeed, I should!' said Reba, 'The man does not lift a finger. Whom is he calling aristocrat? Can I leave him here for a few days, Maloti?'

'No,' said a voice.

'Jonaki ...! Come here,' called out Palash. 'Why, don't you want me to stay here?'

'Because we don't have a room for you?' said the boy, eyeing the Pyrex with the dessert.

'What? You don't have a room in such a large house? Why, I'll share a room with you then,' said Palash.

The boy shook his head. 'I sleep with Baba and Ma. The other room is a room for books and things.'

'Then I will have to sleep in the shed, with that fellow...'

'Yes, I think Mamat needs some company. The poor chap looks miserable most of the time,' said the young man.

'Oh, this is going to be fun, this is going to be a fun-fun afternoon!' said Palash, cavorting in an inelegant twirl. 'Let's come down to business – where's the beer, Sengupta-babu?' The young man returned with a can of Anchor beer and a big glass mug. 'A real beer mug ...' marvelled Palash.

'It came with the case,' said the young man.

'You have a whole case here, man?'

The front gate rattled and Maloti peered out.

Nag stumbled down the driveway in his rubber slippers and introduced himself. 'Utpal Nag. Clerk.' Palash shook his hand.

'Palash Mitra. Dentist.'

Nag was impressed. 'A dentist? Wonderful ... I need to show you something.' He opened his mouth and poked his gum.

Maloti walked up to Nag's wife who was standing awkwardly at the door, a smile suspended on her face. She was fair-skinned and wore an additional coat of white powder on her face. She had a somewhat pneumatic build. A sleeveless blouse exposed her plump, fair arms.

'Please come in, Didi ... Why are you standing by the door?'

Nag's wife walked in timidly and sat down.

'Anchor beer. First class,' said Nag tucking his skinny feet in a yogic pose on the sofa cushion. 'This is my wife, Leela,' he added as an afterthought.

Jonaki sidled his way over to the sofa and waited till Nag had sipped his beer. 'Will your driver take me for a walk in the jungle?' he asked.

Maloti snapped at him. 'Not everyone wants to do that. Behave yourself and stay indoors while we eat lunch.'

Nag looked at Jonaki with commiseration. 'The little fellow is very observant. Send my driver a little something to eat later, will you please?'

'Yes; I did notice you brought the estate jeep. Were you out on work earlier today?' asked the young man.

'Work?' said Nag loudly. 'Work? This is the work, brother. This is hard work.' He grinned at everyone.

They adjourned to the dining room. Nag sat himself at the head of the table. Maloti insisted on serving everyone. Reba objected loudly, 'This is not your large family lunch back home. Sit with us. We can all serve ourselves.'

Jonaki started with the chicken. 'Did you shoot it yourself? Are we eating your hunt?' asked Palash. Maloti laughed.

'Poor boy. He goes out looking for wild animals with his plastic gun and all he sees are hens running around. I think if he had a real gun, he would have shot all of them by now.'

'Madam, do you have any children?' Nag asked Reba loudly.

Palash answered for his wife, 'No, not yet, sir. Soon perhaps. How about you?'

'We have one monkey. He is fifteen,' said Nag.

'Why did you not bring him today?' asked Maloti, feigning ignorance.

'Because he is in Singapore. In a boarding school.'

'Why all the way in Singapore?' Maloti asked.

'You should send him away too,' Nag added, pointing to Jonaki. 'Send him back to Calcutta. He could stay with his grandparents and go to a proper school. Would have saved me a lot of money. But Leela here ...' Leela ate silently.

There was silence after that, except for the sound of Nag chewing on chicken bones. A couple of minutes later, he said, 'I'll be very honest and tell you why I sent my son away. It's not that I think the school here isn't decent. The problem is elsewhere.'

'What is this problem?' asked Palash.

Nag appreciated the question. 'Who are the students there? Tell me. Sons and daughters of the poor plantation workers, right? And some Malay kids from the nearby kampungs. Do you want your boy growing up in that company?'

'But we've come all this way ...' started the young man.

'Yes. We had to come to this strange place to make our livelihoods, but we can certainly shelter our children. I don't want illiterate, slovenly villagers surrounding my boy. I tell you, if Leela were educated, I would not even have sent him to primary school. I would have kept him at home and made him read. You won't have that problem. Maloti here is well educated ... Probably from a high-class family like yours. I wasn't so lucky.'

Reba put her left hand gently on Maloti's leg. She could feel it shaking and she pressed down on it harder. When they went to the kitchen to bring more rice, Maloti turned her back to Reba and faced the sink. Reba put her arm around her, laying her head on the back of Maloti's shoulder.

'Let it go, there are all kinds of people, Maloti. You know this better than I do.'

'Yes. Let's finish up with the meal.'

When they were done with dessert, Palash declared, 'There are few things that heal the soul more than fresh homemade yogurt. Its simple texture ... The way it dissolves in your mouth and this sublime aftertaste. Tell me, friends, do we need to go to the prayer room today?'

Nag scrunched up his face and said, 'Maybe. But I have this problematic tooth. Sala, whenever something cold enters my mouth, it starts complaining.'

'Then just don't eat cold things!' said Leela forcefully.

'Keep quiet. What's gotten into you?' said Nag.

'But men never do the sensible thing do they, Didi?' quipped Reba jokingly.

'No, they don't. They make their own stupid rules.'

The young man got up and said, 'I think the senseless men should retire to the living room and let the ladies clean up in here.'

'Oh no, no', protested Maloti. 'I can do it. Everyone, please go and rest in the other room. We'll have some tea later.'

'Is there something I can do?' asked Leela timidly.

'Just sit here and talk to us, Didi' said Maloti. 'You must miss your son a lot. What is his name?'

Leela nodded slowly. 'We call him Babla at home.' She pulled out a photograph of a tall, strapping boy with glasses, waving from a car.

'So handsome!' exclaimed Reba sincerely.

'You know, when he and his father go out for walks, people don't think he's his son. He is fond of saying, "How did a son of mine end up looking like that?" I think he's secretly jealous.'

'Well, I think we could say that the boy has his mother's lovely looks,' said Reba, smiling. Leela sat quietly and looked at the photograph. Tears welled up in her eyes.

'You know ... I used to love to cook at home. There was nothing for me to do here really, except take care of him. After he left ... I just don't feel like doing much ...' And then she looked at Maloti and said softly, 'Don't listen to anyone; keep your boy with you. Never let him go.'

There was loud laughter in the next room. 'They're drinking again,' said Reba.

'Why did you agree to send him to Singapore?' asked Maloti. Leela looked at her and shrugged.

'I'm not educated ... I didn't finish school or even really read much. His father started yelling at him all the time and blamed me for being so ... illiterate. So, it was decided that he would be sent away ... What could I say?' She got up and went to the sink to wash her face. She turned around. 'I was so young when I was married. I didn't know we would spend the rest of our lives here, alone in this country. But now, at least you are here. The other Bengalis aren't as nice. They talk about buying cars and ... But you seem to be nice.'

Maloti was touched. 'Please come more often. Even if it is just you. I'll cook for you any day, Didi. I miss my own sister.'

'Where is she?' asked Leela.

'Oh. She isn't with us any more.'

Palash walked into the room and barked, 'Attention, attention, important announcement: The men are going out on a tour of the area in Nag-babu's jeep. We'll be back around four. I have been dispatched to ask for your permission.'

'Please do go on your expedition and leave us alone,' said Reba.

'Dearest wife, I shall interpret that as consent,' said Palash bowing.

When the three men approached the jeep, Jonaki was already seated in the front with his seat belt strapped on. 'Where do you think you're going?' asked the young man.

'If you don't take me with you, I will never ever do Bengali homework again,' said Jonaki resolutely.

'He's got you ... he's got you!' said Palash, laughing loudly. 'The Achilles heel of the immigrant ... That ever-primordial issue of the mother tongue! I think you have to accept his demand. No way out.'

The jeep pulled out of the driveway and turned onto the dusty, red lane that led to the main road. Soon, they were cruising by the small kampung on the periphery of the town. 'Look how peaceful it is. A little paradise we have here,' said Nag sincerely.

'Don't you get tired of this?' asked Palash. 'It's been so many years for you, sir.'

'I never tire of this. So many trees, so much order. You have to hand it to the British; they really did an amazing job in these dense jungles. I think these people would still be living in huts in the forests if they hadn't come here and cleared the place out.'

He addressed the driver in Malay and asked him to stay clear of the manager's bungalows. 'Four brown buggers, out on a joyride in the estate car. Doesn't look good, does it now?' he chuckled.

'Do you think they will get their independence soon, Nag-babu?' asked the young man. He rarely got the opportunity to discuss politics.

'Yes, they will. As you say, they will 'get' it – not really 'take' it, like we did in '47,' said Nag with detached pride. 'Not so much for their own demands as for the Empire changing their ways all over the world. So here we are in 1956 ... It may take another year or two – who knows maybe three – but yes, it is most certainly closing down. And I think that when that day comes, quite a few people here will weep. Not necessarily in joy...'

A few bare-chested men recognized Nag and waved at him. 'I see that you are popular here.'

'Ha. Stupid people most of them. They always ask me for advice. Should I buy this? Should we go there?'

'Did you really mean it when you said some people will weep when the British leave?' probed Palash.

'Oh yes, my young man. You see, things here are pretty simple: these Malay people love their many rajahs and, of course, the sultan. Damned loyal subjects they are. And these royals who look over them have handed out contracts to the Whites in return for handsome revenue. The land is lush and rich – rubber, tin, coffee, rice, sugar ... you sprinkle it, it grows here. Even the women are more fertile! The people working in the fields are paid nominally and everybody is happy. Well, almost happy. But imagine what our country went through in the last two decades! What a ruckus they created for the damn sahibs – bombs going off all the time, your good friend Gandhi and his hunger strikes, civil disobedience, Netaji and his ridiculous army marching through the forests, laypeople refusing to cooperate, assassinations ... Who would want to hold on under such miserable conditions? They couldn't get out fast enough. But this place ... this was paradise. Well, until the Japs showed up.'

Palash nodded.

'I am sure the two of you know all this ... after all, you were there when it happened. I was here eating durian.'

Palash and the young man had indeed experienced those heady, harrowing years. That was why they were friends. That was why they were together again.

'What's all this about a "black area"?' asked the young man.

'Ah, yes ...' said Nag. 'That is something to consider. I must admit grudgingly that I have some admiration for the communists here – the only people who really put up a resistance of any sort. You see, the rich people of this nation are pretty much all playboys, quite uninterested in issues of freedom, save for occasional lip service. But the days are numbered for the communists. You can't camp out in the forest and take over a country, can you now? You know ... I even know a few of them and I know where they are right now.'

'Why don't you turn them in?' asked Palash.

'Me?' said Nag incredulously. 'Do I look like a person interested in all that? None of my bloody business. I get asked by the local sergeant all the time if I have any information, if the tappers have reported anything suspicious. That big, loud Irish fellow called O'Brien just barges into my office with his stupid questions. "Just leave them alone," I shout back. "They'll either die of dysentery or get eaten by tiger." Do you know the government will give about two thousand ringgits if you can turn in a bandit? And if they surrender on their own – they are given some money too. The number of leaflets they sprinkled all over the country, goading those chaps to give up. And still those fellahs won't come out of the forest. Look ... look at that ...' A golf course loomed into sight; a smooth, lush, flat stretch of green in the middle of the plantation.

'My goodness,' said Palash. 'How did they make something like that here. It's enormous.'

'Imagine that,' said Nag. 'These planters, lord knows where they came from originally, maybe from some poor hovel of England and Ireland, built a full-sized golf course here. You don't do that unless you are sure that it will be yours to enjoy for a long time. Interesting story I'll tell you: a few years ago, before any of you were here, we had a series of attacks. The communists had started to run out of rice to eat, and they were going to people's homes and demanding food at gunpoint. The locals were terrified and handed over whatever grains they had. So, the government passed a rule: we were not allowed to store rice in our homes any more.'

'What did you eat then?' asked Palash.

'Aha ... huge communal drums of rice were cooked every morning on that golf course and we took just our share for the day, that's all. Kind of a communist thing to do, isn't it?' Nag laughed.

'Did it work?' asked the young man.

'Well, they did stop raiding homes. Of course, you must realize that it was not all attacks. A lot of these forest bandits had local sympathizers who would willingly give them rice. I think they figured out other means of sustenance ... Maybe they grew their own crops in the jungles. I have come across abandoned patches and clearings in the middle of the forest. If they happen to be near a pool, they'll even catch fish by dropping charges of gelignite. Besides, I think they have several collaborators in town, working alongside you and me every day. Who knows, right? Do we know what happens in each and every home after dark?'

'Are you worried?'

'Me? Hah! No one will ever touch me. I'm nobody. A harmless, dark Indian clerk,' said Nag with unshakeable assurance.

When they returned, it was almost four. As they were leaving the house, Nag asked for a cigarette and put it behind his ear. Maloti and Jonaki kept waving and yelling their goodbyes. The Kottiyans and their brood of children joined in as well from across the street. The two cars left the driveway with Palash honking loudly.

BEFORE THE REVOLUTION

They said that he had succumbed to the habit of drink in Scotland, just another uppity Indian falling prey to the licentious ways of the firangs. Sell half your estate and send a young man away to study – and he returns home a drunk, they mocked. But truth be told, the young man had not had his first sip of drink till he was on the month-long journey back home. And there were extenuating circumstances. About two years earlier, he had received a cable from Calcutta that had obliterated everything for him. Nirupoma had died. The conditions were uncertain. To cope with his grief, he reread her telegram-like letters in Budhon's slanted handwriting for several months. His family saw no use in him returning in a rush. And so, clinging to the fading memory of a wife and the apparition of a baby, he morosely continued with his studies. But in 1945, Nirmal Sengupta wrote an apologetic letter, asking him to return home. The family was running out of money.

The young man packed his belongings and scribbled a note of withdrawal to the university. It must have been one of the strangest letters the director of the medical centre had ever received: 'As my wife had met an untimely death at the hand of rural miscreants in the recent past, and my ageing parents and young son are now living in a city recovering from famine and in an inhospitable social climate, I hereby beg to withdraw.'

He would have shared accommodations on the ship, but the suddenness of the booking prevented that. He travelled in a room by himself, a luxury that made him feel guilty. He skimped on food and avoided refreshments, exorbitantly priced on an ocean liner. He would walk out to the patio after dinner, often forgetting to lock his room, and sit on a deck chair. He didn't observe anything or anyone in particular; he just sat. The cabin boy, a middle-aged man really, stopped by three to four times every evening and asked, 'Whiskey, gin, sir?' The young man would wave him away.

A week into the journey, the young man had a slight fever. He skipped dinner and sat by himself, watching the sunset.

'No dinner, sir?'

'No. I'm a little unwell.'

'It is not good, sir, to sit here in the wind. Maybe you have a whiskey, gin sir? It will make you feel warmer.'

'Okay, whiskey–gin.'

The cabin boy–man was walking away when he realized that the young man had finally ordered a drink. Two drinks, actually. He returned with a tray – a glass with a peg of whiskey, a glass with a peg of gin and a bucket of ice. He slipped two cubes deftly into each drink and said, 'Good for health, sir.'

The young man took a swig from the glass that had the clearer liquid and immediately made a gasping sound, loud enough that people turned. He put it down and breathed in deeply. Five minutes later, he felt a pleasant warmth come over his body. He sipped this time. He finished the drink over the course of fifteen minutes. Then he proceeded to drink the whiskey. He emptied it in about ten.

The cabin boy–man – who seemed to have been hiding somewhere in his blind spot – appeared as soon as he put the second glass down. He would do this all night. 'More whiskey–gin?'

By the end of the night, he had consumed five pairs of whiskey–gins. A small group of deck hands, on instructions from the head steward, kept watch over him from a discreet distance. But the young man didn't do anything outrageous. He tried to sing, but only croaked for a while.

The cabin boy carried him back to his room. He asked for yet another whiskey–gin, but when the cabin boy returned for the sixth time with the tray, he had passed out on his small cot.

He awoke the following afternoon with a throbbing headache. He washed his face and stumbled out into the blinding sunlight. He turned around, stumbled back in, and slept again till dinner. He ate his meal quietly and then made his way to his spot on the deck. The cabin boy–man showed up but was promptly waved away.

When the cabin boy–man returned a third time, the young man pondered whether to have more drink. The cabin boy–man leaned in and said, 'Sir, if I may say ... it is not good to drink whiskey and gin together. That is why you are so unwell, sir. Just drink the whiskey. No pain.'

The young man agreed to have just the whiskey. That night, he had five glasses of whisky and when he awoke the next morning, he felt only slightly ill. He got used to the drink. For the next three weeks, he drank himself to oblivion.

As the ship came within a few hours of Calcutta, people on board began to arrange their belongings furiously. The young man drank his whiskey. A coolie helped him get off. He stumbled his way through the port.

'Sengupta, returning from England ...' remarked the landing officer, looking at his particulars. 'Oh, the Senguptas of Hazra? Near that movie theatre, what is it now ... Russa Cinema?'

'Yes,' mumbled the young man in a parched, drunken haze.

'Are you Nirmal Sengupta's son? The one that went to study medicine?'

'Yes,' said the young man feebly.

'Welcome back, Dr Sengupta!'

The young man woke up when the taxi driver yelled, '*Where* in Hazra, sir?' He looked around his old neighbourhood; they were close to home now, driving slowly through the crowded streets. He had expected to see worse – the remnants of the famine, more dilapidated facades – but the old street appeared like it always had. He guided the car to their lane and stumbled out. 'Budhon!' he yelled.

No one was expecting him. His telegram from Glasgow had not arrived. Chaos enveloped the household when the family realized that he had returned. Fair, thin, fat, old, rich, tall, western, gaunt, sad, weak, altered, different–different – these descriptors were deployed within moments and they made him feel loved again. His mother touched his face gently and said, 'Yes, it is him. My boy has come home.' Still in a daze, he made his way up the narrow stairway to the large living room. He sat down wearily, wishing for a drink. A crowd gathered against the far wall, some standing, others squatting on the floor, watching him intently.

A boy of about three was ushered in.

'Look, it's your father ... He came in a big ship just to see you,' said the girl with him. The boy clapped his hands.

'Do you want to play with me?' asked the young man hesitantly. 'Can I take him? Are you his ayah?'

'No,' said Mrs Sengupta, 'This is Maloti ... Nirupoma's sister.' She began weeping. 'She cares for him like her own son. Go on ... take your child into your own arms.'

The young man looked at the child. 'But I am wearing street clothes, Ma ... Let me change first and take a bath?'

'Just hold him for a bit.'

So, the young man took the small boy in his arms and awkwardly paced around the living room. A servant holding a thick garland, outstretched in his arms, entered the room. 'Ma ... where did you want these flowers?' Mrs Sengupta said nothing and sobbed again. The young man noticed that everyone in the room was looking at the wall behind him. He turned around and saw a large photograph of Nirupoma framed in polished Burma teak.

For the next few days, he reacquainted himself with the people and the quotidian rituals he had been away from. He would take naps in odd places – the floor of the storage room or a corner of the terrace where he had played as a child. He read the local papers voraciously, catching up on the complex politics of the city and nation. It would take him several days to come to a basic comprehension of contemporary affairs. He would walk all over the old house, at times mumbling to himself. The old cook who knew the young man from infancy would often be startled to find him sitting on his haunches, staring at her.

'You used to sit right there when you were a child. What are you looking at?'

'You.'

'What's there to see? Do you want to learn how to cook?' He nodded. 'Don't worry, you'll have a wife again. She'll cook and do a lot more for you.'

The cook was the only one among the staff who spoke to him in this candid manner. He found solace in her unguarded banter. Everyone else, including his own parents, were too wary to bring up the issue of Nirupoma's death. A few lines in a letter was

A FLUTTER IN THE COLONY

all the news he had received. But the old cook would give him disconnected pieces of information while serving him pieces of fried fish on a newspaper.

'I thought I had seen it all, but I never dreamed that Budhon was capable of that. We all thought he adored her. But he and that shaitan nayib of your father had been stealing the rice all along. She rushed to the village to confront him, but they said there was a stampede and she was killed on the train for the precious bit of grain she was carrying for her mother. Do you believe that? Your dear wife didn't even tell us she was leaving.'

'No one knew?'

'Not a soul. Left at the crack of dawn the day after her sister came here looking like a corpse.'

'Did they ... bring her back?'

The old cook nodded. 'But I refused to see her body. And her mother's too; who knows if she died of starvation or heartache? Well, maybe a village girl just can't marry a master's son. Maybe the gods didn't like that. But she was special. I used to listen to her sing in the evenings after my cooking was done. Oh, what a divine voice:

Mind, call no longer ma. You will not find her. Had she been alive, she would have come. But she is dead and lives no more. Now go to your stepmother's bank; there burn an image of kuśa-grass; when the time of mourning has finished, leave on the bank your lump of rice. Then let us go to Kāśī.'

'You have a lovely voice too.'

She smiled. 'I sit at the temple in the evenings with the others and sing along for hours. I know many songs. I don't know what they mean though. I just repeat them. Otherwise, my evenings would be empty. A widow doesn't have much else to do.'

'Do you remember what he was like?' asked the young man.

'Who?'

'Your ... husband.'

The old lady smiled. 'We were married for a little while. He had a big moustache and I was scared of him sometimes, but he was gentle. I remember that.' There was no sorrow in her words, just a lingering fondness.

'Don't you have a picture of him?'

'A picture?' she laughed. 'I cannot even remember his face.'

'I can't forget her face.'

The old lady sighed. 'Yes. We were all so sad. Nirmal-babu often sits at the balcony for hours, not speaking a word. But you will forget her. Sooner or later, everyone forgets everything.'

The young man wondered about his place in the household now. He wasn't sure whether he was supposed to start working or remain dependent. He considered talking to his father about the possibility of him eventually returning to Scotland to finish his degree, but he was aware of their deep financial woes.

Early one morning, the young man woke up to find the toilet on his floor occupied. He walked up one flight of stairs to use the lavatory and heard his usually slumbering uncle Potol talking to his wife – a chatter of drifting topics. When he heard his aunt say 'Nirupoma', he paid attention.

Potol was grumbling, 'Dada has been keeping silent about his son returning home without a degree and not looking for work. Remember how angry he was when we suggested that perhaps he shouldn't sell all our properties? As though we were all obligated to him.'

'But he has done a lot for everyone. You've said so many times yourself,' said his wife.

'Yes, but this was also my father's estate. That Scotland-returned fellow is now as good as a locally matriculated schoolboy.'

'Aren't you one too?'

'It was different in my time,' snapped Potol. 'Men from our family didn't have to do anything; we just had to look after the estate. Did your father agree to marry you into this household because of my education or because of our reputation? Anyway, going back to what I was saying, I think Dada says nothing to him because of the guilt he carries within him.'

The young man squatted silently.

'I liked her, she was hard-working. Even though she was rather dark and unattractive, and I never thought she was much of a singer. Poor girl,' said Potol's wife.

'Poor girl? Oh yes, the hardships of coming from a little village and marrying into this family ...' snapped Potol.

'Be a bit open-hearted.'

'Open-hearted? Is that sister going to live here forever? The family is losing money, my nephew returns after three years without a scrap of paper to his name and we are sheltering a destitute.'

There was a long pause, then Potol continued, 'And that little boy – that lucky villager's son – is going to get all of this one day, whatever remains, that is.'

The young man heard rapid footsteps. A moment later, there was a tug at the latch of the bathroom door.

'Is there someone in there?'

Potol was the youngest of the Sengupta siblings. He lived on the third floor of the house. Nirmal Sengupta was the eldest of his generation, the one who made the important decisions in the extended household. They ate their meals together, but for the most part, the families lived separate lives, occasionally mingling during festive events.

Potol had married late in life – when he was almost in his forties. He had shown little interest in his father's business and remained idle throughout his entire youth, sleeping a lot, eating prodigiously, spending his evenings away from the house in the company of friends. This had continued until he suffered a heart attack when he was barely in his mid-thirties.

The doctor had sternly advised Potol to lead a less dissolute life. A week after he returned home from the hospital, gaunt and woeful, he had announced feebly that it was time for him to start a family. The marriage was arranged in less than a month to a girl about twenty years younger than him. Potol embarked on his domestic life with relish.

But five years into their marriage, with all the jealous gossip about their demonstrative amorous ways, Potol and his young bride were yet to have a child. It was assumed that the fault was with the wife, still not twenty-five. Several trips were made to sacred destinations – temples, rivers, mountains, even a hot spring – to receive blessings from famous holy men. She drank potions that were sweet, bitter and salty. At dawn, midday and dusk. All of this was of no avail. Potol, realizing that the situation was hopeless, returned to napping and grumbling. Years later, when Nirupoma became pregnant, someone had uttered less charitably, 'Even a village girl was able to conceive quickly. Surely, the men of this house don't have problems.'

The tragedy of Nirupoma's death led everyone to focus on the child, as a way of assuaging guilt and sorrow. When the young man returned home, he observed that there was little to worry about his son's care. The child now stayed with Maloti, Nirupoma's sister. He awoke from his nap one afternoon to see the little boy sleeping beside him. Maloti explained that Mrs Sengupta had asked her to place the sleeping boy next to his father for the afternoon. This became the routine.

There was one game in particular that father and son played endlessly. Maloti called it the 'finger-biting game.' The child would hold his index finger close to the young man's mouth as he pretended to be asleep. Then, suddenly, he would try to bite it and the boy would have to remove his finger in time. This game brought the child an inexplicable amount of joy. But he would play it only with his father, amidst peals of laughter.

Maloti had an unusual place in the household. She hovered somewhere between ayah and family member. She refused to eat at the family table and took her meals alone in her room. But she graciously accepted used sarees and everyday commodities like soap and oil from Mrs Sengupta.

A tailor arrived one morning to take measurements of the mattresses in the house that needed to be fitted for new sheets and covers. Maloti followed him from room to room. She watched his tape measure closely and mentally added up the numbers. An hour later, after visiting every room in the house, the tailor submitted his total to Mr Sengupta – forty metres of cloth.

Maloti spoke up. 'It should be just under thirty metres.' Everyone stared at her. The tailor had been with the family for years and had never been questioned. Maloti swiftly multiplied the dimensions of each mattress aloud, added extra lengths for folds, tallied the numbers and confirmed her estimate of about thirty metres. Nirmal Sengupta asked the tailor if he was sure it was forty. The tailor admitted that he might have made an error.

After this incident, Nirmal Sengupta started asking Maloti to keep track of household finances. The accounts of the family were exhaustive – market expenses, monthly commodities, municipal bills, servants' wages. Maloti began to feel needed. On the Bengali new year, Mrs Sengupta took two thin gold bangles off her wrist and slipped them on her. Maloti accepted these and wore them on her thin wrists at all times.

One afternoon, while aimlessly loitering around the large house, the young man overheard his mother complain to her husband that her son was turning into his uncle Potol –

unemployed, boorish and unenthusiastic about life. These bits
of conversations that he kept overhearing were starting to grate.
They were never said directly to him. Was it because people pitied
him? How long would the penumbra of his wife's death prevent
everyone from interacting with him normally? He wondered if he
too was relishing in the excuse, finding it convenient to wallow
indefinitely.

'You never say anything to him. You have a stern word for
everyone on this earth, but when it comes to your own son, you
stay silent. Why?' Mrs Sengupta asked of her husband.

'Because I couldn't save Nirupoma when he was away. What
sort of a father am I? A man who could not protect his own son's
wife.'

'You cannot blame yourself for that. It was fated by the gods,
wasn't it?'

Nirmal Sengupta sat in silence.

'Can I bring you some tea?' she asked after a while.

'Yes ... just half a cup please,' said Nirmal Sengupta.

The young man had never heard his father's voice falter before.
He walked away quietly.

Six months after the young man's return from Glasgow, a short,
bespectacled man in a starched kurta appeared at the house
asking for 'the brother who lives here'.

'My goodness ... it's Jyotirmoy!' the young man exclaimed on
entering the living room, surprising himself with the joy in his
own voice. Someone had remembered him. 'Are you a doctor
now?'

'Yes, I am. And I hear that you are one too! Didn't you go to
England?'

'Glasgow. But I didn't finish the degree.'

'Oh. What are you doing now, then?' asked Jyotirmoy.

'Nothing ... I just read the newspaper,' said the young man.

'Nothing? *Nothing*?' said Jyotirmoy and laughed.

'Nothing.'

'Come on, then,' he said. 'We have a lot to talk about.'

They walked to a nearby park. It had rained that morning and the benches were damp. They sat down anyway. Cursory facts about each other's life were exchanged. Jyotirmoy had started working at a small clinic while continuing with his residency at the medical college. But he had become involved in politics. His father had been a freedom fighter who had spent some time in jail and had made Jyotirmoy promise that he would become a certified doctor before participating in a single political demonstration. Jyotirmoy had heeded his father's advice. But now that he finally had an MBBS degree, he was using his free time for the cause of Independence. He didn't say much more, but invited the young man to come visit him at his place of work the following week. 'A man like you would be indispensable for our efforts,' he said.

'Like me?' asked the young man. 'What is so special about me?'

'You look trustworthy. And you read the newspaper. And you have nothing else to do.'

A week later, on a bright July afternoon, the young man set out to visit his school friend. Jyotirmoy's clinic was in Metiabruz, close to the waterfront on Suriname Ghat. It was a densely Muslim-populated area in the city, the reason closely entwined with the history of the settlement. About a hundred years ago, Wajid Ali Shah, the deposed king of Oudh, had stepped off a British ship with a retinue of 500 servants. In time, the nostalgic nawab, benefitting from a prodigious allowance provided by the East India Company, would transform the area into a sort of 'mini-Lucknow', replete with palatial buildings and ornate mosques. While these buildings still stood proud, the area had regressed into considerable squalor over time. Homes sprung up within feet of each other and the narrow streets were numbered haphazardly, making them almost impossible to navigate. The young man showed his chit of paper with an address and asked some men standing idly on the busy street if they knew of a medical clinic. The number meant nothing to them, but when he mentioned 'Dr Jyotirmoy,' they understood instantly and escorted him there.

'Badol, cha!' Jyotirmoy called out to his attendant as soon as he spotted the young man outside his door. The young man sat in the corner of the room on a small stool and sipped his tea while Jyotirmoy attended to an elderly lady and her son.

'For how long have you had this cough, Begum Afreen?' he barked as he listened to her chest.

'I have always had this cough ... years,' she wheezed. She seemed unsure and looked at her son.

'Are you a good son?' Jyotirmoy asked.

'Yes.'

'Do you want your mother to die?'

'No.'

'Then why don't you take care of her? You came here months ago and I told you what to do then. You had promised me that you would look after her. You live right next door to me and yet you don't listen. I had even given you the medicine. For free.' The son lowered his head.

'He is not to blame, doctor ...' said Begum Afreen.

'Of course he is to blame!'

The son shifted around. 'I will do what you say, doctor.'

Jyotirmoy seemed unconvinced, but proceeded to write out the medications and went over them with the son, while the mother stared out the window and picked her nose. The young man watched, filled with a sense of awe.

'He will never do it, but still I must try ... She has tuberculosis, the poor lady. These people are poor, so poor,' said Jyotirmoy in a surprisingly gentle tone. 'What are you staring at?'

'Just looking at you, in that white shirt; so authoritative.'

'Come on, let's go for a stroll,' said Jyotirmoy placing his stethoscope inside its case. 'How did you find the place?'

'A few men escorted me here. You're famous.'

'Badol, close the clinic for now,' Jyotirmoy said loudly. 'And ... try to keep your little girl away from Begum Afreen.'

Badol appeared instantly. 'But she takes care of her, sir. Padma loves her like her own nani.' A small girl of about ten walked in.

'Who is he?' asked Padma, pointing at the young man.

'He is my old friend,' said Jyotirmoy.

'Is he a doctor too?' she asked.

'No, I am not,' intervened the young man.

'Then what do you do?'

'Nothing much, really,' said the young man, smiling at her. Padma looked unimpressed.

'Go on ahead, both of you. Baba and I will lock the place up.'

'Thank you, Padma,' said Jyotirmoy, smiling.

'Yes, if I wasn't here, the thieves would come,' she replied, shutting a window.

As soon as they were outside, Jyotirmoy said, 'One simple question for you. Do you want Bengal to be split in two?' It was a long time since anyone had asked the young man for his opinion.

'What are you thinking about so much? What's your first reaction? Just a simple yes or no would be fine,' said Jyotirmoy. 'There is no correct answer.'

'Uh ... no,' muttered the young man.

'Correct answer!' exclaimed Jyotirmoy. 'Any reasonable man would not want that to happen. And yet ...' he paused. 'What do you think the composition of Hindus and Muslims is in Bengal today, in 1945? Just give me a rough estimate.'

'About half and half...?'

'Incorrect! This is the only state where the Muslim League is in power. It is about 60 per cent Muslim.' He let the young man ruminate on that statistic.

'These people are my patients. Don't think that I am against Muslims. I come here three days a week to treat them. Will I marry a Muslim girl? Of course not!' He chuckled at the last bit. 'What I am trying to say is that I am tolerant of their faith, but intolerant of their demands to create another country.'

'Is that what they are saying? Is that what they want?' asked the young man.

'Oh yes, anyone can see that coming. Attlee has sent a delegation to discuss independence, but the word is that both the Congress and Jinnah are creating obstacles at every stage of the process.'

'Yes, I have read about the Cabinet Missions meetings,' said the young man.

'And people are so stupid, so stupid. Do you read the stupid, perverted, twisted writing in our newspapers about Muslims? And their papers do the same.'

'Where are we going? Isn't it getting dark?'

Jyotirmoy chuckled. 'Concerned about being in this neighbourhood? Don't worry. Nothing would ever happen to us here. You see ... I trust that this country works when we have Hindus and Muslims living and working side by side. You don't kill your neighbour, do you? You don't kill your milkman, do you? Badol – that Hindu attendant fellow – lives inside my clinic with his little daughter. He has never had any problems. And we're right in the thick of a Muslim mohalla! It's all those isolated neighbourhoods, just like the ones that we live in, that breed the hatred.'

The young man considered Jyotirmoy's arguments as he glanced around, taking in the unfamiliar surroundings. They were now at the dock, overlooking the slowly moving steamer ships. Where was Jyotirmoy headed with this line of questions, he wondered.

'Why are you so silent?' asked Jyotirmoy. 'Do you have no opinion on this matter?'

'I agree ...' said the young man slowly. 'Yes, I do hear and read rather disturbing accounts of our attitude towards them. People are mostly scared, I think. And ignorant.'

'We must do something then, don't you think?' asked Jyotirmoy.

'You mean start a movement?'

'Listen,' said Jyotirmoy, stopping in the middle of the street and turning to the young man dramatically. 'I have been thinking about this a lot and I don't think there is a need for armed politics right now. Think of what happened to groups like Master-da's in Chittagong. Or even our own Anushilan Samiti. You know how they started rather peacefully and were supposed to follow the teachings of Bankim Chandra. Who wasn't a part of that movement – even educated women, like Sarala Debi and others, were. But what happened? They grew violent, na? They trained people to assassinate ... They even sent someone to France to learn bomb-making. And, of course, they bought guns. But what good did any of this do? This is a different crisis; we can't solve this by force.'

'Gandhiji's doctrines then?' asked the young man.

'No!' cried out Jyotirmoy, resuming his stride. 'No one cares more about this more than we do, not the Congress leaders, not the Muslim League. Not Gandhi for sure. You of all people should know this – you were a teacher in a village. Tell me, will those people back in that village care about the Cabinet Mission or Jinnah or Gandhi?' Though taken aback by Jyotirmoy's forcefulness, the young man was pleased that he had remembered that odd interlude in his life.

'But what can I do ...?' he asked hesitantly. It was dark now, and the young man could barely make out Jyotirmoy's face, but he sensed that he was smiling.

'You can do a lot. It is encouraging that we have some common thoughts. Now listen ...' he stopped again and faced the young man. 'I know of a few men, all of whom live near your house. They are a lot like you and me, and want to do something. But we need a convenient place to meet and talk. Could we use a room in your large house? Maybe for an hour or two in the evenings?' The young man found himself agreeing readily.

'Thank you,' said Jyotirmoy. 'Let's head back, then.'

They shook hands and parted ways at the bus stop. The young man found an empty seat in the bus, next to the window, and watched the city as it flew by, dotted with the occasional yellow incandescent lamp peeking from inside a home. He saw a calm, ordered, if somewhat forlorn metropolis and could not detect the foreboding that Jyotirmoy felt. Yet, he sensed that Jyotirmoy was right.

The following week Jyotirmoy sent word through Badol that a meeting was on the cards very soon. Three other men planned to be present. The young man brought it up at mealtime. He did not elaborate the context. Mrs Sengupta promptly said, 'Why, that is good news indeed! I wondered how you spend all your time with just the few of us here at home. Now you can talk with your friends and...'

Nirmal Sengupta cut her off. 'Make sure you send some tea and snacks for them. Let Maloti take care of it.'

At about seven that evening, Jyotirmoy appeared with two young men and a little girl. One of the men was Badol; his daughter trailed him. They did not enter the room, but sat outside in the corridor. 'This rangy, bespectacled owl is Ajit. He's an intellectual,' said Jyotirmoy gaily, as they sat down. The doorbell rang; a third visitor had arrived. The young man recognized him as another classmate from school.

'Palash ...' he said, ushering him in. 'Is anyone else coming?'

'No, this is it, for now. Yes, that fat, roguish-looking chap is our dear Palash. He's a famous dentist now, but you wouldn't be able to tell, from those thick stubs he has for fingers, how deftly he can extract a tooth. Can I have an ashtray please?'

Jyotirmoy elaborated on his plan as cigarette smoke filled the small room. He wished to form a group of dedicated men who would write about pressing political issues – mainly about the desire to preserve the province of Bengal from being cleaved along religious lines. There were to be several forms of output, all in print, mostly in pamphlet form. Short articles with clear arguments, longer essays for university students, and guides for volunteers on how to talk to the masses about the issue. 'We will not discriminate nor will we be affiliated to any party,' concluded Jyotirmoy.

There was a light knock on the door. The young man opened it and saw Maloti standing outside with cups of tea, a large bowl of muri and some fried fritters. 'Our future freedom fighters,' smirked Jyotirmoy as he wolfed down the snack. 'And my father was given one roti a day when he was in jail.'

'He has suffered so we can eat our muri in peace,' quipped Palash. Moments later, when he placed the cup of tea down on the table, it broke into pieces.

'Did you leave any for that poor fellow sitting outside?' asked Ajit, as he helped pick up the debris of the teacup.

Jyotirmoy opened the door a crack to see that Badal had been given his own bowl and cup of tea. The little girl was hopping around. 'No class discrimination here,' he said. They decided to meet again in a couple of days to discuss the details.

They began to come to the house regularly, spending long hours in the evenings, shooting the breeze. Maloti would always bring tea

and snacks. There was never any left over. Palash requested that
he be served tea in a tin mug. He confessed that he had a problem
gauging the force and strength to perform simple actions. 'But
then how do you extract teeth, Palash-da?' asked Maloti. A few
days later, Badol moved in to the floor of the room – he listened
but didn't participate. The little girl, if she showed up with her
father, waited in the corridor. But Maloti would take her upstairs
to play with Jonaki. The two children would conduct their own
version of a meeting, mimicking the adults. Padma would pace
around in her little frock, talking and wagging her finger while
Jonaki tried to get her attention with his toys.

One evening, when Maloti entered the room with tea, the two
children trailed in behind her. 'Oh, I am sorry' she said. 'I did not
realize they had been following me. Come on now, Baba is busy,'
she told Jonaki.

Everyone was silent after they left the room. Finally, Palash
blurted, '*Baba*? Is that your own son?'

'Where is your wife?' asked Ajit.

'Is she with your in-laws?' Palash pressed.

'She died a couple of years ago,' shrugged the young man
uncomfortably.

'What happened?' They were all staring now.

He decided that it was time to reveal his situation, to dust off
the cobweb of grief. How much longer could he live in isolation on
the second floor with a son, his late wife's sister, and the memory
of a young bride trapped inside a large teak-framed photograph?

'You have been the best thing that has happened to me since I
returned from abroad, I had no aim or direction,' said the young
man sincerely when he concluded his odd tale of woe.

Short Jyotirmoy reached up and threw his arms around him.

They began drafting articles and reading them to the group. The
young man wrote a short essay about the fallibility of partitioning

the state. 'It thus stands to reason,' he concluded, 'that all major political parties operating in the province of Bengal today – the Congress, the Muslim League, the Communist Party, and the Hindu Mahasabha, even if they merely considered their own selfish interests – would stand to lose if Bengal were to be divided.'

'Sharp,' said the tacit Ajit. 'I think we should name our paper Undivided,' he added.

'Okhondo ...' Jyotirmoy enunciated the Bengali word slowly. 'Yes, it has a firm yet rhythmic ring to it. I like it. What do you all think?'

Everyone repeated 'Okh-ondo' like a chant. It stuck.

One of the issues worrying the fledgling group was, of course, money. In due course, Jyotirmoy came up with a plan: they would approach the wealthy Marwari business community in Calcutta for a handout. 'It takes one of those shops in central Calcutta just five minutes to clear the cost of what they might donate to us,' reasoned Jyotirmoy. 'I have tried hitting up a few rich Bengalis, but they are a stingy lot.'

The Marwaris were mostly aligned with the Akhil Bharatiya Hindu Mahasabha, also known as the All-India Hindu Assembly. Though limited in their cultural influence in Bengal, they harboured considerable wealth. Jyotirmoy had heard from his sources that they had spent a fortune and procured a worrying number of arms from American GIs stationed locally. While he did not know where they stockpiled their ammunition, their meetings were safe, open events, often held in the homes of their patrons. They were keen on having Bengali Hindus join their group to bolster more support in the province. So the small group of men, Badol trailing, went to an evening session of the Mahasabha early in May 1946.

About a hundred men sat on long stretches of cloth covering the floor of a large, brightly lit room. The patron of that evening's event, along with key members of the Calcutta branch of the Mahasabha, sat on a raised dais. Small cups of tea were served. People talked softly amongst themselves. The young men of *Okhondo* had thought that there would be an open forum. The discussions, mostly administrative and conducted in muted tones, were disappointing.

About an hour later, Jyotirmoy said, 'Sitting here will do us no good.' Taking his cue, they made their way to the front of the room in an awkward half-crouch. One of the men seated on the dais beckoned at them.

'Sirs, we have come here to discuss something with you. We are a small literary group called *Okhondo* and here are Palash, Ajit...'

He was cut off. 'All reputable-sounding Bengali names. Tell us what we can do for you. Please sit here,' he indicated a spot on the floor, to the left of where they were seated.

Jyotirmoy continued, 'We urgently feel that we need to do more to spread the word that Bengal should not be divided. We know it is your wish too.'

'Yes, yes ...' said the Mahasabha leader. 'Why divide beautiful sonar Bangla? Ei amaderi Bangla rey; this is our very own dear Bengal, isn't it?'

'Your Bengali is good, sir,' said Ajit.

'Why wouldn't it be, my brother? This is our home.' The leader spoke with the expansive charm of a politician. 'Anyway, what do you need?'

Jyotirmoy said, 'We will go to schools and colleges, we will canvas from house to house and we will send our people to the villages. We intend to appeal to the logic of our people, not their emotions. We do not want to do anything violently.' Jyotirmoy emphasized the last bit and anticipated a rebuttal.

'Are you a follower of Gandhi? You know we left the Congress because of their timid ideas. Do you think that you are larger than the desire of evil men to be violent? Just look around you.'

Jyotirmoy retorted. 'Sir, one does not need to be a follower of anyone to be averse to violence. We do not wish to see our province divided, but we do not want to be a party to bloodshed either. We want to win over our own people, explain to them in various publications in the local vernacular that a divided Bengal would be a tragedy. Is that so unreasonable a plan?'

The Mahasabha leader sighed – as though he were lecturing a group of over-eager schoolboys. 'Listen, young men, we have nothing against Bengalis. We even have several in our party; our party boss as you must know is Mr Shyama Mookerjee, the former head of Calcutta University, son of the famous scientist called the "Tiger of Bengal". Look, he is sitting right there.' He pointed towards a well-dressed, un-tiger-like man with a thick handlebar moustache and a wide, luminous forehead. He sat a few feet away from them, talking in a soft, well-modulated voice. 'Our aim is simple – we too wish to keep Bengal undivided, but we will not allow Muslims to dominate in the legislature. They have taken your own province away from you. How do your families feel about that? Ask your mothers if you're not sure.'

The young man who had silently been following the exchange spoke up, in a voice loud enough that Shyama Prasad Mookerjee could hear him.

'Sirs, what you are saying is a contradiction. It is impossible. In order to save Bengal, you must concede some rights to Muslims. How can you have both? You make no sense. If you do not give them something, they will obviously seek a division. Your way will only create a stalemate. And bloodshed.'

'I make no sense? So you think you understand everything? Like I said, just go home and ask your father and mother what they think!' The leader had lost his composure.

Shyama Prasad Mookerjee turned towards them. 'Don't yell at him. Listen, boys, they do not need to divide Bengal. There is always a special place for disgruntled people. What is your father's name?'

'Nirmal Sengupta, sir,' said the young man.

'I know him.'

That was all he said.

The young men got up to leave. This time, they did not resort to the submissive half-crouch. The leader had the last word, 'You are all boys from good families. I can see that in your eyes. Believe me, you do not have the stomach for this. Go print your newspaper if that gives you some peace. Maybe I can put in an advertisement for my shop and pay you something. Send someone to me tomorrow when we are open.'

They started arguing as soon they returned to the house. They were loud enough that the family upstairs could hear them. 'Why did you take us there?' yelled Palash to Jyotirmoy. 'Did you not know that those people are simply goondas? What do you think they've been buying all those weapons for? Did you see their ugly, pockmarked faces?'

Jyotirmoy replied angrily, 'One should not assume anything until hearing it for themselves. Now we know where we stand and where they stand, and we will look elsewhere. There is nothing wrong with that.'

'Look where?' sighed Ajit. 'They laughed at us, Jyotirmoy. Maybe we are just a group of effete schoolboys. Maybe we shouldn't get involved in all this.'

The young man spoke in Jyotirmoy's defence, 'That is a cowardly thing to say. We must stick to our principles. I do not believe that Shyama Prasad Mookerjee is right. He will soon realize this himself.'

He noticed that Maloti had entered the room and was listening to the altercation. 'Is there any tea today?' asked Ajit.

'Shut up, Ajit,' said Jyotirmoy. 'All we ever do here is drink tea. Why should anyone provide us with tea or money? We need to achieve something or stop this charade.'

The young man spent the following day listlessly. The agitation of the previous evening had left him unsettled. He stayed in his room, napping intermittently. There was a knock on the door. Maloti entered, the small boy asleep on her shoulder. 'Are you awake?'

The young man turned. 'What is it? Is he ill?' he asked.

'No, he is fine. But I have something important to discuss with you – this evening, go downstairs as usual.' She said no more and left the room.

Maloti came to the octagonal room with a cup of tea for the young man and a bowl of the usual snacks. Standing stiffly in front of him, she spoke a little formally, as though she had been rehearsing all day. Her voice was soft, though not timid. 'I know what happens in this room every evening. I read the newspapers every night after they are discarded. What you have been planning for is important. I know what happened last night and I have a solution for you. I can ... help you. So you must listen to me.'

The young man didn't know how to react. He stared back at her. Finally, realizing that she was waiting for his permission to continue, he asked, 'What is it?'

'I think I can give you some of the money that you need.' She pointed to the gold bracelets on her wrist. 'Your mother had given these to me.'

'No, no,' said the young man. 'That is very generous of you, but my mother would not allow it. I would not allow it. It's your gold.'

'What use is gold on a girl if her country is in peril?'

The young man was silent. It was a deep sentiment that couldn't be dismissed easily.

'That is a brave thing to say ... but our family would not understand. They would make a fuss when they notice the bangles missing.'

'I know,' said Maloti. 'But you see, your mother gave an identical pair of bangles to Didi. They are tucked away in her clothes upstairs. After her death, they removed all her belongings from the room, but they overlooked those.'

'They are the same?' asked the young man.

'Yes,' she said. 'The exact same. I want you to pawn my bangles and get some money. I will wear my sister's bangles till you are able to secure these for me again.'

'But that may take years,' said the young man.

'Is there any hurry?'

The young man considered her proposal. They heard a noise in the corridor. It was a servant entering the house.

'Why don't we just pawn hers then?'

'Because these are mine. Please take these bracelets,' said Maloti. She slipped them off her wrists, hid her hands under her shawl and left the room.

The next morning, the young man set out for Jyotirmoy's clinic by the docks. This time, he was able to find it easily. Badol, who was sipping tea outside, waved excitedly. Padma was sitting beside him. 'What are you doing here?' Badol asked. 'Does doctor-babu know you're coming?'

'No.'

'What is Jonaki doing?' asked the girl.

'Why don't you come to the house and find out? He asks for you all the time,' the young man said.

'He's such a baby,' said Padma dismissively. 'I have to teach him everything.' The young man gave her a lollipop and entered the clinic.

'Nice of you to come all this way,' said Jyotirmoy. He sounded morose.

The young man placed the two bangles on the desk. 'Do you know of a good pawnbroker?'

'For what?'

'Our newspaper.'

'But whom do they belong to?'

'They belong to Maloti. It was entirely her idea,' said the young man.

'My goodness, what are you saying, man? Let's go!'

'Right now?'

'Yes, now. Badol, close the place up!'

The two men ran across the street towards a bus going to central Calcutta and jumped in as it pulled away. When they reached the crowded business district, Jyotirmoy strategized, 'There are several stores on this street. You take one bracelet and I can take the other one. We make inquiries; we meet back here in an hour.'

They stopped at about a dozen stores. They compared rates and decided to go with one that Jyotirmoy had negotiated with – while the amount they would receive wasn't the best offer in hand, the interest rate was lower. 'The rest of us from the group will pool together and pay the monthly instalments,' said Jyotirmoy reassuringly. 'That will be our contribution. Come, let's go back to the store.'

The pawnbroker was a bit surprised that there were two bracelets now. 'Are you selling off all your mother's jewellery?' the elderly man asked dispassionately.

'We need the money for something important,' replied the young man.

'Yes, yes ... I am sure there's a mess somewhere that you need to clean up. You don't exactly strike me as men who are desperate to make ends meet.'

The young man looked around the room – there were about five people, all despondently clutching onto something small. He could make out a pair of earrings, a locket, and a thin silver chain. 'They hang around here all day asking me for a bit more than my offer, but what can I do? This is all fixed with the price of gold and the price of silver. Eventually, they agree to my price. Do you?'

'Yes.'

He seemed satisfied with the bracelet and nodded approvingly, 'Yes it's identical to the first one. This is good estate jewellery. If you didn't look well-dressed, I would have worried that they were stolen.'

Jyotirmoy said, 'A hundred-and-twenty rupees for each, correct?'

The pawnbroker nodded and started writing out a receipt. 'Sign here. Remember payments are due before the fifth or the rate doubles.' He counted out the money three times and then handed it over.

'We need the money to start a publication that will raise awareness about preserving the integrity of the province of Bengal...'

The pawnbroker shrugged, 'Just remember to pay me on time.'

The two men stepped back into the blinding afternoon sun. Jyotirmoy was clutching the envelope secured in the inner lining of his shirt.

The next morning Maloti caught the young man alone on the balcony. 'Did you get a good price?' she whispered.

'Yes. Two hundred and forty rupees.'

'Will that be enough?'

'Yes, more than enough for now.'

'What's the big news?' demanded Palash, as he walked into the meeting room later that evening. They had all been summoned urgently.

'Take a seat' said Jyotirmoy. He looked at the young man and indicated that he ought to speak, but the young man nodded back at him. Jyotirmoy explained to the group that they now had enough money to start a publication. He told them the source of the capital. Ajit whistled.

'Who would have thought that girl had so much going on inside her head ...?' And then, almost on cue, Maloti walked in with the usual tray of teacups and the bowl of fritters. Jyotirmoy stood up. The others followed.

'Sister,' he said in a melodramatic but sincere tone, 'we, the members of *Okhondo*, wish to thank you for your kindness and thoughtfulness. We remain in your debt.' Maloti shifted uncomfortably, nodded and then headed back towards the door.

The young man called after her, 'Would you like to say something?'

Maloti turned from the doorway. 'I want to be a part of this too.'

'You already are, sister. You are one of us,' said Jyotirmoy. Maloti nodded and turned to leave the room. Jyotirmoy spoke again, 'Sister, will you take responsibility for a very important job?'

'What?' Maloti asked cautiously.

'Will you be the treasurer? All our expenses will go through you. You will also keep our funds.'

Maloti nodded excitedly and left the room.

The group sat down and started discussing their first publication. They were all given three days to write their articles. These would then be distributed around the city and in adjoining rural areas. Palash, who didn't enjoy writing, was entrusted with the job of finding volunteers.

'I think that in addition to our own small pamphlets, we need a presence in the local newspapers. People need to know who we are,' said Jyotirmoy. The young man was to write an article. Ajit, who knew the editor of *Anandabazar*, was asked to make inquiries about getting something published.

The young man retired to the living room immediately after dinner and wrote till late into the night.

'Packed with punch!' exclaimed Ajit, when he dropped in to collect the writing a few days later. 'You capture our point of view well, but you keep your name a mystery, eh?'

'I think I should just credit it to *Okhondo*. Is that allowed?' asked the young man.

'Perhaps ... I'll run it by my friend,' said Ajit and left.

But Ajit could not be traced for a few days. A week later, he finally sent word that he was dropping in with the editor of *Anandabazar*.

The group reunited. They sat around, silent and anxious. Jyotirmoy lit two cigarettes at the same time absent-mindedly. Finally, they heard Ajit's voice and perked up like watchdogs. Maloti started cleaning the large lampshades in the hallway right outside the meeting room. The newspaperman walked in.

He was close in age to them, but had clearly been battered by life. 'It's been a long day,' he said. 'It's been a long year.' He looked around at the three men and smiled. 'I can see that you want to do something. But I don't know how much I can help.'

'You can't do anything? Perhaps get our writing printed somewhere?'

'I like the writing – it reads smoothly and has impeccable political judgment. But ...' he paused for a minute, 'there is always a "but" isn't there? Who is writing this piece? Who is our author?'

'I am,' said the young man quickly.

'Yes, I know that ...' said the newspaperman. 'What I mean is who are you to a reader?'

'Can you explain?' asked Ajit.

'Good man, our articles are written by our own reporters. Mostly, that is. Sometimes we have commentators contributing. But these people need to have clear affiliations with political groups or organizations. They write as the voice of a party or a university or even a business interest. We just don't have ... how do I say ... an "outlet" for a group like yours. Maybe I could run it if, say, you added a few words about Gandhiji or...'

Jyotirmoy spoke up, 'No, no ... the whole point of this is that we don't want to represent these ideas as political. These are supposed to be common yearnings that reflect the ...' he paused, looking for the right phrase but couldn't find one. The newspaperman nodded. The room fell silent.

Maloti broke the impasse by entering the room with a large bowl of the usual snacks. She handed a separate plateful to the newspaperman with an awkward tilt of her head. She put the large bowl in the centre of the room. 'Oh, why so much for me?' fussed the newspaperman. 'Is there enough for everyone...?'

'Yes, sir,' said Maloti. 'Please have some.'

The newspaperman glanced at her and then asked in a tone that bordered on impropriety, 'What is your name?'

'Her name is Maloti,' said the young man. 'She is one of our family.'

The newspaperman looked unconvinced. 'Where did you grow up, Maloti?'

'In a village ... not far from here.'

At this point, Jonaki walked in and for some inexplicable reason went right up to Palash and kicked him in the shin.

'Stop misbehaving!' Maloti yelled at the small boy, who upon realizing that there was an unfamiliar person in the room, fell silent.

'What is your name?' asked the newspaperman.

'My good name or my pet name?'

'Well ... how about your pet name?'

'His name is Jonaki' said Padma, from the door.

'Oh, and who is that now?' said the newspaper man turning around.

'That's my assistant Badol's daughter,' said Jyotirmoy.

'Go and pranam the sir,' whispered Badol.

'Oh, we don't do that any more. You have a lot of people here. Anyway, that's a funny name for a boy ... Who gave you that name?' The small boy pointed to Maloti and ran out of the room.

'These articles in newspapers – any newspaper – mine or the dozen others floating around every day, are written by someone and there is a name signed at the bottom. But what's in a name? Just a marker that gives something legitimacy. Do you follow?'

Palash nodded, looking unsure.

'Now,' continued the newspaperman, 'let's say you wrote something but had someone else be the person whose name it appeared under ... Hers, for instance,' he said pointing to Maloti.

'Maloti?' asked the young man perplexed.

'Exactly!' exclaimed the newspaperman. 'The newspaper is saturated with articles written by young men like us, telling people what to think. But what if there was a column by a housewife? Someone who said the same things but in a different way – unthreatening, simple – a lady's point of view. Understand?' He got up to his feet.

The young man said, 'Are you leaving now?'

'Yes, I have to be back at the office very early in the morning. I am tired.'

'But what shall we do? Do you have any instructions for us?' asked Jyotirmoy.

'Rewrite that article as though this lovely lady had written it. Think like her. Ask her questions. Then send it to me. I'll see what can be done. Oh, and one more thing ... I have access to a good, inexpensive printing press for all those other materials that Ajit mentioned. I'll send along the details with him.'

He looked at Maloti and said, 'You probably have stories that we could use. Stories about that village of yours. Try recollecting them.' He turned to Jyotirmoy. 'May I have one of your cigarettes for the walk back?'

The next morning, the young man opened his notebook to a fresh page and attempted to fabricate a tale. 'I am a housewife in Bhowanipur,' he began. 'Every morning I can hear the temple bells from my balcony and every evening the azan.' But he found it hard to progress beyond this. The azan was never heard from their house. Nor were they close enough to a temple.

When Maloti walked by later, she saw him at his desk, facing the door, trying to write. She grinned at him. He glared back. The rest of the morning was spent scribbling and crossing out sentences.

By noon, he had one page of dull prose. He considered talking to Potol's wife, hoping to extract some material for this housewives' perspective he had been entrusted with. During the midday meal, he asked casually, 'Kakima, I see you reading the newspapers sometimes. What do you think of all these concerns about the religious divide in Bengal today?'

She stared at him in panic, as though he had asked her to recite multiplication tables. 'What do you mean by "divide"?' she asked finally.

'Hindus and Muslims ... you know, people talking about their own place to live. Remember how Bengal was divided in 1905 and then reunited in 1911 again? What if it were to happen again now ... Would that worry you?'

Nirmal Sengupta shot him a quizzical look. He wondered why his son had chosen to ask Potol's wife – of all people – for her opinion. She looked at her husband for help, but Potol was engrossed in cleaving the flesh off a piece of chicken. She finally said, 'Everyone should be happy.'

Feeling encouraged, the young man prodded, 'But what if that happiness meant dividing up our state? How would you feel about that? Our ancestral village would then become part of a different country. You know the river we cross when going to our village?' Potol's wife nodded. 'What if that part of it, the land on the other side of the Ichamoti, where Maloti grew up, becomes a different country? How would you feel?'

She hesitated for a while and mumbled, 'We could still buy our rice here.' And that was that. Out of the corner of his eye, the young man noticed Maloti smirking.

Later that afternoon, he looked up from his desk and caught her watching him. 'Laughing at me again?' he asked grumpily.

'I want to know what you've written.'

'It's terrible and you won't be able to read my handwriting,' he replied, waving his hand dismissively.

'But I want to,' insisted Maloti.

'All right. Sit outside my room and play with the child. I'll read it out aloud.'

Maloti sat herself down in the corridor while the small boy jumped around. The young man paced around his room and read the two pages with an awkward, halting delivery. He frequently stopped mid-sentence to alter the wording. When he was done, he peered outside. Maloti had fallen asleep.

'Just wonderful,' he exclaimed loudly.

Maloti awoke from her light slumber and said instantly, 'Yes, it was nice!'

'Yes, it was nice ...' he mimicked her. 'You fell asleep!'

'No, I heard it all,' insisted Maloti.

'What was it about then?'

'Well ... a young housewife hears the temple bells in the morning and the Muslim prayers in the evenings. And then one day, she talks to the man who comes to sharpen their kitchen knives and asks him if he is Muslim and then ...' she faltered and stared back at him sheepishly.

'It's not your fault,' he conceded, disappearing into his room. 'It is an awful, boring piece of writing ... And what do I know about how you women think anyway?'

They fell silent for a while and watched the child prance about. Then Maloti spoke softly. 'When I was coming here from the village, I travelled with a girl named Mumtaz. I remember her name because we were both searching for our relatives. I would tell her that all she had to do was go to the Taj Mahal. Anyway, she was my age, but was already married and had not heard from her husband in months. She knew that he lived somewhere in Park Circus; she had his address memorized.

'We were together for days ... many days – people were equally kind or unkind to us, but they didn't care so much that she was Muslim. We shared the little food we could scrape together. She never ate anything without offering me some. Initially, I was a bit selfish – if someone offered me a cup of rice froth, I would gulp it down instantly. But then I too started to save some of what I could scavenge, for her.' She paused.

'You couldn't have been more than fourteen,' said the young man, engrossed. 'Go on.'

'It was a long journey here. God knows how many days we walked for and how we kept up. We asked people where Park Circus was. I insisted that I would take her to her husband; I really wanted to make sure that she had found him, but ... she was stubborn about it. She said her family wouldn't be nice to me.'

Maloti spoke in a distant, even voice. 'I told her that I would wait on the street outside her house, that I just wanted to see her safe. It was difficult to see her go, not knowing whether she would ever find her husband. But I was waiting for so many days to see my sister, too, and so ... I finally put her out of my thoughts. I stayed on the main road and walked down towards Hazra. I remembered the way. I had come less than two years ago with Ma to see Jonaki. He was just a baby then ...' Her voice cracked and she stopped. She got up and left the room silently.

The young man realized he had a story. Two young women from different faiths who had gone through a near-death experience together, parting ways forever in an unknown metropolis wracked by famine. While it bothered him that he could find joy in describing the heart-breaking incident, his spirits picked up.

The next evening, he gave it to Ajit. 'It's a different piece,' he said. 'Let's see what your editor thinks of it now.'

A few days later, the young man asked Ajit if he had heard back from the newspaperman regarding the article. Ajit shrugged. 'He said he would contact me when he was done reading it.'

'Why don't you pay him a visit, then? He's a busy man, maybe he forgot.' Ajit agreed but reported the next day that the newspaperman was not in his office when he had gone to look for him.

Badol had started delivering the printed materials. Piles of boxes were stored in the meeting room. There were some issues with the volunteers. One of them had expected to be paid for his work. Another simply deposited the pamphlets on the platform of a railway station and boarded the next train back. Not everyone agreed that the pamphlets were important. A week later, when Jyotirmoy went to follow up in a village, he was served a snack in a paper packet made from their pamphlet. But the group reasoned that by the end of the month, even if one in twenty pamphlets were read, they would have reached about 5,000 people.

Early one morning, Jyotirmoy stopped by the house.

'What is it?' asked the young man. 'Don't you have to go to the clinic?'

'I'm on my way there. But have you seen today's paper?'

The young man shook his head. 'No ... our paper hasn't been delivered yet for some reason.'

'Well, you wouldn't want to miss it,' said Jyotirmoy and went away briskly. The young man stood on the balcony and waited for the paper. When it arrived, it was soaking wet.

'What is it?' asked the old cook in the kitchen, who was kneading flour for the morning meal.

'Can you hold these pages near the chullah so they can dry?' he said with urgency. When they were less soggy, he scanned the pages but couldn't find anything. And then he spotted it. 'Maloti and Mumtaz' was the name of the story. It was all there, every word he had written. At the bottom of it was the editor's note: 'Will Maloti and Mumtaz live in the same country for long?' The young man took the wrinkled pages of the newspaper and brought it back to the second floor. Maloti was feeding Jonaki, distracting him with imaginary birds. 'Maloti, come down to the meeting room when you are done with him,' barked the young man.

'What is it?' she asked as she entered the room. The young man gave her the newspaper and pointed at the article. She sat on the floor and read it slowly, enunciating each word.

'It's so strange to read about this in a newspaper. Why did it have to be so sad? People should not read about sad things,' she said when she was done.

'But it *was* sad, Maloti,' said the young man. 'And everyone should understand the difficulties that you faced...'

Maloti cut him short, 'We should have put our home address on this. What if she reads this? Or someone in her family reads this? Maybe she will look for me ...' She stopped herself and added rhetorically, 'She would never read a newspaper, would she?'

The young man saw the teardrops well slowly in her eyes. She stood still, not wiping them as they formed, each pulling a fresh one out. She let the tears run. For the first time since he had returned home, the young man glimpsed a sad, orphaned child with a heavy heart. The young man approached her and took her hand. He held it gently till the tears stopped.

'Didi would have been alive today if I had never come here.'

She left the room and went back to her life.

THE PLANTER'S FRIEND CLUB

Rubber plantations have no seasons. There is no sowing or harvesting ritual. An adult tree is bled every day till it expends all of its yield. It is chopped down unceremoniously – a few deft, hard strokes; thirty years tumble and crash. Although the young man was not directly involved in the daily ritual of sap collection, Milne would take him on rounds at times, on the back of his motorcycle. The Indian labourers would line up at dawn as the head foreman, or kepala, called row. 'The Chinese prefer to work on contract,' Milne had explained. 'They get paid by the amount of latex they produce. But the Indians like the security of a fixed wage. So, we need to make sure they show up in the morning.' The tappers trudged on towards the plantation and made cuts into the trees. They were deftly measured incisions; too deep and one could damage the trunk. The oozing latex was preserved by adding ammonia to the cup attached to the trunk. They would then collect the buckets of sap and take them to a weighing station. As the Chinese were paid by weight, they always made sure that not an ounce of latex was left over. A centrifuge took about a third of the stuff out – excess water mostly – and then the tanker lorry, now full of latex concentrate, would head out. This cycle of events occurred every day. There were no exceptions.

The managers at the young man's estate were on their toes on one important date – the biannual reporting of the fiscal and agricultural health of the operation. These submissions were usually followed by visits from higher-ups from Singapore or, on rare occasion, all the way from London. Nag would spend hours after work, dictating passages to a junior clerk banging away at a typewriter. Milne would pace around the office chain-smoking.

'Are you sure, Naaag?' 'Did you say you already have the charts from that, Naaag?' he would ask, and Nag would nod sagaciously – he was used to young, eager, white planters wanting to submit thorough, precise reports. The final document never had Nag's name on it. When this process was over, the office would relax and Milne took a couple of days off to go drinking. The young man knew little about Milne's personal life, though Nag had mentioned that he had a mistress in Penang, a Eurasian woman few years older than him.

The young man suspected that Milne had been tippling between estate trips. He caught a whiff of spirit through the gum he had started chewing in the morning. He seemed to be in a happy haze, sipping on a cup of coffee so dark it resembled Coca-Cola.

'So does your missus let you out in the evenings?' Milne asked early one morning, grinning uncharacteristically. 'Can't claim to know much about the married life, but if you're up for it we could go for a couple of stengahs at the club tonight. You'll be my guest, no problem at all.' He leaned in and added, 'I'd wondered about asking Naag, but then he's a lot older and frankly, I don't feel very, you know ... comfortable.'

The young man nodded and Milne got up, 'Good chap! I'll send you a car this evening. Just keep this between us, ya?' The young man nodded again.

Around seven that evening, a jeep pulled up outside. Maloti peered through the living room window. 'There, sahib has sent you a car.'

The young man appeared dressed in a blue short-sleeved batik shirt and dark trousers. Maloti giggled. 'Be careful, they might mistake you for a barman when everyone gets drunk.'

Milne was already pacing his veranda when the jeep pulled up. A man holding a rifle tailed him.

'Don't worry about that chap,' he said getting into the car. 'We've all been assigned what they're calling a "home guard" for a few weeks now. The company is paranoid that we'll get ambushed and nicked off by a jungle rebel and so ...' Milne leaned to one side and revealed a revolver tucked snugly in a leather holster. 'We are required to carry one of these too. I've got my eye on a couple of roosters that wake me up every morning.' They drove down the road that the young man took on most mornings. As they approached the estate, the jeep took a sharp turn onto a graveled path that he had never noticed before. Large trees and drooping foliage shaded its entrance from view.

'Welcome to the Planter's Friend Club, Mr Sengupta,' said Milne, as they walked up the short flight of steps. The club was a large wooden structure raised on stilts with open veranda-like sides. It was dimly lit, except for the area where people were throwing darts under fluorescent lights buzzing with moths and insects. There were no women on the premises.

Men greeted Milne as they walked in. 'Take a seat right here,' said Milne pointing to one of the short, round, glass-topped tables with Anchor and Tiger beer coasters strewn all over it. He walked up to the bar, slapped a few colleagues on the back and shook hands with some Chinese men who were smoking cigarettes through long, stylish holders. They were better dressed than the white planters.

Milne returned with two drinks and one ruddy-faced gentleman. 'Sengupta please meet Alderson, assistant manager of the Jeram Padang estate. Sengupta works with us at the office.' Alderson was middle-aged and had a strikingly taut posture.

'Sengupta ... Ah, you're a Bengalian, aren't you?' he asked.

The young man stood up and nodded. 'Yes, Bengali.'

'Sit, sit ... enjoy your drink; you'll see the worst of the Empire here tonight,' Alderson chuckled as he walked away.

The young man took his first sip of alcohol in several years and made a face. Milne laughed out. 'Not used to the hard stuff, eh? Probably better that way.' He kept staring at the bar and then to the young man, smiling politely at him. He had downed his first drink and glanced at his empty glass.

'Why don't you go say hello to your friends for a while? I am quite comfortable here, sipping my drink and watching people,' the young man said.

Milne appreciated the gesture and said, 'All right, but I'm keeping an eye on you. As soon as that drink is over I'll bring you another one.' He got up and settled at the bar amidst more backslapping.

The young man looked around. A roomful of pink-faced, drunk Englishmen wobbled about with guns on their hips in the middle of a plantation surrounded by nothing but jungle. He lit a cigarette and walked towards the open side and peered out into the dark, moonless night, the enormous golf course barely visible. He heard voices and noticed the young Malay guards huddled on their haunches, some smoking, with their rifles laying against a wooden beam. When he walked back to his spot, he noticed that an elderly Chinese man had taken the seat across from him. When he saw the young man approach, he got up and said, 'Oh, I have taken someone's table.'

'It's all right, it's all right,' said the young man immediately. 'I am sitting alone. Please, please do sit down.' The man extended his hand and introduced himself: 'I am Lim, I trade in timber around here and sometimes I come over to play golf. And then I stay on for a beer.'

'I work on the estates and am a guest of my manager's this evening,' said the young man pointing at Milne.

Lim laughed. 'God, these chaps can drink, I tell you. Can't blame them really. Must feel so completely out of place in this part of the world. They leave behind their nice plump wives and sweethearts, their families and their mates, to come here to manage these damn estates ... susah lah.' The young man nodded and wondered how rich a Chinese man needed to be to be granted membership to the Planter's Friend Club. The young man was about to ask Lim about his family when an altercation erupted near the bar.

'I would like you to repeat what you said, Mister,' a loud and confrontational voice demanded. It was Alderson, the assistant manager that the young man had just met.

A short man seated on a barstool, clearly drunk and slurring said, '*Mishter?* Who the hell is this "mishter"? I'm Davie, you've known me for donkey's years...'

'All right then, Davie, what was it that you just said about the Queen?' said Alderson, his voice rising again.

'Look, alls I said was that Elizabeth...'

'Do not call her by name, you will call her Queen!' yelled Alderson.

'Okay, okay, easy does it, old chap. Now, the Queen, formerly known as Elishabeth ... Well, she's just plain lucky, inn she?'

'Lucky?'

'Yeah, lucky. There she was riding ponies, learning French and whatnot, and her uncle, the king, decides to marry that American slag, Besshie, probably named after a horse. So dear lover-boy uncle abdicates and good brother George becomes king. The poor man is in horrible health and Elishabeth, oops, pardon me, the Qu-weeeeen, starts filling in for him everywhere, just a wee girl then ... and then, poof, the King dies and suddenly this lassie becomes the queen of bloody England. So I say, no, we should not have her photograph or portrait or horse head or whatever mounted on our club.' He stopped and took a sip of whiskey. Everyone had stopped their chatter now.

'She is still the Queen and you cannot defame her!' thundered Alderson, clenching his fist.

'Listen, mate,' continued Davie in a drunken drawl, 'all I am saying is, she's lucky.'

'Lucky, eh?'

'Yes, lucky, blood ties and all. And not fit to rule. She should be at home raising those kids of hers with that philandering cad Philip. Not qualified to be queen. Simple, mate. Okay, you can hang her picture behind the bar, next to the whiskey bottles. Happy? Now I'd like to drink please. Go away. End of history lesson, ladies and gentlemen. Maybe more tomorrow, if you buy me a round.' Davie took a bow from his seat.

Alderson walked over to Davie. 'Apologize,' he said coldly, standing tall.

'Apologize? To bloody whom?' squeaked Davie.

'Just take back what you said about our Queen!'

'Who do you think you are, mate? Your Air Force days are over ... You're just a small rubber planter in the boonies like the rest of us. Living off the crumbs of this ... bloody, crumbling kingdom in the east. Hang her picture on your living room wall. Hell, in every room of your house if you want to, including in the toilet. But leave us alone.'

An elderly English man walked over to the bar to calm matters down. 'Let it go, Aldie ... he's just a drunk fool right now, right? Ah cummon now ... just walk away. He'll say he's sorry in the morning.' Alderson stood his ground.

'Davie, you'd do best to apologize now. I'm warning you!' screamed Alderson. Davie took a slow sip of his drink and turned around.

'Sod off, Aldie.'

A shot was fired before anyone had the wits to intervene. Davie slumped off the bar stool and fell onto the wooden floor with a thud. A trickle of blood appeared instantly.

'Bloody hell! You've killed him!' someone screamed. A few men bowed down clutching their heads, expecting more shots to follow; others watched stunned and wide-eyed, still holding their drinks. Alderson stood still, the smoking gun in his hand. The elderly gentleman reached out and grabbed it from him; Alderson did not resist and knelt down. He shook the still body lying on the floor. 'Davie, are you all right there ...' he asked hoarsely.

The Malay Home Guards burst into the club and looked for the attacker. One of them saw the elderly man holding the gun and pointed a rifle at him. A couple of men were on the floor now, prodding the limp body. Milne spoke up, 'Come on, let's pick him up carefully, put him in a jeep and drive him to Dr Murray's.'

'No can do ... Murray's gone to Johor for a wedding,' said someone from the bar.

'What? Dr Murray's not here? Let's take him to the hospital in Seremban then,' yelled Milne.

'But that's an hour away,' said the older man. 'Looks like he's bleeding a lot.'

The young man got up. 'I can help! Let me take a look at him,' he yelled, pushing people aside. They moved away from the crumpled body. The young man quickly checked for Davie's vitals – heartbeat, breathing and pulse. Then he rolled him over onto his back. Davie stirred. He unbuttoned his shirt and inspected the wound. The stomach was a bloody mess.

'Oh god, what have I done!' cried Alderman.

'Someone, give him a torchlight.' The young man held it over the wound. The bullet had entered from an angle and appeared to have lodged in the exterior flab of his ample gut. Davie stirred, flapped his arms about and then got up abruptly, knocking the young man over.

'He bloody shot me ... He shot me!' he yelled, looking for Alderman.

'Calm down, sir' said the young man.

'Where's the doctor? Take me to the bloody doctor!'

'Please lie down!' the young man said sternly.

Davie nodded obediently and said, 'Can I have a drinkie? I'm in pain, doctor.' He lay down again as the young man inspected the injured area. 'Is it still in there?' grunted Davie.

'Yes it is, but I will get it out.'

'God! Then take it out before I bloody bleed to death!' yelled Davie.

Lim grabbed the young man by the arm. 'You do know what you're doing, right?' The young man nodded.

It was a fifteen-minute ride back into town, where the local clinic was. Davie let out a moan each time the jeep hit a bump. They waited while the keys were being picked up from Murray's servant. A few minutes later, someone jumped out of a car and rushed to open the metal gate. It took several minutes before the lock disengaged with a reassuring click.

Four men with flashlights barged in, looking for the electric board. The young man held out a torchlight and opened the door to the small doctor's chamber. He found a glass cabinet with sterilized forceps and tweezers. They laid Davie down on the bed. Milne held a small metal pan while the young man glided in a long surgical tweezer and instantly pulled out the bullet, which fell into the pan with a light metallic clink. Everyone cheered.

The young man saw a thin wooden staircase, almost like a hanging ladder leading up to a space above the visiting room.

Peering into the dark, he could see several rows of bottles and large containers for pills stored in bulk, clearly labelled. He located what he needed easily and brought down the capsules. Davie was sitting up in a chair now.

'All I need to do is wrap up your stomach with bandages and give you a shot. But you must be back first thing in the morning to talk to the real doctor.'

'You mean you're not a doctor, mishter Kumar?'

'Who is Mr Kumar?'

'Oh no, wrong chap. He was me doctor back in Surrey,' said Davie in a haze.

'You chaps take Davie back. I'll close up here and drop Sengupta home,' said Milne.

'Are we going back to the club for a quick round? I'll respect the Queen and everything,' Davie asked, grinning, as they carried him out.

It was a short drive back to the house. When the young man opened the door on his side of the car, Milne stepped out as well. 'I don't know who Mr Kumar is, but Mr Sengupta, you were bloody incredible. Really, I can't thank you enough. This town owes you one. And I apologize on behalf of Her Majesty.'

'Careful now, Mr Milne. Her mention has caused enough trouble for one evening.' They laughed and shook hands.

When settling into bed later that night, Maloti said, 'I am getting a whiff of something medicinal; what is it?' The young man didn't respond. He tried to keep the incident at the club from Maloti.

When he arrived at the estate the next morning, he was informed that Milne had taken the day off. A little tired himself, the young man spent the morning in the office, trying to realign a typewriter.

Milne called eventually. 'We don't know what the official version is going to be. Looks like they want to call it an accident. So don't talk to anyone about this, please. Ya? Oh, and I had a chat with Dr Murray; he's really impressed with your work on the wound. Told me to convey a big thank you to you.' The young man put down the phone and went back to his typewriter.

Ganesh popped by in the afternoon, grinning from ear to ear. 'Aha. The local hero.'

'How did you know?'

'The news of a gunshot in a small town travels faster than electricity, Mr Doctor. When something exciting like this happens, everyone talks. White man shooting another white man, OHMIGOD ... first-class drama, mister. Who doesn't like bang-bang-bang!'

'There was only one bang.'

He beckoned Ganesh into the office and closed the door. 'Listen, first of all, I'm not a doctor.'

'Arré ... nobody cares about your certificate,' he interrupted, 'They heard that you removed a bullet. You are doctor. Simple. People here need a hero once in a while – the Indian man who save orang putih.'

The young man sighed and then said, 'How many people are talking about this?'

Ganesh shrugged.

'People in town know about this?'

'Oh, yes. Many different stories also.'

'I need to keep Maloti away from the market.'

'First, I thought you were a clerk, then people tell me you are a doctor, and now I see that you are a mechanic. Very mysterious ...' Ganesh pointed to the disassembled typewriter and the various-sized screws on the desk.

The young man dialled home. He tried to sound calm when Maloti answered. 'Do you need anything from the market?' he asked casually.

'The market ... Why?'

'Because I need to go there for something.'

'But you can't buy fish at this hour,' Maloti reminded him. So don't worry about it. I'll go in the morning.'

The young man persisted, 'I can buy chicken curry from Muttuswamy's, can't I?'

Maloti laughed. 'I see ... father and son are fed up with the fish I make them eat. All right, it would make Jonaki happy and save me some trouble.'

The young man hung up the phone and turned to Ganesh. 'Not a word of this at my home, all right? I just don't want them to worry.'

Ganesh shook his head. 'This will not be easy to hide from the missus.'

'I know ... I know,' said the young man lighting a cigarette. 'But I need some time to explain it to her.'

There was a minor commotion outside. The young man peered out from the window. A few tappers had gathered around a police jeep. They pointed towards the office. A brawny white man in uniform stepped out. 'Keep the engine running! I won't be gone for long.' Loud boots bounded up the steps. What Sergeant O'Brien lacked in perspicacity, he compensated for with ardour.

'Is Sen-Guptu here?' he boomed, police helmet in one hand, a much-worn baton in the other. The young man stood up.

'Yes, I am he,' he said. Ganesh disappeared to a corner.

'You are he? Sen-Guptu? Excellent. Is my good friend Milne here?'

'No, he isn't in today, unfortunately.'

'Not unfortunate at all. It is you I have come to see.'

'Me?'

'Yes, you. Because you are he. He who saved one of our men last night. There was an incident with a gun. The police and shootings, they go hand in hand, you see. We used to have more of them.'

'Police?'

'No, shootings. There used to be one every bloody week. I used to protect this estate from bandits. I caught some of them too. Milne will tell you. They stopped their sneaky attacks after a while. There's still just one damn group lurking around near here. But these jungles are so thick and full of crevasses and caves; you can't spot them from the air. And if you went on a patrol, you'd be turned around in no time.'

'Yes, I have heard some stories ...' the young man didn't think O'Brien would fit in the office chair. They both remained standing. Ganesh watched the exchange from his corner.

'So, this shooting business last night, would you say it was an act of hostility?'

'It was pure stupidity, sir.'

Sergeant O'Brien was cross. 'Yes, yes. They need a permit for those things, you know. Firearms they are. Not for boys. I am supposed to hold all permits at the station. But when the bandits started shooting, we looked the other way if the plantation folk got themselves a gun for protection. And now they're playing bloody cowboys and Indians.'

'He was drunk.'

'Ah. Would you say that Alderman was incapacitated? That he wasn't able to tell right from wrong? Good from evil? Jesus from Mohamed?'

'I don't know about his beliefs, sir.'

'Who cares about his beliefs! I mean was he so drunk that he didn't know what the hell he was doing?'

'Very drunk, yes.'

'Would you say he poses a threat to our town?'

'Maybe he shouldn't have a gun.'

'Yes! Mark my words. As soon as this town is declared safe, I am going to take all these guns away. Would you say Davie instigated him? Gave him no choice but to shoot his head off?'

'No one needed to be shot.'

A few people – clerks, drivers and tappers had gathered outside and were peering into the office from the window. 'Mr Ganesh, son of Murugasu!' O'Brien bellowed. 'What are you doing over there? Did you hear about all this?'

'I did not wish to disturb,' said Ganesh, smiling widely. 'But everyone in the town has heard about this.'

'Really? Already?'

'It is a small town, sir.'

'Yes, very small. I know everyone here. You know, Ganesh, people still come to me and complain about your old man. They tell me Murugasu owes them money.'

'I am sorry. It is not I, but my father who is to blame. Not I.'

'Yes, yes. Not you. Anyway, I tell them that gambling debts are not police matter. Until someone gets hurt.'

'No one will get hurt.'

'Someone always gets hurt, Ganesh. Someone has to get hurt. Or I'd be out of a damn job!'

The room fell very quiet after Sergeant O'Brien stormed out. But moments later, the young man heard him shouting again. The driver had disappeared with the keys to the jeep. 'I told the damn fool to keep it running! Where'd he bugger off to now?' The men shrugged. They were enjoying watching the large white man fuming.

'Damn fool! Damn fool!' O'Brien thundered, looking around. 'Someone find that idiot!'

'He is damn fool,' said Ganesh.

The young man managed to keep the affair from Maloti for a couple of days. Thankfully, the Kottiyans had either not heard anything or had opted not to gossip.

On Sunday, the family went out to lunch. They sat in a small Chinese restaurant on a side road off the main stretch. It was a

popular place called Five Sisters, run by a quintet of hard-working
siblings. They ordered steamed chicken dumplings, chicken fried
rice and a curried chicken dish called 'Five Sister Chicken'.

'Indian people, they like this one ...' said the eldest sister, dressed
in a silk blouse with a taut bust and light-green jade earrings.

'How can they work so hard and yet remain so pretty?'
commented Maloti. 'It's sad, but our Indian people here look so
unhealthy and tired, don't they? And why do all Indians have dark
circles around their eyes?'

The young man shrugged. 'I think it's because the Chinese have
better habits.'

Jonaki noticed his school friend Boon Siew sitting with his
parents and waved at him. The boy yelled back in Chinese and
Jonaki giggled. Then he picked a piece of food with his chopstick
and held it up. This made Jonaki double over laughing.

'What is it?' asked Maloti. 'Why are you laughing like that?'

'He is eating frog, Ma. Do you want some?'

Maloti gasped, wide-eyed. 'They won't mix any of it in our
food, will they?' The young man shrugged and kept eating.

A youthful man in a floral pink shirt walked into the restaurant
with his wife. One of the sisters rushed to seat them. The couple
pointed at a table near a fan, but she sat them next to the Senguptas.
'Put Indian people all together, ah?' said the man under his breath.
The sister dragged out the floor fan and plugged it into the socket
on the wall. Then she handed them the menu and said, 'Maybe
you try the 'Five Sister Chicken' – Indian people like this one.
Spicy one.'

The young man recognized him as a worker from the estate
and nodded. The man took a moment and then waved excitedly.
He turned to his wife and talked to her in Tamil while she stared
at them. As the young man was paying his bill, the estate man
called out to him. Using his thumb and forefinger, he mimicked

the motions of a gun going off and smiled. The young man nodded brusquely and walked out of the restaurant.

'Why did that man pretend he was shooting you?' asked Maloti.

'Too much beer.'

As they walked the short distance to the house, the young man sighed and hunched. 'What is wrong with your slipper?' asked Maloti.

'The stupid strap keeps popping out.'

'Just wear this pair at home. I'll buy you something sturdier.'

A car was parked outside their house.

'Mr Sengupta,' someone called out as they approached. 'Just thought I'd ... come by in person and thank you.' It was Davie and his wife. She smiled at Maloti and held her hand out.

'Hello, I'm Iris,' she said. Maloti touched her hand lightly.

'Please come in for a bit,' said the young man. 'I hope you are better.'

Davie was using a cane for support. Iris tried to help him, but he shrugged her off. 'Would you like something to drink?' asked the young man as they sat down inside.

'Oh no, sir' said Davie. 'We are so sorry to take up your time on a holiday afternoon ...' he started.

'But he wanted to come over as soon as he could walk to thank you,' said Iris, completing his sentence.

'Is the wound healing properly ... No pain is there?' asked the young man. Davie picked up his shirt.

'Dr Murray did another round of bandaging on it. Said it would heal just fine; no stitches needed. Said you did a nifty job of teasing that little bugger out.'

Iris walked up to Maloti and touched her arm. 'Your husband's a kind man, madam.' Maloti simply nodded, mystified by the conversation.

'Yes, who knows what would have happened if I'd bled all night,' said Davie. He got up with the support of his cane. 'Look, we're going to go now, but please accept my thanks and more importantly, my apology. I behaved very, very badly.' He was uncomfortable. 'I would be very grateful if you might accept a small token of appreciation from us.'

Iris pulled out an envelope from her purse and placed it on the table. 'It's really nothing,' she said. 'Please don't say no.' The young man nodded.

'Thank you,' said Davie and walked towards the door. 'Oh, one more thing ... we're dropping the charges against Alderson. We're saying it was an accident. I just don't see the point of dragging this out. Are you all right with that?'

'I am happy that you're recovering well.'

The young man escorted them back to their car. Maloti waited for him on the porch. He returned and sat down on the steps. 'I didn't tell you about something.' He paused, looking around for the boy.

'He's out in the back playing,' said Maloti. 'What happened at the club?'

He narrated the events of that evening.

'Why couldn't you have told me this?' said Maloti when he was done.

'Because ... I didn't want to worry you.' And then he started laughing.

'Why are you laughing like a mad person?'

'Because, in hindsight, it is actually quite funny.'

'Funny, eh? So you keep secrets from me now? You lay beside me night after night and just kept it inside you.' She teared up. 'Do you not remember what I have been through with you before ...?' The young man nodded and cupped her head in his palm.

'That was a long, long time ago. Our lives are different now,' he said.

She wiped her tears with the back of her hand and put a finger on his lip. Then she drew herself very close to him and said, 'I want you to know that I am very proud of you.' She put her arms around him and clutched him tightly. He felt relieved, yet her ardour confused him.

'Is that a fruit on the ground?' asked the young man, pointing.

'Yes!' exclaimed Maloti. 'At last, the kuini have ripened!' She ran to the front of the house and picked it up. 'Number 39,' she called out. 'It has a lovely smell.'

'Are there more ripe ones on the tree?' asked the young man.

'Yes, seems like it.'

'Well, let's collect a few then. I'll get that ladder from Mamat's shed.'

But even before he had made it down the steps, Maloti had started climbing the tree, her sari pulled up and folded into her waist.

'Careful! It's a tall tree ...!' exclaimed the young man.

'You forget where I grew up,' laughed Maloti, deftly going from one branch to the next. She was in the heart of the large tree in moments, inspecting the fruit.

The young man walked over and began pointing out the ripe ones. 'There, that one ... No, no, more to the left ... Yes, *that* one.' Maloti plucked about a dozen kuinis and carefully lobbed them down to the young man. She made her way down the tree and collected them in her sari. Once indoors, she rolled them out on the kitchen table.

'What numbers did we get?' asked the young man. 'Maybe we should line them all up and buy a lottery ticket?'

Maloti stared at the fruits and then started to rearrange them, forming a long row.

'What are you doing?'

'Come here and read the sequence,' she told the young man.

He walked over to the kitchen table and read, '22-22-22-22-29-29-29-77-77-69-4-54-16-104.'

The young man looked puzzled. 'You mean ... he's given the same number to more than one fruit?'

Maloti nodded, smiling.

'That Mamat is either really, really stupid, or a lot smarter than he looks,' said the young man, laughing.

Maloti opened the envelope that Iris had given them. She counted the money and said, 'Let Mamat sell a few fruits. We're doing okay.'

'Why? How much is in there?' asked the young man.

'Enough to pay back Palash-da's loan.'

'Really?' said the young man, surprised.

'Yes. There's money in doctoring,' said Maloti, slicing up kuini number 104.

DEATH OF A PAMPHLETEER

'Baba ... please sit down. Why are you short of breath?' asked the young man, standing up as Nirmal Sengupta entered the octagonal room unannounced. He seldom encroached on their meetings. Jyotirmoy concealed his cigarette in a deft manoeuvre of thumb and forefinger. Badol jumped up from his spot on the floor.

'A long walk from Ballygunj. Don't like taking the car these days ... Vandals everywhere. What are you all doing? What is the discussion about tonight?' He was in a foul mood. He sat down wearily.

'Well, Nirmal-babu, like everyone else, we're really worried about this Direct Action Day coming up. We're wondering how we can help in preventing hysteria from breaking out ... even in our own neighbourhood. You know how it is, sir ... It's so easy to get people agitated over Hindu–Muslim matters,' Jyotirmoy rambled. A thin spiral of smoke rose from his tucked hand.

'Then this is what you four musketeers need to do – print more of those pamphlets and ask shop owners to keep their stores open. We will not cave in to absurd demands. That chief minister of ours is a lapdog. And that useless Governor Burrows has caved in to demands for a holiday. Imagine that, a holiday! The Muslim League's internal meetings are none of our concern. They can meet all they want and they may have the space for that. But Bengal will remain open.' Nirmal Sengupta whacked his cane against the floor and got up to leave the room.

The young man spoke up, 'But, Baba, what if there is a riot here, on our own street? We should never be...'

Nirmal Sengupta cut him off. 'If anyone comes near this house with one of their blunt cleavers, I will blow their heads off. I have done it before. I should not call you musketeers as you have no muskets. Four pamphleteers you are. Oh, and that girl too, I suppose. Now do something with your pamphlets.' He left the room.

Nirmal Sengupta's communal rants were increasing of late. He had lost faith in the colonial government's ability to broker an amicable solution for the escalating rift in the political leadership of the country. Despite efforts to ensure a bloodless transition to independent leadership in India, matters had not proceeded well. In February, the Cabinet Mission established by British Prime Minister Clement Attlee began negotiating with the Congress Party and the All-India Muslim League. Months of political gridlock followed. Finally, in May, the Mission recommended a governing body for an India that was to remain undivided. But just a month later, under considerable pressure from *both* parties, they hurriedly drafted a plan that provided for the creation of a separate state for Muslims. The Congress Party didn't accept the fine print and leaders of the Muslim League grew impatient. They rallied for a Direct Action Day on 16 August so that Muslims could give fair voice to their aspirations for a country of their own. It was unclear what 'action' was to take place on this day and people of both faiths were jittery.

The *Star of India*, a popular newspaper, subscribed to predominantly by the Muslim population, took out an unprecedented two-page 'notification' of the programme for Direct Action Day. As Jyotirmoy had surmised, it was clear that a lot of planning and coordination had taken place. The details were chilling, especially in the references to a 'Holy War.'

It was Jyotirmoy's idea that they attend the rally. He looked up from his copy of the *Star* and paced the room, maintaining eye contact with his colleagues. He had become good at these drawing-room theatrics; he modulated his voice and spoke convincingly, 'Brothers ... is this not our city? Do we not have the right to be anywhere we want to be? If people cower at home, then these rallies and strikes, which the Congress started in the first place, would mean nothing. My "action" will be to go to the maidan in front of the Ochterlony Monument and listen to my minister speak. Yes, that will be my direct action. Remember, Suhrawardy is everyone's chief minister, not just to those of his own religion – *we* put him in power. I will exercise my right as a voter in Bengal to attend. Besides,' he added with finality, 'I don't think anything will happen.'

'No?' asked the young man.

'Nah. Not in the middle of the day in the busiest part of Calcutta. I am sure there will be police protection.' Like most people in the city, the pamphleteers went to bed that night without an inkling that the gates of hell had already been pried open. In the coming days, Calcutta would feed on itself.

There were no vendors or vehicles to disrupt the quiet of dawn on 16 August. The citywide strike made the lane feel communal. Noises that were usually drowned out could be heard – the sounds of toilets flushing, slippers flapping, several radio sets tuning into broadcasts of ragas and gentle hymns, with the occasional crackling of news announcements piercing through – reminding everyone that it was an unusual day.

Around nine, the younger boys in the neighbourhood formed teams for a day of street football. They started warming up. Loud slaps of the ball against palms and feet echoed against the walls lining the street. An hour later Nirmal Sengupta called out to one of them. 'Run out and see if any of the shops have opened yet ... It's a quarter past already.'

The boy ran to the corner, looked around, and yelled, 'No, not a single store is open. And no cars either. We can move our game to the main road!'

'This is not a holiday!' Nirmal Sengupta bellowed. 'Open your shops, you bloody cowards!'

As the morning rolled on, Jyotirmoy came to the house. 'All quiet on the eastern front,' he said in English. 'Where are the rest?' The young man shrugged. Jyotirmoy went to the street and started dribbling the ball as the younger children watched. Badol arrived minutes later.

Maloti yelled from the balcony, 'Jyoti-da, I think you've missed your calling in life. Now you're doomed to be a doctor for the rest of your days and not a famous footballer.'

'Yes, you're absolutely right. Damned shame,' he replied, panting.

'Where's your little sidekick, Badol?' asked Maloti.

'I left her at home, Didi. The ladies in the mohalla are taking care of her. I thought that perhaps she shouldn't stay out of the house all day. Who knows how long this meeting will last...?'

'I've always told you that she can stay with us whenever she needs to,' said Maloti, leaning out from the balcony.

'Yes, Didi. I'll bring her around the next time. She likes it here,' Badol smiled.

The men started the long walk to the maidan. They cut across several shorter streets till they were on Russa Road, a wide conduit that ran through the heart of the city, joining the southern and central sections. It was empty, save for a few pavement dwellers who lay curled up in the narrow slivers of midday shadows. In minutes, the men were dripping with sweat. 'Nothing open at all ... Can't even get a drink,' said the young man. A few minutes later Badol, peering through a window, noticed a large urn inside a house facing the road. An old lady was sitting on its stoop keeping watch over two little girls playing on the pavement. She poured the men some water and they drank thirstily, taking turns. They lifted the tumbler to avoid touching the rim with their mouths.

Refreshed, the men continued their walk. In about an hour, they were within sight of the maidan. They could hear speakers blaring and a din of human voices rising to a discordant pitch every few minutes. Light orange dust hung like a thin cloud over the open expanse, the tall white monument sticking through it like a sabre. 'Lord ... I have never seen so many humans in my life,' said Jyotirmoy. The loudspeakers crackled loudly, drawing everyone's attention. They realized that the crowd was mostly Muslim.

The meeting's objectives were read out and everyone was thanked for coming. The first speaker was Nazumuddin, a senior member of the Muslim League in Bengal. He began with a booming, 'My dear Muslim brothers,' and the people gathered let out a deafening roar. A shopkeeper, still holding the padlock to his store, leaned in to where the young men were standing and said, 'This could get out of hand. Do you think we have time to pull down our pants and snip it off?' He laughed at his own joke. The young man noticed groups of young men clumped together, their fists coiled around metal chains.

Nazumuddin started by asserting that the rally ought to be peaceful and that every Mussalman in India would practice tolerance and restraint – however strong the impulse to destroy and desecrate might be. 'Allah teaches us compassion ... towards everyone ... even Hindus,' he added forcefully. Some in the crowd nodded. But he subsequently undermined the conciliatory tone he was setting up, by saying that Muslims in Calcutta had been unable to show restraint earlier in that day, by retaliating against the Hindus who had started beating and abusing them. 'They were poor and innocent and they did this only for their own defence. I cannot hold that against a man. I hear some died defending their honour.'

The crowd grew restless. The young man turned to Jyotirmoy and asked, 'Is this true? Have you heard anything about this – people being killed earlier today?'

'Yes,' a man standing near them said, 'I heard that some of them ... their people, died. We were told to shut down our shops. But the way he is speaking now is not good. Everyone is getting very agitated. Am I wrong?'

'Dada, have you heard whether there has been any trouble in the Kidderpore side ... the dock area?' asked Badol.

The man shrugged. 'But I heard that the big store for rifles on the corner of Esplanade and Dharamtalla had been robbed right in front of everyone earlier today.'

Finally, around 2 p.m., Chief Minister Suhrawardy took centre stage. The young man, who couldn't see him from where he was, asked, 'Who's this? Who's on the stage now?'

'Don't you recognize your own minister's voice?' snapped Jyotirmoy. Suhrawardy's time at the podium was surprisingly short. He reiterated his colleague Nazumuddin's observation about the death of Muslims and expressed anguish. He informed the crowd that as their elected leader he had personally ordered the police and military to not interfere with the public. The statement was difficult to interpret.

'Does he have the authority to do that?' asked Jyotirmoy. 'Will it not just encourage people to go out on attacks?'

'Look at this unending crowd,' said the man next to them. 'He can say or do anything he wants.'

Suhrawardy ended the rally abruptly. Swarms of angry young men took to the streets immediately – they ran in every direction, screaming. Lorries with more men appeared, some wielding lathis, knives, cleavers and bottles. Badol took in the chaotic surroundings, wide-eyed and palpitating. 'I am going home now,' he said. 'I need to make sure that things are safe.'

'Go, go right now,' said Jyotirmoy.

'Come back to the house with Padma as soon as possible,' the young man shouted after him.

'Before nightfall,' Badol yelled back. The three men exited the maidan as fast as their legs could transport them.

The local shops did not reopen the next morning. While rumours of mayhem had swept through every street and lane in the city, people in secluded enclaves like Nirmal Sengupta's neighbourhood were anxious for official news. The radio had stopped broadcasting, save for one announcement by the chief minister late at night. He insisted that matters were well under control, but people were sceptical. Women blew conches. Normally this made the lane reverberate with piety; today it sounded ominous.

The children decided against playing football in the lane, though it was quieter than the day before. People loitered on their balconies and in the streets, exchanging the bits of information they were picking up – the possibility of the army intervening, more killings in the Entally area, the killing of some policemen in Baigbagan. These locations were new to Maloti. 'Where is this place? Is it near us?' she asked the informants, worried. But she had to attend to her tasks and was soon drawn back indoors. A household's routine must carry on even in the most irregular of days. Rice must be boiled, vegetable diced, potatoes peeled, children fed, clothes washed, and floors swept.

Later that morning, Jyotirmoy turned up at the house, unsure of how to assess the unfolding events. The reporting had been haphazard. 'Should I go to the clinic and see if Badol is alright?' he asked Nirmal Sengupta, who had come down to the octagonal room.

'How will you get there?' he asked. 'Nothing is plying on the streets.'

'Besides Badol said that he would come here,' the young man added.

'Yes, but like I said, there is no transport. How will he make the journey? In any case, I sense that things have died down since last night. Otherwise those hideous mobs would have been at our doorsteps by now.'

They spent the morning listening to radio broadcasts from Delhi. It was a repeat of the same news – riots in western Bengal, curfew on the streets, Gandhi condemning the violence. The same grim, monotone voice made announcements on the hour.

'Why doesn't he just come here instead of speaking to us through the radio?' Nirmal Sengupta grumbled.

'It might send the message that he favours Hindus if he rushes here right now,' Jyotirmoy considered. 'Yes … Let it all die down. Perhaps it's best not to draw too much attention – maybe things have quelled after all.'

The telephone rang around noon. Maloti ran up a flight of stairs to answer it. 'Badol! Badol! It's Badol!' She screamed.

'Where are you Badol?' asked Jyotirmoy, snatching the receiver from her.

'I have been trying to call for hours … The lines were dead. I am at Balu Ghat. I ran as fast as I could.'

'Are you safe?'

'No. We are in grave danger.'

'Why? Where is Padma?'

'I've left her with Begum Afreen. The ladies in the lane are taking care of her. But the men are there.'

'What men? Why didn't you take her with you?'

'I couldn't. There are men everywhere now. Everywhere.'

'What men?'

'Their men, our men ... I can't tell them apart. But they arrived and I ran out the back lane.'

'Arrived where?'

'At the clinic! They are there now, about five of them. Asking about the Hindu doctor. They want to know why you set up a clinic there. I don't think I can keep them away much longer.'

'Are there any police patrols or anything?'

'No police. They left the area after the incidents this morning.'

'What happened?'

'There was a calamity near here earlier. A gang of Muslims attacked the Kesaram cotton mill in Lichubagan. They say they killed the workers in retaliation to some other killings by Hindus in the morning. I am not sure what happened, sir ... But now they are roaming around the area looking for stray Hindus. Someone must have told them about you. Sir, you must come, all of you. They are demanding to know why we have a Hindu doctor making profits and why a Hindu family lives there.'

'Go back home to your daughter, Badol, we are coming right now,' Jyotirmoy said, trying to sound calm as he hung up the telephone.

'Where is he?' asked the young man.

'He is near the clinic. There's a mob there demanding information. Asking for me.'

'I don't think it would be wise to go there.'

'Of course! I must! And so must you!' yelled Jyotirmoy.

'Where is Padma?' asked Maloti.

'She is trapped at the clinic. Badol managed to get away to call us. He's on his way back, but wants me to go there. I can explain matters ... Tell them to leave their family alone.'

'Why have they not attacked yet? What are they waiting for?' asked Nirmal Sengupta entering the room.

'Sir,' said Jyotirmoy turning to Nirmal Sengupta, 'I beg of you to let us borrow your car. We must try.'

'Let's think. Let's think a bit,' he said sitting down. 'Well, if they still haven't harmed them, I agree that we should try. But it would be foolish to just apprehend a mob. I think I can help you. Wait.' He returned moments later, dressed to leave the house. He carried a rifle and a box of cartridges. 'Does anyone know how to use this?' he asked. 'I know my son doesn't.'

'No, sir.'

'I am loading it up. Here, this is the switch. Unlock it if you need to shoot.' With these instructions Nirmal Sengupta handed the long double-barrelled gun to Jyotirmoy. 'Now follow me.'

The driver could not be found. Nirmal Sengupta walked around the ground floor, shouting out his name. 'He's hiding in the storage room,' said the old cook. Nirmal Sengupta kicked open the door.

'What are you doing here?'

'I won't go, babu.'

'Alright then,' said Nirmal Sengupta. 'Give me the keys to the car.'

'You shouldn't go, babu.'

'Give me the keys, you coward!' Nirmal Sengupta yelled. The man got up and walked through the house towards the garage.

'I will drive, sir,' he said starting the car.

'Good. Now, get in, you two,' said Nirmal Sengupta.

'Why do you need to go?' asked Nirmal Sengupta's wife. 'Let the young ...' Nirmal Sengupta waved her away and got into the front seat.

'Where are we going?' asked the driver

'To the police station down the road.'

Jyotirmoy and the young man sat in the back, the gun at their feet. The car drove out of the quiet lane. The police station was about half a kilometre from their house, on the main road across from the typically busy Russa cinema hall, which was shuttered today. Nirmal Sengupta was on amiable terms with the sub-inspector. The portly man often stopped by their house for tea and snacks after work. Or before. Or during. 'Wait here,' he said and strode in to the station. A lone guard was sitting just inside the main entrance. He jumped up.

'Is Sub-inspector Ghosh here?' asked Nirmal Sengupta.

'No, sir,' said the guard.

'Well, who is? Call an ASI. Tell them Nirmal Sengupta is here.'

'There is no one here, sir.'

'What? How can there be no policemen in a police station?' fumed Nirmal Sengupta.

'I don't know, sir.'

'Are you saying there is not a single policeman in there?'

'Yes, sir. No, sir. No one has come from the morning ... Just me, waiting.' The guard seemed lost. The police van and wagons were parked outside in neat rows.

'I see. You come with me then. Come on – get up. We have to go disperse a mob.'

'Me, sir? No, sir. I cannot, sir. I am guarding the station.'

'What exactly are you guarding if there is no one here? Get up! I need a policeman.'

'But I am just like a daroga, sir.'

'But you have a uniform on!' Nirmal Sengupta grabbed him by the arm and dragged him out of the station as he protested. He opened the car door and pushed him into the front seat next to the driver. 'I'll tell Ghosh that I sent you out. Now go with these men. If there's trouble, tell them you're a policeman and a full van is on its way.'

'Yes, sir' he said, nodding at Jyotirmoy and the young man.

'Okay. Go on and keep your heads calm. Agree to everything they ask of you and get them back,' said Nirmal Sengupta.

The streets were deserted and the pavements littered with debris and refuse. Row after row of shops had been stripped bare, down to their walls. The road was strewn with an ensemble of objects that mobs had vandalized but were unable or unwilling to carry with them – plumbing fixtures, remnants of broken furniture, utensils, shards of glass, electrical wires, gas cylinders, construction beams and the odd strip of colourful hosiery. As they left the more insulated areas of the city, bodies appeared – burnt and charred, some bludgeoned, others mutilated and disfigured. The ones that lay intact were distended. Dogs sniffed and tugged at them, no longer interested in the cars casting long, fleeting shadows. Driving through Babu Bazaar, they passed a group of men by the side of the road, sipping tea and wolfing down bread. A couple of them pointed to the car and picked up bricks. The driver said nervously, 'Chhoto-babu ... perhaps we should return home. I kept saying this was a terrible mistake ...' No one answered him. A morbid fascination took over as they travelled on, journeying towards a perilous tryst. A truck appeared in the distance, full of men shouting and jeering. It was impossible to hear what they were saying. They seemed triumphant – an odd set of smiling faces on a grisly, decomposing terrain.

At four in the afternoon, they entered the familiar stretch that led to Jyotirmoy's clinic and stopped where the narrow road began. It was uncharacteristically crowded. Almost everyone who lived in the adjoining houses and hovels had taken to the street, excited and nervous, titillated by the promise of something unexpected, possibly macabre.

People started pointing at Jyotirmoy as soon as he stepped out of the car. They had been expecting him. 'Wait here,' he said to the driver. 'We will go on in and see what is going on first.'

The guard refused to budge. 'I'll guard the car.'

Jyotirmoy walked confidently toward his clinic. A group of about a dozen men – clearly not from the neighbourhood – were milling around. Haggard and angry in appearance, they wielded enough weaponry to fight a small battle. But the local crowd that had gathered seemed unafraid of them. They wouldn't kill their own.

'Your saviour has come at last!' cried out one of the men as he walked up to them. Badol bounded out of the clinic. He was sweating profusely. The man leading the group, who stood with a hand on his green, tattered, blood-stained pyjamas, let out a maniacal laugh. 'Look! He's just a man in a dhoti!'

'This is our doctor,' said Badol.

'What a small man! I thought that we would witness the arrival of Krishna or Vishnu or one of your great gods. The streets would part and he would come to us. So tell me, am I not seeing something yet, are you divine?'

'No,' said Jyotirmoy. 'I'm just a person who helps here.'

'I see. What a person you must be then. We have been on a spree all morning, you know, getting rid of people. Sending them upstairs,' he pointed at the skies. 'But here, all of a sudden, a whole mohalla-ful of people asks us to spare lives. Your lives! So we said, "Let's stop operations, we need to see this magician, this man who can walk in to a Muslim neighbourhood fearlessly and start a shop," didn't we?' The man turned to the mob and they nodded, entertained by the theatrics – some respite from a strange day of mayhem.

'I am no magician. Everyone here knows me. I know them too, I know their illnesses,' said Jyotirmoy pointing to several people in the crowd. 'I just ask you to let go of this man and his daughter.'

'Yes, yes, we know of this daughter,' said the gang leader. 'An old grandmother was covering her with her arm, protecting her when we arrived. Imagine that! A little Hindu girl being saved, on a day like this, by a Muslim grandmother! What a magician you are! You could be a big politician, sahib, you aren't much shorter than Panditji. Teach us how to live happily in our great land.'

'Please. I am no magician. Let us take them away. Let us have peace now.'

'Oh, he comes in peace! We'll tell you about peace. Shall we?' The crowd nodded.

'It has been heard that as of this morning, a Hindu man named Goat, has formed an army of people pledging to take ten Muslim lives for every Hindu life. And another man in the city, near Beliaghata, a big babu like you, called Ghosh, has even authorized a rate – ten taka for killing, five for breaking bones. We're not very expensive, are we?'

'But we haven't killed anyone,' said the young man desperately. 'Nor has Badol. You can't just kill innocent people.'

'Oh, but killing is easy. You don't understand how easy it is till you do it. You speak of innocence? If I said, I'd spare your life if you killed someone else, you'd kill them right away. Trust me.'

'I would not,' said the young man.

'You would. Oh yes, you would. But you still think you're better than me.'

'But the doctor saves lives. He is a good man. He has saved many lives here,' said Badol trembling. 'Just ask anyone here. And I always help him, right by his side.'

'And what else does this magic doctor do? Where do you and the doctor go all the time – villages, schools, meetings with Hindu leaders? What was all that you told me?' Badol began trembling. He looked at Jyotirmoy and then at the young man.

'We know what you do!' screamed the man, losing composure. 'I have been waiting for you, magic-babu. What good would it do to end this miserable servant's life? The streets and gutters are filled today with the bodies of poor, wretched people like him and me. But you, now you are worth something. You don't want us to have our own country, I hear?' He pulled out one of the leaflets tucked in his vest. 'Is this yours? I can't read but they tell me it is.'

'If you could, you would see that...'

'Shut up!' screamed the man. 'Bring that little girl out!' Two men went inside the clinic and dragged Padma out. She stood in the middle of the circle of men, staring at her father. Badol screamed and fell at Jyotirmoy's feet.

'Now why do you go around and spread this filth? Can your Krishna chakra save you now? Can your thousand gods save you now? From the hands of a man like me, a beast who can't read or write?'

'I only did what he asked of me,' cried Badol. 'I didn't know what they were doing. My daughter is small. She has no mother. Let her ... live.'

The man paused. He seemed to be focusing on something in the distance. 'Did you come in that car?'

'Do you want it?' asked the young man quickly. Reason flickered across the man's face. 'Just take it and let them go please. It's a good car.'

'Do you think you can buy us with a car? I could just take it if I wanted to!' sneered the man. But his voice indicated that he was contemplating a compromise.

'It isn't a bribe, it's an offering,' said the young man as deferentially as he could.

'He asks for kindness. Should I let them go?' the man asked the crowd. No one answered.

'You touch this little girl and I will thrash you with my bare hands, you harami goonda!' It was Begum Afreen yelling. She walked up to the man and started to pummel him with her thin arms. He laughed, covering his face from her punches.

'I am more afraid of her than the whole lot of you! Stop beating me up!' The crowd tittered.

'Will you accept the car?' asked the young man again.

The leader turned to the people in the neighbourhood. 'Should I take the car and spare them?' he asked. The crowd agreed that he ought to. 'But if he does not bring the car and runs for his life, then I burn this clinic down, right?' The crowd responded with a roar.

He picked up a kerosene bottle and lit it. Three other men did the same. 'All right, Begumji, ask this polite babu to go and bring us his car. Now, get inside that clinic. You and your girl. Let's see if he comes back.'

'When I return will you release all of them?' asked the young man.

'Gaadi lao!' he yelled. 'I give you two minutes! Jah!'

The young man ran and the crowd went after him chanting, 'Gaadi lao! Gaadi lao!' He looked over his shoulder and saw Jyotirmoy being taken into the clinic. As he approached the car, he noticed that the guard was in the driver's seat. He had already switched the ignition on. The young man opened the side door and jumped in. Even before he had closed the door, the guard hit the accelerator and swerved around.

'Oh no, no, no!' screamed the young man. 'Turn the car back around! We must go back.'

'Are you insane? They will kill us all alive!' said the guard knocking someone over as he made his way out of the crowded lane.

'No! We must bring them the car! STOP!'

The crowd began jeering as they pointed at the car, entertained by the turn in the plot. 'Bhaag gaya, gaadi bhaag gaya!'

'STOP THE CAR NOW!' screamed the young man. He put his arms around the guard's neck and choked him, pulling him away from the wheel. The car swerved. The driver tried to intervene. And then he froze, staring out the rear windshield.

'Oh god,' he whimpered.

The young man turned around and saw Jyotirmoy's clinic implode into giant orange flames.

The Hindu retaliation didn't start till a couple of days later. But when it came, it was pervasive and demonic. The slaughtering wasn't limited to the labouring poor of the metropolis with its huge immigrant population. The myth of the genteel Bengali was dismantled swiftly, as was the secular insurance of neighbourhood or para loyalty. The young man didn't leave his room, even when screams rang out in his lane, from right under his window. The Week of the Long Knives came to a blunt halt after both sides had had their fill and the Hooghly was bloated with naked bodies of unidentifiable faith.

THE DISPENSER

The incident at the Planter's Friend Club was settled swiftly. Davie recovered from his bullet wound and continued drinking merrily at the club, right under a newly framed photograph of Queen Elizabeth. Alderson went on extended home leave, taking his family with him to rural England. Word was that he would not return. A fortnight after the incident, the young man found a note on his desk – a message to call a Dr Murray. After sitting on it for a couple of days, he telephoned him during a lull at work.

'Well, hello, hello, Mr Sengoopta,' answered a booming, breezy voice after the receptionist put him through. 'I have been meaning to call you for a few days.' He sounded pleasant. 'It's about the you-know-what. I want to say thank you. I am sorry that you had to witness that. What a bunch of absolute savages my people can be, Sengoopta.'

'It's quite alright, doctor. It was fortunate that I happened to be there.'

'Damn right you are, Sengoopta! You know what ... Do you think you might be able to come see me at my clinic after work sometime? I'd love to make the acquaintance of the only other person in this town who knows how to use tweezers to pluck more than an eyebrow.'

They decided to meet the next day. The young man walked into the clinic around five. There were a few patients waiting. The young Malay lady at the small reception counter asked, 'First time? Do you have yellow card?'

'It's a personal visit,' said the young man.

'Per-so-nal visit?' she repeated haltingly. 'The doctor is quite busy actually.'

'I can wait for him then.' He took a seat next to an old Chinese man in a singlet. The man smiled at him feebly. The receptionist called out for the next patient, a Malay man named Baharrun. He sprang up immediately.

She looked at the old man seated on the bench and waved her hand emphatically. 'Doctor has no time. Doctor very busy. You go home, lah.' The old man stood up shakily and sauntered away. She turned to the young man and said, 'So ... can you tell me what is the nature of this per-so-nal visit?'

'Well, Dr Murray called me ... and we set up a time to meet this afternoon.' On hearing this, she scurried inside. A moment later, a red-nosed man with a cheerful, doughy face, stuck his head out of the inspection room.

'Well, hello, hello,' he boomed. 'Pleasure to see you here. Please, just give me five more minutes, my good man.' The young man nodded.

A little later, the doctor emerged and walked the young man to a food stall across the street. 'Would you like a beer?' he asked, his hands quivering a bit.

'I'll have a Coca-Cola, please.'

A Tiger beer, a Coca-Cola and a plate of satay were ordered. Murray spoke to the stall owner without the accent the young man usually heard when Europeans spoke.

'Your Malay seems to be very smooth, sir,' he said politely.

'My wife's Malay,' said Murray, looking pleased.

Murray poured the beer into a tall glass and took a long sip. 'So ...' he began in a serious tone, 'you broke into my clinic and used my equipment. And now everyone in this town is giving, not the town doctor, but someone *else*, some clerk from the estates, the credit for saving a life. Even that dimwit policeman O'Brien thinks you're a hero.'

The young man remained silent.

Murray burst out laughing, 'Oh my god, I feel terrible. You're taking me seriously! Like I said on the phone, I am relieved that you were here that night.' He extended his large hand theatrically and the young man shook it. And then he embarked on a long personal narrative in his loud but pleasant voice.

'I am a VMO ... Do you know what that means?' The young man shook his head. 'Visiting Medical Officer. *Visiting*. That should mean temporary, right? But I've been here six years now. I'm ready to leave this town. Lord knows I love it here in Malaya, but it's been thirty years. Penang, Dungun, Bukit Matajam, Malacca ... I've been telling my poor wife for years now that we'll move back to England. I'm old, she wants to live in England, and my boys have grown up ... My mother has a few years left in her. Did I tell you my wife was Malay?' The young man nodded.

'Yes. So, a few years ago they needed someone temporary here and I agreed. But I can't just pack up and leave. No one wants to come here. A couple of Indian doctors looked at the prospects, but bolted in less than a month. I close the clinic at five, but I tell you every bloody evening there are people rattling my gate.'

'"Go to the hospital," Fatimah yells at them, but they say, "Hospital so far away, lah," It's bloody annoying, I tell you.' He downed the beer and asked for a second one.

'Anyway, enough with my nowhere story ... So, moving on to you, sir, I gather you are here to work in the estates but you've got some good medical training?' The young man nodded. Murray considered this for a moment, 'You know what ... there's money to be made here if you're a good nurse. But then again, maybe you like the estate career. Did you train in India?'

The young man shook his head. 'No, in Glasgow.'

'In Glasgow?' said Murray. 'You went to Glasgow to become a nurse?'

'No ... I went to become a doctor. But ... I never finished.'

Murray leaned back, taking in this unexpected piece of information. 'Where did you study?'

'Royal.'

'For how long?'

'About three-and-a-half years ... But I had to return to India.'

'You studied medicine at the Royal Faculty?' Murray whistled. 'Why did you quit?' But before the young man could answer, he said, 'Finances, was it?'

The young man decided that it was the easiest to nod.

'Bloody hell ... three years at Royal and you're shuffling papers in the woods. I don't know what to tell you.' Murray asked for a third beer.

The young man said nothing to Maloti about his conversation with Murray. Being reminded of Glasgow depressed him. But a month later, Murray contacted him again and requested another meeting. Again, at the satay stand.

He arrived a few minutes before five and ordered a soft drink. He could see the clinic across the street. A plain white board over the front of the establishment said, 'Clinic Murray, 7 Main Road. 9–12.30 (morning time), 2.30–5 (afternoon time).'

Murray arrived around quarter past five and sat down with a big heave. He gulped down a Tiger beer in four large sips and got straight to the point.

'I wanted to ask you if you are looking for some extra work ... after hours. The pay will be decent. Just tell me if you have any interest and I'll continue ...' The young man nodded. Some more money would be good.

'The point is that I am bloody tired of this job. I can't stand to spend the entire day in there and then have more patients badgering me in the evenings. I just like to play my old records, read a good book and get a bit lit. I've worked hard all my bloody life. Don't I deserve these simple comforts?' The young man nodded.

Murray continued, 'You know what – can you work in the evenings? You see the patients, listen to their complaints, take their reports. For the most part, it's just basic stuff – fever, body aches, colds ... you know the lot. The Indians often have digestion problems. You would be able to tell them what to take – we have a lot of medicine supplies in there.'

'Yes ... I saw that,' said the young man.

'Right,' nodded Murray. 'And if there's anything serious, you call me ... If it can wait, tell them to come back in the morning. This way the clinic stays open and there is a place for people to go after hours. And I can have my beer in peace.'

'Now ... strictly speaking, this is not ... legal, you see. But there are ways around it. If there is ever any trouble, we will have to present it a little differently ... We explain you are merely refilling prescriptions. I really don't think there will be a problem.'

'Don't you have someone who does that already...?'

'Yes,' said Murray. 'His name is Wong and he's an amazingly organized fellow. I've broached the issue a couple of times with him, but he never warms up to it. I think he just doesn't like dealing with people ... he's a little odd that way. Strange chap. You'd think people around here would want a bit of extra cash, right? Ah, there he is, locking up.'

The young man looked across the street. Wong was in a bright white uniform, on his haunches, working the padlocks. He noticed them but turned away. Every couple of minutes one heard the piercing noise of serrated gears moving rapidly and then the loud clang when the shutters hit the pavement.

'You know what, take your time,' said Murray. 'It's a bit to think about. But we do get maybe a dozen patients and I'll split the fee evenly with you. You don't have to pay for electricity or the staff or anything else.'

'What about my other job?' asked the young man. 'Will they allow it on the estates?'

'Oh yes, I'll have a word with Milne, definitely not an issue. He's a fan of yours anyway and everyone knows that young clerks could do with a bit more income. And frankly ...' Murray dropped his voice, 'I sometimes wonder if the lower pay doesn't give them incentive to become a little creative with their jobs. If you know what I mean.'

They left the stall an hour later and the young man decided to take the longer route back home. He ambled into one of the lanes that ran parallel to the main road and it led him to the clamorous stretch where the market began. Maloti came here in the mornings, three times a week, to do the household shopping. Bright yellow–white lights fell on the street from the stove lamps perched above the food stalls. The town's one movie hall, 'Lucky Theatre', stood at the end of the road. People were seated on small chairs at collapsible wooden tables littered with bowls of noodles, soups, peanuts and other dishes. Young couples, some well-dressed, holding hands and talking softly, were out for their evening stroll. Grandmothers ran after infants, patiently feeding them or pulling them along as they toddled. He noticed an elderly lady feeding a baby no more than a few months old. She nibbled on a piece of meat, took it out of her mouth, and then fed it to the baby, who chewed on it like a tiny bird.

When he got home, Jonaki rushed out and yelled, 'Surprise! Surprise!' Taking his father's hand, he dragged him from the front porch, all the way down the kitchen steps to the back of the house. 'He's been waiting all afternoon for you to come home,' said Maloti smiling.

'A cat,' said the young man. 'You found a stray cat and brought it home?' The boy giggled. The creature made a very un-catlike sound; it went, kirikirikirikiri. 'What is that?' said the young man and jumped back. The little animal shivered and tried to bury itself in the box.

'Ah! It's a porcupine. What are you going to call him?' asked the young man.

'Mr Rambutan,' said Jonaki, giggling uncontrollably.

A few days later, when they were in bed, the young man brought up the proposition made by Dr Murray. To his surprise, Maloti was excited by the news.

'But wouldn't you feel lonely in the evenings?' he asked.

'Yes, I would, but I think this would give you something a bit more meaningful. And ...' Maloti hesitated.

'And what?' pressed the young man.

'And it would make me proud.'

'Will you let me sleep please?' hissed Jonaki.

'So, can you start tomorrow?' Murray asked the young man as soon as he sat down. He extended his hand.

'Yes. I think so,' he replied, taken aback by the simplicity of the agreement. They were back at the satay stall.

'Good! And you know what ... until we start getting a few people in the evenings, you don't need to share anything with me.'

They shook hands. The young man was now the town dispenser. Murray downed two more beers to make it official.

The next day, the young man arrived at the clinic at four. Murray showed him around, pointing at things haphazardly and then introduced him to his staff of two – Zainun and Wong. 'I had them prepare this box of important injections you might need in case of an emergency – rabies, tetanus, an adrenaline jab, that sort of thing. If anything major happens, of course, you'll just call me.'

He spoke to Zainun in Malay, and then turned around to the young man and said, 'She'll help with the older Malay patients and her English is pretty darned good too. She's a city girl; came here from Seremban answering an advertisement I put in the paper. Says she likes it here because it's quiet. Go figure. And Wong will help out with his people, the Chinese patients.' Murray got up to leave. He seemed satisfied with the arrangements.

As he was walking out the door he paused for a moment. 'You know what ... it just occurred to me that this is a historic moment ... it's the dawn of a modern Malaya. We have an Indian, a Malay, and a Chinese working together, and an Englishman going out the door!' Murray bumbled out and crossed the street, straight to the satay stall.

There were no patients on the first two nights. The young man sat in the inspection room looking up drugs for the prescriptions he might have to write. Murray had handed him a hefty book provided by a Salim and Company, which he assumed was the pharmaceutical firm that supplied the medicine for the clinic.

Zainun popped her head through the door on the third evening and said, 'No patient again.'

'But if we are patient, we will have patient,' said the young man, immediately regretting the silly wordplay.

She laughed 'Doctor is funny.'

'I am not a doctor,' said the young man. 'I am just the dispenser.' When he was locking up that night, he noticed the old man in the singlet he had seen in the waiting room when he had first come to meet Murray. He was sitting across the street, on a small stool, watching the clinic intently. 'Who is that man, Zainun?'

'Oh, that man always wanting to see doctor but will not say anything. If you ask him if he is sick, he will just shake his head. I think he just want money, lah.'

On the fourth evening the phone rang, startling the young man. It was Murray, sounding drunk. 'I'm shending you shomeone; fell off a motorcycle. No broken bones, I think. Bones are fine, bones are fine.'

Half an hour later, two Indian men came into the clinic, one of them had a shirt wrapped around his arm. Zainun sent them in promptly, without any forms. 'Hello, doctor,' said the uninjured man, wearing rubber slippers and a purple sarong. 'This my brudder. He fell off the scooter. Lot of blood and scratching.' The young man inspected his arm; there was a large gash running down the anterior side. He cleaned it and applied a bright orange tincture of iodine.

'Can I bring my wife tomorrow also?' he asked. 'She has been having some flu.'

'You should bring her in the daytime, when doctor Murray is here. I am only here for evening emergencies,' explained the young man.

'Aah ... okay,' replied the patient. 'But it is easier for me to come in the evening. You be here tomorrow also, na?' They went to the counter to fill Zainun's yellow card.

The young man's semi-legitimate business picked up when the townspeople realized that they had the option of an evening consultation. Some felt a little more comfortable with a non-white person listening to them, especially if they were Indian. But there were a couple of patients who walked out when they were told that an Indian 'assistant' was filling in for Murray.

The on-the-spot translations provided by Zainun and Wong were adequate. While Zainun would engage the older Malay patients with chatter, often holding their hand or putting a friendly arm on their shoulder, Wong would stick to formal translation. He never made small talk. Often the patient, if he knew Wong, would launch into pleasantries and general small town babble. Wong immediately steered the conversation back to the medical issue. 'Pain? Where pain? How many days pain?'

The young man grew to admire his work ethic and asked him for his opinions. 'Not so serious it seems. Just a decongestant might do, lah. What do you think, Wong?'

Wong would either nod his head or he might say, 'Maybe Mr Sengupta might want to check the patient's lungs again and consider if there is an infection. It is her second visit this month.'

The young man's days were full. From early in the morning till mid-afternoon he worked on the estates. The he went home for a short rest. Upon waking up, he would return to town to change places with Murray. By the end of the first month, the young man was seeing as many as a dozen patients every evening. While making appointments during the day, Zainun would pause, her pen hovering an inch above the yellow card and ask, 'Doctor or assistant?' A few began to prefer visits with the young man.

On the first day of 1956, the young man saw seventeen patients and earned about fifty dollars. Jonaki got a bicycle and Maloti a pair of gold bangles, long overdue.

DRUNK DAYS

The horrific events of August 1946 notwithstanding, Palash and Ajit continued to come to the house regularly. It was a routine they could not shake. Maloti continued to bring them tea. Jonaki was always happy to see his father's friends. He asked for Badol and Padma a couple of times, but eventually forgot about them. Nirmal Sengupta would join them on occasion to discuss politics. Some evenings, the young man's mother would knock on his door, 'Your friends are all here ... Don't you want to see them?' He never left his room.

But one evening he got out of bed and took a long bath. He put on fresh clothes, combed his hair and slipped on his shoes. Everyone observed him from distance, afraid to interrupt or question. 'He's going downstairs to see his friends,' his mother whispered to Maloti. The young man walked down the stairs. And right out the front door.

Palash noticed him. 'Where are you going?' he asked running after him. 'Are you coming back to join us later?'

He nodded nonchalantly and walked on to the main street. His friends waited for him back in the octagonal room till about nine. Much later that night, around 11.30 p.m., a rickshaw stopped in front of the house. One of the servants dozing on the stoop jumped up. 'Does this drunk babu live here?' asked the rickshaw puller pointing to the sleeping young man.

The servant shook his arm, 'Babu ... you are home. Come on, get up!' he urged in a hushed tone. The young man stirred. He realized where he was and climbed down.

'Pay him something,' he said and stumbled into the house. He went straight to the staircase, held on the teak bannister and made it up to his room.

He awoke late the next morning, but for the first time in weeks, came to the table at lunchtime. He ate his food quietly and repaired to his room.

When he went down the stairs the following evening, he noticed a light in the octagonal room; his friends were waiting for him. He turned around, slinked past the kitchen and left from the back of the house.

This continued for days. No one interrupted his routine. Nirmal Sengupta would discreetly inquire about the time of his return from the servants. Sometimes the young man played with his son after lunch and, on occasion, complimented his mother on a good meal. Other than that, he kept mostly to himself.

One evening, as he was slipping out again, Palash, who was urinating in the alley behind the house, spotted him. 'Where are you going?' he asked, zipping up quickly.

The young man hesitated for a moment and then said, 'Tripty.'

'Tripty? The drinks place?'

'Yes.'

'Can we come too?'

The young man shrugged.

'Wait,' said Palash excitedly. He went inside and brought Ajit out. They followed the young man.

It was a fifteen-minute walk to the bar, the only one in Bhowanipur at the time. The entrance was almost hidden –

through a narrow lane, past several vegetable vendors, and then up a flight of dark stairs. The bar was on the second floor of Jadu Bazaar. The market was alive even at that late hour. It was one enormous room facing Russa Road – about thirty tables, with chairs spread around. There were a couple of dozen patrons when they walked in. Some glanced at them and resumed their conversation.

The waiter in a stained, starched tunic, recognized the young man and bowed. 'Would you like to sit next to the window again, sir?' he asked.

'Whiskey?' asked the young man. Ajit and Palash nodded, and he ordered three double pegs. The drinks came with a spicy fried lentil and peanut snack.

Ajit took a sip and said, 'So … is this where you come every evening?' The young man didn't answer.

'Are you hungry?' he asked the two men. Before they could answer, he called the waiter over and said, 'Three kabiraji cutlets.'

'The usual way, sir?' he asked.

'Yes,' said the young man and downed his drink in a swift gulp.

The men ate and drank silently. The young man hummed a tune. Two rounds later, Ajit said, 'I have Dutch courage now.'

'Good. Get some more courage.'

'But I must say something first.'

'Say.'

'Are you angry at us?'

The young man dragged on a cigarette. 'No, not in the least.'

'Then why, why do you avoid us every night and come here to drink?'

'Because I like to drink.'

'Yes, I do feel nice,' said Palash, 'But every night…'

'Yes, every night!' said the young man triumphantly. He ordered another round. 'How's the cutlet?'

By about ten, the three men were quite lit. But the animated conversations cautiously steered away from personal matters. At the end of the evening, however, Ajit, plastered and unsteady, finally leaned over the table. Grabbing the young man's shoulder, he said, 'I just want you to know that I am sorry I wasn't there that morning. I chose to stay with my family and I have regretted ...' The young man lifted his index finger to his lips slowly and beckoned the waiter with his left hand. The last drink was gulped down quickly and the men headed out.

Russa Road was deserted. A couple of rickshaw pullers waved to them from across the street and clinked their dull bells. Palash and Ajit crossed the road and hopped onto a rickshaw. The young man walked away briskly.

'Where do you think you're going at this hour?' yelled Palash from his seat. The young man waved at the rickshaw as it pulled away. He crossed the street, got into a taxi and asked to go to a shebeen that used to be frequented by poor dockworkers but had become more integrated in recent years.

The young man entered Khalashitola and sat on a hard, wooden bench next to a burly man eating his dinner – rice with an amorphous brown curry. There might have been a hundred people on the premises – truck drivers, taxi drivers, off-duty policemen, office clerks, barbers and household helpers. The young man asked for a bottle of Ma Kali No. 1. The boy asked for payment right away. He counted the money, placed the bottle and an earthen cup on the table and walked away.

The young man was about to pour his drink when he saw two men across the table watching him. He asked them if they would like to drink with him. They eagerly pushed their soaked cups forward. The cheap alcohol stung as it went down the young man's throat and he couldn't help making a face. The two men laughed and said, 'You'll get used to it.'

One of them said, 'Babu, you look like the sort who might know some good songs. Why don't you sing one for us?' The young, amused by the forthright nature of the request, cleared his throat. He decided to sing the first verse that entered his head. A few lines from his time in the village appeared from somewhere – a song about an enchanted river named Shonamukhi:

'I'll take you to the golden river of life,
Where men are tossed around like fish,
I'll take you to the golden river of life,
Where human sized waves crash upon this.'

His singing was awful.

'What a wonderful voice,' they exclaimed. 'One more time!' The young man obliged and this time they joined in and the eight people at the table sang along. It was the first time in a couple of months that the young man felt anything. He ordered a second bottle. Soon, it was closing time. He exited the premises and noticed the same taxi waiting for him.

He got in and gave directions to the house. But once they reached the Hazra crossing, he got out. He walked down the deserted streets, the cheap alcohol coursing through him. He thought that his neighbourhood looked quite beautiful late at night. He bent down and picked up the fragrant rosewood flowers that had fallen from the huge tree above. A few stray dogs watched him cautiously and then joined him on his walk home. It was drizzling when he turned onto his lane. The two men who were supposed to stay up waiting for him had fallen asleep on the stoop. He walked past them and pushed the door. It was locked. He stepped out to the front of the house and quietly called out, 'Maloti.'

Maloti heard her name through her light sleep. There it was again, a bit urgent now, louder. 'Maloti!' She got out of bed and ran down the stairs. The young man stumbled in. He grabbed Maloti by the arm as she helped him up the stairs. 'Do you know this song?' He crooned again:

'I'll take you to the golden river of life,
Where men are tossed around like fish.'

The young man modified his routine. He began to visit his friends in the octagonal room. He would joke with them, sip tea and discuss politics. Jyotirmoy's absence prevented them from contemplating action. It was just talk and speculation.

But he didn't give up drinking. He would wait patiently till about eight; when the men would usually leave. If it went to a quarter past, he would stretch his hands and yawn, sending them a clear hint. As soon as they left, the young man would walk to the corner of the street, turn right and wait for one of the empty buses that dropped him right across from Khalashitola.

After drink, song and disconnected conversation, he would find his way home. He would wake up late in the morning, slither down to the kitchen and sit on the floor in front of the old cook. As always, he found her forthrightness comforting.

One morning, after an especially hard night of drinking, he lay crumpled on the kitchen floor. 'You look horrible,' she said, kneading dough. 'I remember your useless uncle – what a handsome fellow he was in his youth, couldn't take your eyes off him when he walked into a room. And now ... lord knows he looks like a toad. But your family is famous and so he was able to get himself a pretty wife. Awful wench that she is.'

'Why don't you give me something to eat?' the young man asked, holding his throbbing head.

Maloti got used to the young man's routine. She had begun to look forward to his stumbling return every night. In an otherwise full, well-ordered day, it was the only moment of unpredictable entertainment. His odd insistence that she – and only she – open the front door, made her feel special. It took just about a minute for him to make it up the stairs to his room, but there were funny moments.

'Do you know what they said today? They said that women should never wear the colour pink. Do you agree with this?' the young man asked one night, stumbling in.

'But I have some pink sarees,' Maloti replied.

'Throw them away. Just throw them away. No more pink!' the young man slurred. Maloti giggled.

'Do you know what my son said today when he saw the fish in the bucket in the kitchen? He said, "Baba, are the fish taking a bath?" Isn't that funny? I kept thinking about that all day,' the young man chuckled.

'I have a very poor friend, works as a clerk somewhere ... He told us a story tonight. He said he saved for two years to buy his wife a silver waistband. They had gone to a shop and measured it for her. When he finally had the money, he placed the order and they made the waistband. But when she tried it on ...' he paused and started to laugh so hard that he couldn't possibly go on.

'What?' asked Maloti, feeling his strong clutch on her shoulder.

'When she tried it on, it didn't fit ... because she had become fat. Now he needs to buy another two inches of silver links!'

'Poor man,' said Maloti, laughing along with him.

These conversations would end abruptly as he reached his room. He would shut the door, and Maloti would change and retire to bed.

One night, the young man gave her a small, white plastic statue of Jesus Christ. 'What is this?' she asked, putting her finger through the hollow base.

'I found it on the side of the road. Funny, isn't it? Right there on the edge of the pavement – this small, white figure facing the street. It glows in the dark, I think.' Maloti kept it on the windowsill in her room, along with her few possessions. A luminous, incongruous item in a Hindu household.

This routine went on for several months. The young man's late-night escapades were generally manageable, except perhaps for the time he stumbled in with two strangers and asked Maloti to feed them. The entire household, however, was beginning to feel that the young man was headed towards an early, inglorious end. But Nirmal Sengupta was incapable of intervention. He disliked the idea of having to talk to his son about drink – it was beneath him. His wife worried that he might lose his temper one night and hit his son, or worse, throw him out on the street. She finally broached the topic that had been on everyone's mind: it was perhaps time to find him a wife. Everyone felt that enough time had elapsed since he had become a widower. The little boy was now close to four.

'You must give a young man a reason for wanting to return home,' said a neighbour to Nirmal Sengupta's wife one afternoon when she expressed some distress about her son. 'It doesn't look good, you know ...' the neighbour added in a lilting tone, 'those calls to Maloti that he makes late at night when he comes home drunk. My husband said that he had heard the girl giggling ...' Nirmal Sengupta's wife gave her a stare that indicated that the topic was off limits. The neighbour said no more.

The family members discussed the situation one evening, while the young man was out on his usual jaunt. 'Fine. But I have two questions – one, does he want to be married, and two, where do we look for a bride? The circumstances are ... a bit different now, aren't they?' said Nirmal Sengupta.

'Don't worry about whether he wants it or not,' said his wife. 'I agreed to his first marriage without reservations; he will have to agree with me on this one. A mother has her place and time to insist on something and I shall assert myself. I won't stand for my son becoming a drunkard in my house, in front of my own eyes, while I am still alive.' She rarely spoke with force; it was convincing. Potol said that he could put an advertisement in the newspaper; it would be a good way to 'strain the market' and see what sort of responses a young widower might get. After that, they could consider using their personal connections.

The next day, when Nirmal Sengupta's wife mentioned the plan, her neighbour pounced on it. Apparently, she had the perfect candidate in mind, but had not felt comfortable bringing it up earlier. This girl was about eighteen, homely, and lived in Hazaribagh with her parents. Her father was a civil servant and was well regarded in the district. He was fond of sponsoring evenings where devotional songs were chanted. They were distant relatives, but she had seen her recently at a wedding and had been taken in with her polite demeanour. 'And this one is fair,' she added.

Nirmal Sengupta, upon hearing about the father's standing, thought that it was reasonable that they travel to Hazaribagh to see the girl. At mealtime that day, Potol broached the topic. 'We are going to make a trip soon, possibly in two Sundays,' he said to the young man.

'Oh,' he appeared absent-minded and continued with his meal. The others at the table looked at each other. After a couple of minutes, he said, 'Where to?'

'Hazaribagh,' said Potol.

'I've heard it's a nice place.'

'Well, there is a nice girl there … daughter of the collector, and we thought that someone like her could possibly make a good addition to the family. No harm in seeing her, is there?'

'I'm not going anywhere,' said the young man and left the table.

'Well, if Muhammad won't go to the mountain, then we'll have to bring the mountain to Muhammad,' remarked Potol.

'Who's Muhammad?' asked his wife.

A few days later, Mrs Sengupta knocked on her son's door. He opened it a crack and peered out. She shoved him aside and entered. Holding his gaze, she said, 'I do not pry into your matters, but you should perhaps stay home tonight. There will be some people coming here from Hazaribagh tomorrow. They should be arriving by lunchtime. I will expect you to be presentable and ready to meet them. You do understand what this is about?'

The young man nodded. For the first evening in months, he stayed home.

The Hazaribagh people had misread Nirmal Sengupta's invitation to lunch and arrived early the next morning. The girl, her parents, their maid, and an uncle came in a taxi from the station. Nirmal Sengupta greeted them while his wife ran inside to make herself presentable. Potol's wife was asked to serve them breakfast immediately. Tea and snacks were followed by luchi and vegetable curry.

The young man, of course, was fast asleep. His mother banged on his door. He opened, sleepy-eyed. 'They are here,' she informed him.

'Who?'

'The Hazaribagh party.'

The young man let out a moan and then said he would get prepared.

'Do you have a pressed punjabi?' She barged into his room and went through his clothes. 'Maloti!' she yelled. Maloti came running. 'Press this immediately ... These people showed up at an odd time ...' Maloti took the crushed garment and sprinkled water on it. She laid a cloth on the dining table and brought in a hot coal iron from the kitchen. She went about ironing ferociously, but started giggling halfway through her chore.

'What are you laughing about?' asked the young man, trying desperately to pat down a stubborn tuft of bed hair.

'You won't like her,' said Maloti.

'Good.'

'Do you know why?'

'Because she looks like a rhinoceros?'

'No … she's pretty, actually. It's because … she's wearing a pink saree!'

'Very funny,' said the young man. 'Now give me that thing.' He put on the cream-coloured punjabi, turned to Maloti and asked, 'Presentable?' She nodded.

The family stood up when he entered the room. 'Oh please sit, sit,' he said in self-effacing parlance. His mother made eyes at him; they kept darting to the floor and back up. She was signalling to him to touch their feet. He bent down in front of the father, who said, 'Oh no, no …' while extending his foot. Then it was the mother's turn and then the uncle's.

He sat across from the girl in the pink saree, who seemed to be staring at a fixed spot on the ground. 'I've heard bits and pieces about your life from your father,' said the collector. 'What is it that you do now?' The young man had not expected questions.

'He works for me in the family business,' said Nirmal Sengupta.

'That's good. That's good,' said the collector. 'We have heard about your tragedy … and we wish to tell you directly that we are a very modern family. Bad luck can strike any of us at any time, but the challenge is to look past it and move on. So we understand … I think it's brave the way you are going on with your life.' He said this with absolute sincerity. The young man felt embarrassed.

Thankfully, his parents did not ask the girl too many questions other than her favourite activities, which were predictably singing and cooking. She had just completed her intermediate exams. 'Do you wish to study further?' asked Nirmal Sengupta, and the girl remained silent. 'Well, it's my turn to tell you that we are a modern family and we would support you should you ever wish to study further.'

'Of course, never at the expense of her familial duties,' chipped in her father.

When breakfast was over, they all stood up at the same time taking a cue from the collector. He walked up to the young man, put his hand on his shoulder said warmly, 'Come visit us in Hazaribagh one of these days. You'll like the fresh outdoors and open skies.' The young man nodded courteously.

At the doorstep, there seemed to be some confusion. The girl in the pink saree kept looking around. 'What is it?' asked Mrs Sengupta, but the girl was too nervous to answer her.

When her mother asked her the same question she whispered, 'I can't find my slippers.' They searched the entrance area of the house and the steps leading to the first floor. All the ladies glanced down at their feet just to make sure that they hadn't slid the wrong pair on. They were nowhere to be found.

Nirmal Sengupta seemed more mystified than embarrassed, 'Where on earth could they have gone?' he kept saying while scouring the floor. Potol's wife brought down one of her own slippers and insisted that the girl take them. She gratefully put them on and the group said their final pleasantries.

But just as they were walking out the front door, a slipper came flying and hit the girl on the shoulder. She shouted out and almost instantly, the second one fell right on her head. Everyone stood around stupefied. Then they heard a small boy's laughter.

Nirmal Sengupta, who had never raised his voice to his adored grandson, gave him a sharp scolding. Maloti spanked him a couple of times and apologized for not keeping an eye on him. But the young boy didn't seem repentant at all.

'But why did you do something like that?' asked his grandmother.

'Because I felt like it,' he said.

Later that night, lying in bed, the young man realized that there was a part of him that wished that he were like the person the collector had imagined him to be. He wondered what would happen if the gentleman did indeed approve of him. But a few days later, a letter arrived for Nirmal Sengupta. The collector expressed his approval of the young man and congratulated Mr Sengupta for having a nice family. But his daughter had seen the slipper incident as a bad omen and could not rid her mind of it. With great regret, he was forced to retract her hand. Nirmal Sengupta left the postcard on the young man's desk. The incident was never brought up again.

The groundwork for a second alliance began the very next week when Potol ran into an old college friend at Hogg's market. Potol's wife had a monthly ritual of wrapping herself in a gaudy saree and dragging him to the Metro Cinema to watch a movie. She would then purchase cashews, walnuts and pistachio to hoard in her cupboard. It was while she was sampling (a little too generously) two kinds of walnuts that Potol spotted his friend. The two had not seen each other since their debauchery-filled bachelor days and hugged tightly, despite their protruding bellies. A précis history of recent years began. The friend remembered the well-mannered young nephew he had once met at their house.

'Ah,' said Potol. 'He is well. But a sad story there.' He filled him in on the tragedy.

'You know,' said the long-lost friend, eyeing Potol's wife askew, 'I have a niece, not the most beautiful girl to be quite honest, but very lovely in nature; the only daughter of a fairly wealthy man. Her father is looking for a suitable groom to help him with his business and eventually bequeath to. Maybe something to consider? We could be relatives!' He laughed out loud.

'How unattractive is this girl?'

'Oh, she's all right' said the friend's wife. 'Though nothing like boudi here.' She pointed at Potol's wife. 'But maybe they could be good friends; she's probably not too far in age from you.' Potol's wife tittered like a schoolgirl.

'All right, then,' said Potol. 'I'll have a word with Dada and let you know.'

'Wonderful. Do you still live at...'

'Yes, at the same house in Bhowanipur.'

A Sunday matrimonial rendezvous was arranged once again. The prospective bride's family was invited to lunch, but they said that they had a prior engagement and would be available only a little later in the afternoon. Nirmal Sengupta had heard of the gentleman before, a small-time garment importer, who didn't have the most savoury reputation. Still, about half the Europeanized population of the city wore underwear that went through his godowns and distributing stores. His nickname in Calcutta was 'Underwear-babu'. It was rumoured that he had once put up a huge billboard of a man posing just in his briefs, nothing else, right at the main crossing on Chowringhee. The municipality had taken it down within hours, citing an archaic decency clause. Storming into the assistant commissioner's office, he had shouted, 'Don't you wear underwear, sir? How about we take those down too!'

Underwear-babu and his entourage arrived around four. They were a boisterous, narking lot. The mother sat down and immediately asked for a cold drink, 'Preferably coconut water with ice.' The daughter was doughy and had the attitude of a dogged circus animal. Indeed, it soon transpired that they had just spent the afternoon at the house of another prospective groom. 'Cheap people, no class,' said Underwear-babu, sucking on a gold-tipped cigarette holder. 'Invited us to lunch and fed us vegetarian food. They made some excuse about a pujo ... Hindus and their 10,000 pujos ...' Nirmal Sengupta went back into the house and made sure that thick mutton cutlets were promptly ordered from a nearby eatery.

The young man was to wait for his mother's call. But he grew tired of waiting. Dressed in his one resplendent silk punjabi, he wandered down to the kitchen and sat at his favourite spot across from the old cook. She was frying snacks for the guests – nimki to go with the tea. She looked at him and grinned. 'Looking like a groom. Once you brought back a dark one, maybe this time you'll get a fair one. Dark wife, fair wife, you'll get it all in one life. But not this one upstairs.'

'Oh really?' asked the young man.

'Yes, I took a peek upstairs; this one's ugly like a toad.'

The young man laughed. 'You call everyone an ugly toad.'

'You'll see for yourself in a moment. But why your parents have to go looking while the obvious ...' her comments were cut short by a shrill call from Mrs Sengupta looking for her son.

He got off his haunches and went to the living room. Luckily, his mother did not insist that he touch anyone's feet. Underwear-babu looked at him and said, 'Handsome boy. Waist size ... about thirty?' He beckoned to his assistant sitting at the door, who ran down to the car.

'Do you have any experience in running shops?' he asked.

The young man shook his head.

'Not a problem ... It's not that difficult, you just have to be strict. You can be strict, can't you? Why the hell should the Europeans make all the money in this city? What say you? I hear that you are a bit of a nationalist. There's nothing like a native operating a successful business. That is my brand of swadesh!'

Just as he ended his short, exultant speech, the assistant appeared with a box. 'Here,' said Underwear-babu to the young man, 'three of my new designs. You'll look handsome in them.' The young man took the box graciously and went back to his seat.

'My daughter does not sing much,' said the mother abruptly, 'but she does have one gift.' The girl made a face at her mother. 'She dances quite well.'

'That's lovely,' said Nirmal Sengupta's wife politely. 'What style?'

'Well,' said the First Lady of inner garments to her daughter, 'why don't you show us a little?' Potol came to the rescue quickly by insisting that the hard living room floor could certainly not do justice to a trained danseuse. The mother seemed disappointed.

The cutlets arrived and everyone ate in awkward silence. Right as he was departing, the father turned to Nirmal Sengupta and said haughtily, 'You'll be hearing from us soon.' There were no episodes this time during their exit; Maloti had been asked to spend the entire duration of the visit with Jonaki.

'He should have chucked the slippers at those people,' said Nirmal Sengupta after they had left.

'Who rang the doorbell?' shouted out Potol's wife while they were all at lunch the following day. Of late, several charming and persistent Afghani shawl sellers had been frequenting the house and she had been haggling and flirting with them. This time, it was a deliveryman with a small parcel. The servant put it on the table. Potol inspected it with his clean left hand.

'It's from the family that visited yesterday,' he said. 'Did they send us some sweets ... but such a small, light box.' He shook it and something rattled.

'Go on ... open it, will you?' his wife egged him on. The box contained a brief thank-you note and a set of gold buttons encrusted with small diamonds for the young man.

It was passed around the table. Even Maloti took a long, admiring look.

'Well,' said Potol, 'it would be rude to send it back right away. Let's hold on to it for a couple of days, until we come up with

an appropriately judicious response and send it back with a box
of sweets. Unless, of course, someone wishes to entertain the
proposal...'

The young man shook his head. 'I'd like to keep the underpants
though.'

But two days later, a letter arrived via the same delivery man. It
was addressed to Nirmal Sengupta. 'Why won't this underwear-
man leave us alone?' he grumbled as he sat at his desk and opened
it. He read the contents and slumped back in his chair.

'What is it?' asked his wife and he pointed to the letter.

Dear Mr Sengupta,

I hereby retract any possibility of an alliance with your family.
We have made inquiries about your son. He is NOT a man
who works responsibly at your side, nor is he someone with
much love for our MOTHERLAND as you falsely claim. He
is a FAILED doctor and a DRUNKARD. I will under NO
CIRCUMSTANCES allow my only daughter to be allied with
such a person. This is my FINAL correspondence on the
matter.

Megnath Bhowmik, BA

Nirmal Sengupta forbade further solicitation for his son's
marriage.

A TIME FOR MOTHS

Nirmal Sengupta wrote to his son on the first Sunday of every month. The young man preserved these letters in a cavernous drawer next to his bed. He was re-reading his father's many admonishments, late one evening, when he heard a child's cry. Then he heard it again. 'Meester Sen-gooop-tah,' a voice called out from the night.

'Who is it?' shouted out the young man, tightening the drawstring on his pyjama bottom as he looked out of the living room window. There was a woman on the street outside.

'My son is hurt. Can you help … tolong?'

'I see someone with her,' said Jonaki, peering into the darkness. The young man shone a torchlight. It was a Chinese woman carrying a small boy of about five. The child was wailing. The young man directed the light so they could make their way in. She put the boy down from her hip.

'So sorry. But I need help.'

'What is it?' asked the young man. The child was doubled over, sobbing.

'His thing stuck in the pant, doctor.'

The young man laid him down on the rattan sofa. His mother pinned down his upper body. Then, with the boy writhing to free himself, the young man held his legs firmly and inspected his crotch. The zipper had gotten stuck in two places, but there was no bleeding.

'I need to dismantle the zipper,' said the young man. He returned a moment later with a wire cutter. The boy let out a piercing scream. The young man tried to cut the front of the small zip plate, but with the boy twisting and turning, it was dangerous. He kept staring at the implement from the corner of his eye. His face had turned bright red.

Jonaki entered the room with Mr Rambutan, the porcupine. Upon observing the little grey creature, the boy became subdued. Jonaki brought him closer to the table.

'You can touch him like this.'

The young man deftly cut the metal bridge and then slowly separated the two sides of the zipper, releasing the trapped pinch of flesh. The boy winced a bit, but stayed engrossed with the small creature. Mr Rambutan called out, 'Kiri ... kiri.' The boy smiled. There were welts on his scrotum and foreskin, but everything was intact.

About fifteen minutes later, after the boy had chased the porcupine around the house, his mother told him that it was time to leave. 'I am Wong's wife,' she revealed.

'Wong from the clinic?' asked the young man.

'Yes,' she said. She picked the boy up. As she was about to leave, she said, 'Sometimes after work he goes to meet the friends. I send people to two houses, but he was not there. So, I come here myself. Sorry.'

'Can I escort you home?' asked the young man. 'How far do you have to go?'

'Oh, don't worry; it's just short-short through the forest here,' she said.

'But you have the little boy ... are you sure?' asked the young man.

'Oh, I grow up here. No problem for me.' She walked out of the front door.

Maloti tugged at the young man's sleeve and whispered, 'You must accompany her back to her house!'

'But she said ...' started the young man.

'Have you no sense!'

The young man ran out to the porch. 'Mrs Wong ... I must walk you to your house.'

'Baba ... can I come?' Jonaki called out.

'Absolutely not. You need to stay at home with Ma.'

The woods were dark, but there was a pathway of sorts. Wong's wife walked easily, occasionally turning to see if the young man was still following her. The child seemed unaffected by the darkness, bouncing along on his mother's hip.

'Nothing change here since I was small girl,' she said. 'Some places of town now no more forest ... They cut down the tree but here still same-same.'

'Are there animals here?' asked the young man.

'No animal. Empty. Snakes got.'

'Hantu?'

Mrs. Wong laughed. 'Chinese people don't believe so much in the hantu. That one usually for Malay people.'

'I saw some moths on my veranda. Do they fly about in the forest?'

'Ah ... you see the moths.'

'Oh, yes. Never seen such big moths in my life.'

'They are not moths. They are spirits.'

The child had fallen asleep. The young man waited for her to say more. 'What did you just say about spirits, Mrs Wong? Spirits, not hantu?'

She turned around and said, 'Yes, different. That one is a long story.' They kept on walking.

'Can you tell me, please?'

'Ah, my English so bad! But I try for you, doctor.' She paused for a minute to collect her thoughts and then started.

'Actually, when I was quite young, had not married his father yet, the Japanese came to Malaya, is it not?'

'Yes, I heard. They almost came to India too,' said the young man.

'They came here also to our town. You know the place that is the police station now, just after Main Road? They had an office there, more like military centre. Sometimes the soldiers would come out to the villages or to our houses and look for food. My mother always told us to hide as soon as they saw them. If you don't give them, they come inside and look and look. Sometimes they take away the pretty girls. Lucky for me, I was ugly one,' she laughed and continued. 'But people were so scared all the time. Or if they have news that you are trying to fight them or something like that, then you are in big trouble. They used to take the men to the station there and tell the kempetei the problem. Only for small reason, they yell 'banzai' and just cut the head off.'

'Did they kill a lot of people?'

'Yes, lot of peoples. Mostly the Chinese peoples. At night, sometimes we heard the sound of motor from our house. They stop at the road here and then drag the body and just leave it in the forest. Right here, where we walk now.'

'Did you lose anyone from your family?'

'No. But my father-in-law – they kill him later. Never found him.'

'Ah, the Japanese killed him.'

She was silent. 'They say is that the moths are the spirit of all those who were killed. At night, they fly around trying to escape maybe ... I don't know.'

They approached a clearing and several electric lights were visible.

'Our house over here,' said Wong's wife. 'Do you want to come for some tea? I think my husband back by now.'

'No, no,' said the young man. 'Don't want to leave my wife waiting for too long. I hope Wong is home by now. He'll know how to take care of the cuts.' Wong's wife made a short bow in the dark.

The trail was easier to follow the second time around. The young man shone his torch, illuminating the clearing ahead of him. Halfway through, he thought he heard someone follow him. He walked a few more steps and stopped to listen. The trees were ricocheting a faint echo and he was unable to separate it from the soft crunch of his own footsteps. He paused again and turned around, flashing his torch light. It was an odd sensation, as though he was being guided along, rather than followed. Soon, he saw the light on the porch of his own house. As he looked behind for the last time, he thought he saw a form recede into the darkness.

Maloti was asleep at the kitchen table. She woke up as he was taking off his shoes. 'Wong called a little while ago,' she said. 'All I could tell him was "All okay",' she said, giggling.

The young man thought it a bit odd that Wong had not gone looking for him. 'What time did he call?' asked the young man.

'Maybe ten minutes after you left. Did the boy cry any more? Poor baby...'

'No,' said the young man. 'He fell asleep on his mother's shoulder.'

Maloti got up from the table and turned off the ceiling fan. 'Are we always going to live here?' she asked.

'I don't know,' said the young man. 'Do you want to live here?'

'Why not?' said Maloti, smiling. 'But we have to take holidays sometimes, when we have money.'

'Yes, we will go on a long pilgrimage back home,' teased the young man.

'Pilgrimage? Since when do you even look at a temple? Do you know that there are temples here, in this country?'

'When I am about to die, I will think about god and all my sins. We'll go then.'

'Oh, like those old couples you see on benches at train stations, sitting quietly, not even looking at each other? With a water bottle between them?'

'Yes. That will be us someday.'

'You know ... Jonaki is doing well in school. I was so worried that I wouldn't be able to take care of him here, so far away from home,' said Maloti, hugging him. 'Come to bed.'

The young man felt the crush of her breasts on his back. He nodded and said, 'Yes, it's very late.' Maloti got into bed and tucked in the mosquito net securely. Jonaki slept between them.

The next evening, as the young man was clearing his desk and arranging Murray's papers in a neat pile, Wong knocked softly. He looked up; he had been expecting him. 'Mr Sengupta ...' began Wong in a soft voice, 'I came to thank you. My wife sends you her gratitude too.'

'How is the little fellow?'

'Oh, he is fine. He went to school today. But it could have been quite bad...'

'Yes, these things happen to small boys,' said the young man.

'If you had not done the right thing, there could have been some damage ... I don't know how to thank you enough.'

It was uncomfortable for him to watch someone as tacit and modest as Wong repeatedly express his gratitude. 'Wong, I did my duty as a medical professional. You would have done the same, I am sure. But, Wong ... where were you?'

Wong looked embarrassed. 'Sometimes I go out with my friends in the evening for a few hours. It was the wrong night to go out.' He looked down at the floor.

'Don't be hard on yourself,' said the young man, feeling bad for having asked. 'Okay, let's see the patients now. Is there anyone?'

Wong shook his head. 'But you have a guest.'

The young man opened the door and saw Ganesh sitting in the waiting room in a bright red shirt, reading a newspaper. 'Ganesh,' he called out. He sprang to his feet immediately.

'Where have you been, Ganesh? Gallivanting around as usual?'

Ganesh looked around the inner chamber admiringly. 'I go away for a few days and everything in this town changes. You become doctor and I hear that Nag might be made assistant manager.'

'I am not a doctor. I still work hard all day at the estate. But where were you? They've been asking every day at home.'

'I went to my father-in-law's house in Perak. My wife wanted to move there for a while, so I just ikut and spent some time with her father. That fellah wanted some help repairing the house, so I stayed back,' said Ganesh.

'That fellah?' said the young man. 'You call your own father-in-law "fellah"?' What do you call me behind my back, Ganesh?' He was laughing. 'And I didn't even know you had a wife, man. Did she leave you and go back?'

Ganesh shook his head, 'No, no, just for a few weeks till ...' he stopped himself mid-sentence. 'Just for a while, lah,' he said.

The young man pounced on his slip. 'Oh, Mr Ganesh, you are fumbling. Why do I think your wife is going to have a baby?' Ganesh sheepishly put his finger to his lips.

'Okay,' said the young man, 'it's a secret from everyone else, but I must tell Maloti the good news. And what's this about Nag becoming assistant? I thought he avoided all that for good reason.'

Ganesh slammed his hand on the desk. 'Nag got everything, now he going to get the *respect*.'

The phone rang and the young man picked it up. He chatted in Bengali for a moment and then he called out for Wong. He poked his head in through the door.

'Wong, what is this nonsense? It seems your wife came to the house with enough food for twenty people!'

Wong smiled and said, 'It is nothing, Doctor. Just some makan-makan,' and went back to work.

'That fellah ... your assistant, is it?' asked Ganesh looking concerned.

'Yes, why?' asked the young man.

'He has deep pockets,' said Ganesh and got up to leave abruptly. 'I have somewhere to be.'

'Ganesh ... sit down for a moment,' said the young man firmly. 'Today you must come to my house for dinner. There is so much extra food. I will not take no for an answer. Okay?'

Ganesh grinned, 'Hokay, hokay.' As the young man started to tidy up, Ganesh said, 'Say encik, can I ask for a favour from you? Only for short-term.'

'Yes, Ganesh?'

'I need about 100. Some stuffs...'

'One hundred? All right, Ganesh. Can.'

The spread on the table was spectacular. Jonaki squealed when he heard Ganesh's voice on the porch and came bounding outside.

'I say, what a lovely smell of the sweet kuini,' said Ganesh, as he got off his bicycle. 'Can smell it even from the street.'

'Uncle Ganesh! I have a new pet, but you must guess what it is!' the boy said breathlessly.

Maloti made a face. 'I don't know a single dish here ... but it is all so beautiful.'

'Ganesh,' called out the young man, 'after you are done inspecting that miserable creature, you must tell us what these dishes are.'

Ganesh looked around the table. Pointing first to a set of dumplings in a soft, paper-thin crepe-like wrapping, he said, 'Poh Pia ... this one inside probably got prawns and meat and you eat with that sweet sauce. Okay ... this one inside the bamboo basket is the Mandarin-style Tim Sum, which is king prawn dumplings steamed.' He lifted the dainty baskets. 'They make it inside the basket, you see.' Ganesh picked up a large dish in the middle of the table, 'Aah ... This is of course the main one, Laksa Lemak – noodles with pieces of chicken, prawns ... see all floating inside the spicy coconut curry soup?' Everyone peered into the bowl.

Jonaki pointed at a chicken dish, 'This is just chicken, right?'

'Yes ... Okay, here we now got Nasi Ayam that this young man will simply love – roast chicken with rice, cucumber and all the usual sauces ... Oh my god ...' He pointed to a large spread of prawns glistening in a thin coat of oil. 'And we also have the udang, which is again tiger prawns crisply fried. Just amazing, I tell you ... Why the celebration? Wong had a baby, is it?'

The young man burst out laughing, 'Ganesh ... baby on your mind, ah?'

'I have food on my mind right now,' said Ganesh quickly.

'Makan, lah,' said Maloti. Ganesh's eyes lit up. 'Oh-ho ... somebody is picking up the local language I see. Things, they change fast, no?'

They ate for well over an hour. When they were finally done, Jonaki said, 'Ma, can you make this food next week?'

Maloti laughed. 'I don't think I can eat for a week.'

The porcupine went, 'Kiri-kiri-kiri-kiri.'

'Ganesh Uncle, listen ... he's calling you,' said Jonaki, giggling.

'Enough of all this,' said Maloti. 'Jonaki, go and get ready for bed right now.'

'Ganesh Uncle must tell a story first.'

'What type of story?'

'Ghost story.'

'Can you tell me the Malay word for ghost, mister?'

'"Hantu", of course. Even Ma knows that now.'

'Good! Okay, I will tell you a hantu story then.'

Jonaki clapped and sat on the floor.

'About two years ago, your father's friend Dr Murray was going to a party in Kuala Lumpur. His missus stayed at home; it was only he and his driver in the big car. It was just getting dark and they were driving on a straight road. But his steering wheel kept going to one side, the side of a large field. He tried to move the car back, but could not. Suddenly, a cow appeared on the road. The driver braked quickly to avoid hitting it. Dr Murray looked out to the field and under a huge tree, he saw the most beautiful girl smiling. A Malay girl in a sarong, and her hair open and lovely.'

Maloti moved over and sat next to the young man. She whispered to him to translate. She had difficulty following Ganesh when he spoke quickly.

'But the driver yelled out immediately, "Don't get out of the car, Tuan. It's a trap, it's a trap!"

'"Why, what would happen if I got out?" asked Dr Murray angrily.

'"This is a well-known place, Tuan. Very dangerous! You go inside the dunia-putih. Then cannot come back again. Once a Tuan got out and followed the girl under the tree. A few days later, they found him walking around like a madman, talking to himself." So, Dr Murray just laughed and said, "All right, just keep driving, then."

'What is the dunia-putih?' asked the young man.

'That one means like another world, that is just like ours happening at the same time, but somewhere else. It is white and pure and very beautiful. You meet beautiful lady there and never return to this world. So they went to Kuala Lumpur. It was very, very hot that night. Do you know where Dr Murray is from, Jonaki?'

'England.'

'Correct. And how is the weather in the England?'

'It is very, very cold in the England.'

'Correct! So, Dr Murray was feeling very, very hot that night. He took off his shoes, he took off his pants, he took off his tie, he took off his shirt and he lay in the back of the car, trying to sleep. But he had a lot of the beer, so he needed to pass water. What is the word to say "stop" in Malay?'

'Berhenti.'

'Yes, very good. So, he told the driver, "Berhenti ... berhenti." The driver stopped the car and Dr Murray went to the side of the road to do the kencing. Suddenly, the driver realized that they had stopped in the exact same spot where he had almost hit that cow a few hours ago. He looked out of the window and saw the exact same tree and the same pretty lady.'

Jonaki moved next to Maloti.

'"Tuan!" he screamed. "You must come back! Cepat!" A moment later, he heard the door shut and he drove back home as fast as he could. Mrs Murray was waiting for her husband. So, when she heard the car, she went outside to receive him. The guard ran to open the door. But no one came out of the car.'

'Why?' asked Jonaki.

'"He must be sleeping," said Mrs Murray. "Two of you carry him out." She is a very small Malay lady, you see. But when the guard and the driver looked in the back seat, POOF! No Dr Murray.

'The guard climbed inside and checked, "Alamak! Got shirt, got pant, got tie, got shoes ... all got here ... but no Tuan!"

'"Where is Tuan?" the missus yelled, grabbing the driver by the collar. The driver trembled. The guard said, "The clothes are here, but the body is gone. Must be a hantu took him."

'The driver nodded and said, "I told the Tuan not to go near the girl under the tree. But the Tuan did not listen and went to kencing and she caught him. He run away with her. Sorry, mem." The missus was furious now. "What girl? What tree? What are you talking about?" The driver tried to explain the story of the girl under the tree, but the missus said, "Rubbish! Take me back there right now."

'The driver shook with fear as he drove back in the middle of night.

'The missus got out when they arrived at the spot. "There, that tree there," said the driver, pointing into the dark. "The girl now gone." The missus started walking in the middle of the road. Guess what she saw?' Ganesh paused.

'What?' asked Maloti.

'What did she see?' repeated Jonaki.

'She saw Dr Murray sleeping peacefully in his underwear at the side of the road, next to the milestone. She woke him up. He got up and looked around him very surprised.

'"Tuan is alive! Tuan is alive!" shouted the driver.

'"Shut up, you fool," said the doctor, standing up in his underwear. He hugged the missus. "Oh, thank god you came back for me, darling. I took a piss and just as I was walking back to the car, there was a gust of wind and the bloody door slammed shut. And before I could get there, the idiot just took off at top speed!"

'Then he and the missus went home in peace.'

'She should have left him on the road in his underwear. Why do the English men drink so much?' asked Maloti.

The young man laughed. The porcupine scurried across the floor.

'All the men drink, madam. English man, Indian man, China man, French man, Negro man, Eskimo man ... Okay, now I must go,' said Ganesh, getting up.

Jonaki helped his father lock the gate and yelled out to Ganesh as he cycled away. 'Don't stop under any trees!'

One evening, Murray dropped by the clinic unannounced. He hopped onto the inspection bed and dangled his legs like a child. 'I was on my way to the club, but there is something I need to discuss with you.'

'Is it something serious?' asked the young man, concerned.

'Serious? Oh no, no. I have an assignment for you,' he said. 'Actually, it was for me, but I am shamelessly passing it on to you. It's the sort of thing I am fed up with. But you, being new to these parts, might find it quite fascinating.'

'Assignment?'

The eldest son of the raja of the state, the heir apparent, even though he was 'born on the wrong side of the pillow', as Murray phrased it, was fascinated by the phenomenon of turtles beaching. The young man looked blankly at him, as this term was new to him. Murray explained.

At a spot off the long, wide western coastline of the country, along a brief one-mile stretch, large sea turtles come at particular times of the year to lay eggs. The young crown prince, the raja muda, wished to watch the turtles come to beach. 'He sent one of his fellows to ask me to accompany him; it's an all-night affair and they want to have a doctor with them. I'm too old to camp outdoors on the sand. So, I told them that I was indisposed, and that my very capable assistant would take over for me. Sorry, I didn't ask for your permission before I made the switch.'

The young man realized that he didn't have a choice. Nevertheless, going to a beach at night with a prince and his followers sounded exciting.

'All right, I'll go. So, what do I need to do now?

'They'll call you in a few days or send someone here,' reassured Murray. 'Don't worry, they make all the arrangements; you just need to tag along and bow to that silly young prince if you see him.'

The following week, two men from the istana came in a car to pick him up for the four-hour-long journey to the coast. He carried a small medical bag with essentials. It was dusk when they reached the deserted beach. The prince had not arrived, but the helpers were preparing makeshift tents and laying down bedding for the night. The waves crashed on the shore and their sounds echoed on the low cliffs surrounding the inlet. It was nothing like the crowded beaches the young man had been to in Bengal; it was calm and desolate here.

Eventually, the prince arrived with a retinue. He walked right up to the edge of the water, his followers trailing. The young man noticed that there was an old Englishman in the crowd, who seemed to be directing affairs. He walked up to him and said, 'I am on medical duty tonight, sir. Good evening.'

'Ah yes, you're the replacement for Murray,' he said. 'What's he doing tonight?'

'I think he is unwell, sir.'

'Unwell, is it? How original,' he chortled. 'Anyway, you'll do. Come on, let's say hello to the raja muda.'

The prince was seated now, on the only chair within miles, a strategic prop to emphasize his otherwise doubtful regality. He was short and fair and had a thin, wispy moustache. The handler bent over and talked to him, pointing at the young man. The prince nodded. The young man stood for a minute and then walked away gracefully, stepping backwards. The handler called out, 'Make yourself comfortable. Just pick a spot anywhere.'

About fifty feet away from the royal tent, the young man found a tarpaulin spread out on the beach with blankets and pillows. He lay down and stared at the efflorescent sky. He realized that this was the first night in about eight years of marriage that he was not next to Maloti.

He fell into a light sleep, awakening a few hours later to shouts and shrieks. He walked over to where several men were scurrying around, holding bright lanterns. They were pointing at a spot in the ocean. Small, dark mounds were approaching like a naval fleet on the rippling waters. One by one, a dozen large turtles climbed onto the beach. They made their way slowly, digging into the sand with their stubbly, wing-like limbs. The men followed them from a few feet away, pointing and flashing their torchlights. Some carried lanterns. They were large creatures; the smallest one was about three feet in length and there were several that were about twice that size. They made their way resolutely to what mysteriously appeared to be predetermined spots and then began using their hind flippers to dig holes. They grunted loudly, oblivious to the crowd around them.

The group gathered around the two largest turtles, beached a few feet apart from each other. Within a quarter of an hour, they had dug shallow ditches. The young man noticed that the effort made the turtles weep. The men cheered as the white slippery eggs began to emerge. A couple of men brought large buckets to collect them. The turtles laid several dozen eggs; smooth, luminous objects glistening in the night.

The prince walked right up to the largest turtle and sat on it. The helpless creature grunted. People cheered. Flashbulbs went off. Then much to the delight of his audience, the raja lay on the back of the turtle. He propped the side of his face with his right palm, elbow resting on the hard shell. The turtle protested again.

The young man walked around, inspecting the other turtles. It seemed they operated on an ancient, pre-ordained schedule. In just under an hour after they had beached, they started to cover up their eggs. He marvelled at how, with just the two hind flippers, they began to repack the sand to smoothen the ditches they had carved. Then they returned to the edge of the water and slithered back into the sea.

Later, everyone was served fresh steaming rice cooked in turmeric with boiled turtle egg – 'Nasi Kuning,' said a small boy handing him a plate. It tasted faintly like the ocean.

The party left the beach at dawn. It was mid-morning when the young man reached home. Jonaki was at school and Maloti had just finished her morning chores. He went to the bedroom and plopped himself down on the bed. Maloti came and stretched out beside him. 'Tell me what you saw last night,' she asked.

The young man described the story of the fantastic sea turtles. When he was done, he said, 'The curry wasn't that tasty though.' Maloti remained silent. 'Did you fall asleep?' asked the young man. He rolled her over and saw that she was crying. 'What is it?' he asked. 'What happened?' Maloti shook her head.

'The story makes me so sad. Please don't go there again.' She cradled her head in his lap and sobbed.

Milne had not invited the young man back to the club since the shooting episode. But he dropped by the clinic one evening. Zainun, startled by the strapping white man walking into the clinic, ran to open the door to the inspection room. The young man looked up, mid-examination.

'Hello, Mr Milne,' he said, taken aback. The patient, a tapper with his shirt unbuttoned, stared at him too.

'Just a-passing through town and saw the lights on,' he said in a longer-than-usual drawl. 'And I thought, "Wait a minute, this is where Sengupta's been hiding." Well, by the looks of it, mate, you're making more dough here than on the old estate. I'll have only myself to blame if I lose you.' He began laughing loudly.

'Drunk,' whispered Zainun.

'Good chap, this chap,' he informed everyone in the waiting room on his way out.

The work at the estate had reached a comfortable routine. The local contractors with whom the young man interacted with regularly had stopped hinting at dubious deals. Maybe they had understood that he was never going to be amenable to under-the-table activities. Or possibly Nag was truly in clean-up mode and all shady brokering across the estate had ceased. The young man wondered if they had a new-found respect for him because of his medical reputation.

Like Murray, he too had started avoiding patients who came to his house. He instructed Maloti to go to the porch and yell, 'Doktor tidak rumah!' when they arrived at odd hours.

'I hate lying,' she would grumble. 'What if someone is really sick?'

One Sunday afternoon, their post-lunch nap was interrupted by long, painful grunts of 'Doctor … doctor…'

'Get up … I think someone is hurt,' said Maloti, shaking the young man.

The young man put on a shirt and went outside. An old shirtless man was bleeding from the chest.

'Bull …' he whimpered. 'Biiig bull.'

The young man lay him down on the living room floor and inspected the wound. He ascertained that the lung had not been punctured. He went to work – a few stitches and a taut job of bandaging. 'You must lie down and rest for one week.'

'Doctor … money, how much money?' asked the old cow herder.

'No money,' said the young man. 'You just wait here till your son comes.'

He smiled gratefully and sat on the porch, waiting for his son. Maloti served him a glass of water. He hesitated to drink from it. He lifted it up and poured the water into his mouth from a height of about two feet.

A few minutes later, the son showed up on a bicycle. The young man recognized him from the plantation. No sooner than he had walked in through the gate, he started to yell at his father in Tamil. The old man looked around helplessly as the son continued berating him.

The young man lost his temper. He walked up to the son and slapped him across the face. 'If you ever talk to your father like that again I will make sure you have no job on the estate. Do you follow?' he thundered.

Stunned, the lad fell on his knees and said, 'I am sorry, doctor.'

'Just get up,' said the young man. 'Make sure he rests completely. Take him to Dr Murray tomorrow morning for more medicine. Now, walk home carefully.'

They trudged towards the main road – the old man's arm around his son's shoulder, as he pulled his bicycle along. Maloti watched them leave and clutched the young man's arm. 'You did the right thing by slapping that stupid boy. You will be a good father when Jonaki grows up.'

'But I don't want to slap him,' said the young man.

'Everyone needs a slap sometimes,' said Maloti. 'Even you.'

A week later, while stirring payesh for Jonaki's birthday, Maloti heard a clanging at the gate. She walked around from the back of the house and saw the old cow herder. 'No doctor,' she shouted. But the old man beckoned to her. She noticed that he had a tray with him. He passed it through the gap in the gate and said, 'For ciruvan ... ciruvan.' He tried to depict a boy with his hands. He was still wearing the bandage, but it did not look like he was in much pain. Maloti smiled and took the tray. The old man shuffled away on the dusty road.

Back in the house, Maloti inspected the tray – it was full of golden-yellow jalebis. A light coat of ghee made them glisten. She remembered the time when she was a little girl. Once a month, after her father got his salary from the school, he would give her a few annas to buy a couple of hundred grams of small, curly jalebis. She would watch the sweet seller's scale like a hawk, making sure he erred in her favour. She thought it was a lovely coincidence that the sweets had arrived at their house on Jonaki's birthday.

In the afternoon, the young man came home with a cake. There were three school friends of Jonaki's at the party, and of course, Uncle Ganesh. Jonaki blew out thirteen candles and Boon Siew yelled, 'Happy tiga-belas!'

A normalcy had begun to creep into their lives and, with it, a stirring in Maloti.

AFTER MIDNIGHT

14 August 1947. As midnight approached, Nehru's speech blared through cheap, cone-shaped speakers. It was in English and most of the men where the young man was sipping cheap liquor, could not comprehend any of it. There were two words in Hindi uttered at the end, and the crowd unanimously shouted, 'Jai Hind!' As the tricolour was raised, they stood up respectfully, reacting to a tenuous, yet primordial sense of fealty.

The young man looked around him and saw hundreds of poor, beaten, sweaty men, workers of menial tasks, rejoicing without much comprehension, but with sheer devotion to that inexplicable human need to belong to something bigger than themselves – a validation that they were more than their ignoble lives. He drank himself to oblivion. As he stumbled out, a taxi knocked him down.

The young man woke up in an undersized, narrow musty cot, his head bandaged. He was fortunate that some of his drinking companions were considerate enough to take him to a local hospital when he had not stirred after being splashed with water repeatedly. They did, however, clean him of the money he was carrying. He managed to make it home and stumble up the stairs, a bloodied bandage on his head. A servant rushed past him and informed everyone about the return of the young man. His mother ran up to him and inspected him, gently touching every part of his body. She held him close to her. 'Please don't ... vanish like your friend did. I wouldn't be able to go on if that happened.'

Nirmal Sengupta emerged from his room. He walked up to the young man, still reeking of cheap drink and the last whiffs of rank, colonial-era sweat. He stood still for a moment and then said softly, 'If you ever go drinking again, I will disinherit you.'

The following morning, the young man woke up before dawn and went up to the terrace. The absence of alcohol had made it difficult for him to asleep. His head throbbed. He sat huddled in a corner as the sun rose, smoking cigarettes and watching the neighbourhood spring into life.

When Maloti brought him tea, he was dozing. The little boy came up with her and woke him up. 'How long will you wear that turban, Baba?' he asked. The young man smiled and asked him if he wanted to go to the park around the corner. The boy ran down the stairs, shrieking, 'I need my shoes! I need my shoes!'

The young man slipped on a pair of slippers and walked his son across the street, still in his pyjama bottoms.

A neighbour peered at him from her balcony. 'What happened to your head?'

'The sky fell on it,' he said.

He soon went back indoors and sat near the old cook. 'Can you get me another cup?' he pleaded. She shouted out at someone from the inner kitchen to boil more tea leaves. The young man lit a cigarette.

'Be careful,' she said. 'You don't want to risk it all. You have your entire life ahead of you and a young child to think about. I heard what your father said to you yesterday.'

'How did you hear about that?'

'What else do we have to gossip about down here?' she said, gutting and cleaning a fish.

The young man lay down on the cool floor. Covering his face with his hands, he groaned softly.

'I wonder sometimes if you are unlucky, or if you are foolish. I think you might be both,' said the old cook, waiting for the oil in a large skillet to warm.

'Why are you calling me foolish?'

'Because I am not sure you realize what fate has bequeathed to you, despite it all.'

'I know, I know. I am the fortunate son of a rich man and I take everything for granted, this house, money, the servants, you ...' said the young man miserably.

'You're going to be in trouble when she leaves.'

'When who leaves?' he asked, vertical in an instant.

'The girl who your son thinks is his mother.'

'Maloti is leaving?'

The old cook would say no more.

The young man went to his mother's room. 'What is it?' she asked. 'How is your head today?'

'Listen, Ma, have you heard anything about Maloti leaving our house?'

Mrs Sengupta motioned to the young man to sit beside her on the bed. She closed the door. Indeed, an unfortunate situation with regard to Maloti's stay at their house had been developing for almost a year now. Her voice cracked as she explained.

Maloti, it transpired, had an uncle who worked for the railways in Madras. He was not close to his only brother, the headmaster. They had not communicated in years. Starting from his early twenties, this uncle had taken postings all over the country and had never visited home, not even when the headmaster had passed away.

Upon returning to the village after his contract with the government was over, decades after he had left, he heard about what the family had been through – Nirupoma's marriage, the move to Calcutta and then, of course, the deaths of his brother and of his niece. In time, he tracked Maloti down. He showed up at the house in Calcutta. A widower with no offspring, she was his only remaining family. He wanted to claim her.

They could not get rid of the uncle easily. He returned the following month and demanded compensation for Maloti's service to the family. Nirmal Sengupta agreed and said that he would open a bank account for Maloti and deposit a reasonable sum in it every month. But the uncle said that the amount was owed to Maloti's family. At this, Nirmal Sengupta told him that he could not make such claims, especially considering that he had been absent for decades. But the man – well-versed in government bureaucracy – knew the law and said that he was legally Maloti's guardian and could take her away if he so wished. He had even gone to the length of creating a notarized document ratifying his status as sole custodian.

The man's shrewdness rattled Nirmal Sengupta. Not wanting to separate his grandson from Maloti, he agreed to his terms. The man came once a month, collected his money and reminded Maloti that he would be back to bring her home someday. Maloti, having never seen him before, refused to speak to him.

'So we are in trouble now. He wants to take her away,' said Mrs Sengupta.

The young man had no recollection of such a person coming to their house; he paid scant attention to Nirmal Sengupta's many visitors. 'How old is Maloti?' he asked, his hands clammy.

'She is about sixteen, I think.'

'So if she did have to go away, could we not bring her back in a while, when she is of legal age?' he reasoned.

'Not if he gets her married off before that. I think he's very aware of the timing.'

The young man asked the all-important question. 'Does Maloti know?'

His mother shook her head.

'No. But we are planning to tell her very soon. I just don't know how to do it.'

The young man felt powerless: something he was getting used to. He could not imagine Maloti back in the village, tending to an uncle she barely knew. And what was it that the old man really wanted with her? He also considered that she had never let on that she was unhappy in Calcutta. What if she did, in fact, wish to leave and return to the familiar surroundings where she had lived as a child?

A couple of days later, Mrs Sengupta summoned Maloti to the living room. Nirmal Sengupta quickly laid out the facts – he explained that he would be legally unable to keep her in the house should her uncle come to take her away. She surprised everyone by saying that she had missed her village and was looking forward to going home, even though the situation was not ideal. She said that Jonaki needed to be fed and excused herself.

'I suppose a pining for your childhood remains deep in your heart,' said Nirmal Sengupta after she left, looking somewhat befuddled.

His wife kept shaking her head. 'But she's still a child. *This* is her childhood. I can't believe it. I thought that she would cry and beg us to help her stay. But she actually wishes to go...'

The next few days were awkward. While no one knew quite how to behave around Maloti, they could not mask their disappointment. Maloti took care of the child and continued as though nothing had changed. The young man found himself unable to talk to her.

Late one evening, he slipped up to the terrace to smoke a cigarette. He noticed Maloti standing dangerously close to the periphery. For an instant, he wondered if she was contemplating jumping. He rushed towards her, calling out her name. Maloti turned, startled. She walked away from the edge of the terrace, keeping her back to him. He heard her sobbing.

'Maloti ... what is it?' he asked touching her shoulder gently.

'I don't want you to see me cry,' she said.

'Why are you crying? I thought you wanted to go back to the village.'

'I didn't wish for your parents to feel guilty. Now please, please go away.'

'You've seen me a lot worse, haven't you?'

They both stood in silence while she tried to stifle her sobs.

'Please go away,' she pleaded again, embarrassed and afraid. The young man started walking back toward the house.

He paused for a moment and asked, his back still to her, 'Just tell me one thing, Maloti. Do you really want to go back to the village?' He turned around. She remained silent, but he thought he saw her shake her head in the dark. For the first time in years, the young man felt a stirring of conviction within him.

'Would you like to stay here? I'll take care of you ... as my wife,' he found himself asking Maloti tenderly.

She nodded again.

He based the rest of their lives on that slow, shadowy nod.

The wedding took place a fortnight later. When Nirmal Sengupta and his wife broached the issue, Maloti took it as though she was being informed about the next phase of her life. When asked how she felt, she did not smile nor offer hints of excitement or submission. She left the room and went to prepare the child's meal. 'She is sixteen,' said Nirmal Sengupta, disturbed with the lack of emotion on her part. 'Yes. She sees him as a deity,' said his wife.

But Maloti had never been in awe of their son. She had considered the young man a family member – an older brother type of figure – before she was to be his wife. That relationship remained unchanged. Being much younger, she had understood neither the glamour nor the depravity of her sister's union – a village girl marrying a rich city boy. So she saw the upcoming marriage as her destiny, an obligation to her sister's unfulfilled station in the household. And she also adored Jonaki; a life without him was unbearable to her.

There was no bridal night with a marital cot strewn with fragrant flowers, the usual salacious set-up of impending unions. The only new item in his, now their, room was a bright-red cover for the bed. Tired from the day's fasting, they both fell asleep promptly. Having inherited the family gene, Maloti snored lightly through most of the night, something the young man had to get used to again. Jonaki slept in between them and upon awakening, announced, 'I am hungry,' startling both bride and groom.

If an erotic attraction for Nirupoma had driven the young man years ago when he felt an intertwined stirring of lust and social rebellion, he saw Maloti almost as a child. He could not bear to look at exposed sections of her body that invariably wobbled in their intimate setting, revealing themselves at times. Over time, he developed an instinct to look away.

Maloti did eventually fall in love – with her new life. She moved from her room on the third floor to the young man's bedroom unceremoniously and put her few belongings on the lowest shelf of the cupboard, where some of Nirupoma's clothes still lay folded. She was too married, too soon, too entrenched in her new role to reflect on its very premise. She was second wife, sister, aunt and mother. These myriad associations diluted the carnal focus expected of most newly-weds. But they were happy.

One evening, as Maloti was folding Jonaki's clothes, the young man crept up behind her and put his palms around her face, covering her eyes. Maloti let out a playful shriek.

'I never hear you laugh,' said the young man.

'I am too busy for silliness,' said Maloti, pushing him away. But the young man could see her suppressing a smile.

'Indeed. You could have gone back to your village and had all your time to yourself. Here, you need to care for a household of people.'

'Indeed.'

'Do you dream about your village sometimes? You must. How can you not?'

'Yes, I do. But had I moved back there, I would have dreamt about this house,' said Maloti evenly.

'Can you see yourself growing old with me? In this house? Or will you run away one day? To that village of yours?'

'I don't know. When you grow old, will you make me serve you a half-cup of tea every hour?'

'What?'

'Your father asks your mother for a fresh half-cup of tea on the hour. He says that the full cup gets cold by the time he finishes it.'

The young man laughed. 'And he never allows any of the servants to make the tea for him.'

'He doesn't even let me prepare it. I've asked him.'

'She's been making him tea since she was fourteen. No, Maloti, you never have to feel obliged to make me tea. We have servants for that. You should have it with me, though.'

Maloti nodded. 'Go away. I have to fold clothes.'

If the young man had expected a calm, sheltered married life under his father's patronage, he was to be rudely jolted. Financial misfortunes swiftly exposed the Senguptas to unaccustomed hardships. Their dwindling wealth could not buffer them from the social and commercial tumultuousness of Bengal, following India's Independence. And yet, the young man remained idle, refusing to find work by taking advantage of connections in the elite circles of his well-known family. He became reclusive, venturing out on occasion to the ground floor only to meet his set of friends – the failed pamphleteers. But this ineffectual surrender to his fate did have one good consequence; he grew very close to Maloti and his son. And perhaps that was all he wished for in the aftermath of the shocks he had suffered when he was only in his twenties. He grew to be an attentive and caring father. And he could not bear to be apart from Maloti. The two indulged in an emotional pining for each other, feeling fully reassured of their deepening bond. But if their closest thoughts, fits of rage and moments of craving were expressed and demanded unabashedly, they never shared their sweat and senses.

This idyllic, platonic romance amid looming depravity was, however, not to last for long. If the pawning of Maloti's bangles had been the extent of the young man's financial adventurousness, he would find out later that his father and uncle had gambled with and lost the family wealth with grave, irreversible consequences.

Much of the Sengupta wealth was inherited – money, jewellery and estate. There was also an unglamorous but profitable family business in selling small, mechanical widgets across the city. Several land-ceiling and anti-wealth reforms had been passed in the 1930s, to protect the local population in the eastern parts of the province, where the family's largest ancestral holdings were. Nirmal Sengupta had anticipated that much of his property would be re-distributed to the local residents; the idea of the school had been to preserve some of it as a trust.

In the early 1940s, sensing that commerce in Calcutta
was soon to enter extreme unpredictability, Nirmal Sengupta
decided to liquidate his assets. He felt that he did not have the
energy or the acumen to navigate his business through complex
wartime dealings and he certainly had no faith in his brother,
Potol. Needing money to pay for the young man's expenses in
Scotland, he had first sold the several metal bolts–manufacturing
workshops that they owned. But the proceeds would soon dip to
half of their original worth due to skyrocketing inflation. Next, on
the ill-timed advice of friends, Nirmal Sengupta had decided to
buy up land on the outskirts of Calcutta. The projection was that
the city would grow in the years after independence and the cost
of land would appreciate steeply as new, indigenous businesses
would start to look for property to develop their factories. After
scouring the periphery of Calcutta, the two brothers had bought
several acres on land in the north of the city, plots near the airport
in Dum Dum and then in an area called Kanchrapara, further up.
Nirmal Sengupta had spared no expense in hiring the best lawyers
in the city to negotiate and work with the brokerage firms, and
drew up iron-clad contracts detailing exact boundaries of the
plots. Most of the family money had been sunk in this venture and
a hefty ream of legal documents were locked away in bank vaults.
But it all became worthless in a few years; the fracturing of Bengal
did not protect the rich.

The momentum to partition Bengal increased after the Week
of the Long Knives in 1946 and a majority in legislatures in the
state eventually voted for a division by the middle of 1947. Bengal
would be split along religious lines in keeping with the larger
two-nation ideology: one nation for Hindus and one for Muslims.
The border of the new country would run along the Ichamoti
river, thus Nirmal Sengupta's ancestral home would lie just a few
kilometres outside of India, beyond claim. It was, however, the
location of those new properties bought to the north of Calcutta,

which led to the ruin of the Sengupta family. It was poached on in a manner nobody could have anticipated.

Soon after Independence, insecure, uprooted Bengali Hindus from the newly formed Muslim state of East Bengal, started arriving in Calcutta. Several thousand people would get off the train at the Sealdah station, to be cordoned in with rope. They would spend days in horrific squalor, waiting to be granted permission to be moved to relief camps. A snack of chirey (puffed rice) along with some molasses was all they would get to eat on most days. When they did move, the conditions were almost as sordid; families contained in suffocating huts with contaminated water and decaying wholemeal flour serving as the main diet. They were not allowed to find employment in the city. While there was a skeletal effort in the form of relief assistance, there was no plan to relocate them. Soon it was impossible to physically contain the hundreds of thousands of refugees. About three quarters of them fled the camps. Many were middle-class folk who felt it beneath their dignity to remain in the filthy surroundings. They sought out relatives in the city. Maloti's uncle, who had not long ago threatened to take her away, now turned up and begged for a place to stay. The family relented. He set up a room in the small, triangle-shaped space under the stairwell on the first floor. He used the toilet reserved for the servants to bathe and relieve himself.

The hundreds of thousands still wandering in the city were forming groups. A people that had left their homes in the middle of the night with nothing to their name, were now facing starvation. The cash-strapped government, seeing no value in the desperately poor without voting rights, did not have the incentive to organize welfare programs. Left to their own means, they began forming clusters under internally elected leaders and began a forcible occupation of fallow land in the city and its outskirts. It was under these conditions that they took over parts of the property belonging to the Senguptas. A few thousand shacks and shanties sprang up in a few weeks, and a colony formed quickly, with capable, articulate and desperate leaders protecting the interests of the several hundreds of thousands of peddlers, ragpickers and beggars. The government served numerous legal notices, attempting to evacuate the area. They harassed the new settlers with police checks. But it was impossible to dislodge a sea of people with nothing to lose and nowhere to go.

Several legal cases were filed in the High Court in Calcutta. After a while, Nirmal Sengupta stopped attending the hearings, in the rare instance that there even was one. Maloti's uncle, who had toiled the streets for days and had managed to find work in a pipe manufacturing plant, offered to pay twenty-five rupees in rent. Nirmal Sengupta agreed to this initially. But when he decided that he would try to sell a part of the house to help with expenses, the uncle proved impossible to dislodge. 'You were very clever in trapping my niece, weren't you?' he said dryly. 'Let's see how you can move me out now.' And truly, no one could, not in that political climate. Nirmal Sengupta sold his cars and let go of most of the servants. The house looked shabby. When electric bulbs burnt out, they were not replaced.

When Jonaki reached the age of seven, his father's inheritance ran out completely. Yet, the young man did nothing. He mostly pottered around the house. Maloti, shrugging patriarchal admonishments, started working. Having no skills or much education, the only job she was able to secure was as an ayah of sorts at the local primary school that Nirmal Sengupta, Potol and the young man had all attended as children. The principal, an ageing man originally from East Bengal himself, took pity on Maloti and paid her a generous salary of sixty rupees. It was a glorified servant's job. She had to spend time with several five to twelve-year-olds, take care of them and carefully hand them over to their parents or guardians. Jonaki was allowed to study there for free. He and his mother would wave goodbye to the young man and leave together for school. It was unusual, reversal of traditional roles – Maloti late for work and the young man scurrying around to find her purse, lipstick and shawl, often cooling her tea by blowing on it. He would rush to Jonaki and ask to borrow his small sharpener to acuminate her eyebrow pencil. But no matter how much in a hurry she was, she would always stop at the door on her way out, turn for an instant and smile.

When evening fell, the young man would pace around, peering out of the window, waiting for her. But when he heard her footsteps coming up the stairs, he would sit down with the newspaper he had filched from Potol's room. When she would enter the room, he would not look up. She would lean in and try to catch his eye till they both laughed.

Maloti's salary at the school was insufficient. Relatives took pity on Jonaki and invited him to their homes for meals, especially on Sundays. Jonaki's parents had begun to look worried and the constant, friendly banter between them receded. He noticed his father adding up numbers on the edge of newspapers while pacing around. The young man had also stopped going downstairs in the evenings to meet friends. If someone came to inquire after him, he pretended he was not home. The evening sessions in the octagonal room went on, mostly without him. The young man had instructed Maloti to keep sending tea downstairs. One day, Jonaki overheard her say, 'We don't have any money and yet we make tea and snacks for people every evening. Don't your friends understand that we can't afford it any more?'

They did understand. At first, the visits reduced to once or twice a week. And then they stopped coming altogether. The room remained empty and Jonaki would go there and play – climbing the large windows or bouncing a small rubber ball on the wall until it was spotted with its prints. One evening, as he was about to enter the room with his ball, Jonaki heard two people. He recognized their voices. It was Ajit and his father's uncle, Potol.

'What do you think will happen to him, Potol kaku?'

'I don't know. Still unstable.'

'Well, who wouldn't be? Under the circumstances.'

'But why doesn't he work? I don't understand that. That wife of his ... What an angel. Just imagine, sending her out to earn.'

'It was very difficult and strange – his life. Unusual tragedies.'

'But how many years does a man need to pick himself up again? He couldn't become a doctor ... I understand that it was difficult. And, of course, the terrible events happened ... his wife and then your friend ... But why can he not swallow his pride and get on?'

'He has too many regrets.'

'Do you think I have no regrets? Do I hide in my room all day? Show me one man who has no regrets.'

'Maybe he needs a chance. Palash wrote me a letter from Malaya. He said he might be able to find something for him there.'

'My nephew, son of this ancient crumbling house in the heart of the city, working in a banana plantation, on a clerk's salary? Oh no. I think his time is gone. A man like that just fades away.'

'You don't think we should talk to him, Potol kaku?'

'No point. He's finished. Maybe if we sold a floor of this house he could rent a room somewhere.'

Jonaki walked silently up the stairs to his room and wept. But he hadn't known then that his father would be one of those rare people who would change. The new life at the edge of the Malayan plantation would heal them.

HOSPITAL

Malaya, 1956. Not once in a decade of a marriage brought to order in haste had Maloti and the young man shared a conjugal moment. That was to change. Far away from sad memories, the crush of poverty and the constant spectre of society, in a land where they had found peace and respectability, a carnal canopy stealthily enveloped them. It had taken time for that intimacy to blossom, almost a year after their arrival in Malaya.

They had trysts in the afternoon, when the house was empty. The young man would telephone Maloti when he was able to arrange for a ride from the estate – typically between eleven and noon. Maloti's heart would race. She would bathe and dry her hair vigorously. They would customarily sit for lunch as soon as he would arrive, but they would barely be able to complete their meal. They had the rank ardour of people having an extramarital affair.

One afternoon, she asked, 'How did you remember after all these years?'

'Remember?'

'That.'

The young man shrugged. 'It's like learning to ride a bicycle – once you know it, you never forget.'

She asked him how often he had made love to Nirupoma. The young man shrugged again and said, 'Not much at all at first, and then a bit more...'

'Did you enjoy it?'

He hesitated for a moment.

'Well?'

'I think so,' he said, as though recollecting the taste of a fruit he had tried a long time ago.

'Very much?'

'Probably,' he said offhandedly.

'Were you sweet and gentle with her?'

'I must have been.'

Maloti lay still on him for a moment and then slapped him hard across the face. He glared at her as her mouth hovered a few inches above his. He grasped her soft, narrow waist and used his strength to move her hips over his. Maloti leaned in instinctively – he felt her tears on his neck and shoulder. He pinched her nipple between his thumb and forefinger, and squeezed it till she gasped. She kissed him fervently even though he had caught her in a vice-like grip and was hurting her. As their breathing eased again, he put his face to where his fingers had rouged her breast. He stroked her buttocks gently. He could still feel the long spasms inside her.

'These marks ...' said Maloti softly, looking down at her body.

'I don't mean to hurt you,' said the young man.

'I didn't mind it,' whispered Maloti and rolled over on her stomach.

A few weeks into their heady, altered life, Maloti began to feel unwell. She shrugged it off. But the fatigue would not lift. Dark circles formed under her eyes and she was constantly tired, her normal lissomness frayed. She coughed frequently and found it difficult to concentrate on Jonaki's tutorials. A trip to the market would exhaust her; she would return home and collapse on the bed. The young man suggested that she see a doctor, but Maloti refused, thinking it would pass. She did not, however, reveal to him the one thing that had begun to scare her.

One night, when they were in bed, she had a coughing fit. She got up and rushed to the bathroom. 'Are you all right?' asked the young man. Maloti mumbled something. He turned the light on. He noticed a fresh blood stain on her pillow.

When she came back into the room, Maloti sat on the edge of the bed. The young man asked gently, 'How long has this been going on?' Maloti was silent. 'Come inside and lie down,' he said. Maloti pulled herself through the net and tucked the edges in. They lay in the dark, quietly.

'Earlier, every once in a while, a bit of blood would come out when I coughed. But now it's every day.'

'How long has this been happening for?'

'Many years ... since I came back to the house. But just sometimes ... maybe once a month,' Maloti replied. 'What is it?'

'Don't worry,' said the young man. 'There are medicines for this.' He lay in bed wondering how he could not have noticed, in so many years of marriage, that his wife had been harbouring tuberculosis.

After a restless night, the young man stopped by the clinic the following morning. Murray didn't seem alarmed by Maloti's prognosis. He recommended a specialist in Malacca, promising to make the appointment personally. Wracked with anxiety, the young man spent the morning absent-mindedly typing one of Milne's regional reports. What about Jonaki? Had he been infected too? And if Maloti had to go away for treatment, how would he take care of the boy?

Milne noticed the young man staring out the window. 'Is everything all right?' he asked. The young man nodded and looked at his papers. The phone rang. It was Murray.

'I've arranged for everything,' he said in his paternal boom. 'You have an appointment tomorrow morning at eleven at the Tuberculosis Centre at the Hospital Besar in Malacca. They've got an excellent man there, an Indian chap actually – Dr Jesudasan.'

'Thank you so much, Dr Murray...'

'Now,' continued Murray, 'tell you what, I will send you my car with the driver in the morning. You will probably need to stay overnight; they've got reasonably priced places near the hospital, just ask for a main road called Bendahara. Come back the next day, when you can.'

'Dr Murray ... you really don't need to ...' The young man started protesting feebly, but he realized that it was a favour he needed.

'One more thing,' said Murray, dropping his voice, 'don't talk about it. It's not something everyone needs to know.'

The young man went home early that afternoon and found Maloti fast asleep. He pottered around for a while till she woke up.

'What are you doing home at this hour?' she asked groggily, a bit embarrassed.

The young man explained to Maloti that they would have to go to Malacca right away to get a thorough check-up.

'They'll probably have to keep me there, won't they?' she asked. The young man nodded.

'But Jonaki's school holidays won't start for another month ...' said Maloti,

The young man looked at her blankly. 'I don't know ... The most important thing now is for you to get better.'

Maloti spent the rest of the afternoon packing a small suitcase with clothes and toiletries. 'If I have to stay there, you can bring me some things later, can't you?' she asked. The young man nodded.

Jonaki was delighted to be able to miss school.

Dr Jesudasan at the Tuberculosis Centre had a jovial demeanour. He pulled up a chair for Maloti. She sat down gratefully, exhausted after the three-hour-long drive. 'And you, young mister,' he said to Jonaki, 'will have to follow Ismael to another room where people wait, okay? Don't worry, we won't talk about your school marks.' He smiled at the boy.

The office was bright and airy. There was a small statute of Ganesh inside a cubby on the wall. There was evidence of recent ash on the floor from joss sticks. 'My wife,' said Jesudasan, noticing the young man looking at it. 'She insists on some divine presence in the hospital.' He asked Maloti several diagnostic questions; she kept looking at the young man, answering hesitantly.

Jesudasan was matter-of-fact. 'Well, as you may know already ... it is very hard to diagnose tuberculosis accurately in a short time. I will order some X-rays, which will be ready by tomorrow for further study. If something serious shows up, then we may do a very invasive operation called plombage.'

The young man nodded and said, 'Is that the same term as pneumothorax?'

Jesudasan was surprised. 'How do you know this? Yes, we basically put something under the ribcage and collapse the bad lung. Then it heals over time ... or we hope that it does.' Noticing the look of alarm on Maloti's face, he added quickly, 'I must say though, that I think she is all right. We will take a sample of her sputum when you come back here early in the morning tomorrow. We have to grow a culture of it in our laboratory.'

'For how long will I have to stay here, doctor?'

'One day at a time, no?'

They left the hospital and found an inexpensive hotel room on Jalan Bendahara. They ate off a newspaper spread out on the bed and went to bed early. Murray's driver insisted on sleeping in the car.

When they returned to the hospital early the next morning, Jesudasan waved from the corridor. 'Good news!'

'How good is the good news?' asked the young man, striding towards him.

'Well, the X-rays showed no real damage. So, surgery is ruled out ... for now. We must monitor her improvement though. I must advise you to keep her here with us, Mr Sengupta.' They followed Jesudasan back to his office.

'How long do you think she needs to be here?' asked the young man.

'I don't know ... a few weeks, maybe a few months. She is young, has a very hearty constitution and so I hope she'll get better fairly quickly. We take good care of our patients here.'

The young man went to look for the car. He found Jonaki asleep inside. He opened the door and slid in next to his son.

'Jonaki,' said the young man, 'I need to talk to you.'

'I know. Ma's going to stay here.'

'How did you know?'

'I saw her pack the suitcase.'

'There's one more thing, Jonaki ...' The boy looked up at him.

'Are you going to have to be here too?' he asked.

'No ... I'll be home with you. We will both come sometimes to see Ma. But, for a few days, you cannot get too close to her. She has a bad cough that can infect us. So we must all be careful. I need to go back inside now, okay?' Jonaki nodded.

Maloti was adamant that she would not take a private room. 'I will never let you spend so much money on me. I will be happy in the group rooms.'

The young man spent a long time convincing her that he could well afford the expense. 'Besides, I do not want you to be exposed to anything else. Now stop making a fuss,' he said sternly. Maloti uttered a sound of resignation; she didn't have the energy to argue further.

When they returned home, the young man found a blue aerogramme in the mailbox. This surprised him as he had received a letter from Nirmal Sengupta just the previous day. Nirmal Sengupta wrote exactly one letter a month, never more, never less. In a hurry, he used his index finger to rip the fold open. The letter tore in half. Joining both portions together, he read that his mother had passed away.

That evening, they had some difficulty securing the mosquito net. They looked around the bedroom, trying to figure out how Maloti did it every night – taut and symmetrical. They tried tying one corner to a window grille and the other to a lampshade on the wall, but the net wouldn't hang properly. In the end, the bed had to be moved to solve the problem.

The next morning, they awoke later than usual and ambled down to the stalls near the market for their breakfast. Jonaki asked for greasy mee goreng and drank two glasses of Milo. The young man sipped sweet, frothy tea. When they returned home, Ganesh was waiting for them. He was sitting on the porch steps like a bill collector, patient and resolute.

'Ganesh, I need to talk to you about something … Come, let's go in and sit under the fan,' said the young man, unlocking the front door. But as soon as he opened it, Jonaki sprang out.

'The back door was open!' he said, giggling.

'I have a problem …' began the young man, switching on the ceiling fan. 'I need someone to work here immediately. A lady who can cook and clean the house and keep an eye on that fellah,' he said, pointing to Jonaki.

Ganesh leaned against the wall. After five minutes of pondering on the matter and some mumbling, he said, 'Next house.'

'Next house?' repeated the young man.

'Yes, Kottiyan's house.'

'I should leave him in Kottiyan's house?' said the young man.

Ganesh laughed. 'Oh no, no. Kottiyan has the mother-in-law living with him. Wait …' said Ganesh, getting up suddenly. 'I bring her now. She is also distant cousin of my mother. You wait.'

Ganesh called from the kitchen a few minutes later and the young man found him holding the arm of a thin, elderly lady, with stained teeth, in a prim hair bun and neat sari.

'This is Amma,' said Ganesh. The young man nodded.

Amma, taking that as an invitation to sit, squatted on the floor. Ganesh spoke to her in Tamil. He pointed to the young man and then to Jonaki. He pointed at the kitchen, the house, the garden and once, at the ceiling.

'Okay, I told her everything' said Ganesh. Amma got up, walked over to the sink and started to wash teacups.

'Has she started working already?'

'Yes,' said Ganesh. 'She will cook and wash the clothes, and she can buy some vegetables, dal, rice, that type of thing. But for meat and the fish, you can go to market on Sunday and put in fridge.'

The young man nodded; it seemed like a workable plan. 'Can she speak any English …? What shall we call her?'

She turned around and said, 'I, Amma.'

Then she leaned over and grabbed Jonaki by the arm. Startled, the boy tried to pull himself free, but she proceeded to button up his shirt while mumbling something incomprehensible, yet oddly soothing.

In Maloti's absence, the house fell silent. Their small family had never been separated. Jonaki coped quietly, expressing little. One night though, after they had turned the lights out, the young man heard a faint, stifled sob. He reached out and stroked Jonaki's head and felt a small hand grip his arm. But the next morning, Jonaki woke up and went about his day responsibly. When they called Maloti in the middle of the week, she wanted to know details of what they were eating at every meal. Jonaki felt shy and answered 'yes' and 'no' to most questions, and when the young man goaded him to speak further, he handed the receiver to him and ran away. Some days when the young man returned from the estate, Jonaki would not be home. He would be spending time at the Wongs', going there directly after school. Mrs Wong didn't seem to mind and would walk him to the clinic before closing time.

Amma proved to be efficient and mindful of domestic details. She brought to the daily cuisine a new southern Indian flavour that they enjoyed. She kept constant vigil on Jonaki, rarely leaving him unattended. In the afternoons, while he played in the garden, she would sit on the grass outside, doing small chores, sewing clothes or dicing vegetables. She was forthright with money, counting every cent aloud as she returned change from the market. The young man had told her to keep the change in a tin box in the kitchen and use it as needed. She insisted on counting the money out in front of him before putting it away.

On the evenings that Jonaki came to the dispensary, he sat next to Zainun behind the reception area and prattled away, dangling his legs from the wooden counter. She would give him treats of small pastel-coloured glutinous Malay cake that he happily ate.

Wong would emerge once in a while to check on a prescription and Jonaki would stop talking immediately.

'Why you scared of Wong?' Zainun would ask.

'I don't know, Auntie Zainun. Mr Wong so quiet, like he is doing something,' said Jonaki. 'What does he do upstairs?'

'Why don't you go see for yourself?'

Jonaki went as far as the narrow stairs that led to the attic, but didn't dare climb them.

The young man would come out to check on him sometimes. Jonaki became an expert at listening for the slight creak of the chamber door and would pretend to read as soon as his father would appear. When the last patient was gone, father and son would walk home together, sometimes they would take the back roads near the market and the young man would buy Jonaki a steamed pork pao. 'I wouldn't tell Ma,' he advised. 'I don't know if she would approve of pork.' Amma would invariably be waiting for them, seated on the porch, humming tunes of indecipherable origin.

Wong knocked softly one evening as the young man was settling in to work. 'Do you have some extra minutes?'

'What is it, Wong?'

'Someone wants to see you.'

'Who?'

A man walked in. The young man recognized him as the thin old man in the singlet he often saw near the clinic.

'What's wrong with him?'

'He is not sick,' said Wong.

'Then what does he want?'

From his pocket, the old man carefully pulled out an envelope. In it was a small photograph, the sort taken at a studio. It was of a young couple and two small boys in front of a fake bookcase.

'Who are they?'

'These are his family. His son, his son's wife and their children.' The old man looked at Wong and indicated to him to keep speaking.

'He wants me to tell you about them. His son died. The wife died. Killed by the Japanese. The two boys now live in the forest.'

'In the forest? With whom?'

'No one. They have no relatives there.'

'Tan King. Tan King,' said the old man emphatically.

'What is he saying?'

'They work in the forest with a local leader. And the old man heard that they may be ill. He wants you to see them.'

'Of course, I'll see them. But someone must bring them here. I can't make a house visit to the forest!'

The old man seemed to understand what the young man said. He gestured at Wong. He pointed at the photograph and shook his head.

'Is he saying the boys won't come?'

'They are not allowed to come,' said Wong.

The old man said 'Tan King' again and shook his head.

He got up slowly and shuffled out.

Weeks passed. Jonaki stopped visiting his mother after a couple of trips, choosing to spend his time at the Wongs' instead. The long bus rides bored him. The young man would travel to Malacca every Sunday, taking the morning bus, arriving around lunchtime. He would bring Maloti a letter from Jonaki and food cooked by Amma, which they would eat together. Then he would take a nap in the common area till it was teatime, when everyone shared snacks brought from home. Maloti's indulgence was Kyeldsens Danish butter cookies, which the young man replenished regularly.

One afternoon, just as they were finishing lunch, seated side-by-side at a small table in the hallway, Maloti asked the young man if there was any news from Calcutta. He usually read his father's monthly letters aloud to her. However, this had not happened since she had been admitted to the hospital. The young man remained silent. 'Have you not told me something?' pressed Maloti gently. The young man barely nodded.

'Is it bad news?'

He nodded again.

'Very bad news?'

'Yes,' he said in a whisper.

'Was it ... Baba?' asked Maloti with difficulty.

The young man shook his head. 'No. It was Ma.'

He got up to wash his hands, walking over to the sink across the hallway. Maloti sat quietly, wondering whether he had not gone home because of her illness. 'There was no point in returning. Potol took care of matters,' he said, his back to her. Then he went and lay down in the common area for guests.

Later that same afternoon, he was awakened gently by a nurse. 'Doctor calling you,' she mouthed. The young man washed his face in a hurry and went to the medical wing. Jesudasan was at his desk, wearing everyday clothes. 'Mr Sengupta! They told me you were here and so I asked them to call you in. I don't like going to the ward on Sundays unless I absolutely have to. But I have something to tell you. Please do sit.'

'Is Maloti all right?' asked the young man.

'Yes,' said Jesudasen immediately. He explained that Maloti had been responding well to the medication, and her chills and fevers had almost subsided. But she was still coughing and he wished to keep her for a few more weeks. The matron had reported that she had gained six pounds.

'Weight gain is one of the best indicators for us. We've had patients come in here thin as a rail and leave looking all plump and roly-poly,' he said. 'Indians, Chinese, Malays ... they are so happy when they put on weight.'

'But the Whites are different. I once had a pretty English lady here. Her husband was away at sea and had left her here for several months. She was so upset by the weight she was putting on that she stopped eating. I would tell the matron to instruct the nurse to force her to eat. And what a fuss she put up! Finally, her husband's ship returned; she was waiting for him in the common room, all dressed up with make up on and all that you know. "Darling," he called out as he walked in, so handsome in his white sailor's uniform. He looked at her lovingly and said, "By golly, you've put on some pounds, sweetheart." The poor lady burst out crying and ran straight back to her room!

'But,' continued Jesudasen smiling now, 'fortunately, I was able to give them both a piece of good news that I am about to give you too, Mr Sengupta.'

'News?'

'Congratulations. You are going to be a father again.'

A SMALLER LIFE

When Maloti returned, her arms were plump and her face less oval. She continued with her household chores, but with less intensity. She often sat on the steps in the kitchen, observing Amma dice vegetables. Thik-thik-thik-thik. Amma watched over her lovingly, as she did with Jonaki. 'Minum many, many water. All day must minum water. Good for small, small baby inside,' she'd say handing her a glass. Sometimes, she would collect ripe kuinis from the tree at the front of the house and prepare a tangy, cool beverage for her.

When Maloti went back to the market, the fishmongers welcomed her back. They immediately commented on her altered looks. 'Wah, so fat and fair, and your face round,' said her favourite seller, her gold tooth gleaming. Feeling embarrassed, she smiled and looked at the catch. Soon, when she started showing, the sellers at the market would not hesitate to place their palms on her belly. 'I think boy,' said one. 'Kicking like football player.'

A light reserve had crept into Jonaki's demeanour. He did not hanker for Maloti's attention as before. He had found a different world at the Wongs', spending much time with their two boys who were about his age. With them, he spoke in a spitfire hodgepodge patois of English and Malay. At home, he reserved this for Amma; 'Amma cepat just give me the susu, gula no need, must go main now, lah,' he would say impatiently, standing at the back door, ready to run across the woods. One Sunday morning, he slipped out before Ganesh made his usual appearance at the house. Ganesh waited for almost an hour, chatting with Amma and the young man, but Jonaki was nowhere to be seen. Ganesh was no longer his sole companion on Sundays. The Wong brothers were local and they took Jonaki along with them on their jaunts across town. Jonaki had also stopped sleeping in his parent's bedroom. The Wong brothers did not sleep with their mother, he said, and Mrs Wong had repeatedly warned him to be 'very, very, very careful near your mother, because she has small baby inside'. But they had one enduring ritual. Every night, Maloti would slide next to him in the narrow bed and sing him a lullaby.

'Ma, who taught you how to sing so well?'
'My sister.'
'You have a sister?'
'She used to sing this song to you.'

Mamat approached the young man one afternoon, just as he had sat down for his afternoon tea with Maloti, before heading out to the clinic. The bomoh had to be brought back, he explained. 'Why, did you see a ghost again?' the young man asked, smirking.

'No. For baby. The bomoh give something.'
'What?'
'Come, encik. I show you.'
'I have to go outside?'

Mamat led the young man to the side of the house and pointed to a spot under a pillar.

'This thing he give. Nenas.'

'What? Pineapples? Why?'

'Because ada one hantu, Hantu Penanggal, who likes the blood of the new baby. So, if new baby coming to house, must put nenas with many leafs. Then the hantu get trap. Cannot go inside!'

'Okay. Thank you, Mamat. Now the hantu will be caught. With the pineapple.'

'Yes.' Mamat looked pleased. The young man got up from his haunches and started walking back to the house. 'Eh, Tuan, bomoh need the money.'

'Money for what?'

'Nenas.'

'I see. How much?'

'Ten ringgits.'

'Ten ringgits for pineapple!'

'Yes, encik, this one special one. Bomoh give only for you.'

'Did you ask me first?'

'No, encik. Sorry.'

'Then I cannot give you any money. And listen, if you tell the madam about all this hantu and baby business, I will throw you out. Understand?'

'Yes, Tuan. Give five ringgit only can?'

The young man walked off. Maloti was waiting for him at the kitchen table.

'That Reba-di of yours called me and asked me what your favourite dishes were,' said the young man.

'Reba-di? Why?'

'She wants to organize your shaadh!'

Reba insisted on celebrating Maloti's maturing pregnancy. 'I will expect you to do the same for me should I ever be lucky. I will ask Leela-di to come as well,' she said on the long-distance call. Maloti realized why the celebration was so important for Reba; she wished it for herself.

On a rainy Sunday morning a week later, Palash and Reba arrived at the house bearing several containers of home-cooked food. Among them was Maloti's favourite – a standard fare for Bengali indulgence, ilish fish cooked with mustard seed paste.

Palash pulled the young man aside to the balcony and said, 'Listen ... why don't we let the ladies have their time today? Let's go drink, sir!'

'That's a good plan.'

'When that thug friend of yours shows up, I think we fellows should go to town and have lunch somewhere. Accompanied by a few beers. Good plan?'

'Good plan, good plan.'

Moments later Nag's jeep pulled up. He leapt out, leaving his wife in the vehicle. 'Greetings, friends!' he yelled. 'It's been months since I've had a real Bengali meal ... I tell you ... nothing like a great home-cooked meal on a Sunday. Anyone have a cigarette?' Leela followed him inside, carrying food. The young man ran over to help.

'So ... we are now full house,' said Palash in dismay, realizing that his plan of getting away had been foiled. They sat down in the living room for the payesh-eating ritual.

'Amma, we need dishes and small spoons here,' called out Maloti.

There was a soft rap on the door. Mrs Wong peeked in. She carried what looked like a box of pastries.

'Mrs Wong,' exclaimed Maloti. 'Come, come ... Please sit. These are our friends. All from Calcutta, where we lived before.' But Mrs Wong stood at her spot near the door, not daring to displace the huddle of Bengalis.

'Okay Palash-babu, feed her the payesh,' said Reba ceremoniously.

'One moment,' said Palash. 'Perhaps we should explain to our guest what is going on here.' Mrs Wong, looking awkward at being the centre of attention, shook her head to indicate that it was not necessary. But Palash continued. 'You see, madam, the brother of the husband feeds this sweet Indian milk dish called payesh to the lady who is expecting a baby. It's for good luck.'

'Ah, for the good luck,' said Mrs Wong, nodding. Palash picked up a teaspoon of payesh, closed his eyes, mumbled something vaguely Vedic and put it in Maloti's mouth. The Bengalis made a ridiculous amount of noise devouring the payesh, their spoons clanking against the ceramic. Mrs Wong ate a couple of spoonfuls quietly.

Nag spoke up. 'Madam!' he said, addressing Mrs Wong. 'Let me tell you why we really have this ceremony.'

Leela tried to interrupt, 'But didn't Palash-babu just talk about it?' Nag waved her away.

'You see ... in the old days, many, many girls used to die while giving birth. And so, before they had the baby, their family would tell the expecting girls that she could eat anything her heart desired, just in case, you know ... she didn't live. So this is sort of like the last meal they serve someone who might meet their creator soon.' He laughed loudly.

'Oh, that is very scary story,' said Mrs Wong.

Leela leaned over to Maloti: 'Don't worry, I hear the second one is much easier.'

They moved to the dining room for the main meal. Mrs Wong handed the box of Chinese cookies to Maloti and took her leave.

'The Chinese lady ran away,' observed Palash. 'We can be quite unbearable at times.'

'Who is she, anyway?' asked Reba.

'She is my best friend's mother,' snapped Jonaki.

Maloti nodded. 'Yes, when I was in the hospital, she's the one who took care of Jonaki almost every evening ... She did so much for us.'

'Oh,' said Reba, sounding apologetic, and then added, 'Well, I told you to send him to us. You didn't have to send him to a Chinese family.'

Maloti decided not to argue. 'I know, Reba-di ... but I wanted him to stay in school.'

Nag had the last word. 'Just as well she left ... Makes things a bit more comfortable, na? I know she is nice, but I hate having to speak in English. I speak in bloody English all day.'

Amma came to clear the dishes when they had finished eating. She eyed Palash and smiled nervously when he caught her staring, making an odd half-bow.

'I've never seen Amma smile. What's your magic, Palash da?' asked Maloti.

'I think she sees him as a deity, or worse, a living holy man,' ribbed Reba.

'Be careful what you say, Reba' said Palash. 'I think I can get quite a following ... Then you'll just have to be one among many, many devotees.' Leela giggled.

'There is definitely something going on,' concurred the young man. 'I've been watching her for a while; she's been peeking at Palash from the kitchen.'

When they finally went outside, hours later, after three rounds of tea over the Chinese cookies, Amma was standing at the porch with two boys. She barked at them and they swooped in, touched Palash's feet and ran away. Amma folded her hands and went to the back of the house.

'What on earth is going on?' asked Nag.

'Amma,' shouted the young man. She appeared again, looking nervous. 'Nag-babu, can you translate please?'

'Yes, Malay is no problem for me, almost a damn local now,' chuckled Nag. 'Amma, who are those boys? Your grandchildren?' Amma nodded.

'Amma, why are they touching his feet?' Nag prodded.

'Same face,' Amma said in English, clasping her hands.

'Same face? Same face as whom?'

'Great man.'

'Great man? What great man?'

'Yes, great man. I see with this eyes. He come here … with many, many soldier,' she pointed towards the woods, suddenly animated. 'We all give our money and we give …' she mimed taking off her earrings and bracelets. 'My gold I give. He also. My sister also.' The story was touching, but no one could follow it.

'Whom did you give your gold to?' asked the young man.

'Netaji,' said Nag before she replied.

Amma nodded excitedly. Palash was taken aback. 'She thinks … I'm Netaji Subhas Bose's family member?' he said.

'Perhaps. Or at least some close relative,' reasoned Nag. 'You should give her that pleasure, Palash. She's clearly besotted.'

Palash looked uncomfortable. And he was moved by the realization that this dark old woman, who cleaned and cooked for scraps in the back of the beyond, had given up her precious belongings and money because she believed in the freedom of her people so far away. She had sacrificed more than he ever had.

'Have you ever been to India?' he finally asked. Amma shook her head.

'No. But I go one day. Good, na?'

BONNIE GIRL BORN STOP MOTHER WELL STOP ACCEPT OUR PRONAMS STOP.

The young man was at the General Post Office, Malacca, perspiring uncontrollably. 'How much for eight words?' he asked.

The clerk scribbled and said. 'Thirty-two ringgits.' The young man tore it up and asked for another form.

MOTHER DAUGHTER WELL STOP PRONAMS STOP
'Sixteen ringgits.'
A baby girl was born to Maloti at Malacca General Hospital on
a balmy Saturday afternoon.
The young man jumped up as soon as he heard the screams. A
janitor passing by said, 'Don't worry, mister. Cry is good.'
'Boy or girl?' he asked breathlessly, walking into the delivery
room.
Maloti smiled weakly when she saw him. The baby lay next
to her, swaddled in a white sheet. Unable to help himself, he
moved the thin cloth aside. 'The first girl in the family after a
long time.'
An older nurse laughed and said, 'You know, they always say
that the man wants a boy, right? But I tell you, lah, I always see the
father so happy when it's a beautiful little girl.'

Unlike the time when she had just arrived in Malaya, Maloti
barely looked out of the window during the drive home from
the hospital. She clutched the baby every time the car jostled
and glared at the young man. He asked the driver to slow down.
When they stopped at the house, Jonaki peered in through the car
window. 'It's so small ... so small,' he said.
Amma scooped the baby up without asking. For the next few
days, she spent much time with her. Maloti rested. Amma didn't
smile or coo. She spoke to her in her normal voice. She would
come into the bedroom early in the morning, take the baby from
the cot and set her down on the dining table, at a spot visible from
the kitchen, where she did her chores. Amma used an enormous
red, netted plastic shield – usually used to protect food from flies
– to cover the baby. Sometimes, Maloti, waking up at dawn, would
find the cot empty. But she would hear Amma's voice saying,
'Sayang, Sayang ...', and she would roll over and try to sleep again.

Every evening, either Ganesh or Mrs Wong would stop by to see the infant.

'So, what is going to be her name, then?' asked Mrs Wong, after two weeks. Maloti shrugged.

'Don't know, lah.'

In solemn matters, such as naming family members, the young man preferred to defer to tradition. He waited for a letter from Calcutta with the name for the new baby. Maloti refrained from making suggestions. She remembered the household being annoyed when Nirupoma had started calling her infant boy Jonaki. When no letter arrived in two months, the young man decided to name her after his late mother.

'Do you really like that name?' asked Maloti, trying to be tactful.

'Yes. She was my mother.'

Amma was unable to pronounce 'Swatilekha' and preferred calling her 'Sayang' (precious one). Since this was, strictly speaking, not a name but a term of affection, the young man didn't object.

Maloti tried calling her Swatilekha, but in all her conversations with Amma, she referred to the baby as Sayang. 'Did Sayang sleep through the night?' 'Sayang has a rash on her face.' 'Sayang was laughing in her sleep today', and so on.

The young man would come home from work, pick up the little baby and whisper 'Swatilekha ... Swatilekha.' Even from his lips, the name sounded odd.

One evening, when the baby had felt hot to the touch, Maloti called up the young man at the clinic. 'Sayang has a fever. You need to...'

He interrupted her. 'We have a name for her, Maloti. Please use her proper name.'

A few days later, Jonaki brought the Wong brothers home from school to see his baby sister. 'Sleeping all the time, is she?' asked one of them, peering through the red plastic fly guard. Just at that moment, the baby smiled. 'Wah, I think she can hear me! So, what's her name?'

'Sayang,' said Jonaki.

'Sayang, Sayang ... can hear me or not? If can, then smile again,' said the boy.

'Her name is Swatilekha!' thundered the young man from the living room.

'I think we go play now,' said the elder Wong brother, and the three boys ran out the back door. In the end, it was decided that the baby would be called Sayang at home. Swatilekha would be her formal name.

There was a calmness in the house after Sayang's birth. The family had gotten used to the smallness of the town, its friendly inhabitants, narrow streets and colourful shops. The constant attentions of Ganesh, the Kottiyans next door and Mrs Wong, provided a sense of security and well-being. Amma was invaluable. She had identified that Sayang tended to fall asleep easily when the loud, high-pitched spice-grinding contraption next door was turned *on*. On afternoons the baby refused to sleep, Maloti would wearily ask Amma to go across the street and request the Kottiyans to turn their spice machine on. And, like a charm, the baby would be asleep within moments.

Jonaki had adjusted well to his new world – he liked his school and he had found fast friends in the Wong brothers. He remained more or less diligent about his home-taught Bengali lessons, which made Maloti happy.

'I will teach it to you too, one day,' she would say to Sayang, cradling her as she checked Jonaki's spellings. The young man worried less about issues at home and focused on his estate work. The number of patients coming to see him kept growing.

One lazy Sunday afternoon, the couple found themselves in front of the dressing table, admiring their half-clothed reflections.

'Look at those two lovers in the mirror ... They look happy, don't they?' asked the young man.

Maloti scowled and buried her face in the young man's neck. He felt her nod against his shoulder.

Even Ganesh commented on their well-being as he chatted in the kitchen one Sunday. 'Amma, your bosses looking very healthy nowadays, all fair and getting round-round. What you putting in the food, aa? Secret?'

Amma looked up at him and said, 'Not my food. Silver tonic.' There was truth to that; they had never been more solvent.

One unsavoury thing did occur in the household during those early days after Sayang came home. Jonaki had spent the day with the Wongs and when he returned home, Mr Rambutan was nowhere to be found. He spent hours searching for his pet. When the entire household started looking for it, Mamat joined in the hunt, calling out 'Rambutan, mana Rambutan ...' and then shrugged and said, 'Maybe run away.'

But the next day, the young man got a call from Ganesh at the estate. 'I have some news for you. Not good news. Your fellah Mamat sold the boy's porcupine.'

'Sold it! Who wants a porcupine?'

'Oh, Chinese people, they eat the meat. Considered delicacy if the right age. He got ten ringgit payment.'

'Thank you, Ganesh. I don't know how you find these things out.' He went home and confronted Mamat, who didn't try to lie. The young man fired him immediately and told him to clear his shed out.

'But, encik, I try help you only, eh.'

'Help? How you help by selling my son's pet animal, EH?'

'That one is not animal, encik.'

THE VANQUISHED

The telephone shattered their rice-induced, deep Sunday afternoon slumber. Maloti answered groggily and then shook the young man. 'I don't know who this is.'

'Doctor?' It was a faint but familiar voice.

'Who is this?'

'Zainun from clinic.'

'Zainun, is it? What happened? Got problem, is it?' The young man had adapted to the town's locution.

She continued shakily. 'I am scared.'

'Why are you whispering, Zainun? Are you at the clinic?'

'No, I am home. But my husband sleeping. I don't want to disturb him.'

'Is he sick?'

'No, not sick. But I am scared.' The young man surmised that she was in the midst of a domestic rift.

'Listen, Zainun ... maybe you should call your parents?'

'No, no ... please listen to me.'

'What is it about?'

'I must come to your house.'

An hour later, Zainun rattled the gate. The young man beckoned her from the living room window. It was a typically hot afternoon and she was perspiring. Her white powdery makeup had started to drip down the sides of her face. She sat on the rattan sofa and looked around. The young man asked Amma to bring her a glass of iced water. After a few sips, Zainun pulled out a small handkerchief from her handbag to wipe her face. She smeared her makeup. Nervous, she began speaking, occasionally hesitating.

'I have been seeing some things for many months. I never tell anyone. I said to myself, "Zainun, this is not your business." But now I am scared something will happen, and Dr Murray will find out.' She paused. The young man decided not to interrupt. She continued, 'I just tell you this, but you cannot tell anyone I tell you this, please.' She waited for the young man to nod. He hadn't the faintest idea what she was talking about.

'So what did you see, Zainun?'

'I saw some things.'

'What things?'

'Medicines stealing.'

'What?'

'The salesman from Salim company asked me why we are buying so many special medicine of all types, more and more every month. Dr Murray lets Wong do all that, so I never ask. But then I kept an eye out.' She pointed to her eye.

'Special medicine?'

'Yes. Good penicillin. And what I see make me sure that Wong was also stealing the streptomycin.'

'Are you sure?'

Zainun nodded. 'At first, I could not believe this because he is so properful, is it not? And always doing everything correctly and nicely. But then I just started to track the orders and something going wrong. So wrong. Mr Wong is doing the wrong things.'

'Come on, Zainun, how are you sure it was Wong?'

'It was him or his toyol.'

'What?'

'Toyol is a small ghost. You tell it to steal and it will steal for you. And it never steal anything else. Just the thing you want.'

'And this yo-yo has been stealing penicillin?'

'Yes, *toyol*. I even leave out some shiny things for it. Like marble and button. Because if the toyol see this, it will play and forget to steal. But the medicine still gone.'

'Zainun, are you sure about all this?'

Zainun leaned forward and clutched his arm. 'Please, you cannot tell anyone. I don't want problem, you know. But I swear on my god that I am saying the truth. You tell me where the medicine go? No answer for that.' The young man nodded grimly and removed her hands from his arm.

He rang Palash up as soon as Zainun had left the house. Palash's take on the matter was simple. 'Apprehend him this evening.'

'Why the hell should I even get in the middle of this? And what is all this hantu nonsense with the people here?' the young man countered angrily.

'Because if what she is saying is true, you could find yourself accused of theft,' said Palash. 'Wong reports to you in the evenings and so you're sort of a supervisor there, aren't you? Start using a lock for the medicine cabinets immediately.'

'It's not that easy. It's all in Wong's attic and I hardly go up there.'

'Then just question him.'

'I have no proof.'

'Then you have to catch him with his pants down, right in the act,' chuckled Palash. 'You know that friend of yours ... That know-all Tamil fellow who wanders around town...'

'Ganesh? What has he got to do with this?'

'Ask him whether he knows anything. He seems like someone with a lot of unusual knowledge.'

'Unusual knowledge?'

'Yes. Unusual knowledge. You shouldn't go to Murray unless you feel sure about this.'

'Pet yo-yos! Unusual knowledge! What next?' The young man huffed and hung up the receiver.

The rest of the week was uneventful. Wong was diligent and orderly, as usual. The young man wondered if Zainun might have made a mistake. It was hard to see Wong as a petty crook, stealing vials of penicillin for the black market. When Ganesh came by the house the following Sunday, the young man interrupted his morning tea with Amma. 'Let's go out to the front.'

Out of earshot, the young man narrated Zainun's strange report of thievery. Ganesh didn't seem surprised. He shrugged.

'So you think Wong could be stealing, Ganesh?'

'Maybe. But if so, not because he is just a simple thief.'

'What exactly do you mean by that?'

'Ayo, that fellah, a very strange fellah,' Ganesh ventured. 'I have seen him in very odd places quite late at night, wearing clothes that make him look like someone else. You know the Wong of perfect white clothes and shoe?' The young man nodded. 'You should see him in slipper and white vest and uncombed hair, walking around. You won't even know him. Looks like kopi shop owner. And he has deep wound on his arm. That's why that fellah always wearing full sleeve.'

'That doesn't prove anything,' said the young man.

'Aah, yes ... but one more very significant thing to consider. People say that Wong donates money. Wong is just a medical compounder. Where he getting that money?'

'Donate money to whom?' asked the young man. Ganesh did not answer. 'Money to whom Ganesh?' he repeated.

'People in the forest.'

'What people in the forest?'

Ganesh deliberated. 'Listen. Wong's family has been here for long, long time. Everybody here know them. Wong's father was businessman, but also a well-known communist. He was part of the original party. Good friends with the famous Teng Fook Long.'

'Ten-foot-long?'

Ganesh laughed. 'Actually, yes. Some people called him that because he was tall and big. People here were scared of him. They said to children, "Study hard and don't do bad things or else Ten-Foot-Long will catch you."'

'Is he alive?'

'We don't know 100 per cent. But I think yes. Wong's father was the one who got killed. They caught him supplying weapons to the gang. So Wong had to support the family. But before, Wong went to very good Catholic school, that's why his English better than mines.'

'It doesn't mean that Wong is involved in anything. Besides, where would he find the time? He is at the clinic all day.'

'Ah. Clinic can be a perfect place for him. We don't know anything. But we know people here are loyal, lah. If somebody murder your father, they will take the revenge probably.'

'His wife told me that the Japanese killed him.'

'Japanese? No, no, mister; the English man kill him.'

'What? Why was he killed?'

'British army force killed him. It was so terrible. He was communist, na?

'Should I tell Murray all this?'

'All this, what this? Everybody knows this. We don't think about this any more. We have a normal-style life here now. But, of course, we all know that very easily something can still happen to anyone.'

'My god, what should I do with Wong?'

'I don't know. But don't make Wong your enemy.'

'Ganesh, is my house safe?'

'Safe, lah. Safe, safe. All that happen in past. Country is safe now. Normal-style.'

'Normal-style, you say?'

'Yes. One thing, if it's okay, may I borrow fifty more from you? I pay back all very soon. Promise, mister.'

The young man went inside and pulled five crisp bills from his pay packet.

'I have another request,' said Ganesh when the young man returned with the money.

'Oh, what?'

'My small girl, I give her madam's name, can?'

'What? I don't understand.'

'The name of madam. Very nice one.'

'Oh! You want to name her "Maloti"?' Ganesh nodded. 'Ask her yourself, lah,' said the young man and called for Maloti. She appeared at the veranda a moment later. 'He has a special request for you,' said the young man, grinning.

'Yes, Ganesh?' asked Maloti.

'No, no, no. It's hokay,' said Ganesh, reconsidering his request, feeling embarrassed.

'What is it, Ganesh?' asked Maloti again. Ganesh smiled and shook his head.

'He wants to name his little girl "Maloti",' said the young man. 'And he wants your permission.'

'Yes, Ganesh!' she said immediately. 'When you will bring her to our house?'

'Ah, coming, coming. The wife still at father house. Maybe some more months.'

'And what is your wife's name?' asked Maloti.

'Oh, never mind that one. Just simple local name for her,' replied Ganesh, hopping on his bicycle.

Murray rang the young man a few days later and requested that they meet to discuss 'matters of some importance.' He suggested that they rendezvous at the Planter's Friend Club instead of the usual satay stall across the street from the clinic.

It was a Monday evening and the club was almost empty. A few men were at the bar and a lone woman sat in the front parlour, sipping a cocktail. Murray doffed his cap at her. A man, balancing a bit precariously on a barstool, yelled out, 'Why, it's Dr Murray! And he's going to deliver us from the *blackness*, isn't he?' His companions laughed. Murray waved.

When they sat down, Murray said, 'You know what, you're not going to refuse me the pleasure of buying you a stengah this evening. Enough of that cola rubbish.'

'Okay. I'll have what you're having,' said the young man.

Murray's face lit up. He waved at the bartender and held up two fingers. Someone shouted out, 'Two stengahs for the good doctor! The bearer of hope! We're waiting for yer speech!'

'Shut your gob and drink up!' Murray yelled back. The young man watched the drunken men. He didn't recognize any of them. 'Do you know what that chap is going on about?' asked Murray.

The young man shrugged. 'Drunks. I hope no one draws a gun tonight.'

'Well, yes, he is wasted as always, but there is a reference to an important event coming up.'

'An event? At this club?'

'No, not here. In the middle of town, really. The government has decided that this place will no longer be called a "black area". I don't think it's been announced publicly yet.'

'I did read something about this in the newspaper ... That's good news, right doctor?'

'Oh, it's out to the public already? Yes, it is indeed good news. You see the "black area" designation, was for towns and districts that the government felt was still under terrorist influence. So there is extra scrutiny and security. The Chinese businessmen have been waiting so long for this day. The check posts holding up traffic, long lines for the goods lorries. Merchants having to reassure their creditors that the town is safe. Why do you think no one wants my job in this tiny bandit outpost?'

Murray lifted his glass, 'To becoming a white area.'

'The white area,' repeated the young man.

'But, most importantly, the government wants the entire country to be "white" before Independence Day. I mean, if you handed a country back to its rightful owners while there were still killers lurking around ... that doesn't look too good, does it? You have to return something that's not broken. Right?'

'Right.'

'Imagine this piece of conversation, Sengoopta, "Dear Tunku, here is Malaya, lush and beautiful, all yours now. We're giving her back. But there is one small issue, your Highness, a few commie bandits are still lurking around, killing people. Sorry, but that's your problem now." Wouldn't that be a hoot?' Murray laughed.

'Yes, hoot.'

'As it turns out, I have to play a bit role in it,' said Murray.

'How so, doctor?'

'Well,' continued Murray, wiping sweat and beer off his moustache, 'they are going to have a celebration of sorts in town – you know ... a band, speech-making, some food, maybe a bit of goyang-goyang ... that sort of mild Malay ribald stuff. So the local committee that is overseeing all this wants me to make the official declaration.'

'Declaration?'

'Yes. As I said, the town is still "black" now because it is an area under surveillance for communist infiltration. They said that there are sympathizers here.'

'Sympathy for what?'

'Sympathy for *what*? You've been hard at work, haven't you, young man? Right. Let me give you a little sketch of those days, Sengoopta. You see, when the Japs were here, we armed the local communists to help us fight them. We had to.'

'Who are we?'

'*We*, my lad! My government. The Brits. With the help of many others, of course – Americans, Australians, and, of course, you Indians. You see, when the Japs suddenly turned up on bicycles and started taking over Malaya, a special team was set up underground to train the Malayan commie buggers. We gave them all sorts of stuff. I mean the real stuff – Lewis guns, Tommy guns, Bren machine guns, grenades, rifles ... you wanted it and Her Majesty provided it. But when it was all over, and I knew it would be a matter of time before we scorched those bastards, the bandits hid some of the weapons. Some stayed on in the jungles. And blimey, now ... they're pointing those same guns at us!'

'Oh. Have you ever been threatened?'

'Oh, haven't I now! I was driving near here a few years ago and there was a lorry that had broken down. So we stopped to investigate. Bad idea. Bang! Bang! They started firing. It was an ambush, of course. One chap got a bullet in his shoulder. I just hit the floor and we got away. They didn't have a real plan. Just some raids here and there. Killed a lot of people in the early days, though.'

'Are they still dangerous?' asked the young man, suddenly worried about his decision to stay on.

'Nah. We figured it all out. You see, the government set up these areas called "new villages". And maybe a few hundred thousand people, who lived in the interiors, were moved into them. The plan was to starve the bastards out. "Operation Starvation" I think it was imaginatively code-named.'

'You moved the communists to these villages and starved them?'

'Oh no, no! We moved the local people – mostly Chinese – who lived in more remote areas into these fenced places. That way, they wouldn't be able to supply food or anything else to those jungle bandits.'

'So it's all over now?'

'Mostly over. There is one pesky group around here somewhere, but there hasn't been a problem in months. Thank god. As a bloody physician, I've seen the worst of it.'

'You saw murders?'

'Oh yes, many. One time, I was called to an area – you know, that place where they load the latex into lorries. Four people had been shot. All Tamils. And another time, they called me to see a planter in the forest. They had stabbed him, then chopped off his fingers, joint by joint, and they were strewn around in pieces around him. He remained alive to witness it. Christ, what a way to go.' Murray downed his stengah.

The young man wanted more reassurance. 'But all okay now?'

'Ah, and who could forget good Johnny Johnson, manager of Ladang Geddes. Shot him at his dining table. I'll never, ever, ever forget that.' The young man looked horrified. 'Don't worry, my good man. We won. They lost. It's all in the past. Look around you.'

'Yes ...' agreed the young man. 'Looks all right.'

'That's why they want me to be the one to declare this place "open." You know, open for business and visitors. A new era in a new country.'

'That is ... excellent, Dr Murray,' said the young man. 'And perfectly befitting, if I may say so; you are, after all, the respected town doctor.'

Murray smiled and shrugged. 'I don't need respect. I just want to retire in peace. Another stengah?' The young man nodded.

'Well, there's also another issue why hardly anyone else wants to do this. Make the speech, that is.'

'Why not?'

'Why not? Think about it ... The Chinese are still worried. One never knows who might take revenge; they have complex ties with the jungle guerrilla stuff. It's genetic, my friend. You're a man of science, you understand. One inherits that instinct, right? The Malay chaps hate giving speeches, even the ones around these parts who are, you know, pretty upscale. Speaking in English intimidates them, I think. And so, they chose the drunk town doctor. Cheers!'

'I think they chose you because they respect you.'

'Ah, that respect business again. Interferes with everything. Thank you though, mister, you are most kind,' said Murray. 'But they decided to even things out by inviting an Indian chap to give a speech as well. You probably know him well – his name's Naag. I think he worked with Milne, but now he's been made manager.'

'Nag?' asked the young man, stupefied.

'Yes, it will be a ridiculous event,' said Murray. 'But you should come, and bring your wife along. I think the whole town is going to show up.' He excused himself and went to the loo. The young man sipped his drink and realized he wanted a third one.

Murray ordered two more stengahs. 'Now, before I get too drunk, the important stuff; what I want to talk to you about. It's about our clinic – I'm not sure where it's headed exactly. You see ...' he paused for a moment and looked out at the golf course. 'Lovely course, isn't it? Built it with our own hands...'

The young man nodded.

'Sorry. You see, Sengoopta, this town is starting to become quite attractive now. All this white–black business sorted out, the Malayan independence looming ... this area will grow, the businesses will grow.' The young man nodded again.

'I'll come to the point. A young Chinese doctor paid me a visit the other day. He was born here, a local lad, and is speculating whether this is a good time to return home. Obviously, he wanted to know my plans. He suggested that he might even buy out my little shop, which is frankly, something very attractive for me right now.'

The young man spoke up, 'I see, Dr Murray. So you might close your practice.'

'I may or I may not,' said Murray. 'I have no idea if this chap is serious. But, Sengoopta, what is clear is that there will be added scrutiny on this area. And frankly ...' Murray paused and looked at the young man. 'Frankly ... our arrangement isn't exactly legitimate. It worked well for a while. But people might start asking things ...'

'So we need to stop?'

'I am sorry.'

They sipped their drinks quietly. Milne walked into the club with a couple of friends. He spotted the young man and waved at him, but proceeded to the bar.

'Sengoopta, there's more. I have a plan,' said Murray abruptly.

'Plan?'

'Do you remember after I had thanked you for doing that bullet removal, I had waited a few weeks before offering you the work?'

'Yes, a month.'

'Well, I wasn't convinced that you had actually studied at medical university in Glasgow. Don't take it personally. I didn't know you at all and you have to admit that it was a rather unusual detail.'

'You checked on me?' asked the young man.

'Bingo!' said Murray. 'And they wrote back saying that you were indeed a student there.'

'Yes, I was. Once.' The young man sounded sad.

'But I wrote to them again recently.'

'Why?'

'Because I have plans for you! They say that if you went back for about a year and took the exams, you could still get a medical degree. Wouldn't that be something?'

'Oh, I can't do that any more ... It's been so long and my family and the estate work ...' his voice faltered.

Murray leaned forward and shook the young man by the shoulder. 'Listen ... I'm bloody sure you can do it. I'll lend you what you need. I mean it. I like you. And the way this country is looking right now, you'll be paying me back pretty quickly too.'

The young man was at a loss.

'Think about what I said, will you? You know what – let's have another one!'

They had three more stengahs.

Murray dropped the young man off. He walked into the clinic unsteadily, waving at Zainun and then at the patients waiting for him. 'Send them in,' he said loudly, plopping down in his chair. Wong walked in and stiffened. The small room reeked of cheap club stengah.

'We have a young patient who is going to need a pox vaccine. Should I prepare one, Mr Sengupta?' he asked.

'Yes-yes-yes, Wong. You prepare a ... vac-sheen for the patient.' The young man spoke slowly, choosing his words. He walked over to the small sink in the hallway. He washed his face and rinsed his mouth. Settling in at Murray's desk, still light-headed, he observed Wong going about his work. It still baffled him as to why Wong hadn't taken the job of the evening dispenser; he was clearly qualified. This man, one who could diagnose illnesses promptly, expertly mix reagents and concentrates, meticulously label every pill container, bottle of syrup and vial of medicine by strength and expiration date ... was possibly a crook? It occurred to the young man that if he weren't going to be a part of the clinic for much longer, he wouldn't have to worry about the whole stealing matter. The thought relieved him. Besides, he was almost convinced that Zainun had imagined it all.

'The next patient,' Wong announced as he opened the door and walked in. He stood by the young man's desk. The young man's gaze went to Wong's hips and he marvelled at how perfectly well-creased his white trousers were. He traced the smart seam down his legs, but his eyes stopped at a spot near the ankle. He noticed a bulge. Wong caught his gaze and moved, blocking his view using the side of the table. The patient sat down. Wong translated, not moving from his spot. As soon as the consultation was over, he turned around and left the room. He could be heard going up the stairs to his attic. The young man got up and went to the back of the clinic. The stairs to Wong's medicine room were steep, almost perpendicular. With effort, he managed to make it up the ten narrow rungs. Panting, he hoisted his body up, dropping himself on the wooden mezzanine floor.

'Mr Sengupta?' Wong asked, startled.

'Wong, I've come to your office for once.'

'It's not an office. Just a storage place.'

'I was in here once before, the night I removed that bullet. It's very tidy up here. Very neat...'

'Can I help you look for something, Mr Sengupta?'

'Wong, please put your hand in your pockets ... left-left-left pocket.' The young man slurred his words, unsure of himself. Wong did as asked.

'Yes?'

'I think your pocket goes deeper, Wong. I want you to put your hand in as far as it will go.'

'Okay?'

'Deeper, Wong!' And deep it went, all the way past his knees, down to his ankles. 'Now pull out what you have in there.' Slowly, Wong pulled out small tubes of ointment, four slim injection vials and a strip of tablets. 'Put them on the floor, Wong. Now the other pocket.'

'There's nothing in that one,' said Wong.

The young man got up. Wong took a couple of steps backwards, towards one of the shelves and took out his handkerchief.

'So, Mr Wong ... Did your pet hantu do this for you?'

'What?'

'Never mind.' The young man inched towards him.

'Please, when you report to Dr Murray about this ... ask him to consider the fact that my wife knows nothing.' He spoke calmly.

'Oh, Mr Wong. So you are afraid now?'

'No. I am not afraid.'

The young man shook his head. 'You know, Wong, I didn't want to believe that you could do this ... I thought that Zainun was a silly girl ... bored and making up stories.' He was standing a couple of feet away from Wong now.

'I am sorry.'

'Sorry? Just sorry? That's all you are going to say?'

'There may be reasons why people do things, Mr Sengupta.'

'*Reasons?* What reasons? I invited you to my home. My boy plays with your children. I didn't know you were a scoundrel.'

Wong walked towards the opening in the floor. 'No. I am not that word.'

'Oh, no? Don't climb down. Come on, tell me these reasons of yours.'

'You will not understand,' said Wong.

'Why not? You have no reasons, Wong. You're talking big. A thief doesn't need reasons.'

'Yes, you may say I am a thief.'

'Ooh? I *may* say that? What else are you? A sage?'

'Mr Sengupta, I think you are saying foolish things because you are drunk.'

'You think I am a fool, Wong? A fool?' The young man lunged forward, attempting to strike. It was a clumsy effort. Wong moved out of the way, and the young man lost his footing and fell. He smashed against a shelf stocked with containers. Pills, bottles and reagents spilled everywhere. He sat on the floor, winded. When he struggled to get up again, Wong gave him a hand.

'Are you hurt, Mr Sengupta?

'No.' He had a cut on his palm. The young man stared at him for a moment, still breathing heavily. 'Why don't you tell me what's happening? Why have you been stealing all the damn medicine?'

'You cannot understand this, Mr Sengupta.'

'Why not?'

'Because ... it is a long and difficult matter.'

The young man leaned against the wall. The altercation had sobered him.

'Wong, I don't believe you are a thief.'

'You called me a worse thing.'

'Tell me what you are. What you do ... I have a right to know.'

'And Dr Murray?'

'I don't know, Wong. Should I report this? Why the hell did you take these?' He pointed to the pills scattered on the floor.

'Very easy, Mr Sengupta. My people need the medicine.'

'But maybe Murray would give it to you if you asked! He's a good man.'

'It's not for my family. Surely, you know that much.'

'Yes, I think I do actually.'

'So you know. Then why keep asking me?'

'But tell me. Wong, why do you support those people? Is it because of your father?'

'Ah, I see you know about my father also.'

'Everyone in this small town knows everything about everyone. He was killed. Right-hand man to the leader.'

'I was still young when it happened. My father made me promise that if anything ever happened, I would look after our family and not join them. But I help how I can. I have to.'

'How did he die?'

'Do you really want to know?'

'Yes.'

'Okay. I tell you.' Wong sat himself on the floor of the cramped room, across from the young man. 'My father was going in and out of the forest. When he went, sometimes it was for days, sometimes weeks. They were deep inside and the British forces couldn't find them. They searched and searched. They used airplanes, helicopter, everything ... sent many men. Then they used a new strategy; they brought in Dayak to help find them. Do you know who Dayak are?'

The young man shook his head.

'They are a tribe. From Borneo. Expert in tracking. So, they led the British and local troops till they got them.'

'And killed them?'

'Yes. But the Dayak used to be head-hunters a long time ago. So, the British officers said they could chop off their heads so they don't have to carry the bodies back.'

'They ... decapitated them?'

'Yes, that's the good word. But before that, they took pictures. Many pictures. This war has more pictures than children's birthday parties. So they brought the pictures back to the local station. I hear they put them up outside for the public. We are not sure if they were pictures of just the head or the whole body.'

'To warn people ...' murmured the young man.

'Also, to identify people. They wanted to see who came, who cried, who were the relatives and friends, and then they would be tracked. So my mother and I, we never went to see the pictures. We never saw him again.'

The young man groaned. 'That is horrible. But ... The wars are over, Wong ... The Japanese are gone. The communists too are, I suppose, finished. They tell me that good days are coming. Peace. Independence. Your children, Wong ... they will have a new country. Murray said to me today that this was going to be a rich country. Not like India or China, with millions and millions and millions of people. There's enough for all of us here.'

'In our country, we should decide matters. Not be hunted like wild animals. My father fought for the British, on their side. Now I don't even know where his head is. What kind of a betrayal is that?'

'You know, I too tried to fight the British.' The young man laughed tremulously. 'I was useless. But I had braver friends. I guess, I must admit that I have some admiration for you.'

'Do you want me to resign on my own? I can write a letter to Dr Murray.'

'No. Stay. I won't be here for too long anyway.'

'Oh ... I will put back the medicine then,' said Wong abruptly, picking up the bottles and pills from the floor. He had not expected the young man to change his mind so easily.

'Hey, Wong.'

'Yes?'

'Can I go see them? Help them?'

'Whom?'

'Your friends in the jungle?'

'What? Why do you want to do that?' asked Wong, surprised.

'Ah ... I had friends once, and we did things and we wanted to put up a resistance ...' The young man was rambling. 'I just want to understand this land a bit better...'

Wong shook his head. 'That is not a good plan, Mr Sengupta. Don't get involved just out of curiosity. People watch everything here. Everything.'

The young man nodded. 'You are right. It's not my country.' He climbed down the steep ladder and washed his hands. The last patient for the evening had been waiting for him.

The young man took the road by the market. This time, he went past the turn to his house and continued on, towards the train tracks. Just one train came through the town. It stopped for a few minutes every midnight, en route to Kuala Lumpur from Gemas. He walked along the middle of the track in the darkness. The small stones chips rattled underfoot. Still somewhat light-headed, he attempted to understand why he had initially been angry with Wong for stealing from Murray, but had weakened mid-altercation. He realized that he had glimpsed in Wong a clarity that he had long lost. Wong had persevered despite personal tragedy, while he had folded in. Perhaps Wong's story of defiance had roused dormant feelings within him. After all, it was not hard to identify with a group of people trying to fight the British, regardless of the setting. It was a primal battle line, driven in from childhood – Asian versus White. It was easy to stoke; nostalgia for a war you never fought. But what good was it to wallow in such thoughts? Entertaining the idea that one could be of any use was dangerous, irrational and utterly presumptuous. The young man turned around and headed home.

Maloti smelt the alcohol on his breath as he got into bed. 'My goodness, what have you been doing?' she asked, more amused than concerned.

'I'm going to become a doctor, Maloti,' said the young man, gravely. 'And we are going to get out of all this. I will earn well, buy a good house and send Jonaki to the best school in Kuala Lumpur.'

Maloti got up to switch the lights off. She spoke from outside the net, 'Yes, you like this place. I wonder sometimes if you'll keep us here forever. I worry about your father. He must be ... lonely.'

'Don't worry about Baba. There is much for him to do in Calcutta.'

The young man had actually considered bringing his father to
Malaya to live with them. He had mailed a letter a few weeks earlier
to Potol, asking for his opinion. But Potol's reply was disheartening.
Nirmal Sengupta had become reclusive, he explained, refusing to
go anywhere or talk to anyone. When not praying in the secluded
room on the terrace, he spent hours sitting in the living room
staring catatonically at his late wife's framed photograph. He had
turned frail, eating and sleeping little. He was often found in the
early hours of the morning slumped over the chair at the foot of
his late wife's image. Among his many worrying ailments were
severe constipation and headaches as he had stopped drinking
tea. Potol had written two more aerogrammes, beseeching the
young man to return home. The young man hadn't shown these
letters to Maloti. He had tucked them away, out of sight.

On a sunny Monday morning, 400 chairs were arranged in rows.
A small, makeshift stage was set up on the steps of Lucky Cinema.
A large fluttering banner read, 'Liberation Day, 27 April 1957.' It
was dwarfed by an enormous marquee of Frank Sinatra cavorting
in *From Here to Eternity*. People started to take their seats at about
10.30 a.m. The event would take place between 11 a.m. and 1
p.m., when the shadow of the one tall building on the street would
provide shade. The town council had set up a food station serving
cold drinks with Chinese, Malay and Indian snacks. Save the three
policemen chasing a confused cow that had ambled in, all was
calm. There was one grievous oversight – the Malays were fasting
and didn't go near the stalls.

Many locals as well as a few white planters had come with
their families. A group of almost 300 estate workers sat in the
back rows. Ganesh scanned the crowd and saw the young man
with Maloti and Jonaki. He began ranting as soon he sat down
next to them.

'They are calling this Liberation Day. Nonsense Day, I say. Liberation from what? A few starving people in the forest? Like I tell you always, these people need special entertainment, that's why all this circus ... Now only romantic American movie is all they are getting. This is Nonsense Day.'

The young man grinned and said, 'And our good friend Nag will be making a speech. What do you say about that?'

Ganesh took the bait. 'Yes, yes ... how absurd, how *com-plit-lee absurd*! That fellah thief number one, now making speech about safety and unity? See all those buggers in the back? They are Nag's union people.'

The young man put his finger to his lips and pointed to the front row – Leela was sitting next to a fair, plump teenaged boy. 'Is that her son?' asked Maloti.

'Yes, that fat fellah son of skinny Nag,' said Ganesh.

A band started playing. The percussion drowned out the two singers. But it was a popular Cantonese tune and a few older men in the crowd continued to hum along.

'Look at this perfect system,' said Ganesh. 'The Chinese sitting with Chinese, Malay with the Malay and us dark buggers, all over here.' The young man looked around and realized it was true. 'And they want to make country for everybody. Everybody talking about making country nowadays. Look at the India. Fighting, still all fighting.'

Jonaki spotted Mrs Wong and her two boys. He waved to them. 'Can I go play over there, Ma?' Maloti turned to the young man. The Wong boys had not visited their house in several days. Jonaki ran towards them, knocking a chair over.

'Ei mister, any development on that stealing medicine story?' whispered Ganesh. The young man shook his head. He had refrained from telling Ganesh about his drunken truce with Wong.

Murray staggered onto the platform before he was expected to. Someone rushed over and asked the band to stop playing. A short

Malay girl in a sarong and kebaya came onstage with a garland. She held her arms up as high as she could, but Murray had to bend quite a bit to allow her to put the garland around his neck. For a moment, it looked like he might lose his balance and topple over. He straightened himself up, clutching his back in pain.

The speech was short and slurred. He spoke for a while about a home away from home and then thanked the town for taking the initiative to petition for the change to 'white' status. He ended by hollering, 'You know what, ladies and gentlemen – no more threats, there are no more darn damn CT threats! We have prevailed!' The planters and the few officials from the municipality clapped.

The announcer called Nag to the stage next. The tappers cheered. The girl held up a garland again, so Murray could put it around Nag. But he took it from her and put it around his own neck. The girl pointed at Nag awkwardly. The crowd laughed. Murray, oblivious and doubly garlanded, bowed again and shouted, 'And now I give you Mr Out-pal Naag, a true son of this town ... a man who has battled Japanese and communists right in these fields...'

'Look, Nag wearing the Englishman's suit!' exclaimed Ganesh.

Nag looked almost distinguished. He did not have his usual frenetic way about him as he smiled calmly at the people seated close to the stage. He began by addressing everyone as his 'brothers and sisters' who, like him, 'had suffered many years of danger and threats of murder'. Unlike Murray, he thanked people, including Gerald Templer, the famous 'tiger of Malaya' who had come up with and executed several far-reaching anti-communist operations. He mentioned by name Sergeant O'Brien and other members of the local police, individuals he knew only too well through his years of local dealings. In conclusion, with his voice cracking dramatically, he declared, 'Only good days lie ahead now in this land and this town that has made me the small but proud man I am today. I hereby state, that as of this moment, our town is no longer a black area. We are white and bright as this sunny day. No communist insurgent or CT will threaten us ever again. We habis the last one of them!' He mimed shooting a rifle. There was a drum roll and the crowd applauded.

'My good lord,' said Ganesh, in disbelief. 'He has become politician.'

'Maybe we should go up to him,' suggested Maloti. Nag was surrounded by people. The young man waved, imagining he had caught his eye, but Nag continued with his post-speech chatter with an array of Indian and Chinese men.

'Sengoopta!' a voice boomed from across the street. It was Murray. He shuffled up to them and bowed gallantly on seeing Maloti. 'Ma'am ... you know I think the world of this fine gentleman here. Let me tell you about a time when he took charge and saved a stupid, drunk Englishman's life from another stupid, drunk Englishman's bullet.' The young man watched their exchange – a drunk, sweaty Murray blathering away and Maloti, impeccable in her sari, nodding intermittently. She followed little of his excited jabber, but had a great knack for smiling just at the right moments.

'He's grinning, this husband of yours,' said Murray. 'Always has that handsome smile, doesn't he? A good-looking fella. But you know what, we both want to see this chap get ahead, don't we?' Maloti nodded. 'I tell you – he should just go for it. Seize it, the opportunity right now, and become Dr Sengoopta!' Murray punched the air and Maloti leapt out of the way.

The morning was over. The town was white.

It was a time of festivity and frolic for a town that rarely had anything to celebrate. A week after the Liberation Day event, the local Malay population observed Hari Raya. To atone for their previous oversight, the municipality (headed by an all-Chinese council) allocated funds for a lavish party. People drank thick, sweetened beverages and ate staggering amounts of freshly slaughtered goat meat, followed by colourful, glutinous cake. Ribald joget parties abounded. Callipygous Malay maidens, constantly in demand for performances, swayed around the town coquettishly, deflecting catcalls. If that was not enough, the country celebrated independence just a few months later.

The Independence Day event was sombre compared to the festivities preceding it. People started to gather near the large padang in front of the local school at nine in the morning for a flag-hoisting ceremony. About a hundred students in uniform stood in attention. The Stripes of Glory had officially been raised at midnight, but the enormous public celebration was taking place in Kuala Lumpur, at the newly built Stadium Merdeka. It was broadcast across the peninsula and the live medium-wave transmission blared through the school speakers. The market people went about their business on the edges of the road, as locals began crowding the streets, walking towards the school. People stood in clumps at the periphery of the padang, speaking softly. Milne spotted the young man and walked over.

'Feels like a sudden end, doesn't it?' asked Milne.

'Well, it took a few decades, actually,' said the young man.

'Yes ... I know. It makes even me happy. I wonder though how it must feel for these chaps here.' The young man noticed Ganesh loitering around, looking disconsolate. He beckoned to him to come and join them.

'Why no food, aa?' he said, looking around.

'Wait for Deepavali,' said the young man. 'Maloti will cook us a feast.'

Ganesh nodded. 'One thing we all Malayans have in common, I must say, we like to eat. It is food that will bring this country together someday. You will see. But now we will try with flag.'

Ganesh noticed Maloti standing behind them. 'Madam!' he called out, 'where is little master?' Maloti pointed to Jonaki, in a white, starched school uniform, standing in attention with his classmates as the Tunku's speech went on.

The leader of the fledgling nation suddenly yelled 'Merdeka' startling everyone. Then he yelled it again, followed by the thunderous echo of a few hundred thousand people at the Stadium Merdeka, transported across the airwaves. It was so loud that the speakers crackled and people stopped talking. When the Tunku yelled 'Merdeka' for the third time, the locals joined in – Indian, Chinese and Malay – everyone screamed in unison.

'Look,' said the young man, pointing to Jonaki. He was shouting at the top of his lungs, like his classmates. That single word – freedom – was shouted seven times in all. Then it fell quiet. A minor problem came up as the British flag was to be lowered. The school principal ran up to Milne.

'Will you lower the flag, please?'

'Me?' asked Milne, dumbfounded. 'But I'm Australian.'

'Yes, we know, but Dr Murray has not arrived. Please, we must not delay.'

'Look,' Milne pointed. 'There's an English lady right there, I think.'

'Mrs Swaine is one of our teachers. But she's a half. A Eurasian. Please follow me.' Milne shrugged and walked toward the flagpole. He went right up to it and decided to salute it first. Just then a commotion broke out; Murray had arrived, driving his car right into the padang.

'Berhenti! Berhenti!' he yelled, parking it just meters away from the flagpole. Assisted by a few schoolboys, he huffed and puffed and managed to lower the Union Jack. The crowd broke out in applause. Next, the Malayan flag was raised as *Negaraku* played for the first time.

'Hey, are you crying?' asked the young man.

'Ah. No, lah,' said Ganesh, embarrassed. 'This damn flag business, this song ... That cloth has magic, I tell you. It can make the people forget all the old wars and the bad bloods. For some time, at least. Then we see, lah. God bless our damn country. Godbless-godbless-godbless.'

'Whose god, Ganesh?'

'All the gods, lah. Allah, Vishnu and ... even that Confucius fellah.'

The school staff brought out biscuits, nasi lemak, ais Bandung and lemonade. Malaya was free.

The telephone rang just after midnight. Maloti groaned.

'Sala patient ... they'll stop after a while,' said the young man.

'No, they won't ...' said Maloti shaking him. 'Sayang will wake up and start crying.' The ringing stopped.

When it rang again, the young man stumbled to the living room and lifted the receiver to his ear. There was an odd whimpering sound at the other end. 'Who is this?' he shouted angrily.

'It's me ...' said a hoarse, ghastly voice.

'Who?'

'Leela ... Nag-babu's wife.'

'Leela-di? What is it?' he asked alarmed.

'They took him away ...' said Leela, 'I couldn't stop them ... I begged of them. I fell at their feet. They took him away!'

'Nag-babu has been taken away?'

'Yes, yes, yes, yes,' she repeated hysterically.

'Who took him away? The police?'

'No ... not police ... men,' whimpered Leela. 'They said horrible things and took him away.'

'Stay at home. Don't go anywhere,' instructed the young man. 'I'm coming.'

'Maybe you should call Ganesh,' Maloti suggested as he put the phone down. 'Didn't you say his neighbour has a phone?'

'Why Ganesh?'

'Because he is a local.'

The young man relented. Ganesh arrived in about twenty minutes. He didn't think it was a good idea to call the police right away. 'Let's visit Nag wife first,' he said, breathless from the fast pedalling.

A manic, quivering Leela narrated a strange tale of abduction. She spoke haltingly, in English. 'There was knock-knock on door. We are still awake because we are fighting tonight. We stopped and listened, and then it was again! So he got up and walked very quietly towards the door. We heard the sound of peoples outside. A voice said, "Encik ... Encik Nag. There has been problem at the estate."

'So of course he asked, "What problem?" The man replied, "Very sad affair, encik. One worker took poison and kill himself." So he opened the door and I saw the men.'

'How many men were there?' asked the young man.

'Maybe five, maybe six, maybe seven.'

'Did he know any of them?' asked Ganesh.

'No ... because he asked them, "What estate are you all come from? Who asked you to come here?" Then one of them pulled him out. He yelled at them and they held him very tightly. He shouted, "What are you doing?" And so I also shouted. One of them said, "I have a knife, so stop making noise." So he said, "Okay, okay, don't do anything to us. We will give you what you want." But they said, "We got what we want. We got you." I was so afraid I just screamed. A big man said, "If you scream, I will hit your husband till his bones break." So I kept quiet. But he was making eyes at me and I knew what he wanted me to say. So I said quickly, "I will give you money. Come, I give you money." Then he also said, "Yes, my wife will bring the money and some jewellery. I will wait here with you." But they started dragging him down the stairs. At first, he was fighting a bit, but then he stopped. When they went down to the bottom step, he tried to run. Then ...' Leela started shaking. The young man took her hand.

She whispered, 'Then they kick him like a dog. He made a noise ... Oh ma, I cannot forget the noise. He begged, "Please, don't kill me. I will give you what you want." They said, "We will talk to your wife later." They said to me, "If you tell police, you will not get him alive." Then they dragged him and went down the road. I waited outside for five minutes. And then I made the telephone, but when I was talking, I saw that somebody was there.' She pointed at the window.

'Did they say anything more?' Ganesh asked.

'They said he had stolen for years and we become rich. And they said something about being a Japanese dog ... Something about a part of the animal.' She could not go on and banged her head on the table. The young man tapped Ganesh on the arm.

'We're going out to take a quick look around. Stay right here, Leela-di.' She looked up and nodded like a frightened child.

They heard a chicken scurrying away when they opened the back door. It was windy, and the trees beyond the house swayed. The young man lit a cigarette.

'They are gone,' said Ganesh, looking around. 'They are gone to the forest now. Damn, the Nag hides so much stolen estate materials here.'

'Ganesh ...' said the young man, 'do you think they'll kill him?'

'No.'

'No?'

'No, lah,' he said with confidence. 'They will not kill. Before, they killed. Even a few years ago they killed … They wanted to cause fear. Now they need some money and they don't want too much trouble. Killing is lot of trouble – police, special troops, helicopter up in sky, raids down in the forests.'

'But what do they want?'

'I think they make some demands, few thousand ringgits … they can also ask for gold, rice, goat, whatnot. Life is susah … *difficult*, in the jungle … hiding in there. Almost starving now maybe. No killing.'

The young man peered into the house through an open window. Leela was staring at a wall.

'Whom will they make the demand to?' he asked.

'We have to wait and see. They will take all the precaution first.'

'That is all we can do now? Wait?'

Ganesh nodded. 'Yes. Wait and see.'

The two men went inside. They gently told Leela that there was nothing to be done at the moment. That was, unless, she wished to inform the police. 'What you think?' she asked.

'We think that we should wait,' said the young man. Ganesh nodded.

'Yes, yes. They said no police. Do you know how long we need to wait?'

'We don't know. But it will be very soon, Leela-di.'

'Will they send someone here at night again?' She was afraid. The young man looked at Ganesh.

'If they do, it won't be to hurt you. Just listen carefully to what they say. And then call me,' said the young man. Leela nodded.

'Will you stay here please?' she asked the young man. 'Please?'

He looked away. 'Leela-di, call us if you need something.'

She stood at the door of the house, staring as they pedalled away. Daylight had just begun to edge its way in over the horizon. The young man made his way towards the forest. When he arrived

at its edge, he hopped off his bicycle and walked in the direction
of Wong's house.

There had been an incident in town, involving the ambush and
killing of two communists that Ganesh often remembered. It was
in 1951, after the British had outlawed the resurgent Malayan
Communist Party. To preserve themselves, they had vanished
into the caverns and folds of the enormous Malayan jungles.
But they carried on with their mission – sneak attacks on estate
personnel and vehicles. The white managers were assigned
uniformed constables, usually locals, to guard them at all hours.
The insurgents would often target a police station, striking in the
middle of the night, killing two or three policemen. Looting guns
and other armoury, they would vanish into the night. Sometimes
they'd execute white planters. Frustrated and demoralized, the
government started an extensive propaganda campaign. They
dropped leaflets over the dense jungles asking them to surrender.
Cash and other incentives were promised. Civilians, suspected of
helping the guerrillas in any way, were punished. Support for the
communists died down, but the insurgents rarely gave themselves
up. Finally, the authorities began to move the squatter Chinese
population to areas called 'new villages' to safeguard them from
the guerrilla's demands. They were restricted behind barbed wires
with strict patrolling and curfew hours. Their supplies cut-off, the
communists became desperate.

Ganesh's father, Murugasu, had been a kepala at one of the
smaller plantations and had come to know about a clandestine
meeting being planned. A couple of insurgents had contacted the
tapper groups and had asked to meet in the dead of night. Murugasu
had mentioned this to his colleague, a Chinese kepala. A few days
later, the newspapers carried a gruesome, yet celebratory, story.

Two bandits, who had been trying to secretly meet with estate workers for money and recruitment, were ambushed. It had happened in pitch darkness, in an empty shed at the edge of the town. The local police led by Sergeant O'Brien had come prepared. His aim had been so clean that both died instantly; the bullets went through the back of their skulls and out the front of their faces. The images, published on the front page of the local paper, were horrifying. They were meant to act as a deterrent. But what Ganesh remembered most was this: the Chinese kepala, who had tipped the police off, received 3,000 dollars as a gift. His drunk father with gambling debts, had grumbled about this injustice till his last days. Murugasu would lie in his cot, facing the window and hiss, 'Bloody Chinese fellow. Took the money. All the money. Don't trust the damn Chinese fellows.'

Wong was startled to see the young man at his door.

'You know why I am here?' he asked, arms folded. The young man tried to sound stern.

'No, Mr Sengupta,' said Wong, clearly surprised. It was barely daybreak.

This confused the young man. He was certain that Wong would be cognizant of, if not directly involved with, Nag's abduction. 'You don't know what happened last night?'

'What happened last night?'

The young man looked around. Wong's one-storey wooden house was camouflaged by an uneven thicket around it. Bright bougainvillea bloomed along the wired fence. The homes were spaced apart. Despite the tumult of the previous few hours, it felt calm at this edge of the jungle. Wong asked him to come inside. The young man took off his sandals and sat on a hard, low sofa. On hearing voices, the children peered through the curtain.

'So, this is where my son comes and plays all the time?' he asked.

'Yes, or they go out in the back. I have a small court for badminton.'

Wong's wife came in with tea. It was without sugar or milk in a tall glass with dragons etched on its sides. She smiled at the young man, but didn't stay in the room.

'So, what happened?'

'Wong, I need your help.'

When the young man returned to his house, it was still dark. He saw Maloti curled up on his side of the bed. He attempted to lie down without disturbing her, but the pressure on the mattress woke her up. 'Where is Nag-babu?' she asked immediately.

'Maybe in the forest.'

'Forest?'

'Yes, forest.' The young man explained the developments of the night, after he and Ganesh had cycled away. He didn't mention his visit to Wong's.

'But who is with Leela-di right now? Did Ganesh stay back with her?' asked Maloti.

'No ... Ganesh went home.'

'So, who is she with?'

'Let's not worry about Leela-di any more. We can't do much.'

'You left Leela-di alone?'

The young man shrugged. 'I told her that she could call if she needed to ...' He felt Maloti's body tense up. Before she could respond, he said, 'Listen, I am not bringing Leela-di here to our house. And I am not going to stay at her house. This is a serious matter. It involves dangerous people. Very dangerous people.' He turned over.

Maloti lay on her back and stared at the dark ceiling. A few minutes later, sensing she was still awake, the young man shouted, 'Why do you care so much about other people?' Maloti got up and carried Sayang to Jonaki's room.

The news of Nag's abduction spread through the town quickly. But it didn't garner sympathy. When Amma returned home after taking Jonaki to school, she wagged a finger and said, 'They take him to jungle. Now, he will see.'

'You don't like Nag, Amma?'

'He take my brother son away and sell him to Japan people. Now he will see, he will see. Give me duit.' She motioned in the direction of the market. Maloti counted out the shopping money and handed it to Amma.

'No fish, Amma. I go tomorrow.'

'Even Ganesh family,' said Amma.

'What?'

'Ganesh father, Murugasu, very drunk and playing with money of people in estate. So, the brother take some money from Nag and gave his father. Then he go to work for Japan people. He never come back.'

Later in the morning, Maloti found the nerve to call Leela.

'Maloti ... I was waiting for you to call.'

'Hello, Leela-di ...' She didn't know what to say next.

'What will happen, Maloti?'

'Are you alone, Leela-di?'

'They have taken him, Maloti. There is no one here now.' She sounded devastated. Maloti wanted to ask her to come to their house for lunch, to stay the day and the night. But helpless, she put down the receiver and wept. Amma watched her from the kitchen.

Milne had somehow not heard about the abduction till mid-morning. At ten, returning from his estate rounds, he bounded up the stairs shouting, 'Sengoopta! Sengoopta! Have you heard about Naag?'

'Yes, I know,' said the young man. He decided against telling Milne about his involvement in the matter.

'It's awful ... it's godawful! They got him. And from his own home!' He sat down, shaking his head. 'It's a bloody shame. I thought we had gone past all this. Jesus Christ ... Naag's been here for ages. He probably knows all those buggers too.'

'Yes, he knows a lot of people.'

'A bloody shame! We should have gotten every single one of those bastards when we could! They can be pretty ruthless. What do they want anyway? The country's soon to be independent. What're they still fighting for?' He slammed his fist down and the table fan fell on the floor with a crash. The sleepy office boy came in running. The young man wondered about that demonstration. Milne was clearly affected by the news. But there was a weakness to it, not unlike the shooting at the club – a flaring of emotions because of a sense of order being challenged.

'Small-time hoodlums. Those remaining jungle monkey bastards living off tree barks. Do they really think they can scare us? It's bloody absurd, isn't it? They know they're doomed. They've no way out now – maybe that's why they're on a suicide mission,' Milne ranted. 'O'Brien's got approval from Special Branch to put a 10,000-dollar bounty on anyone directly involved with the kidnapping. The estate's paying for half of it.'

Nag's abduction, pondered the young man, could be seen in many ways – violent, mercenary, or perhaps even patriotic. But it was certainly not absurd. He remembered Wong's words. In hindsight, it almost seemed inevitable.

'But it is still their country ... in some ways. Nag didn't have a very good reputation among the locals. Do you really think it's that absurd?' he countered.

Milne stared testily at the young man. 'So, do you sympathize with them, Sengoopta? All the bloody hacking and blowing up and murdering they've been doing!'

The young man shook his head, 'No. Of course not.'

'Good. Because I know of a fine place to send sympathizers.' Milne opened his drawer and pulled out a flask.

The town reverted to black status. The police resumed their operations – they set up roadblocks, checked car registrations and turned away vehicles after sunset. While no special forces were deployed to search the forests – it was, after all, just an Indian clerk – O'Brien went to the adjoining Chinese kampongs and threatened local dwellers with severe punishment if they were withholding information. "You're all lying bastards," he hollered from his jeep, driving slowly past crowds of people.

When Leela had yet to hear from anyone in three days, Wong discreetly advised the young man to put an advertisement in the newspapers, offering money for the whereabouts of Nag. This way, he explained, the abductors would be intimated that a barter of cash and hostage return was being considered. He did not divulge if he had any information on the whereabouts of Nag.

The young man told Leela to put an advertisement in the newspaper, but he otherwise kept to himself. He did not discuss the issue with Maloti. Murray had showed him a way out of the plantation life and he was engrossed with planning for his immediate future. He had received communication from the Royal Faculty of Physicians and Surgeons in Glasgow in response to his inquiries to be reinstated. He read the letter about a dozen times, formulating a strategy. He could complete the degree in about fifteen to eighteen months. His family could stay in Calcutta during that time. He had some savings. He would need to borrow some money from Murray, or possibly sell his share of the house in Calcutta to fund his studies. 'Perhaps I should go to Calcutta soon and discuss this with Baba and Potol-kaku,' he said to Maloti. She listened sadly. This plan would disrupt their small life she had become so used to.

'You should go home to see your father, regardless. He would be happy to see you,' she said. Maloti had raised this matter a few times. She had felt that Nirmal Sengupta, in his current hapless and sad condition, would benefit from seeing his only child. The young man insisted that it would not help matters.

'I need to save money. It's the only thing that matters now.'

The announcement placed in the *Malay Mail* bore a photograph of Nag, clipped from his passport. It was a short column and made the front page:

Utpal Nag, manager of the JCP Estate, was forcibly abducted from his house on the night of 20 September by a group of unknown men. Mr Nag is 51 years of age and 160 cm tall. He has a black moustache and, at the time of disappearance, was wearing a light-blue pyjama bottoms and white singlet. Any knowledge of his whereabouts should be reported to the local police station. His wife has offered a reward.

Late that evening, Wong and the young man met on a bench at the small outdoor railway platform. It wasn't Wong of the smart white uniform, but the *other* Wong, the one in slippers and a half shirt, looking like any other local Chinese man. The station was deserted as the only train that passed through the town came at midnight. A man selling sweet buns started to make his way towards them, walking with his bicycle, the weight of the large tin containers almost tipping it over. Wong waved him away.

'Anything?' the young man asked.

'I saw the advertisement. Good,' replied Wong.

'Good? What's good?'

'Good. She will get some notice from them soon.'

'When?'

Wong shrugged.

'Can you tell me more?'

'No. Don't worry so much. Your family is safe.'

'Are they, Wong? You understand why I am doing this? Because she is a friend.'

'No, Mr Sengupta.'

'No?'

'You are doing this because she is an Indian. In fact, exactly from your area of India. That is how it always happens.' The young man pondered over Wong's statement. He was right. He felt nothing for Nag. Yet, his hapless wife, Leela, was a sit-in for many people he knew in the old world and had extracted a primordial loyalty from him.

'It's because we speak the same language, Wong.'

'Yes, language is a big matter in this life. In the next life, maybe everyone speak same and look same. Then no fighting.' The two men sat in silence for a while.

'Wong, I don't know what I am doing here right now. Don't stay quiet. Did you meet those people? Where is Nag now?'

'I don't know so much.'

'Wong, is he alive? I need to tell his wife.'

'Yes, alive, I can tell you that. They just want some money. I am sure that some action will take place very soon.' Wong went quiet again. He stared ahead at the lights from the small town. From where they were seated, they could see a murmuration of sparrows swooping in dense formation over the rooftops, under the telegraph poles. Then the birds took a sharp turn left and vanished from sight.

The young man got up. 'Can I go and tell Leela that Nag is alive? Promise me?'

Wong nodded.

'Can I tell her that he is well?'

Wong shrugged.

On reaching home, the young man called up Leela and informed her that her husband was alive and well. She wailed and pressed for more information. Who had informed him? When? And how soon would they release him? The young man could tell her no more. 'Will you please bring him back?' she pleaded.

'Yes, of course, Leela-di. He will be back soon.'

'You are like my younger brother ...' she wept.

'I promise you, Leela-di.' The young man considered handing Maloti the receiver, but changed his mind and secured it onto the phone. She was standing next to him.

'You see, I do care about her. I am trying. My best!'

'How do you know about Nag-babu?'

'Never mind how I know. Do you think I would lie to her? All of a sudden, I am her "younger brother." Never heard more than three words from her before.'

'Why can't we invite Leela-di to stay with us?' asked Maloti.

'Because it is dangerous! Don't you understand that! I don't want to do any more than what we simply must.' The young man was yelling now. Jonaki peeked from his room. He had been quiet throughout the episode. He had sensed that his friends, the Wongs, were somehow involved in the recent debacle raging in his house. It was his hunch that he would be better off not asking any questions.

The next morning, while chopping vegetables, Amma asked Maloti, 'Sir shouting-shouting. Angry?'

'Yes, sir angry.'

'Oh,' murmured Amma, and continued dicing potatoes on her haunches.

'But Nag is alive, Amma.'

'Ah.'

'I feel sad for his wife.'

'Yes, sad.'

'Poor lady ... so nice also.'

'You send food for poor lady? I cook and take.'

Maloti smiled. This had not occurred to her. It was a small gesture, but it would surely help Leela.

The following morning, Ganesh arrived and sat on the steps of the kitchen. Amma handed him a tall glass of sweet tea and some bread. Noisily sipping the frothy tea, he noticed the containers of food on the table. 'Guest coming, is it?'

'No, for madam's friend.'

'Who friend?'

'The wife of Hindu man in jungle. He will see.'

This caught Ganesh's attention. He had been trying for days to get some information about the abduction and had not heard of any developments. The young man had been silent. The people in the estate had not heard anything either. Apparently, Milne had read the announcement in the newspaper to every tapper group. That would be close to 2000 men and women. Still, no one had heard anything. In a town rife with gossip, a strange, stubborn silence prevailed. He had even cycled by Nag's house once and had not observed anything interesting. But he noticed that Leela was still living there; she made an appearance in the kitchen, looking dishevelled. She had almost caught him peeking through the window.

'Who is delivering the food?' he asked.

'I.'

Ganesh acted immediately. He informed Amma that he would take the food himself.

'Good boy, Ganesh,' said Amma, relieved that she wouldn't have to walk three miles in the sun.

Ganesh knocked on Leela's door, waking her up from a deep sleep. Unaware of the time, she lay still in her bed. There it was again. Tat-tat-tat. She peered at the watch on the side of her bed; it was almost noon. She walked to the living room and stood silently next to the door. When Ganesh knocked again, she asked feebly, 'Who is there?'

Ganesh answered loudly, 'Hello, Madam Nag. I have come from Mr Sengupta's house with the food.'

Leela turned the lock and opened the door cautiously. She stared at Ganesh, unable to place him. 'Hello. Remember me?' he asked with a broad smile. She was wearing the same clothes he had last seen her in. She looked haggard.

'No,' said Leela, patting her hair down.

'Oh. Maybe you forget. I come here the other night. The ... night when sir was taken away.'

Leela'e eyes widened. 'You came here to take him?'

'No, no, no. I came with Mr Sengupta, after.'

Now Leela recognized Ganesh. She opened the door and moved to the side. Ganesh took a step into the house.

'Well, they have sent you some food. I just want to give you.' He held out the containers neatly fastened together by Amma.

'It is so much. Your name is...?'

'Ganesh,' he folded his palms politely.

'Yes ... Ganesh. Thank you, Ganesh.'

'How are you, madam?' he asked, trying to engage her in conversation. Leela seemed unsure about whether to invite him in. The living room was usually for officers of the estate and relatives.

'It is my meal time now...'

'May I wash the hands in your kitchen, madam? Some fish curry leaking, I think ...' Ganesh looked at his palms.

'Yes, come, come in, please.'

Ganesh headed to the kitchen; the layout of the bungalows in the area was identical and he knew where it was. The interior was neat and not ostentatious – simple furniture, wall decorations from India and a few dull brass figurines. Like the home of a clerk ought to be. Leela was comfortable with Ganesh in the kitchen, the part of any house in Malaya that acted as a social leveller. As he washed his hands elaborately, she asked, 'Did you know Mr Nag?'

'Oh yes, of course, madam!'

'Do you work on the estate?'

'No, no. My father knew him very well also.'

'You have lived here many years?'

'All of my life, madam. I seen Mr Nag since I was a young boy.' Ganesh kept washing his hands.

'He was a good man, no?' Leela realized that Ganesh had probably known her husband for longer than she had.

'Yes, madam. A very good man.' He continued to wash his hands.

'Look at this.' Leela pointed to a framed picture on the wall. Nag was next to two Englishmen, in an oversized blazer and a tie, holding up a certificate. 'He went to England to train about the workers' unions. He cared for his workers.'

'Yes, madam. Before, Indians never have any union. But now, all working on strict contract. I think in 1953 he started to make the workers' groups.'

'Yes, he told me that if the Chinese can have their unions, so must the Indians. And he wanted to help them. But now nobody cares...'

'I care, madam.'

'You care?'

'Jealous people have taken him away, madam. But I saw the newspaper. Very good quality plan. He will return. You don't worry, na.'

Leela's face lightened. 'Yes, Maloti's husband told me what to do. He also just heard news that he is safe and well.'

'What, madam? He has news of Mr Nag?'

'Oh yes, they tell him things every day. He gets news for me.'

'Who tells him things?'

'I don't know that.'

'Does he know where Mr Nag is?'

'I don't know that.'

'Is this your son, madam?' Ganesh pointed to a small, framed photograph above a cabinet in the kitchen. He was fishing for time now.

'Yes. I keep it there so I can see his face when I cook. He goes to boarding school in Singapore.'

'Very handsome boy, madam.'

'I did not tell him anything about this. I wrote him a letter yesterday, but did not say one word about his father. He will be upset.'

'Yes, madam. That is a good thing. Why to make the children worry unnecessary? Will affect the studies, no?'

'Do you have children?'

'Yes, madam, small baby daughter. Very mischievous one. Always want to ride on bicycle with me.' Leela smiled.

'Ganesh, would you like some coconut water?'

'Ah ... it's okay, madam ... I have the work ...' Ganesh tried to sound unconvincing.

'Sit, sit for a few minutes.' Leela went to the refrigerator. Ganesh pulled out a chair at the small, round kitchen table.

'Hokay. I will have the coconut, madam.'

Later that afternoon, Leela telephoned Maloti to thank her for the food. She was surprised to hear that it was Ganesh who had delivered it.

'Amma, did you tell Ganesh to take the food?' she asked from the kitchen steps.

'No.'

Maloti decided against telling the young man about the food delivery. It was her personal support to Leela and a minor mutiny. She had felt hurt that the young man had distanced her from Nag's tragedy. He had not even considered her gesture of asking Leela to stay with them. In fact, they had not been speaking much to each other of late. The young man had conveniently acquired the male Indian habit of grunting at everything.

'Will you need to take lunch to the estate tomorrow?'

'Gmm.'

'Jonaki did rather well in the mid-year exam.'

'Gmm?'

'Ganesh came by today.'

'Gmmh!'

'Why don't you say anything properly any more?' asked Maloti.

They had not been sleeping well. The young man had begun to look harried and lay in bed long after the alarm rang. The driver would have to wait several minutes every morning before he was ready to leave the house.

In the days after the abduction, the young man would sleepily stare out of the jeep as it chugged along the asphalt road leading to the estate. He observed the early morning landscape, a mundane view by now – rows of trees awaiting laceration. Where did the perfect symmetry of trees end and where did the abyss of the jungle start? How far in from that demarcation of order and entropy were the people he had only heard of and imagined about? How many of them were there? What if they remained hidden for years, managing to survive using only their wits, never participating in all the changes that were enveloping the new country? Nag's misfortune had not traumatized him. But the sudden realization that an entirely different set of aspirations and histories had existed in the small town all along – while he worked for Milne, drank with Murray, joked with Ganesh, and while Maloti cooed Sayang to bed – gave him pause. Was the birth of every country an unsolved puzzle?

He went about his daily duties in an inattentive haze. He ticked charts, added columns and subtracted wages. No one noticed the somnolent condition he was in. He wondered one morning, as his head hurt and he smiled at a group of kepalas, whether that was how alcoholics went about their business. But while he felt that he was slipping in his duties, his value in the eyes of the estate corporation had been rising.

Milne called him in one morning, just before lunch. He seemed fidgety and asked the young man to take a seat in his cluttered office. He paced around the room, smoking. 'I can't say this delicately, Sengoopta, but with Naag ... well, let's just say "indefinitely gone", you're rather important to us now. My superiors have intimated that we should give you a bonus payment if you assure us that you'll stay with us for two more years.'

'But Nag might return. It's just been a few days ...' said the young man, surprised by this quick turn of events.

'Oh, we do hope so. But even if he returns, or if a new person takes his place ... you'll have more responsibilities, more stake with us. We'd up your salary, of course. And give you a permanent contract, with a nice pension for retirement or ... if something untoward were to happen.'

'Why would you hire a new person?'

Milne shrugged defensively. 'Well, Nag may not want to be here any more. Maybe a different estate. Or retirement. We just don't know what to expect. Will he return ... Will he be himself even if he does ... Who knows, right?'

The young man composed himself. The extra money, even if for the short run, would be of much help. 'Yes, I would like to stay here.'

'I thought so too, Sengoopta. Of course, I told them that your work was excellent.'

'That was kind of you.'

'Not to mention. Just be careful till this passes over. And it will soon; O'Brien's on it.'

The young man went to the cafeteria to find some sugary tea to keep him awake. He had left his tiffin container at home. He saw Ganesh sitting there, sipping a drink. He looked up at the young man as he walked in.

'Ah, here for the lunch?'

'No, just tea, Mr Ganesh.' He pulled up a chair next to Ganesh. 'I think we met here first time, no?'

'Indeed. You taught me Malay numbers.'

Ganesh laughed out loud. 'Correct! Already seem like so much time pass, na? So many thing happen so quickly. Sometimes time flies like the English man's golf ball. Whoooosh!'

'Yes, time travels fast, Ganesh. Like the golf ball.'

'You looking tired, mister,' Ganesh said. 'You hear any news about Nag?' The young man shook his head.

'No news.'

'No news at all?' Ganesh pressed.

'No news at all.'

'Strange ... Hokay, enjoy the teh tarik, mister. I come on Sunday again to your house.' Ganesh got up and left the small canteen. The young man felt a prick of guilt for lying to him. Ganesh had, after all, always been an extremely helpful and a calming presence to his family. But his dealings with Wong were off limits. He didn't discuss them even with Maloti.

When the young man entered the house that afternoon, Maloti took his hand and rushed him to the bedroom. She looked nervous and conspiratorial.

'What is it?' he asked, wondering for a fleeting moment if she was pregnant again. Or was experiencing a particularly strong knock of affection.

It was about a phone call. 'Leela called many times. You have to call her.'

'What did she say?'

Maloti lowered her voice even though they were in their own house. 'I think she has some news about Nag-babu. She said she tried you all afternoon at the estate.'

'She shouldn't do that,' said the young man, alarmed.

'Just call her, Lokkhi-ti. She needs to talk to you.'

The young man nodded. He was helpless when she called him Lokkhi. He made his way to the phone. Leela picked up on the first ring. 'Leela-di, I hear you have some news...'

She didn't let him finish his sentence, '20,000!' she screamed.

'What?'

'They are asking for 20,000!'

'I see. Who told you?'

'Someone telephoned. He said, "Get 20,000 ready by tomorrow". Then he put the phone down. I shouted and then waited. But he never called again. Just one time.'

'How will he collect it?'

'I don't know.'

'Do you have the money?'

'No.'

'No?'

'I have 10,000. I am trying to get more. He has a relative in Penang ... and I have some other places to go and ask ...' Leela's voce was cracking. 'Please give me a week.'

'Oh Leela-di, it's not up to me...'

Leela started sobbing. 'Tell them. Please understand. Can you tell them to return him to me now? I promise I will give the money soon. If he comes back ... we can find it quickly. I don't know how else ...' The young man was taken aback at the request. Leela didn't seem to realize the logic behind a kidnapping operation.

'Leela-di ... all right. You start collecting the rest of the money. I'll see what we can do.'

'Yes, you must bring him back. Right away. Now we know what they want. They will get it. They must believe me ... they must.' Leela was speaking in a maniacal tone that unnerved the young man.

'Yes, we will,' he said and hung up the phone. He wondered what on earth it was that he was about to get into. He looked at Maloti, standing beside him.

'Did you understand any of that?' he asked.

'No. Tell me.'

'Someone called Leela-di and asked for money. She's very excited. But she doesn't have it all.'

'Some news at last. Is it a lot of money?'

'Not so much that she can't pay. But she doesn't have all of it.'

'Can we help her?'

The young man shot her an exasperated look. 'Now you want me to help her with money? Money? We don't even know these people and you want us to give up our little savings? Bills that we have carefully put away for Jonaki and Sayang? Is that why I work all day while you sleep at home?'

'I don't sleep all day!' cried Maloti.

The young man followed her to the bedroom. 'Yes, yes, I know you don't. But do you understand me? Do you understand that I shouldn't get involved any more than I have already?'

'But what will happen to them now?' asked Maloti.

'I don't know what will happen now. She will take a few more days to find the money. I am sure they will wait. But she doesn't want to wait.'

'What do you mean?'

'She wants me to find a way to secure his return before she pays the money. Can you believe that stupid lady?'

'Can you do that for her?'

'Of course not!' exclaimed the young man.

'Why not?'

'Have you womenfolk all gone crazy? What kind of kidnapper gives up his victim before getting his money?' the young man chortled, exasperated.

Maloti persisted, 'But surely you can do something, Lokkhi-ti?'

The young man grunted.

That evening, as soon as he entered the clinic, he signalled to Wong. Zainun caught their exchange. Of late, she had noticed these strange moments between them. She had been on the other side of the door when they had had their altercation, and had heard the commotion and the yelling. Wong followed the young man to the inspection room and shut the door.

'She doesn't have 20,000. It will take her days and days.'

'I know,' said Wong. He was in his starched uniform, preparing a nebulizer for an asthma patient.

'You know what? That they asked for the money?'

'Yes. But I did not know how much.'

'Is it not a lot of money? How can she find so much money so quickly?'

'I don't know.' Wong shrugged.

'Wong!' exclaimed the young man. 'That woman is going mad. She is calling me at the estate now. My wife is yelling at me at home. Help me, please.'

'I don't think they can reduce the amount,' said Wong calmly. 'But I am quite sure that no harm will come to him. Might just take some more days, right?'

The young man nodded. 'You can't do anything?'

'Sorry, but no. Can do nothing. These things are only told to me. I don't know who decides or even where they meet.'

'Do you know where Nag is?'

'No.'

'Then how do you know he is even alive?'

'You think I lie to you?'

'No. But I can't see how you know so much and yet can do nothing.'

Wong startled the young man by sitting down on the chair reserved for patients. 'Listen,' said Wong, dropping his voice, 'I know the older people. They were my father's friends. Now you know that I help them sometimes. When they tell me something, I know it is the truth. They will never lie to me. But they don't tell me everything.'

The young man clutched Wong's arm. 'Can you make a request to them?'

'No, I can't ask them that … You must pay what they demanded. Cannot bargain. Not fish market.'

'No, not change the amount. But to release Nag. Now. If we promise to pay.'

'You mean let him go before delivery of money?' Wong asked.

The young man nodded vigorously, surprising himself with his own insistence. 'Yes, you tell them that we promise to give the money. Full money in one week. One week. That's all. You explain everything to them. If they trust you, they should agree to it. Tell them I give my word. Tell them we need Nag to get the money.'

There was a knock on the door.

'Okay. I will ask for you,' said Wong and got up.

Zainun peeked inside. 'The old nenek from yesterday is here. Say she still vomiting.'

'Let her in,' said the young man. 'Eating rubbish oily paratha all the time.'

Later that evening, Ganesh popped by. 'Your secretary always look at me in strange way,' he said, walking in unannounced. It was a bit like the early days.

'She is doing her work, Ganesh. Can't let any old fellah off the street walk in, lah. What is your ailment?'

'I got the pain in my heart, doctor.'

'Did your wife run away?'

'No. But I pray to Shiva every day that she will!' Ganesh filled the room with his boisterous laugh. All seemed well, if for a moment. He noticed Wong attending to his medical station. 'How he? All okay now?'

'Yes,' said the young man.

'No more ...' Ganesh acted like he was Wong, stuffing things into a pocket.

'No more of that.'

'Then okay, what.'

'Yes, I hope so.'

'You hear any news of Nag?'

The young man paused. 'No news of Nag, Ganesh. You keep asking me the same thing every day.'

'Very strange. What the fellahs want with that man ... still keep him in jungle.'

The young man shrugged. He felt that guilt yet again for not disclosing anything to Ganesh. He had, after all, taken him into confidence the very night the abduction had occurred.

'I go now,' said Ganesh cheerfully. 'You make the money. Plenty people waiting.' 'Come to the house on Sunday. Jonaki was asking about you.'

'Hokay. I come.'

'Ganesh...'

'Yes, doctor?

'Can you pay me back soon?'

'Of course, doctor. I pay soon.'

The young man didn't realize that Ganesh knew about the 20,000. He had been visiting Leela regularly and drinking cool coconut water in her kitchen.

Nag's absence had doubled the young man's work. In addition to his usual tasks, he had to go to the locations that required Nag's supervision. When he arrived at these sites, the tappers wanted to gossip and waste time. Some claimed to have seen Nag at night, wandering around the plantations. Others insisted that he had returned to India because the Malayan government was after him for taxes. The most outlandish story going around was that he had engineered his own kidnapping to collect the ransom money. The young man tried to reign in some order, but met with little success.

Evenings at the clinic were difficult as well. On account of Deepavali approaching, many people showed up with indigestion, forcing the young man to stay on for hours. One such evening, he felt exhausted when he finally made it home after attending to flatulent patients. He took a bath and asked Maloti to bring his dinner to the bedroom. When Jonaki entered the room and announced that there was someone at the gate, the young man mumbled wearily, 'Tell him to get lost.'

But moments later, Jonaki returned to say that it was Wong waiting outside.

The young man put on a shirt. Jonaki went out and opened the gate. He was happy to see Wong. Maloti, who had actually never met Wong but carried an image of him in bright, white professional attire, was surprised to see a weary man in a crumpled shirt, dragging his rubber slippers. But his eyes, peering through thick dark-rimmed glasses, were intense. She inquired about his wife and went to the kitchen to pack some Bengali sweets, which she had fortunately made just that evening.

Wong brought astonishing news. Nag's kidnappers were willing to release him immediately. They had two conditions though. First, half the ransom, or 10,000 dollars, was to be paid right away. And the young man would have to go make the payment himself.

'Why do they want me?' he asked, perplexed.

'They want you to take your medicine bag too.'

'Why?'

'Because there are sick people there. They need help. You help them, they help you. This way.'

'I cannot do this,' said the young man, trying to sound as firm as he could. 'How do I know they won't kidnap me?'

'Why will they kidnap you?'

'Because ... they want more money?' said the young man, a bit offended.

'No, no kidnapping.'

'Will you come with me then?' asked the young man, finger on his lips, realizing that words like 'kidnap' and 'ransom' were being discussed in his house.

Wong shook his head. 'Cannot.'

'Cannot?'

Wong shook his head.

'Then tell them that we can give the money. If they send anyone to the clinic, I will treat them for free. But I won't go to the jungle to meet them.'

'They cannot come to clinic.'

'Then I can't help.'

'This is your final answer?'

'Yes.'

Wong got up and walked to the door. Maloti gave him the container of sweets. He made a half-bow. 'My missus always tell me about you...'

The young man spoke up, 'One thing, Wong...'

'Yes?'

'If they ask why I didn't want to come, tell them my missus wouldn't let me.'

'Okay.'

Wong pedalled slowly back to the edge of the forest, sweets dangling from the handle bar.

'I heard what happened,' said Maloti, when they retired to bed. She was securing the mosquito net, a ritual that usually calmed her at bedtime. But tonight she was agitated. The young man didn't respond and lay reading. The diaphanous cloth brushed against his face as Maloti adjusted the position of the net. 'Aren't you going to tell Leela-di?' she asked.

'No. No, Leela-di.'

'I think you should tell her,' said Maloti, tucking the net under the mattress.

'No, no! Why confuse her? Let her just get the money and then we'll send it over.' The young man tried to sound reasonable.

'How could you say no to that man after all that his family has done for us?'

'I did not say no to *him*. I just gave him a message. This is not concerning him, correct?'

'But do you know how long it would take for Leela-di to get all the money? What about Nag-babu? Is he going to remain in the forest?'

'Who cares about Nag-babu? He'll live. The workers don't seem too upset. You told me even Amma said that it serves him right.'

'Can you imagine how I would feel if they had taken you away instead? And if no one in this town helped me get you back?'

'But I am helping...'

'It's not enough. You should go. Wong said it was safe.'

'Oh, so you've been listening in to everything! And now you trust Wong's "yes" and "no" answers more than my judgment?'

'But you know what happens when people make mistakes!' Maloti shrieked. It was a thinly veiled, deliberate reference to an old, deep wound.

'Stop raising your voice, Maloti! I am the head of this household and I decide what keeps us safe. You want me, a clerk from Calcutta, to go to the Malayan jungles to negotiate with communist terrorists? Do you realize how absurd that sounds? No. I won't compromise our safety!'

'But time is slipping away...'

'Shut up, Maloti!' he yelled.

'You'll wake the children up.'

'Oh, I think my boy has heard everything, thanks to your hysteria. I stay calm. But you women ... Why do you yell when you don't understand simple things?'

'I listen very well and I understand very well. Don't you say I'm hysterical,' said Maloti sharply.

'Listen, listen some more then ...' said the young man, attempting to inject reason into their argument. 'We aren't sure of anything, are we? How do we know what goes on in the minds of these people? How they see us? What if they get me too if I do go there ... deep in the forest?' He stood up and walked over to the door that opened onto the balcony. He stared into the balmy night, enveloped by the sound of cicadas. 'And honestly, I suppose I don't really care so much. As Wong reminded me, this isn't our country after all.'

Maloti moved towards the door. She stood a couple of feet behind him. 'Tell me something, it is better for your position at the estate if Nag doesn't return, isn't it?'

The young man turned around. 'What did you just say?'

'I think you've become selfish.'

'Big words for a slight village girl, Maloti.'

'You had noble ideas once. You talked about oppression and freedom with your friends. Now you think like a man who wears rubber slippers to work. And then bows to his sahib boss. Jyotirmoy-da would have laughed at you.'

It was a hard slap, much harder than he had intended it to be. Maloti stumbled, lost her footing and fell. She got up slowly and leaned against the wall, breathing heavily, her heart palpitating. The young man stood still for a moment and then rushed towards her. But she shook her head and moaned in a way that stopped him. He had never seen her look at him with fear. He moved away slowly and sat down on the edge of the bed.

When Maloti spoke again, she was no longer sobbing. The humiliation had dried up. 'Do you want to hit me again?'

'No.'

'Will hitting me keep us safe?'

'No.'

'Then don't hit me again.'

'No, I won't.'

'I feel that a spirit has entered here tonight.'

'A spirit?'

'Yes, you know ... a spirit from the jungle ... or somewhere.'

'A good spirit or an evil spirit?'

'Both, I think.'

'How can a spirit be both good and evil?'

'Why not? They might be like we are, good, bad, unsure.'

'Oh. So, I am not to blame?'

'Of course, you are to blame,' said Maloti.

'What does the spirit tell you?' asked the young man, pursuing swift reconciliation.

'It tells me some things. Things I have thought of before ... but I see more clearly now.'

'What do you see?'

Maloti was on the floor in front of him, her back resting against the wall. 'I was just a child when I arrived at your house. Yes, a slight village girl. That large, grand house. Full of servants running around. Fans and electric bulbs in every room. Important people dropping in every day. I was afraid of everyone and everything. And I was lonely. And I was so guilty that I had caused my sister's death. But, in time, I grew to love all of you. Loving helps make matters easier and a cruel world bearable. I learnt that quickly in this life. But you don't seem to believe that.'

'I don't?'

'No. Not any more. You did many years ago. Now, I see my husband full of doubt.'

'Why?'

'Why? I think it's because you are hiding someone deep inside you. Someone who has already died – a corpse sitting inside your heart. That's why you cry at night sometimes. Because he remains in there, still alive.'

Maloti paused. She had spoken too much. The young man remained silent, startled by her eloquence and the weight of her words. She walked over to him now. She sat on the edge of the bed next to him. 'You wish to go away someday and become a doctor, don't you? You have finally found a path to become complete. To become a respectable person.' She paused. 'And maybe you will become one. But please do what you know is right in your heart. You must help this lady now.'

'You really want me to go? Is this so important?'

'I beg you to, Lokkhi-ti. I want to see the good man in you again. And there is one more thing.'

'Yes?'

'After this is all over, you must go home to see your father. I know about those letters.'

The young man put his arms around Maloti and held her tightly.

MOONLIGHT

Wong arrived the following evening, but did not rattle the gate. He stood silently till the young man came out to the veranda. He pointed to someone and walked away. The young man beckoned several times to the shadowy figure in the street. But he didn't come towards the house. Carrying the money distributed in three thick envelopes secured inside his medical case, the young man went out to meet him. The man would not touch the money. He started walking immediately, leading the way, taking the path away from the house towards the narrow dirt lane that coiled around the perimeter of the town.

About a minute into the woods, where stray city lights could not penetrate, the young man switched on a small torchlight. The guide, who was moving about ten yards ahead, immediately motioned him to turn it off. Soon, they were walking through dense foliage. The amount of parasitic growth around the trees was formidable. Tendrils, thicker than a man's thigh, wound the trunks of trees. It was easy to see why the Malayan forests provided a natural camouflage to anyone choosing to hide. The guide used a long parang to hack his way through the jungle. The

young man's body itched from insect and mosquito bites. He felt
fresh cuts lacerating his feet. Soon they arrived at a stream.

'Must cross,' said the guide and waded right into it.

The young man followed and the water soon reached up to
his chest. He held the medical case above his head. Drenched, he
took the guide's hand to hoist himself onto land again. Moments
later, the young man stumbled. He managed to catch himself
by clutching blindly onto the low hanging foliage, but his face
smashed against a protruding branch. As he continued trudging
through the darkness, the streak of blood on his face dried. Finally,
after about two hours of travelling, they reached a clearing. The
young man could see glowing embers and made out six skeletal
attap huts in the distance. A whiff of cheap tobacco blew in with
the light breeze.

The guide motioned to him to wait and walked towards the
clearing. The young man peered at the huts. Moments later, he
heard footsteps – three men had approached him from behind.

'Is Mr Nag here?' he asked, turning around.

'Yes,' said one of them from the darkness.

'I want to see him.'

'Okay, but not now. We give back your friend later.'

'Why not now?' the young man asked.

'Because he is not here.'

'You just said he was here.'

'We do not keep him here. You want him to be here, hah? He
will try to run in the jungle and die. Once we have the money, we
inform the other place. So tomorrow, you get him.'

The young man nodded in the dark. He opened his medical
case and took out the three envelopes. One of the men snatched
them out of his hands.

'You give us the next money next week. Correct?'

'Yes. One week. Now you must let Mr Nag go.'

'We must, is it? Come now. Follow, follow.'

'Where are we going?' asked the young man.

'You, mister, follow, follow.'

The young man's eyes had adjusted to the darkness. He took in the camp. It had little symmetry or organization. Empty tins and paper packets lay scattered around. The attap huts, secured with thick rattan and covered with fronds, were on one side. Men sat around listlessly. Some looked at him. He wondered if there was a commander or person in charge. They soon came to a clearing under some trees. A person lay huddled under blankets. On closer inspection, he appeared to be a boy, somewhere in his mid-teens. He looked up wearily.

'Fever. Sick. Got demam,' grunted a short, pot-bellied man, striding over. He had authority. The young man sat down on the forest floor and checked the boy's pulse. He was certain that he was malarial.

'Doctor,' gasped the boy feebly. He had rheumy, yet expressive eyes despite the raging fever. Another boy came over to where they were and squatted next to the patient.

'Haha! Doctor give you cucuk now! Oiiie! Oieee!' he said, poking with his finger. The sick boy tried to slap his hand away.

'Not strong this boy. Catch fever. That other one never sick,' said the pot-bellied man.

'Are you Tan King?'

'Yes, I Tan King. I am famous, is it not?' he laughed. He had a round, youthful face with large piercing, inquisitive eyes – like a bright schoolboy's. It was hard to see him as the leader of a guerrilla gang.

'I think he has dengue. It comes from mosquitos.'

'Yes, yes, we know it comes from mosquito, doctor. Why he sick?' Tan King snapped.

'He couldn't have prevented it.' The young man had been bit all over since the evening had started.

'Yes. We know the dengue. Everyone here got. *Everyone.* But if you are strong you cannot be sick. This boy weak … Now we must carry him everywhere.'

'I think you have to send him to a hospital,' said the young man. The boy shook his head vigorously.

'Aya! He don't want to go. You need to fight, what?' The sick boy nodded.

His friend, hovering nearby, picked up an imaginary machine gun and fired it into the air – 'ack-ack-ack-ack-ack'!

'Jūju!' Tan King yelled. The boy stopped immediately. 'Real monkey, this one. A little gila – up there a little loose.' Tan King pointed to his head. The boy sat down quietly, next to his friend. The young man noticed that he had a withered, bandy leg, most likely from polio.

'There is nothing much I can do for him,' the young man said. 'I can leave you some Panadol, so the fever goes down.'

'Okay, okay. You give us the obat.' The young man pulled out two glass bottles full of white Panadol pills and put them down. The boys looked at the medicine. Tan King yelled out into the darkness and someone ran over carrying a rusty Nestlé tin with water in it. 'How many, biji?'

'Give him two,' said the young man. He opened the case again and took out cotton, gauze, bandages, sulphanilamide and Mercurochrome. 'Here, just keep these.'

'Thank you, doctor' said Tan King. 'We need.'

'Yes, I can see that.'

'Doctor, do you have cucuk? So he can stand up and walk, lah.'

'You want me to give him an injection?' asked the young man.

'Yes. One shot and everything feel so nice!' Tan King laughed.

The young man prepared a shot of paracetamol. And a booster of Vitamin B. Some men crowded around to watch. He had to peer in the dark to squeeze the bubbles out of the syringe. As he was about to prick his young patient in the shoulder, Jūju, the other boy, cradled his head and stroked his forehead gently with a white towel that said 'Good Morning' in small red letters. It was a tender, adult-like gesture.

'See, making face! This boy so weak. Cannot take one cucuk! Want to shoot gun!' Tan King laughed again. The men around them joined in. 'This one strong, even with the bad kaki. But we cannot give him gun.' He pointed to Jūju. The young man noticed him properly now; even by the standards of forest dwellers, he looked particularly tatty. He missed a couple of front teeth and had longish matted hair. But he held onto his sick friend's hand with the sereneness of a caregiver. The young man realized they were brothers. They had identical faces and builds, save the bad leg.

'They are twins, aren't they?' he asked.

'You guess, is it? Yes. Born same time. But very different. When they were small, same-same. But after the mother die, this one become a little gila. We have to watch him, you know. But he never complain, never sick, so strong, can jump and run quickly. Ah, he can also move like snake!'

'Like snake?'

'Jūju, show doctor that one,' said Tan King gently. The boy lay down on his belly on the forest floor and slithered with amazing speed, circling the men. He used his good leg to propel his thin body forward. The sick boy watched his brother's antics and smiled.

'I know your grandfather,' said the young man.

'My grandfather ... the old man, is it?' he asked.

'Yes, quite old. He always has a picture of you with him. He came to see me one day.'

'Your friend?'

Before the young man could answer him, the slithering twin stood up and said, 'Hello, do-toh,' and formally extended his hand.

'What is your name?' the young man asked. Tan King laughed.

'His name Caoyin, but we all call him Jūju.' The others started laughing now. The boy walked away. 'You know what it means?' The young man shook his head. Tan King pointed to his crotch. 'It means pee-pee of the little boy. Jūju come back, lah.'

'Doctor, can you give us vitamin injection osso?' someone asked from the dark.

'Sorry, I just had enough for the boy.'

'Look, my foot here.' The man came forward and extended his leg. It was doughy near the ankle. He poked it with a finger and it hollowed inwards, making a small dimple. It was an obvious case of beriberi. The other men found this funny, and soon several of them did the same – exposing their distended joints, pinching and poking them.

'You come back again, doctor. We can pay you osso,' said one of the men.

The young man didn't know how to respond. 'I will try,' he said, getting up. He looked for his medicine bag.

'Okay, you go now,' said Tan King abruptly.

'Who will take me back?'

'Just follow him again,' he said, pointing to the guide.

Jūju walked up to him, limping slightly, 'Do-toh, I carry your bag can?'

'Give doctor his bag,' Tan King instructed the boy.

'Yes, Bóbo,' he said immediately.

'Are you the leader here?'

'Maybe.'

'Please let go of Mr Nag as you promised.' He looked at the ill boy lying on the forest floor, his body temporarily pacified by the painkiller.

'Yes, can. But one thing, doctor. You are smart man, correct? You don't talk with no other people, correct? We trust you because you are Wong's friend. Otherwise, cannot come here. Nobody ever come here before. Not even Wong.' Now Tan King looked like someone who could easily maim a person without thinking too much about it. What the young man had perceived as schoolboyish was the unconflicted gaze of a man whose mind had given impunity to his conscience.

As they started to walk away, one of the men said, 'Do you think we should punish your friend?'

'No, please do not punish him.' The young man felt nauseous.

'But what about all the bad things he has done? All the stealing? The police never punish him; the planters never punish him. So tell me, who will punish him?'

'He is already punished by now,' the young man said. 'Please let him go home to his family.'

After a pause, the man said, 'Okay. We will let him go. But maybe we punish him a little bit. Otherwise not fair, what?'

'No, please don't. He is old.'

'Old? Does an old man's life have more value than the young man's one? What about the boys he give to the Japanese for making the railway? Indian boys, Malay boys, Chinese ... all boys. He say to them, "Go to Thailand, lot of rice, you won't be hungry. Just makan-makan all day." The stupid boys followed him and then the Japanese send them far away to work as slaves. And then, only a few come back home. They were as thin as the hungry street dog.'

'He should not have done that,' said the young man. He wasn't sure why he was being told these details.

'Doctor, you think we hate you?'

'I don't know.'

'We have Indian people here in our camp, you know, and we treat everyone like the same way. How do you think your people will be treated now – when they are make a new country?' The young man didn't know. He didn't care to know. One of the other men said something in Cantonese, and the two spoke amongst themselves.

'Can I go now?' asked the young man.

'Go. But remember one simple thing: your friend cannot be seen by anyone till we get what we agree. He must hide in the house. Cannot go out. Cannot go to estate. If we see him, we will take him again and he will never return.'

'Yes, I will make sure of that,' the young man promised, anxious to end the strange outing. He was exhausted.

'Goodbye, do-toh!' shouted Jūju from the edge of the camp as they walked back into the jungle. They took a different route on the way back. When they emerged from the woods almost three hours later, the young man found himself on the other side of town. He realized that this was to ensure that he would not be able to trace the path back to the camp. The guide disappeared.

Maloti had stayed up. Soon after the young man had left the house, she lulled Sayang to sleep. Jonaki usually hovered around when it was his sister's bedtime. He liked listening to his mother sing these lullabies – soft, dulcet berceuses of love. But he sensed that Maloti's heart was not in her voice. She was distracted and seemed to recite the words, rather than evoke them.

'Don't stay up too late,' Maloti said softly, as Jonaki slipped out of the room.

'Ma?'

'What?'

'Where has Baba gone?' He was whispering.

'With Wong, to the clinic.'

'Why?'

'Because some extra medicine was delivered this evening,' said Maloti abruptly. Jonaki didn't believe her, but sensed that his mother was lying to him because she had to.

After Sayang fell asleep, Maloti went to the veranda. She spent the next five hours pacing, occasionally checking in on the baby. When the young man eventually returned in the dark of night, he found her asleep on the steps. He shook her gently. Maloti opened her eyes and took his hand. They went in and turned on the light in the living room. She screamed. The young man's face was caked with blood; he had forgotten his encounter with the tree branch. He put his arms around her and whispered, 'It's all right, it's all right ...' several times.

'What do you mean by that? What happened to you?' she asked, stifling her voice. 'And why are you wet?'

'It's just the blood from a small cut. Really. Take me to your kitchen sink so I can wash it off.' They walked through the dining room and down the short steps to the kitchen. The young man turned on the faucet and splashed water on his face. As the crust peeled, he felt the sting of the wound. He opened his medicine case only to realize that he had left the Mercurochrome at the camp. He wandered into the bathroom and dabbed some Old Spice onto the wound. Maloti waited for him, sitting anxiously the bed. When he slid in under the mosquito net, she clutched his arm.

'I was alone with my thoughts for hours. And I grew afraid that I had made a terrible mistake,' she sobbed.

'It was the right thing to do,' said the young man soothingly.

'Was it? Will they let Nag-babu go now?'

'They promised.'

'You were right ... We need to think of ourselves now. Just us. But thank god he is safe.'

'Yes, everything went well,' said the young man. 'But there was a boy there. About fifteen, maybe less. I can't forget his sad face.'

'Why was he sad?'

'He was very sick – a high fever. As I was giving him a shot, he just looked at me with large, hopeless eyes. Like he didn't know who he was any more.'

'Why do they send such small boys there?' said Maloti. 'How can their mothers let them go? You always say that this country is richer than ours. Why can't they find a way to live ... like the people I see in the market or in the shops every day.'

'He doesn't have parents. He had a twin brother there who takes care of him. That's his only surviving family.'

'What happened to their father and mother?'

'I was told that the Japanese killed them. Or maybe the British. I don't remember.'

'Why do you smell of aftershave?'

'Never mind.'

Nag was thrown in the back of a van the following evening. He lay curled up and silent on the hard floor as the vehicle sped along rough back roads, wondering where he was being taken. The driver and a second man began arguing. The van stopped. Nag raised his head stealthily and saw the driver pointing to some lights about a quarter of a mile away. It looked like a roadblock.

The driver swerved the vehicle around and drove back in the direction they had come from. The other man started yelling. The driver stopped on the side of the road. It was pitch dark without the van lights. The two men got out. One of them opened the back of the vehicle. They pulled Nag out by his feet and he tumbled to the ground. As they untied him, Nag noticed a rifle. He stood up shakily.

'You go.' They pointed in the direction of the rubber trees. Even in the dark, Nag could make out exactly where they were. It was a long way from the town, in a deserted spot between two wayside kampongs. Nag was familiar with scenarios like this – people being shot in the back as they ran away. He had witnessed one himself. He assessed that his only chance of survival was if he managed to get the gun. He got on his knees and began to thank the two men profusely. A minute into it, one of them said, 'Okay, okay, cukup ... Yes, yes, thank you. Now you just go.' But Nag continued with his grovelling. The man with the gun walked up to him and said, 'You go now! Go!'

Nag leapt up and lunged for the gun. But his movement was poorly timed and he fell to the ground, several feet short. The man shouted, first in surprise and then in anger. He slammed the hard, wooden butt into Nag's back. He did it again.

'Bodoh! Bodoh!' he yelled. 'We let you go home already. Idiot, bodoh, stupid!' They got in to the van and drove away.

Nag lost consciousness. When he came to, he felt excruciating pain. But he was able to get on his feet and stagger forward. He did this for about an hour, falling down several times, till he came to the part of the road where they had seen lights. But as he drew closer, he realized that the bright lights were not from a roadblock—they were safety beams, illuminating a railway crossing. He followed the railway tracks.

An hour later, his back had swollen so much that it was becoming impossible for him to stay on his feet. He began crawling on all fours, following the tracks. He approached the town at dawn. With difficulty, he managed to lift himself up onto his feet again. A group of street dogs surrounded him. They followed him, escorting him home. They left as he turned onto the lane near his house.

Leela woke up to the sensation of persistent thuds reverberating through the house. She knew instantly it was her husband.

'Leela ... I am here. Leela ...' cried Nag. She opened the door and Nag stumbled in. He lay on the floor, curled up and whimpering. He looked ten kilograms thinner; his eyes were bloodshot and sunken. He smelt of the forest and faeces.

When Ganesh visited the house three days later, Nag was still discombobulated from his days and nights in the wilderness, where he had been blindfolded and tied up against a tree. He had a raging fever and spoke hoarsely. While Leela spoon-fed him soft, boiled fish with rice, he divulged all the information he had – including the upcoming arrangements for the next pickup of the money. Ganesh paid attention and took laborious, detailed notes, like the schoolboy he had never been. The details could free him from a life of debt bondage.

It was late the following evening, just as O'Brien was alighting from his jeep at his bungalow, when Ganesh approached him.

'Who is it there? What do you want?' he said peering into the fading light.

'Sergeant, I have some information for you.'

Ganesh leaned his bicycle against a tree and adjusted his collar. He had a deal to strike.

O'Brien was captivated by the local man's incredible tale of surveillance. He listened to every word, making Ganesh repeat himself several times. With advance information of this nature, there was time to strategize a foolproof ambush plan. The 7th Gurkha Rifles could be brought in to supplement his constabulary. Hell, thought O'Brien, could he perhaps even request a Dragonfly Chopper for backup? He would snare his guerrillas finally. The jungle would give up its last secret, Tan King with it. All this would play out in the presence of top-calibre journalists. Maybe he'd even get his picture in a magazine back home.

In the days following his strange medical mission to the forest, the young man tried to focus on the challenges of his extended workday. He had done his good deed for Nag. And while that did provide relief and a sense of vindication, he remained distracted. He had inadvertently stumbled upon another world and now it was difficult for him to reconcile with his surroundings. It seemed almost absurd that the highly systematized extraction of rubber, made possible because of cogs like himself, existed alongside what he had seen a few nights ago. The perfectly manicured, vast golf course he drove by every morning was a constant reminder of that startling discrepancy. While the small town prepared itself for independence and everyone went about as though the dark days were behind them, there existed, right at that very moment, people in the forests, not too far away, clinging to a fading dream of a nation that was not to be. The young man had seen them with his own eyes; a tribe that had refused to accept whatever status quo everyone else seemed to have made their peace with. He had expected hostility, but had encountered gaunt looks with flickers of a receding pride. There was a screaming fault line in the aspirations of the new country and yet, it was hidden from view. He found himself unable to judge the situation, locate its moral centre. While Milne seemed like a decent enough man, it was indisputable that the system he represented had subjugated entire races for aeons. The young man knew how brutally violent the British were capable of being, how they could lash out with tight-lipped sanctimony when threatened with irrelevance, or worse, dwindling profits. But he had heard of the killings perpetrated by the communists in Malaya – by Wong's extended ilk, the likes of Tan King and his swiftly deflating band of guerrillas. He could not rid his mind of the image of the severed fingers strewn around the dying British planter in the story that Murray had told him. Both parties were historically brutal. Perhaps the answer lay in gauging whose violence was more forgivable. No land was ever given or taken honestly.

Leela called the young man a few days after Nag's return. An acknowledgement of gratitude was in order. While he had been expecting to hear from her, he was uncomfortable.

'I know we cannot keep bothering you,' said Leela. She realized that brevity was necessary.

'Health alright?' asked the young man, concerned that Nag might have been physically attacked.

'Yes, thank the lord. Health is alright now,' said Leela, her voice cracking. She did not let on that Nag had lost weight and had suffered deep bruises on his back, hands and face.

'Good, good, Leela-di. You know you can dial me if you need to.'

'We know. I don't let anyone in the house these days. I can't as you know … I told the servant girl to return to her kampong for a while.'

'I must go now,' said the young man abruptly. He had caught Milne staring at him. He hung up the phone and looked away.

'You seem a bit down, Sengoopta. Is it the … Naag business?'

'Oh, no. Just need to catch up on things.' He picked up some papers.

'Yes. We appreciate that it's been hardest on you probably, this whole mess.'

'Not to worry,' said the young man uncomfortably.

'Listen, I want to apologize for the other day.'

'Other day?'

'Yes. We're all a bit on edge, but I might have overstepped my role there.'

'All is forgotten,' said the young man and left the office in a hurry. He kept his interactions with Milne to a minimum. The relevance of office politics was receding in light of his larger, complex plans.

That evening, he struggled to stay awake at Murray's desk. There had been a crisis in the estate earlier; a lorry had backed into a tapper. Fortunately, the man had survived, dislocating only a knee. The young man did not get time for his crucial afternoon nap that day. He went straight to the clinic, where there was a long line of people waiting. When he saw the last patient, it was close to nine. Wong walked into the room to refrigerate some medicine. They had avoided talking about the forest, other than quick nods to indicate that matters were generally under control.

'Wong ... I can't help asking you ... Those young boys the other night. How are they?'

'I did not hear anything about them.'

'Sorry, I just assume that you know everything about what goes on. You know, there were the teenaged boys ... the twins.'

Wong interrupted. 'Yes, of course. I know one is sick and you took care of him.'

'Oh, I don't think I did much for them. They should be in a hospital,' said the young man, getting up to leave.

'Cannot hospital,' said Wong, shaking his head as he left the room. But a few moments later, he returned. 'Actually, there is someone to see you.' The grandfather to the twins walked in. He shuffled up to the young man and took his hands.

'There is no need of this please,' said the young man, realizing that the man had just slipped him a twenty-dollar bill. The old man looked at him with teary, grateful eyes.

'How old are you?' asked the young man. Wong translated his question. The old man showed him seven fingers and then five.

'He's exactly my father's age. Is his wife still alive?'

The old man understood. He shook his head and pointed upward.

'My mother died too,' said the young man. 'Wong, tell him that his grandsons are doing well.'

The man bowed and left.

As the young man was about to exit the building, Zainun came up to him. 'I forgot to say you something.'

'Yes, Zainun? Say me.'

'Before you come this evening, after Dr Murray go, when there was no one here, someone came here.'

'Who?'

'I was doing my work in the backside of the clinic and did not see. There was a funny smell. Then I heard sound and so I went to your room and I say, "Hey, why you in here? Cannot till doctor is here." And then he go away.'

'Smell?'

'Yes, like smoke.'

'Who was it?'

Zainun looked unsure. 'I don't know. But I think it was the bomoh, the one they are calling Tok Modin. He went away very quickly.'

'The bomoh? For how long was he in the chamber?'

'I don't know. Maybe five–ten minute something.'

'Doing what?'

'I don't know, but I think you should check everything nicely.'

'Check for what?' asked the young man puzzled.

'I don't know.'

He went back to the inspection room and turned the light back on. He looked around carefully. Nothing seemed amiss.

When the young man reached home, he found Jonaki asleep on the sofa. His body covered most of it, his arms dangled off the side. Wisps of hair had begun to sprout on his upper lip. The young man realized that he had started to resemble Nirupoma. Maloti was asleep too, in the bedroom, next to Sayang. The young man went to the kitchen and foraged clumsily for food. He tried to pry an unidentified bowl out from the meat safe, but its lid slipped and crashed onto the floor. As he started to pick up the pieces, Maloti came rushing with a broom. The young man looked up sheepishly.

'Oh, it's you. I thought it was a cat,' said Maloti.

'Meow.'

Maloti laughed. 'Are you drunk?'

'No, but I feel like I am. I'm tired.'

'Sit down.'

'What are all those packets of rice and dal and whatnot for?' asked the young man when Maloti opened the refrigerator.

'Those are for Leela-di.'

'You send her food?

'Yes. Every other day.'

'Who takes the food there?'

'I had asked Amma to, but it seems that Ganesh delivers it.'

'Ganesh goes to Nag-babu's house?'

'Isn't that nice of him?'

'No one tells me anything these days,' the young man grumbled, sitting down to eat.

'I think you're the one keeping the secrets, Sengupta-babu' said Maloti.

'Yes. Maybe so. It's for your own good. Send them more food now.'

'I know.'

'You know? What do you know? How did you know?'

'Ganesh told Amma, Amma told me.'

'Ganesh was right. Indians cannot keep secrets. Doesn't matter who they are. Bengali, Tamil, doctors, housewives, bloody tappers ... gossip makes our worlds go around. I suppose Nag-babu will start walking down Main Road tomorrow. I'm not going to save him again.'

'You don't need to save anyone any more,' said Maloti. 'Are you angry that I sent food to Leela-di?'

'You're a village girl. You just can't bear to think of people not eating. You almost starved to death once yourself.' The young man stopped speaking.

'Please eat. You look very tired.'

He nodded. He could hear Jonaki from the living room.

'Why does your entire clan snore?'

The young man did not anticipate that he would return to the forest. But it was to happen just four days later. Despite his best efforts to distance himself from the Nag debacle, one image kept tormenting him – the quivering, malarial boy. He wondered if the others at the camp – the men – had taken away his paracetamol. Dengue unchecked could lead to haemorrhagic fevers, and if it did, he would have to fight an uphill battle to stay alive in those conditions. He asked Wong if he would be able to send them some more medicine.

'Later, later,' said Wong gruffly.

They planned to meet at the train station, an hour after shutting down the clinic. It was almost pitch dark, but the freshly laid, white stones chips on the tracks helped outline the lone, long bench on the platform. The young man spotted Wong's silhouette; he had come to recognize his lay-clothing and hurried gait by now. Wong had brought a companion. The two men down sat a few feet away, at the end of the bench. The companion lit a match and the young man caught a glimpse of his face. He looked familiar; many people in the town did now.

'You know, doctor?' the man asked.

'Know what?'

'You know me?'

'I am not sure.'

'But I know you. Better this way.' He laughed.

'Who are you?' asked the young man.

'Wong told me that you have some questions. So, he ask you to meet me. Easier this way. Or else, Wong have to go come and go come and go.'

'All right. Yes. I just wanted to know something.'

'I can answer simple question. Perhaps yes. But perhaps no. No guarantee, no?'

Wong said something to him in Cantonese. The man turned, his glowing cigarette moving with his face.

'Ah. Yes ... those boys. You want the boy to become strong.'

'Yes. I want to help him.'

'Yes, yes. So, one of them is unfortunately sick. Quite sick. See, I am speaking the good-good English now. *Quite* sick. Means he is very sick, no?' The man laughed. 'Other one, the one with bad leg, okay, lah. But this one fella, he just screaming and saying rubbish. I hear he has fever and he wants to go home. Like that. *Quite* sick.'

'So why don't you send him home? You don't want him to die, do you?'

'He won't die. Is it so easy to die? But we will send him away soon.'

'When? He needs to get out of those jungles right now. Do you know what could happen to him there?'

The man said something to Wong, a short sentence punctuated with a chuckle.

'It's not funny, mister,' said the young man angrily.

'No, not funny. But it is like an army, my doctor. There are rules. Do you think any army just let a soldier go if he has a fever and cries?'

'He's not a soldier! He's a child. And armies have doctors to help. He's starving in the forest.'

'Okay. You be army doctor, then.'

'Me? What do you want me to do? I can send some medicine.'

'Did the grandfather not pay you? Haha! Now you are a collaborator!'

'No. I just want the boy to live. He can really die over there if he is so sick. And his grandfather keeps asking me about them.'

'Okay. Then you come back to camp. Army doctor.'

'I don't need to go. Wong can handle this perfectly well.' He could not see Wong's face in the dark.

The glowing cigarette moved. 'Your friends say it is all ready to go now. So you just bring it again and check your favourite baby soldiers. Easy, no? Or we make sure the grandfather don't bother you any more.'

'What is it? What is ready to go now?'

'Doctor, doctor, haiya. Do I have to say everything?' The man laughed again. 'Actually, the men happy to see you. They always asking if you return. So, bring your bag again also. Can? We drop the money to you. And then you bring it to us like the last time.'

'Do you know where I live?' asked the young man.

'Of course, everyone know where you live. Left and then right, and then left-left, and then small road, and then big gate, and then kuini tree on left, then steps up, then veranda with fuse light, and then your yellow door with bad handle. Then just masuk. Dining room, go right your room, go left small boy's room, then got the prayer room, correct?'

'How do you know the handle is broken?' asked the young man, uneasily.

'Because I have been inside your house. You want me to tell you what is inside osso? You want me to tell you where you keep your small knife?'

'No.' He was trying not to tremble.

'Don't be frightened, doctor. We protecting you. Just make sure nobody can know. I will send someone like last time. No one can know, correct? And then you don't have to be scared, correct?'

'No one will know.'

'Good. All okay then. Here, take a cigarette please.'

'No. Thank you.'

'Come on, lah, doctor, we are friends now.' He extended his arm. The young man took the cigarette. The man leaned in and lit it for him. It had the same odour of cheap tobacco he had smelt at the camp.

'Good. Now, everything is okay. One last thing, doctor. I feel so stupid, but can I show you something?'

'Yes?'

The man mumbled something in Cantonese. Wong sighed, then stood up and turned his torchlight on. The man unbuckled his pants and dropped them.

'Sorry, aah? But I have a boil down here ... Can see or not?'

The young man leaned in for a closer look at his groin. Wong adjusted the light, as he did at the clinic. The man's nether region reeked.

'Yes. I will bring some medicine for you. I'll tell Wong what to do.'

'Ah. Good, good. So much pain when I kencing. And I cannot even do that thing any more! No fun for me.'

'You shouldn't have intercourse with your wife.'

'Haha, who got wife? If have wife, then I don't get like this!' The man laughed again. Wong cut the light. 'See you, doctor. You orang baik. Maybe you don't believe me, but we are also orang baik. We same-same, lah. We have to do these things in life, no? You know why?'

'Why?'

'Come, I sing you a song. In Chinese. Then Wong tell you the words. His English so good, he study in the Jesus school.' The man started singing as he buckled his pants – lines resembling a rhythmic but tuneless military marching song. When he was done, he laughed and looked at Wong, who translated haltingly:

'I love my Malaya. Malaya is my home
During the Japanese occupation, we were not free.
Now we are in more misery
Who knew when the dogs had gone, the monkeys would
return,
And turn Malaya into a bitter sea
Oh, my brothers, my sisters. We can wait no more
Oh, my … companions, let us all stand up.
We cannot wait no more.'

The man grinned. 'Nice, what, doctor!'

'Yes. Nice.'

'You understood it? The dogs are the Japanese and the
monkeys…?'

'The British?'

'Yes! And they return now. Flag come up. Still don't go away.
They will be here for years and years from now. You will see.
Selamat malam, doctor.'

The young man walked home, perspiring heavily. Later that
night, a few thick envelopes were slid in through a pried open
living room window. Nag had managed his last payment.

The young man came down with a fever the following morning
and was unable to go to work. This delighted Maloti. She
instructed him to remain in bed, in his pyjamas. After Jonaki
had gone to school and Amma had left for the market, she made
him a breakfast of a light dal, his favourite okra curry, and some
chapatis glazed with a hint of ghee. 'But I am sick …' the young
man protested as she brought the food to him on a tray.

She felt his forehead. 'You are not that sick.'

'You almost seem disappointed. The mysteries of women,'
mumbled the young man, tearing the bread.

'Why am I a mystery? Have I not always been clear?' asked Maloti playfully.

'Yes. Very clear. I wish you were less clear.'

'Now eat and I'll watch you. I haven't even seen you properly in many days. You've been busy helping goondas.'

'I have to go out tonight. So it's just as well that I stay home and rest,' said the young man, spilling some watery dal on the bed.

'No clinic tonight for you. You should stay home.'

'No. The jungle.'

'The jungle again? Why? I thought you said that it was just one time. Who told you to go?'

'I think I talked myself into this somehow.'

'No,' said Maloti sharply. 'You will not go.'

'I have to now. And you're the one who insisted in the first place,' reasoned the young man defensively.

'I did. But not any more. Why do you need to go anyway? What do they want?'

The young man sat up. 'Remember the boys I told you about?' Maloti nodded. 'One of them is still very ill. So I said I would take some medicine to him. And others wanted me to visit too.'

'Why you? Why can't Wong do this?'

'I don't know. I suggested that. They want to be my friend. I think they like me.'

'I thought you said this wasn't our country.'

'Yes, but I also said that countries don't matter. Do you want to come along?'

'Never!'

The young man laughed. 'Why? You might enjoy it all. It's very romantic – roaming the forest with knives and pots, cooking tapioca, sleeping under the stars and bathing in the stream.'

'I would grab those boys by their necks and bring them all back.'

'And what if they indoctrinate Jonaki with their rebel ways?'

'Well, they seem to have indoctrinated you. Why do you have to start all this now? Your time for being a revolutionary is over. You are an old man now. Are you going to start printing pamphlets again?'

The young man laughed. 'But just the other day, it was you who demanded that I do this! You said I needed to find my soul and heart and ... a spirit came inside our house and whatnot. Do you remember what happened? And I am not an old man.'

'As you just said, women are mysterious. And, yes, you are an old man.'

'I gave them my word. It won't be long. Old man out at midnight, young man back by morning.' Maloti shook her head.

'What? Why are you crying now? What has gotten into you?' asked the young man. Maloti held her head between her hands.

The young man drew her close. 'Nothing will happen to me. I've been there before, to their camp. If those people had intentions of harming me, they would have done it by now. As long as Nag doesn't short-change them, it will all be fine. I'm just a bit worried about those twins.'

Maloti nodded. 'Be careful.'

'I will.'

'How ill are you feeling now?' she asked, askance.

'I don't feel ill. Why?'

Maloti turned to him and smiled. She ran her fingers through a tuft of his hair. The young man laughed. 'Don't you have pujo later today? Aren't you worried about our ... purity?' He grabbed her arm.

'Can you think of much else that is purer?' she demurred.

'Come here, my old man.'

The smell of Muttuswamy's joss sticks wafted through the house. On Thursday evenings, Maloti typically conducted Lokkhi Pujo.

It was a small affair – flowers from the garden, three or four kinds of fresh fruit as offering and a sonorous prayer, recited for about twenty minutes. She knew the lines by rote; the ritual had trailed her from her childhood in the village to the home in Calcutta, and now here, across the seas. Maloti lit the oil lamp in her makeshift prayer area. A weak, yellow light filled the room. Jonaki's eyes were drawn to the grey figurine of the goddess. There was an all-knowing sanctimoniousness about her that unsettled him. He sat behind Maloti and the young man, and chanted along in a hoarse, adolescent voice. Sayang rolled around on the floor and cooed. When the short ritual was over, Maloti picked up a wedge of apple and touched it to the young man's forehead. He took her arm lightly, shutting his eyes. She fed him the fruit. Although the display of affection was legitimized by piety, Jonaki turned his eyes away. After he had received his share of fruit, he bounded out of the room like a caged animal just released. He wouldn't have to encounter the all-knowing goddess for another week.

'Did you know that it is a full moon tonight?' asked Maloti.

'Really? Did you read that in your almanac?' The young man pointed to a small, battered book resting beside Lokkhi.

'No. I looked up at the sky.'

'It's a sign then. An auspicious day,' said the young man. 'Did you ask her to guide me and keep me safe?' He pointed at the goddess.

'You shouldn't point like that. Yes, of course I did.'

'I talked to her too.'

'Oh? And what did you tell her?' asked Maloti.

'I told her I would never do what I did to you the other night again.'

Maloti felt embarrassed. 'We're not Christians; you don't have to confess everything to her.'

'Then how would she know?'

'She understands without being told.'

'Do you?' asked the young man gently.

'Yes.'

The young man walked out of the house a little after midnight. Someone was waiting in the street again, just yards away from the gate. 'Be safe,' Maloti mouthed from the porch. The young man pointed to the sky and they both looked up. The luminous full moon fell upon them. Maloti remained at the door long after he was out of sight.

As they entered the forest, the young man realized that he was still wearing his rubber slippers. To make matters worse, the strap kept snapping off. Unlike the previous trip, the guide tonight was talkative and helpful. He walked alongside the young man, at times moving ahead, to cut foliage out of his way. When they startled a large group of flying, screeching creatures, he said, 'Kelawar, doctor' and grinned. The young man took in the flurry around them and realized that they had scared a colony of bats. Soon, they came to the stream. The young man had wrapped Nag's money in plastic. He felt something swim past his legs as he trudged through the water and slush.

They approached the clearing in the forest around three in the morning. The young man could make out the campsite from a distance. But there was something amiss. As they drew closer, he realized that it was eerily silent.

'Where all go?' said the guide, puzzled. There was no one there. And yet, it did not seem uninhabited. The young man noticed a kettle on a low, wooden stove. He touched its side. It was still warm. And that familiar smell of cheap tobacco lingered in the air. They walked around silently. It was all there – clothes, bedding, some books, knives, utensils.

'I think we should go back,' said the young man. The guide nodded.

'But where, lah?' he repeated, looking around, confused. 'Maybe they leave this area. Okay, come; we go from that way now,' he pointed, walking towards a clearing. But they had barely gone a hundred yards when a voice shouted, 'D-O-K-T-O-R ... D-O-K-T-O-O-O-R ...' Someone was running towards them. The young man could make out that it was Tan King. He was shirtless. His thin frame drew attention to his potbelly. When he drew closer, it became apparent that he was drenched in sweat.

'Sit, sit,' he said, gasping for breath, pointing to a large tree stump in the middle of the clearing. The young man looked past him and noticed about two-dozen men – the rest of the group. They were walking slowly, almost noiselessly.

'Where did you all go at this hour?' asked the young man.

'No problem. No problem. We had some meeting.' The guide spoke to Tan King in Cantonese. They looked at the young man and then at his medicine bag.

'Yes, I brought the rest of the money, of course,' said the young man. He spoke calmly. Unlike his previous visit, he was not anxious this time.

'Yes, yes. We know. No problem with money. Sit, sit.' He shouted to someone who picked up the kettle. The others gathered around. They were silent. They seemed to have been interrupted. The young man noticed that the men were all shirtless and sweating. Two of them were carrying shovels. The young man saw Jūju.

'Hello, mister, how are you?' he asked. The boy remained silent.

'Haha. He don't know English,' said one of the men in the circle.

'My English more good than your busuk English,' snarled the boy, picking up a shovel menacingly. The man yelled at him.

'How is your brother?' asked the young man. 'Is he feeling better?'

The boy looked at the leader. Some men turned away. 'Actually, he is not here,' said Tan King.

'Not here? Did you send him to a hospital?'

'No. He went away.'

'He went away? By himself?'

'Yes. Himself go away.'

'Did he run away? When?'

'Just now.'

'Just now?' repeated the young man, perplexed. He looked around, but no one offered an answer.

'Come, we have some tea.' Tan King motioned the cook to put down the cups. They young man opened the medicine case to pull out the envelopes. And then Jūju started screaming in Cantonese. He went on for a full minute till a short, bald man rushed over and smacked him on the head. He grabbed him by the front of his tattered shirt, but the boy pried himself away, kicking him with his good leg.

'No more already, do-toh!' Jūju screamed and hobbled quickly towards the thick of the forest. A couple of men went chasing after him. 'Jūju, where you hide the gun!'

'What happened to his brother?' asked the young man, his chest tightening.

'Sudah mati. Dead already.' Tan King spoke slowly.

'What?'

'Ayo. He was sick. He began to talk loud in his sleep and disturb everyone. He want to go home. Crying and shouting, crying and shouting...'

'Why did you not take him somewhere?' exclaimed the young man.

'Ya, ya. My fault, is it? Maybe you should have come back.'

'I said many, many times that he needed to be taken away from here,' shouted the young man. 'When did he die? How did he die? Did you kill him?'

'No, no, no. Why we kill him? Are we orang gila? When he was angry and had high fever, he shouted one or two times, "I will do that ... then you will see", you know, with the rope. But we just laughed at him. Everybody laugh at him, right? We called him silly boy. We say, "Look your monkey brother, so strong." ... All these things, you know.' Tan King spoke matter-of-factly.

'When did this happen?' asked the young man.

'Tonight.'

'He was alive till tonight?'

'Yes. Just now alive. Maybe one–two hour now.'

'Are you sure he is dead? Can I see him?'

'Yes. We thought he going to the bathroom because stomach bad all the time. But he did not return for long time.'

'Who found him?'

'Jūju.'

'Oh god. Are you sure he's dead?'

'Come, we show you'

They walked in the direction the boy had run towards. Fifty yards on, the young man saw the body, limned by moonlight, hanging from a low branch at the edge of the clearing.

'Yes, dead,' the guide announced, walking right up to it.

The perspiring men, the meeting away from the camp, and the shovels – all of it made sense now. 'So, you were digging a grave?' asked the young man.

'Yes.'

'Will you inform anyone?'

'Who to inform, doctor? No father, no mother. Come, we must take him down.'

Two men climbed the tree and attempted to untangle the rope that was tethered to the high branch. But the deceased youth, skilled with years of guerrilla training, had done a thorough job. So they gave up and started cutting through it. Jūju watched intently, without expression. No one paid much attention to him. When the body fell with a soft thud, a few men rushed forward. The eyes were still open, hauntingly expressive. A couple of the men dragged the body by the arm. 'Maybe you take this one back to the grandfather,' Tan King said, pointing to Jūju.

They slid the body down into the freshly dug pit. It wasn't a neat rectangle, but an odd gape in the earth, studded with large rocks lodged too deeply to dig out. The body had to be curled into a foetal position to fit it into the space. After some manoeuvring, they could not properly fit it in and one of the men leaned in and cracked a leg, then folded it over the body. They packed in the soil and debris with shovels and with their feet. Jūju circled the plot, occasionally cupping some dirt with his bare hands and throwing it in. Then he suddenly yelled for the men to stop. He ran to the campsite and returned clutching something. Everyone watched as he scooped some of the dirt away till the tattered, white shirt of his brother was visible again.

'What is that?' asked Tan King gently.

'Nothing. It's my one.'

'Show me, Jūju...'

The boy brought over the small, square piece of paper he was clutching. The young man leaned in. It was a photograph of the two of them as children, about five or six, arms circled tightly around each other. Tan King nodded and the boy went over to the pit, folded the 'Good Morning' towel around it, and tucked it under his brother's shirt. The men stomped over the closed pit to flatten out the site and then they arranged themselves in even rows. The young man moved aside. 'You know the "Yīngdénàxióngnǎ'ěr" song?' Tan King asked the young man. He shook his head and moved aside. The group began singing, hand on chest, in surprising harmony.

The young man realized he recognized the tune, even though it was being sung in Chinese. It was 'The Internationale'. The sight of the mangy, weathered men, singing in the middle of the forest in the moonlight, for a lost child, moved him. He joined in the chorus, humming softly. It tapped into an old well of regrets buried deep within him and he started to sob. One of the men looked at him and smiled. The boy didn't sing along. He was without expression, without tears, watching everyone. The stars were dimming now and a pink hue streaked the sky.

The loud rat-a-tat sequence of Bren gunfire shattered the dawn. The group stopped singing mid-syllable and, an instant later, scattered as fast as they could – men of all ages darted in panic for their lives. It was not till the young man saw the bullets spitting on the dirt that he realized that they were being shot at. There were shouts from every direction, volleys of gunfire, and then the sudden explosion of a grenade, followed by people screaming.

'I got him, I got him!' The young man could make out a figure in fatigues, pushing Tan King in front of him, an enormous Alsatian at his heels. A photographer trailed them. A flashbulb went off. 'I promised I wouldn't shoot anyone. Got a good, good picture, right? Me, my dog and the bloody bandit?'

'Do-toh, mister Do-toh!' a voice hissed. The young man turned around and noticed Jūju about twenty meters away, slithering away on his belly. Confused, he ran towards him. The shouts and barks continued, as they entered an empty hut. No one seemed to have noticed them.

The young man peered through a slat in the straw front. Tan King was in the middle of the quad, next to the broad tree stump. O'Brien stood behind him with a rifle. Several other policemen with raised guns stood a few feet away, covering him. 'Kneel!' he barked. Tan King got down slowly. 'And you, put that camera away.' A moment later, a woman came running out from one of the huts and threw herself at the police chief's feet. Tan King looked at her and then expressionlessly ahead, resigned to the situation. The shots continued in the dark as the squads chased men at the periphery of the camp and shepherded them into the central quad where they were made to kneel, hands on head. The woman continued wailing, but O'Brien barely looked at her. He kept glancing around, his gun trained on Tan King. He picked up a megaphone with his free hand. 'Surrender! Or I shoot him!' The gunshots petered out. The forest was silent again. Tan King shouted out something in Cantonese. 'Shut up!' screamed O'Brien. The young man heard laboured breathing and saw the boy in a corner of the hut, crouching. It took him a moment to realize what he was doing. Jūju was taking aim.

'No-no-no!' implored the young man. The boy didn't flinch, keeping his eye on the crosshairs. The young man looked at the clearing and saw one of the policemen approaching, clutching a wide, flaming torch.

'Let's light up this place and get out!' yelled O'Brien. The man ran to the first attap hut. The straw went up in flames within moments and a thick cloud of smoke filled the area. Four women came out coughing and howling. He went down the row, setting alight the huts, one by one, as people emerged wailing and running – teenaged girls in pyjamas, women in sarongs, two older men, a toddler.

Jūju said, 'Shoot, Bóbo,' and then mumbled something in Cantonese.

'No, they won't shoot him. Come on! We must get out!' hissed the young man. The boy didn't flinch. He kept his eye on the target. The young man saw the man with the torch approach their hut. He looked to his left and saw the boy squint, taking aim.

'Don't shoot! Donshoot-donshoot-donshoot!' shouted the young man and ran out, with his arms up. 'Donshoot!'

'What the hell!' exclaimed O'Brien, startled. 'Aren't you that clerk who works as a nurse in town?' The policemen lowered their guns.

'Yes, yes,' said the young man, panting. 'Don't shoot. Please. And don't bomb that hut.'

'Not to worry, not to worry. You're safe with us,' said O'Brien, still pointing his gun at Tan King. 'Just go on to where those people are; they're my men. What are you doing here, anyway?' He turned to the hut. 'Go on then, light that last one!'

'No!' the young man screamed.

'What? What are you going on about?'

'There's a boy in there.'

'What do you say? Someone still in there?'

'Yes … just a boy. He's scared. But he'll come out.'

'Bloody CT in there!' screamed O'Brien. The man moved away from the hut. Things were still for a moment, except for the sound of the roaring fires.

Tan King looked up and yelled in Cantonese. No one emerged.

'Torch it! That's an order,' bellowed O'Brien, pushing Tan King down with the butt of his gun.

The young man ran towards the hut as the soldier started lighting it.

'Hey you, stop goddammit!' shouted O'Brien.

The young man entered the smoking hut. He heard the boy cough. Somewhere. He waited for the boy to cough again. There was no more. The young man held his breath and thrashed his arms around the small room hoping to find the boy. He finally ran out gasping, his eyes streaming.

'Come here, nurse,' shouted O'Brien. 'What the bloody hell is going on with you?'

The young man walked towards him slowly. He noticed Tan King watching him from his low, kneeling position, without expression. As he tried to catch his eye, he realized that Tan King was looking at something else, something past him. The young man looked to his right and saw it. A swift, slippery movement, like an iguana's, circumventing everyone, stealthily making its way to O'Brien, approaching from the rear. The young man slowed down his gait, trying to buy time. It seemed as though

O'Brien was waiting for him to be out of the way before making his next move.

No one else noticed the nozzle of the gun lift slowly through the grass. It was about a hundred yards between the young man and where Jūju lay concealed. He decided to make a run for it – a clumsy, flailing run, right past O'Brien, who was too startled to react. The young man screamed out a breathless, 'No!' as he approached the boy and stumbled in front of him. Jūju got up slowly, leaving his gun on the forest floor, a disgusted expression on his face. He stared at O'Brien defiantly, his plan now foiled.

O'Brien, realizing what had almost happened, growled, 'The little bastard! Oh, you're done for, you thug.' He took aim.

'Officer, you can't do that!' the young man yelled back, getting up on his feet.

'Just watch me.'

'I'll report this.'

'Who the hell would believe *you*? That bastard almost shot me. Now move! Move! Move!'

Jūju had both hands on his hips. The young man considered shielding him, but remained immobile. He was paralyzed with fear. They were both facing O'Brien, who was about forty metres away, nozzle in air. One could see the whites of his eyes. The young man looked at Jūju – a fourteen-year-old ragamuffin staring down the barrel of Empire. A feeling of utter admiration enveloped him and he regretted sabotaging the boy's one mission. He had never been as patriotic, as decisive, as sure of his beliefs as this child in front of him. He finally found his voice again and said, 'I beg you, sir, please. He's still young. Let him live.'

A distant whir distracted everyone. Within moments, the sound of a loud helicopter cut through the dawn. It appeared seconds later, enormous over the tress, silhouetted against the soft light. The young man felt the rotor wind on his face as the tall grass parted. It grew into a deafening roar. A man with a camera jutted out from it. The helicopter was now hovering right above where the young man and Jūju were standing. The boy kept staring, transfixed by the enormity of it.

O'Brien pulled the trigger. He missed.

Swift, lucid images flashed as the young man's consciousness dimmed. They were not of the endearing moments from his short life – not of that evening he had seen Nirupoma sing in the village, not of Jonaki's childhood antics. He did not glimpse his happier days with the pamphleteers or see the face or body of the slight village girl he had once saved from jumping off the terrace. They weren't of the horrors either – of the burning house where people dear to him had gone up in flames or of the cold and numbness he had felt upon reading about his wife's death. In his last moments, he was a shrieking child of five again, bounding down the stairs, his mother hollering after him. He darted into the kitchen and looked for a place to hide. Mother yelled again, her voice now just one floor above. He felt his heart pounding. The old cook pointed to the corner with her ladle, where the door formed a triangular wedge with the wall.

'Can I hide in there?'

'Yes.'

He saw a small boy hug his knees, tucking himself into the corner. All that the boy heard now was the crackle of fish frying.

'Do you want some?'

The boy nodded. The old cook in the dank white saree deftly edged out two small pieces with her ladle and dropped them onto a newspaper. The boy watched the paper absorb the oil as it expanded outward. She beckoned to him to come and sit beside her. He crawled out from his hiding spot and picked up a piece of fish with his small fingers. It was soft and hot to the touch.

'Will you blow on it for me?'

The old lady picked up a hand fan and moved it back and forth, cooling down the fish.

'Will they find me here?'

'No.'

The boy took a small bite. It tasted of salt and turmeric. And of the river. 'Can I stay here with you till everyone forgets everything?'

The old cook nodded. 'Sooner, or later, everyone forgets everything.'

THE TRIAL

The trial remained on everyone's lips for weeks. It was a tale of mystery and bravado, the sort that sells newspapers. A clandestine police operation led by a British officer commanding a multiracial force had succeeded in cracking open one of the last guerrilla cells deep in the jungle. There was the pesky issue of the death of an Indian clerk, but the courtroom drama kept the story of the raid alive. It gave the police force in the nascent nation much-needed publicity – after waging war for a decade, the communists were caving in to the last person. The country was finally safe.

The young man's salary from the estate had stopped. The office delivered a letter to Maloti stating that pending the outcome of the trial, the company would be freezing payments. She barely registered the legal documents that were arriving, hankering for her attention with growing frequency. Her life was consumed by a seemingly unending series of trips to the courtroom. Amma took care of Sayang around the clock. Jonaki ran amok. Murray, who drove Maloti to the courthouse every day, sat a translator next to her. People made statements in front of her, not acknowledging her presence. Photographs of her husband's mutilated body were displayed, both by the defence and the prosecution. On one occasion, the prosecuting barrister, provided by a national legal team representing Tamil labourers came up to her and whispered, 'When I show his picture tomorrow, wail really loudly, madam. Cry out and say, "Oh my god, oh my god, he will never come back." Can you practice at home?' Maloti sat silently though the proceedings.

The defence had it easy; it was British police officer versus Chinese bandit. In an archaic legal system with no jury, the judge had to ask for the opinions of just two 'assessors' who followed the trial. A European could request for both assessors to be white. So, O'Brien had an English judge and two Australian assessors. Confident of protection, he claimed that the young man had been shot in crossfire. His jungle squad, to the person, attested to more or less a similar sequence of events – they were ambushed in mid-raid, by a lone guerrilla shooting at them. O'Brien had no choice but to open fire. Ironically, Jūju was not allowed to testify on account of his young age. But the defence painted the image of a deranged 'almost adult' bandit on a rampage with a Bren gun. People banged on their benches and cheered kangaroo court style when O'Brien testified. He played up the archetype of the brave, ever-in-uniform Mat Salleh, who went into the heart of the jungle to face a showdown with CTs. Desperate, the prosecution requested the testimony of every single guerrilla that had been caught in the raid. They were paraded in, one by one. Both defiant and terrified, they stared at the roomful of people. Tan King provided an especially moving statement where he thanked the young man for saving the life of a child. He insisted that the boy had been unarmed when he was shot. But the judge dismissed these eyewitness accounts with help from the assessors. The defence argued successfully that since the bandits were kneeling on the forest floor, and were not at eye level, they could not have had a reliable vantage point.

The strongest and most surprising indictment on the young man's character came from Milne. He insisted under oath that he had long suspected that 'there was something else going on' with the young man. And that he had clearly told Milne one afternoon that the guerrillas were not in the wrong for their actions. This started an inquiry into why the young man was in the camp that night. The medical case found at the location suggested that he was treating CTs. Tan King's insistence that he had been coerced into coming to the camp was disqualified as hearsay. Protected by his contract as a witness for the police, Ganesh could not be subpoenaed.

A small miracle turned the case on its head. A copy assistant, working in New York for *Life* magazine, read about the trial when researching for captions for the negatives the team from Southeast Asia had shipped. Realizing the importance of the images to the ongoing case, she placed five eight by ten black-and-white prints and mailed them in a stiff envelope before they were reviewed by anyone higher up. The photographs, taken from the helicopter with a wide lens, were in clear focus. They showed the exact positions of the jungle squad, the kneeling guerrillas and the blazing huts. In one, O'Brien had his barrel facing the young man and the boy. The boy's weapon – a service rifle – was on the floor and he was staring upward, directly at the helicopter, oblivious of the gun aimed at him. In light of this irrefutable evidence, one of the two assessors had the conscience to find O'Brien at fault. The judge charged him with 'accidental shooting during combat', a misdemeanour akin to killing a pet dog under the special Emergency Regulations. Close to retirement, O'Brien relinquished his post and returned to Ireland. Tan King was hanged a month later for illegal possession of firearms.

On the morning of the verdict, an old Chinese man walked up to Maloti and bowed deeply as he wept. Maloti had noticed him sitting in a bench at the back of the courtroom every morning. 'That's the grandfather of the boy your husband saved,' said

Murray. She indicated to him to sit next to her, but he declined and shuffled back to the back of the room. Later that day, the judge ruled that Maloti would receive reparation from the government and ordered the estate to provide her a lifelong pension.

That night, after Jonaki and Sayang had gone to bed, she pulled out a chair and sat on the veranda. Released from months of turmoil, she fell into a deep sleep. The sky started to lighten when she awoke. Maloti stood up. Holding onto the railing, she looked towards the horizon. She had a fleeting recollection of the time she had been on the ship deck alone at daybreak, waiting for her new life to begin. A large moth appeared and flitted around, circling her before flying away towards the jungle. Maloti followed it, holding her gaze for as long as she could, till it meshed with the wilderness.

Venus was still visible on the horizon, its bright, blue solitary light shining through like a gem stuck to the sky. She realized that she would stay on in Malaya. Here, she had been happy; she had been loved. The soil where you bury your adored one can stake a strange claim. It is not in birth but in death sometimes that we plot our home under the slow arc of stars.

ACKNOWLEDGEMENTS

No story is written in isolation – certainly not one shelved under the fluid category of 'historical fiction'. There were disparate influences – some traceable, others evanescent – that shaped this book. I will attempt to acknowledge them. There will be lapses.

An essay titled 'In the Time of Moths' submitted many years ago to historian Rudolf Mrazek formed the kernel for this book. He implored us to stay away from the trappings of academic writing, asking instead that we try somehow to 'touch the past'. British army officer Freddie Spencer Chapman's autobiographical *The Jungle is Neutral* was significant in imagining the psychological and physical terrains of the Malayan Communist Party and their collaborators. Chin Peng's controversial *My Side of History* was key in providing a counter-perspective to the Allied narratives of the Malayan Emergency. Articles published in the *Journal of Southeast Asian Studies* helped clarify events. John Dodd's *A Company of Planters* was a quotidian, ethnographic window into the goings-on in the isolated lives of expatriate estate officers. Numerous audio recordings of interviews, discussing the

Emergency, archived at the Imperial War Museum in London and the National Archives of Singapore provided detail and ground-level coherence. Cheryl L. Nicholas' dissertation on ghosts was instructive. Papers read by colleagues with varying accents at the history seminar room on the fifth floor at the National University of Singapore as we looked at the Indian Ocean, highlighted the undeniably intertwined pasts of South and Southeast Asia.

Madhusree Mukherjee's landmark analysis of the Bengal famine of 1943 and Janam Mukherjee's *Hungry Bengal* clarified the political machinations of a complex and disastrous calamity. Suranjan Das' extensive research on Direct Action Day and its aftermath, along with the evocative primary sources, edited and referenced by Debjani Sengupta, were instructive in fathoming the internecine tragedy of that time. Ashutosh Varshney stoked a curiosity to explore further that irrepressible, primordial urge in people to identify with a nation.

Robin Bush perused the very first pages as they emerged from a borrowed printer in Jakarta, a decade ago. Friends and colleagues – Antara Datta, Ludmila de Souza Maia, Indu Jain, Katherine Demopolous, Debarati Bhattacharya, Julienne Chen – read drafts and their comments helped confront an evolving narrative. Flora Majumder added commas and caught errant apostrophes. The Red Ink Literary Agency was invaluable in its support in developing the project. Prema Govindan of HarperCollins India expertly shepherded the final stages, from manuscript to book. The voices of Sanat Majumder, Sarthak Roychowdhury, Sion Dey, Sananda Banerjee, Swati Ray, Mala Banerjee, Sugato Banerjee, Joydeep Ray, the Pillais of Bahau, Kanishka Raja (1969–2018), Juli Raja, Marieangeles DeFrutos (1967–2012), Sawda, Saswato Das, Afreen Alam, Ronojoy Sen, Lydia Ruddy, Tariq Khalil, Avi Basu, Ratna Subrahmanyam, Thanh Pham, Sarika Chandra, Debjani Chakravarty, Archana Ghosh, Indranil Ghosh, Paromita Chakravarti, Arati Bardhan, Sushil Biswas (1924–2013), Putri

Minangsari, Mary Hardy, John Marshall (1932–2005), Cynthia Close, Irene Doyle, Sameetah Agha, Steven Murphy, Owen O'Gorman, and the Thek-at-large, percolated in my hippocampus for years. We shared stories.

Recording sessions with my father J.B. Ray, who removed bullets, delivered babies and sutured souls as his life ebbed, gave me inspiration to recreate the social texture and terrain of a land so many people with varying persuasions and ambitions came to call home. Somewhere through the last hours of his gravelly voice embossed on thin TDK and BASF tapes, Malaya ceased to be a far country.

Sandeep Ray
Jakarta, 2019

ABOUT THE AUTHOR

Sandeep Ray was born off the Straits of Malacca, on the edge of a rubber plantation. Educated in India and in the United States, he began his career as a film-maker, travelling widely and producing award-winning documentaries. A historian now, he explores woven pasts in *A Flutter in the Colony*, his first novel.